Simon J Patel is a degree-educated engineer by trade. His interest in books and reading spans his whole life, and it is this obsession that has led him to start on his own path in writing. Being a huge horror fan, there was only one direction for him with regards to genre. He is currently writing his second novel, and already has plans for a third.

He is also a musician and has played bass guitar for many years in a relatively successful heavy metal band. This has afforded him a chance to travel the world (most of the gigs have been international) and they have played in everything—from smaller clubs to much larger events.

Living in Gloucestershire, he is a family man with four children and two grandchildren, and has been with his partner for nearly 30 years.

Thanks to the following friends for their encouragement and input along the way:

Matt Chapman
Lee Ireland
Chris Dalton

This novel is dedicated to my two grandchildren, Finley and Isla, for allowing me to relive my childhood for the third time.

# Simon J Patel

## CLONE

AUSTIN MACAULEY PUBLISHERS™

LONDON * CAMBRIDGE * NEW YORK * SHARJAH

A CIP catalogue record for this title is available from the British Library.

ISBN 9781035843909 (Paperback)
ISBN 9781035843916 (ePub e-book)

www.austinmacauley.com

First Published 2024
Austin Macauley Publishers Ltd®
1 Canada Square
Canary Wharf
London
E14 5AA

Artwork created by Lee Ireland

# Part I

# Chapter One

Liam Connelly eyed the large, clinical-looking building with a mixture of interest and apprehension as he pulled his BMW into the spacious car park in front of it. The front of the building was fairly busy, with people bustling both in and out of the automatic doors, above which was emblazoned 'Future Medical Advancements LTD' in large black letters, stark contrast to the pristine white front of the building.

His appointment was at 10.30 am, he was about 15 minutes early. The journey didn't take long—Jen didn't actually know he was there, and he justified this to himself by means of telling himself this was a preliminary consultation; if it didn't seem like the right thing to do, then no problem. If it promised to be a worthy investment, then he would talk to Jen about it and arrange a further consultation with both of them, he saw little point in wasting both of their time if it wasn't to be. And besides, she wasn't even pregnant yet, so you could argue that the meeting was premature…but not entirely so, as certain things needed to happen at the correct time in order for the program to run correctly.

The program in question was a developing technology that had been coming to fruition over the last ten years or so by the FMA Group. The medical business offered other services and products, everything from tailored health care packages (often which included access to emerging drug trialling for specific conditions) to specialist cutting-edge intensive treatment courses for a variety of conditions and illnesses. Throw some standard services in such as chiropractic therapy, paediatrics and cosmetic and dental treatments and you ended up with a very exclusive, lucrative medical business, predominantly catering for the well-off.

Liam put a few things into his bag ('man-bag' as Jen called it and taunted him frequently) and pulled down the visor to have a quick check on his appearance. He was doing well, so he thought the small mirror told him—not long turned forty, he had a full head of thick wavy brown hair which still required cutting regularly. He had it short with no parting as such, and it framed his face well. He had good, lightly tanned skin with a modest amount of stubble sitting on an angular, strong jawline. A few crow's feet gathered at the corners of his eyes, but apart from that he looked at least eight or ten years younger. Throw light blue eyes and a fairly straight nose into the mix and you were looking at quite a catch—or so he told himself. Self-confidence had never been an issue for Liam—right from the onset he had always had self-belief which in turn had rewarded him in life. He was popular in both his social and work life, often appearing to others as the man who had everything…apart from a son or daughter. All the other boxes were ticked—a good career working for a global civil engineering company that not only paid him well but had actively promoted him into ever more desirable management positions with the salary to suit. Liam and his wife had a beautiful home, set back from a quiet street in a small, desirable village not too far from the coast. The only issue with the house was too many spare rooms. And of course, there was Jen. His thirty-eight-year-old wife was a sight to behold, and not just in his eyes—his friends and peers were always commenting on her, and how lucky he was to have her. She was beautiful, but in the most simplistic way. She never really had to try too hard with make up or hair products and styles because no matter what she did or didn't do to her face and hair, what she did or didn't wear, she always looked radiant. And of course, her figure had not been yet ravaged by the onslaught of childbirth.

In a way, Jen was directly responsible for him being there—it was an after-dinner conversation with their good friends, John and Janet Lee. John was a successful consultant for FMA, and up until recently Liam had not known too much about his profession—they had met through their wives' mutual friendship. Janet and Jen had met randomly while Jen was at work a few years back now. Jen worked as a manageress for a national hotel chain and travelled to various hotels across the country depending on business need. She happened to be working a full week in a hotel out in the countryside (about half of the hotels were situated like this—the other half were city or town based). There was a convention happening there one particular evening, and a chance meeting in the reception area had led to a couple of drinks in the bar once all the conference activities were over…the rest was history. They became firm friends, and it wasn't long before regular social events were happening. That was three years ago. The conversation about potential engagement with FMA's services had occurred about six months ago and had not really been discussed or thought about since by neither Liam nor Jen until recently. Liam found himself mulling over the prospects of what had been mentioned as a medical breakthrough giving parents peace of mind over their child ever since he and Jen had been talking about a family. Having a child was a natural progression for the couple—they weren't getting any younger, Jen's biological clock was ticking away and they both yearned for a little ray of sunshine in their lives, a child to dote on—Liam felt this was the last piece of the puzzle for their near perfect lives.

And now he was here. Surprisingly, he found himself feeling slightly nervous about the whole thing, which was out of character for Liam. The butterflies fluttering around in his stomach wasn't a feeling he was used to, and he resisted the urge to pull his tie askew from his collar, his neck feeling ever so slightly clammy underneath it. Maybe it was a combination of the unknown mixed with the fact he was actually meeting with the director of FMA, Dr Nathan Ellis. This had been swung by John following a chat about what FMA could potentially do for them. Liam was intrigued by the concept of what could be offered should he become a father. He was aware that not all consultations happened with the big man and that he was privileged to say the least at having the opportunity.

He got out of the car and walked, perhaps over confidently, towards the building entrance, locking the car on the way. Weaving in and out of more people as he approached, Liam headed towards the large reception desk just off to the left of the main doors. The lobby area was spacious and boasted minimalist décor in order to accentuate the airy building. Marble effect flooring, several large very well looked after plants and small trees along with enough seating in the form of modern pristine sofas and chairs for at least twenty people gave it an effortlessly classy feel. Everything was white—the furniture, the reception desk, the walls and pillars. This added to the minimalist feel, and accentuated the spacious interior as well as adding to the already present feel of a medical institution. Liam was suitably impressed—*there's no lack of money here*, he thought.

"Hello sir, how can I help?" The receptionist greeted him with a well-practised smile, showing off perfectly white teeth. *No doubt she's taken advantage of her position in the form of discounted treatment for employees,* Liam thought. And why not? He had not looked into all the company might be able to offer but was starting to think that it may well be quite a lot.

"I have an appointment with Dr Ellis at 10.30.," he said, slightly apologetic in tone if anything. "I'm a little early." Much to Liam's surprise, he felt a little out of his depth. He had never done anything like this before and felt off-guard.

He noticed her name badge on the left of her white blouse—Jayne Reynolds. She was sat behind the huge reception desk and looked very petite from where he was standing. Quite pretty, too. *Now is not the time to be distracted*, he thought to himself. Jayne gave him an acknowledging look and quickly diverted her attention to the computer monitor in front of her. After a few clicks, she said "Ah yes, Mr Connelly. Please take a seat and help yourself to any refreshments you may want from our vending machines over in the corner. There's tea, coffee and a selection of cold drinks, all complimentary of course. Please make yourself comfortable, someone will be down within five minutes to escort you to Dr Ellis' office."

"Thank you very much… Jayne," he said, with a subtle nod and smile towards her.

"It's my pleasure Mr Connelly, I hope your appointment goes well," Jayne returned. The smile returned, and again he was struck with her attractiveness.

"Thanks—so do I." Liam smiled again and turned away to find a seat as the receptionist again returned her attention to her monitor. He wandered over to the vending machines in the hope of a decent coffee—he was not disappointed. They looked every bit as expensive as any other piece of furniture in the place.

Coffee in hand, he sat on a chair close by and put his bag down at his feet. A quick look around the lobby confirmed that this place was oozing cash—and the clientele too. There were strategically placed tall office type plants, but they didn't look cheap. The pots were huge and very ornate, and the tropical palm tree-type vegetation that sprouted from them were vibrant and healthy. The floor looked like it was polished every hour and wouldn't have been misplaced in a sultan's living quarters.

Liam checked his phone—no messages or missed calls. Good. Jen thought he was at work, and so did everyone else apart from his work colleagues—he had told his secretary that he had a private appointment and would not be available via phone, email or any other means until later that day, after lunch. And that was pretty much true; he just hadn't divulged the specifics of the appointment in question.

A tall gentleman in a smart white uniform approached him. "Good morning, Mr Connelly. I believe you have an appointment with Dr Ellis?" His voice was low and had an undertone of warmth in it which made the formality of his speech less on the stuffy side and ultimately more amenable.

Liam stood up and offered his hand. "Yes, at 10.30 I believe." The man shook his hand with a firm grip.

"Excellent—please follow me," the man said. Liam wondered what other duties he performed when not meeting and greeting clients—open heart surgery, perhaps? Expert holistic guidance and counselling, maybe? He smiled to himself as he followed the man across the lobby and headed towards a small annex set off the main room. This was home to the building elevators, he discovered as they turned the corner.

"Dr Ellis' office is situated on the sixth floor," the guide explained as he pressed the elevator button. The lift doors glided open immediately, revealing a plush interior with highly polished mirrors and brass hand rails. They entered and proceeded to the sixth floor. "I hope you have a productive meeting with Dr Ellis—I will be there afterwards, to escort you back down," the guide explained. The elevator came to a buffered stop, and the doors opened. The guide stepped out, followed by Liam, into a pristine white corridor with a tiled floor. There were framed pictures exactly evenly spaced along the matching walls. All the images were intrinsically linked to the company's products and services one way or another: An idyllic, happy family of mother, father and child running on a beach, pictures of handsome men and beautiful women smiling, a picture of a man relaxing on a sun drenched decking with a cocktail in hand, at total peace with the world. As they walked down the corridor, Liam slightly behind his guide, he noticed the doors and name plaques that adorned them. They were large and well-spaced apart, meaning the spaces behind them were big. He wasn't wrong. They approached Dr Ellis' office and the guide quietly rapped on the door.

"Come," came the loud, authoritative reply. The guide opened the door and said "Dr Ellis, your 10.30 appointment is here."

"Ah, please send him in, George. And thank you." George nodded slightly and turned to Liam. "Please go in, Dr Ellis will see you now Mr Connelly," he said.

"Thanks George," Liam replied, wondering why he hadn't taken notice of his name badge as he had Jayne's…his mind on his appointment, no doubt. He walked into a large, spotless office with minimal décor, mimicking the reception area. There was a large bureau, behind which sat Dr Ellis. He was in his late fifties or early sixties by the looks of it, and had been reaping the rewards of his successful career. He was portly in his upper body, and Liam saw as he stood that this applied more so to his sizeable midriff. Many restaurant meals accompanied with plentiful glasses of red had played a major part in that, Liam concluded.

"Pleased to meet you Mr Connelly," he said in a formal but pleasant manner. His upper body jiggled slightly as the men shook hands across the desk. He was obviously aware of the connection that had facilitated this meeting in the first place. "I'm Dr Ellis, founder and chairman of Future Medical Advancements. I hope that we can be of service to you. You come highly recommended from my colleague, John Lee, our Principal Consultant here at FMA. I understand that you know John on a social basis?"

"Yes, John and his wife are good friends of mine and my wife Jen's. I've known him for a good few years now, and he is largely responsible for me being here. I hope we can discuss some of the services offered by FMA, one in particular." Liam saw little point in beating around the bush—the consultation was expensive despite his connections, and he didn't really want to waste any precious time he might have on small talk rather than picking Dr Ellis' brains.

"Please have a seat," Dr Ellis gestured to the leather-bound chair on Liam's side of the bureau. "Are you happy on first name terms? Please call me Nathan."

"Yes, please call me Liam. Thanks for agreeing to see me, Nathan," Liam responded. He felt a little more at ease now the appointment was finally underway, all the previous apprehension seeping out of his body and mind, allowing him to be himself again.

"No problem, Liam. We hold consultations here every day, but I only conduct a limited amount myself—there is much to do, you understand. That's where my colleagues usually step in, but I am happy to make the odd exception. In your case, my notes tell me you may have an interest in a new, developing technology we are offering here at FMA. These are very exciting times indeed, Liam." Nathan had sat back down, his chair releasing a slight groan as he did so, and was looking at Liam in a friendly, almost excited manner, bushy eyebrows slightly raised above his small, twinkling eyes.

"Yes, that's right, Nathan. John told me quite a lot about the on-going project you are running here, and I must say it captured my interest straight away. I tried to absorb as much information as I could from John, but please excuse my ignorance—it was a lot to take in, especially after a few late night brandies." Nathan chuckled at this last comment.

"You are forgiven Liam; I wouldn't have remembered anything, ha ha! And the subject matter is daunting. But none less real because of it, I assure you. We are very excited and proud to offer what we do in all areas of medical development, but our DNA advancements are world class. We unequivocally lead the field in this area of expertise. Here at FMA we employ experts in their fields—geneticists, biological scientists, specialist paediatricians, growth developmental experts, the list goes on and on, all so we can develop and hone this very special area of our business." Nathan looked at Liam intently following this little speech, to try and gauge reaction. He himself was obviously very keen for Liam to understand the magnitude of what they were talking about. "We are, of course, talking about the genetic cloning of our subjects, and the subsequent development of an exact human replica, grown in laboratory conditions. Exactly the same in every way to its real-life counterpart. The same weight, height, age and DNA. A twin, if you like. A perfectly identical twin. But a twin with a specific role in life—the ultimate insurance for your child." Nathan paused, as if for dramatic effect. In his defence, this was about as dramatic a conversation Liam had ever had. He took the opportunity to interject.

"Yes, that's the gist of what I got from John. It certainly sounds very exciting, Nathan. You must be very proud of your achievement. Can I ask a question?" So far Liam was impressed. Nathan was obviously very talented in his field and was also quite likeable. There didn't appear to be any of the underlying pompous attitude that so often can accompany a person who has elevated themselves to the top of their given field. He didn't get any hint of a subliminal hard sell that he had been positive there would be—Nathan just seemed to be putting the facts on the table for him to assess, albeit in an obviously biased way.

"Of course—ask away, while I get some information for you," Nathan said, opening a drawer in the bureau. He reached inside and started bringing out some glossy pamphlets for Liam's attention.

"How long have you been running this program? I'm aware the business has been around for some time. Are there any real-life case studies I could look at?" Liam glanced at the information Nathan had put on the table. A strap line caught his eye: "Life is precious in every way. Protect it as best you can."

"Well, the research feels like it's been going on forever, Liam. And it continues, every day. It is at the very heart of what we do here and is our jewel in the crown, if you like. We started DNA twinning experiments back in the early eighties and continued to develop this process for the next twenty or so years. In that time, many breakthroughs were made around the world, many of which were documented through television and in books, scientific journals and the like. We kept our developments and advances under wraps from the outside world as best we could. Not for any other reason than we knew and firmly believed that we were forerunners in the field. And we were specialised, too. We focussed purely on what we offer today—DNA cloning as an insurance policy. Our goal was always to offer this niche service to those who believe that their child should have the best in medical care should any circumstance force the requirement." Nathan paused. Liam had absorbed what he had said. He certainly talked a good game. "We have case studies dating back to the eighties when couples first started engaging with us and our development of our research, helping us mould and grow our offering into what it is today. We also have recent and on-going case studies that you are welcome to look at as well. Every client we have engaged with has been paramount to our success. Their needs are the priority in every way. I have an information pack that contains much more information than I can give you in this consultation. You can read this in your own time, and there are links to online case studies for you to look at with your wife." Nathan sat back in his chair and regarded Liam, as if to assess how the meeting was going— did he have a potential client here, or another person who likes the idea, but doesn't want to commit to what it may entail to enter into the program? He thought and hoped for the former. He liked the man's demeanour, and Nathan had a knack of getting the measure of people quickly. Rarely was he wrong on his initial view of somebody.

Liam looked briefly at the brochures that Nathan had pushed towards him on the desk, leafing through the glossy pages. "How many successful clients have you had that engaged in your twinning program?" Liam asked.

"Oh, there are too numerous cases to know exactly offhand, I would have to do some digging into our records for an exact number, but there are about forty parents that have successfully taken part in the program to date." Nathan paused briefly. "The program is not too well known about, as we do not actively advertise the service offered. This is for a few reasons—it's very expensive for starters. This means a limited market of wealthy parents. Also, the program requires engagement from the parents and child in order for us to further develop the technology, as it is ever evolving. This makes the nature of our business very symbiotic with our clients. They are as responsible for the growth and success as much as FMA. We treat our clients with the utmost respect and care and always put their best interests first."

"When does the program have to start? I am aware that the timing in the initial stages is key to the program." Liam looked at Nathan expectantly for his reply.

"Yes, you are correct. We must make sure certain things happen at certain times in the early stages to align the growth of the child with the twin. But don't worry—it's all tightly controlled and been done many times before, so the procedures for this initial stage is well mapped out, as well as the program that follows it. It will involve minor surgical procedures from your wife once pregnant, but nothing too invasive or traumatic. A small biopsy must be taken in order to extract the DNA information we require to begin the cloning." Nathan stood and turned towards the wall to wall window behind him, surveying the view. Countryside dominated, with the hint of metropolitan growth in the distance. "Are you and your wife actively trying for a baby, Liam?" He turned to face Liam.

"No...not yet. But it's on the cards. Jen is desperate, but I have persuaded her to wait a little while longer... I must confess, she doesn't know I'm here. Or that the real reason for me stalling is because I wanted to find out more about your service." Liam looked at Nathan. "I'm glad we waited. Can I take this information and discuss with Jen? Then, hopefully we can make a further appointment with the pair of us." Liam was sold—he was even before the consultation began, if the truth be known.

"Of course, Liam. You'll find plenty of information both in the pack and also online—there is a password in the brochure to allow you to access our website. You'll have to sign a confidentiality agreement to ensure that the security of the site is not compromised. I hope you understand, it's just a formality really. As I alluded to earlier, we are not a secret organisation, but lots of our activity is not in the public domain. We would like to keep it that way for the moment." Nathan opened the drawer on his left, had a brief rummage, and produced two sheets of paper, both identical. He handed both to Liam. "Please read and ensure you're happy, it's not a complex legal document, however it is binding."

Liam took the paper and quickly scanned the contents. It was a simple non-disclosure agreement; he had seen many similar in his line of work, contracts drawn up between customer and supplier. This appeared to be no different in principle, so he reached into his top pocket for his pen and signed the documents. He passed them back to Nathan.

"Excellent, thank you Liam. It may seem a bit MI5, but I assure you it's just precautionary on our part. One of these is for you." Nathan signed both papers also, and put one of them in a white envelope before passing it back to Liam. The other he filed away in his drawer.

"No problem, I don't appear to have signed my life away," Liam said with an air of light-heartedness. After the signing, things felt a little more set in stone to Liam.

Nathan smiled. "No, nothing so sinister, Liam. Do you have any further questions that I can answer for you?" He sat and looked at Liam across the desk. He liked him and got the feeling it was mutual.

Liam looked thoughtful for a second and then said: "Well, just one. How long does the program actually last for?"

"That's a good question, Liam. The program runs for the entire lifespan of your child. In the event of your child outliving either his or her parents, which hopefully will be the case, the program will continue to run, and your adult child will continue to benefit from the peace of mind their parents have given to them." Liam took this in. Of course, the program would run for his child's entire life, regardless of what happened to him or Jen. What did he think would happen, that it would just stop once their child turned eighteen? All of a sudden, he felt the commitment of what he was considering, and it felt weighty. This was something he was really going to have to think about. And Jen would need to think hard too. Did they really want such a lifelong commitment? And there was the question of finances. How much was something of this magnitude going to cost? There would be little point in investing in the program if it meant bankrupting them both.

"Okay Nathan, I guess I need some time to think. I've had an information overload for one day, as I'm sure you can appreciate." Liam stood up and straightened his jacket, picking his bag up from the side of the chair.

"Yes, of course, I know it's a lot to take in. But this could be a very exciting and rewarding opportunity for your future family, Liam. Please think carefully. If you have questions over and above what is available in the pack and on our website, then please call me. I've written my office number on the inside of the pack. I am happy to talk if you need to." Nathan stood also. The consultation had drawn naturally to a close. Liam offered his hand, which Nathan shook, smiling at his new potential client.

"It's been a pleasure to meet you, Liam," Nathan said genuinely. "I hope to meet with you again in the near future. Please, take all the time you need to read the information I've given you, and also be sure to visit our website."

"Thank you for your time Nathan and it's been a pleasure also. I'm sure we will speak again."

Nathan picked up his desk phone. "Jayne—can you send George to escort Liam out, please? Thank you." He replaced the receiver. "George will be here in a moment. Take care, Liam."

"Thanks—and you too, Nathan. I'm sure I'll be in touch shortly." There was a soft rapping at the door. Liam nodded goodbye to Nathan and walked to the door. George was waiting.

# Chapter Two

The oven beeped to the world that it was up to temperature, demanding attention. Jen turned her head towards it, as if acknowledging the fact she was behind schedule. The dish wasn't ready to go in yet—the vegetables were halfway through prep. Oh well, kill the planet with unwanted heat and loss of energy while she messed around with carrots, she thought. Her mood was light—she had finished early from work, and the weekend began here. She hoped to time dinner for six, hopefully Liam would be just in time. They hadn't seen much of each other recently, mainly due to working life. She had spent Monday and Tuesday away at a hotel in Devon, and Liam had been doing overtime every night to keep on top of the new contract he was involved with in work. It would mean more time away for him in the near future once things were cemented in, at the customer site in France.

Jen secretly resented the fact that Liam's career could take him away from her and their home for relatively long periods of time whenever the opportunity presented itself. But every time she had those types of thoughts, her mind countered it with the knowledge that his job brought so much to their lives—they were lucky. And no different to countless other working couples all over the world. It seemed to be a pre-requisite in order for their lives to be 'comfortable', and as such, needed to be just accepted.

The veg was done. She unceremoniously dumped the peeled vegetables and a reasonably-sized piece of beef in the oven dish. A few bits and pieces later, she could put it in the oven and forget about it for three hours, apart from a few stirs here and there. Hopefully she would be able to spend some time with Liam tonight—something to eat, and maybe head out for a drink if he felt like it later. She missed him, even though they lived together. She guessed that's just modern life; all work, no downtime. Jen knew they were in a peak. Their lives were peaks and troughs. In the troughs, there was less pressure from work and more time not only alone, but they were able to socialise. It wouldn't last forever. The contract would be done, and the initial site visits would be done, and then he could relax. Not to mention her. The knock-on effect of Liam's work was significant for Jen. In a way, they were quite an insular couple; immediate family were at arm's length, and friends were lifelong friends that they had the pleasure of a few times a year, if that.

She checked the time—four in the afternoon, plenty of time. Liam wouldn't appear until at least six, if she was lucky. Maybe a glass of Chardonnay would help…? Jen reached towards the fridge door, while opening the cupboard door above it simultaneously. Before she knew it, the cork was out, and the glass was poured.

After the casserole was in the oven, she relaxed and sat down at the table. The table was large—big enough to seat eight, and it was well placed in what could be described as a very spacious kitchen/dining room. Jen unlocked her phone and had a quick check—two social media notifications, four emails. They could wait. No message from Liam, though—she sent him a text, *hi big guy, when you home…? I'm cooking! XX*, and left it at that: *Hopefully, he will get the idea I want him home on time*, she thought. Her mind wandered as she thought of her husband—he had been behaving ever so slightly differently lately. It would be imperceptible to anyone else, his friends, or even his mother for example, and Jen was convinced that no one could possibly detect this apart from her. They were so close after ten years of marriage that surely only she could know there was something slightly out of kilter with him. It was odd; she sort of felt suspicious of him, felt resentful that he may be harbouring a secret, not letting her know there was something wrong, something he was not telling her. They shared every part of their life with each other, so why conceal anything from her? She was his soul mate, and vice versa—there were no secrets. *Well, up until now at least*, she thought uneasily.

This train of thought was dangerous—it could result in an argument rather than a rare relaxing evening together. She couldn't remember the last time they had an argument. Jen told herself that she was overreacting, and deliberately steered herself away from her paranoia. Maybe she would scroll through social media and look at her unread emails about irrelevant job opportunities from agents she didn't know after all. After ten minutes or so of phone-based technology, most of which was either pointless or fairly dull, her thoughts automatically turned to her and Liam again. She glanced at the clock—twenty to five. Still loads of time before dinner, the casserole had at least another hour and a quarter minimum. She had some fresh olive bread to accompany it, and that would do. She was handy in the kitchen, and rarely turned out an unpalatable offering. When were they going to think about their goals in life, and start a family? Neither of them were getting any younger, and conversations about the patter of tiny feet had dried up lately…she couldn't help but think this may be something to do with the slight change in his demeanour. Maybe he was having an affair—but who with? She toyed with the stem of her glass as she pondered this unnerving thought. It could be a number of known candidates: Jess, the intern from work, Georgia the artistic director at Liam's office branch, or any number of unknowns—women that Jen didn't know about. There was no point in tormenting herself this way, but could not help it just the same. Maybe he had lost interest in her and having a family because he was having an extra marital relationship with someone… *STOP IT!* She thought to herself. Well, there was no doubt about it now, there was bound to be a conversation about this whole thing later tonight. She would have to make sure she didn't have one too many, and outright accuse him of sleeping with someone else and losing interest in her. That would be a disaster, especially if she was wrong.

Jen drained her glass, got up to pour another and check on dinner. All seemed okay in the oven, so at least one thing was going well. At that moment, she heard the front door open.

"Hi, sweetheart!" Liam called as he paused in the hallway to check a small pile of unopened letters on the footstool inside the large heavy front door. He heeled his shoes off as he slid envelope past envelope, looking up to the kitchen for Jen. She was pottering at the stove—something smelt great, he was starving. "How's your day? Plenty of R and R?" She looked sideways towards him from the kitchen. "Hi Liam, did you get my text? I'm doing that cooking thing again, thought you might be hungry." She walked towards him, leaving the wine on the island.

After deciding there was nothing too interesting in the mail, he extended both arms to her. "Did you miss me?" he said. She came to him and folded herself into his hug. He still smelt good after a full days' work. He kissed her lightly on the lips. "Of course, I did," she said. "But we have dinner in the oven and I'm on my second glass of wine, so what are you having?"

"Apart from you, my love?" he joked. "Maybe I've earned a vodka tonic. I'll get it." He headed towards the kitchen before she could offer to make it for him. He felt like he needed a stiffer drink than usual after his meeting with Nathan earlier. She followed him in and sat at the table. "How was your day? Busier than mine I bet," she said. "I've done next to nothing, cleaned the guest rooms and bleached all the bathrooms, done all the laundry, went shopping, cooking tea…just the usual. I don't know what you see in a boring old girl like me, sometimes," she commented. Although she was obviously joking, there was still that undertone in her mind—a remnant from her earlier thoughts of infidelity.

He glanced at her over his shoulder while he rummaged in the fridge freezer for ice and tonic. "Oh, not much then eh, Mary Poppins? Did you put the bins out too?" he countered, with a wry grin. There was rarely any tension between them, and tonight was no exception, despite her earlier paranoia attack.

"I thought I'd leave that for you as it's your favourite job…can't remember the last time I had to actually ask you to do it…oh, wait… Monday." Her mood had lifted considerably, the wine helping. Maybe they would get some decent time together tonight after all. Liam took a large gulp of his drink and set it down. Jen checked the oven and took some fresh bread out of the cupboard. "Dinner should be ready in about half an hour. Are you hungry? It's beef casserole."

"Starving," he replied. He hadn't eaten since before his morning meeting. After the meeting, he made what was supposed to be a brief stop at the office, but it had turned into a lengthier visit than expected for one reason or another. He was still mulling over the information given to him by Nathan. The brochures were still in the car, stashed away in the dashboard. *I need to talk to her about it tonight really,* he thought to himself. No time like the present. It could wait until after they had eaten, and maybe a few more drinks for Dutch courage. Liam was slightly perplexed at his own reaction to all of this—it wasn't like him to be so…well, anxious. He generally met things head on and rationalised logically, but that didn't appear to be happening with this subject. Strange.

"I'm away next Tuesday with work," Jen said, while opening the oven. "Not far, but I need to stay overnight. It's in Somerset." She drew the bread knife from the block. "Should just be the one night."

"No problem—I'll take the opportunity to do some overtime, there's still loads of loose ends to tidy up on this project. As ever." His glass was empty already, and his thirst had been whetted. He turned and started making another.

"Thirsty, are we?" Jen commented, with a raised eyebrow. Liam usually had one with his evening meal, but rarely set about two or more before eating. A small sliver of nagging doubt wormed its way back into her mind—damn! She had forgotten her worries briefly, until then.

"It's been a funny day, hon. Just need to unwind. Don't worry, I won't get out of hand and make any unwelcome advances." Her backwards glance caught his mischievous eyes, and she smiled. "Oh, don't worry; I can look after myself, big guy. Fill your boots." Her doubt disappearing again, she laughed and said "I can't really say much—my next will be my third! What the hell, it's the weekend. Let's pretend we're teenagers again and get totally shitfaced!" He laughed with her. And there it was. The entire reason he loved her so much, summed up in a moment. He moved towards her and slipped his arms around her tiny waist from behind. "I love you, Jen." She turned to face him and kissed him, just insistently enough to create a stir from within him. Boy, she was good. "I love you too, Liam. I'm so glad you're here tonight, and not at that stupid office. Feels like we never spend any time together nowadays…it's not like we have a busy family life to contend with, it's all just work, work, and more work." She hugged him tightly. "Why don't you get changed, and by that time it'll be on the table?"

"Deal, I'm taking this with me," he replied, picking up his drink. "Don't burn anything while I'm gone." He left the kitchen and disappeared upstairs.

Jen bustled around while he was upstairs, and sure enough by the time he came back down the table had been laid, and dinner was ready.

"Smells great, love," Liam said, sitting at his usual place. Jen sat too and started dishing out heaps of steaming casserole onto their plates. Liam started wolfing it down immediately, mopping gravy with a big piece of freshly cut bread and butter. Rarely did they eat takeaways—Jen was always keen to cook and was accomplished in the kitchen. He never complained, and although he had the odd occasion where he cooked some 'speciality' dishes he was happy for her to take the reins. They ate in silence for a few minutes, Jen realising that he was hungry. The wine had given her an appetite too, so they ate comfortably in each other's company. In a surprisingly short space of time, both plates were empty, and she began clearing the table.

"I've had a bit of a strange day today, Jen," Liam ventured. Well it was now or never—why was he so goddamned nervous about talking to her about this? "Mostly, because I didn't spend all day in the office. I had a meeting this morning." He paused, waiting for a reaction, or comment.

"Oh, really? What kind of meeting? Work related?" she inquired. She felt a small wave of relief come over her; how could she even think that he'd be screwing someone else? They were the perfect match in every way, and Liam was devoutly loyal in character—especially when it came to Jen.

"Well…you know where John works?" he said cautiously. "I had an appointment there. With the director, Dr Nathan Ellis." He paused again, awaiting her reaction. Jen stopped her tidying and turned to him. He was still sat at the table, sipping his drink now rather than gulping.

Her mind raced a little—why would he go there? Why had he not mentioned this meeting before? All of a sudden, things started to fall into place for Jen. *This is why he's been acting a little strangely! It's not an affair at all, far from it— he's been exploring the option that they had discussed a few months prior with John and Janet. The cloning thing, or twinning thing or whatever they called it.*

"Oh really?" She inquired. "What for?" She looked at him expectantly, and he in turn looked a little shifty. The guilt of even such a simple deception did not sit well with Liam, and he made a mental vow to himself never to keep a secret from her again.

"Well, I got thinking about the conversation we had a little while ago, about the service that FMA offers. My curiosity got the better of me, so I arranged an appointment there with their MD. It's not what you know, it's who you know." He laughed a little nervously. This felt as much of an inquisition as the meeting earlier… "We just discussed what they could offer, and I took away some information. It's in the car; shall I get it and talk you through what we discussed?" The end of his sentence rose a notch in hope. He felt a little flushed, his face pinker than usual, a mix of alcohol and apprehension.

Jen was awash with mixed emotions. She had thought he was cheating, and he had been…well, she knew only too well what she had suspected and now felt guilty for it. And now it turns out he's been sat in a meeting at a medical company…ridiculous. But he had acted without her knowledge, which meant a secret—they didn't do secrets, and that stung a little. But only a little—he had been acting ultimately in both of their interests. And underlying all her feelings of secrets, and the betrayal that comes with them, was a feeling of excitement— this meant that he was seriously considering starting a family, something they had discussed many times but never taken the plunge. Liam was looking at her expectantly, trying to gauge her reaction. "I don't see why not, considering that you have already done all the leg work by the looks of it. Why didn't you tell me?" She moved to the table, sitting by him and taking his hand. "I would have come as well, you know." Liam felt relieved that this was all out in the open now, and in retrospect maybe he *should* have been more open with his wife.

"I know honey, and I'm sorry for not telling you, I really am. I just wanted to make sure it wasn't a pie in the sky idea that would go nowhere before talking to you about it. I never meant to keep it hush-hush from you. I thought if they can convince me it's a good idea, then that's half the battle." He squeezed her hand. "If we decide no, then its no. If we decide it's a goer, then we do it together." He pulled her towards him and hugged her tightly. "I'll go and get the information, and you can judge yourself." He got up and grabbed his keys on the way out of the front door. Two minutes later, Jen was leafing through the brochures and booklets that Liam had retrieved from the car. Liam sat quietly, drinking and casually observing her while she took in the detail he had tried to absorb earlier in Nathan's office. There were still pieces he would need to refresh himself on—he would read through the information later, provided Jen didn't immediately throw the whole idea out of the window. She took her time, and appeared suitably engrossed for the next ten minutes or so.

Finally, Jen looked up. "Well, that's a lot to take in," she said. "On the face of it, it seems like the perfect solution for the over-concerned parents out there, but we need to consider this carefully, Liam. There are a lot of factors to take into account, by the looks of it." She had leafed through the majority of the information on the table, and now tidied it into a neat pile.

"Yes, I know, hon. Why don't we sleep on it and talk later in the week? It may give us both a chance to digest it properly." Liam paused. "I don't want to rush into anything, and I want us both to agree on whatever we decide," he finished.

"Okay, that sounds like a plan." She smiled, and took his hand, squeezing lightly. "Now, how about one last drink?" She raised her glass and tilted it temptingly.

"Oh well, when in Rome. Jen, you are a bad influence, I swear your mum has had you all wrong all these years. Only I know the real truth," He raised an eyebrow at her and offered her his empty glass. "Do the honours then, love?"

# Chapter Three

The woman sat in her parked car, clammy with sweat and her nerves jangling. *Am I really going to do this?* She thought to herself, asking this same question again and again. It had felt like an eternity since she had lost her little girl, Sammi, and her initial all-consuming grief had now turned into something else. Sammi had died over two months ago, and her mother Naomi's sadness had turned to a deep-rooted rage in this time period. Her rage was directed at the company that owned the building that was directly in her line of sight—FMA. Just looking at it made her feel physically sick. She had only been here a handful of times during her pregnancy, and that was over eight years ago—FMA were obviously doing well, as it was now a much bigger affair than she remembered. This very thought fuelled her anger even more and she clenched her fists, her whole body taut. She brushed her dank, limp hair away from her gaunt face, teeth gritted. She had work to do.

She had parked a reasonable distance from the building, so as not to attract any unwanted attention. It was dark when she arrived, and she had not moved from her front seat for an hour. She had a small pair of binoculars on the passenger seat which she had been using to try and figure out the security guard patterns. So far, she had seen only one guard patrol the perimeter of the building. There didn't appear to be any patrol of the outer grounds and the fence that surrounded them. She would need to wait until the guard did another patrol before doing anything. She needed to know the timeframe in which she would have to complete the job. So far so good—she was hoping for hourly patrols, and it had gone past the half hour mark, so she was confident that this was the case. This should give her plenty of time. She was aware that there were security cameras, both on the building itself and on the perimeter fence at intervals, but this didn't bother her too much. She had a balaclava, and was dressed in black pretty much from head to toe, so identification from CCTV footage would be difficult. At least, that's what she told herself. And, in truth, she didn't really care about any consequences or repercussions from her planned actions—this was the only way she was going to get any sort of release from her living hell.

Naomi glanced at the rucksack in the foot well of the passenger seat. She had spent considerable time getting its contents to a point where she thought it could be capable of inflicting the damage she intended. For someone who had literally no idea about home-made explosives, she was quite proud of herself. The 'ingredients' had been fairly easy to procure once she knew what she needed, and the electronics side of it also was relatively straight forward. With so many tiny electronic devices readily available, it had been a case of some simple modifications, and then the remote detonation side of it had been done. As she pondered this, a distant movement caught her eye—the security guard was on his rounds again at FMA. She checked her watch. It had been an hour since she'd seen him last. She exhaled nervously as she eyed him through her binoculars. *Well, it's now or never...* She thought.

Naomi moved the rucksack onto the passenger seat, and picked up the bolt croppers in the foot well. These were more than man enough for the job—she was hoping to snip through the perimeter fence quickly and easily. She had a few things to check before leaving the car. She got her mobile out and checked her signal. It seemed fine, three bars. She was also using a hotspot for Wi-Fi. Satisfied, she put it in the dash. Once she had planted her improvised explosive and returned to the car, she would use the video doorbell App to detonate...simple. After checking the contents of the rucksack, she exited the car, closing the door as quietly as she could. She didn't bother locking it—escape needed to be as slick as it could possibly be, and fumbling with keys did not appeal.

Naomi crept along the fence, sweating profusely underneath the balaclava and hood. The bolt croppers felt slippery in her oily palm. The guard had disappeared around the back of the building. From her previous observations, he would not be seen from this side of the building again—he obviously must enter at a door around the back. The only unknown for Naomi was how long the round actually was, as she had never seen him re-enter the building. She thought about this briefly, and then dismissed any risk. *It's too fucking late to worry about details now!* She told herself. She stopped by the fence, crouching. There was cover from a decent sized tree inside the perimeter, blocking at least a direct line of sight. She pulled at the bottom of the fence, and was pleasantly surprised at the amount of give in it. This would make her entry significantly easier—she had imagined it being buried beneath the ground for several feet. She quickly snipped a right-angled hole in the fence and pulled it back towards her. The hole looked easily big enough to allow easy access, and more importantly, an easy exit.

Satisfied she would be able to duck straight back through the fence when the time came, she stayed crouched and got the rucksack off her back. She left the bolt croppers on the grass, hoping that she would remember to pick them up on the way back. Gingerly, she lifted the piece of plastic piping from the bag. During her 'development' of the IED, she initially thought of using heavy metal piping, but quickly dismissed it once she felt the weight of it. That was a shame, as she had quite liked the idea of dangerous, high-speed flying shrapnel. However, it was part of a spare length of plastic downpipe in the garage that had got the gig in the end. She fumbled in the side pocket of the rucksack and brought out a battery. It slid into place easily on the doorbell taped to the outside of the pipe, the click confirming it was pushed home properly. The disc on the doorbell flashed a light blue, which sent Naomi into a panic as she instantly had her mind filled with horrible images of it detonating there and then. After a few seconds of staring at it bug-eyed, she spurred herself into action—*If it was going to go off I'd be splattered over a fifty metre radius by now*, she convinced herself. Still, her heart hammered in her chest so hard that it gave her a head rush as the blood surged around her body, her bloodstream flooded with adrenaline.

Naomi carefully placed the IED on the other side of the fence to one side and clambered through, successfully avoiding getting snagged by the fence. Still crouched, pipe in hand, she surveyed the grounds of FMA for the hundredth time that evening. Once satisfied that there were no people around, she remained crouched as she scampered her way towards the building. She knew she was on a time limit now. She didn't know for sure if the perimeter fence CCTV would detect her (she had made sure to pick an entry point as far away from any cameras as possible), but she sure as hell knew the ones on the outside of the building would. This would have to be swift. The cameras would detect her for sure, but whether someone inside monitoring picked her up straight away was another matter…another unknown risk in the plan.

Naomi didn't have an exact location in mind for her device, but she knew she wanted it as near to the back of the building as she could risk without extending her stay within the confines of FMA for any longer than she had to. The nearer it was to the back, then the nearer to the laboratory that housed the twins. She saw a corner where the back of the FMA facility widened to accommodate its laboratories, and her mind was made up. She straightened up and broke into a quick, light-footed jog, making a direct line for the shadowed corner. As she encroached on the tarmac towards the nearest wall the night lights tripped on, bathing her black form in a clinical white glare. She always knew this would happen but it shocked her nonetheless, making her feel totally exposed and vulnerable, like an insect pinned to a microscope slide. She had two choices: remain rooted to the spot, frozen, waiting for capture, or get her ass in gear, get the job done and get the fuck out of there—she chose the latter.

She broke into a full sprint and was at the corner of the building within seconds. Panting heavily beneath the balaclava and drenched in greasy sweat, she placed the pipe down as carefully as she could, nestling it right into the recess of the brickwork where the two walls adjoined. After a quick, nervous glance around, she made her retreat at a full sprint. She knew she would have been detected at this point, so crouching and trying to be invisible was pointless. The objective now was to get back to the car as quickly as possible, detonate the bomb and get away.

Naomi's breathing was heavy and laboured as she clambered back through the fence. She paused momentarily to look back at the building—no security guards there yet. She was dizzy with adrenaline as she ran to the car and reached for the door. As she opened it, she felt a rough prod at the back of her head, and heard a clicking noise. A low whisper came:

"Don't fucking move lady, or I'll blow your head off."

# Chapter Four

Life went on for the Connellys. Jen was wrapped up in work with a few overnight stops here and there, and the rest of her day to day routine carried on as per usual. It was a similar story for Liam, doing overtime into the early evening when required, and desperately trying to down tools and relax when the opportunity arose. They had spoken about FMA, and the result was positive from both of them. They had made an appointment to see Dr George Baker on the 19th of August in the morning. Dr Baker was a paediatric consultant at FMA and had spent a large proportion of his previous life as a paediatric surgeon. He was well known in such circles, and a quick internet search proved that this was so. In the few days before the meeting, Jen started experiencing a similar feeling of anxiety just as Liam had prior to his first appointment. Liam on the other hand, felt differently this time round. He was excitedly expectant of a conclusion and a decision following the meeting. This was a welcome difference to his previous feelings about the whole matter. He was positively looking forward to it.

Neither of them had spoken to anyone else about FMA or what they were considering. This was unusual for Jen at least—she shared almost everything with her mother. It was a good job Liam liked Jen's mum Alison—Jen often spoke to her three or four times a week, letting her know every minute detail of their lives (except the obvious stuff). Liam was in regular contact with his own mother Jessica, also. His father, Adrian, had died many years ago when Liam was a teenager from lung cancer. Even though this was devastating to a young Liam, it did bring some good—it had made the bond between him and his mother stronger than ever. For that he was glad. But neither parent knew what was potentially on the cards should there be a grandchild in the mix, and that was for the best at this stage.

Days turned quickly into weeks, and before they both knew it, the 19th had arrived in all its glory. Jen and Liam went about their normal routine in the morning of the appointment, exchanging some light banter during the preparations for the journey. The FMA centre was not far away, perhaps twenty miles into the middle of nowhere from the cosy little coastal town of Cleedon on the south coast, where they had lived since the start of their marriage. They both busied themselves with smart clothes choices from their wardrobes followed by overly picky assessments of footwear—*these don't match my dress as well as these, these need a quick polish, where's the shoe stuff...?*

Finally, they both made their way out of the front door and into Liam's car. He knew where he was going, so no sat nav—he'd been there before. "All set, honey?" Liam asked her. She looked at him nervously.

"Yep, it's now or never, so hit the gas." Liam started the car and pulled out of the drive.

During the drive to the FMA centre, not an awful lot got said between them. *It's like we're on a first date, for God's sake,* thought Liam. The silence was mainly comfortable though, so there was no added tension to the trip, which was good. Jen kept thinking *just relax, it's only a consultation, and we don't have to commit to anything if we don't want to.* It didn't really help her nerves, which were busy trying to rack themselves up to 'full jangling mode'.

They arrived at the facility about fifteen minutes early. Jen started fussing, checking her bag, the mirror, her jacket pockets and just about anything else that could be obsessed over. Liam was much less jumpy—after all, he'd done this before, and with the big man too. He wondered if Dr Baker would pitch it any differently than Nathan did. *It would probably be more of the same*, he thought.

"Ready, Jen?" he inquired. She looked at him, and quickly squeezed his hand.

"Do I look OK?" she asked. She looked stunning, same as ever. Her golden brown hair framed her face perfectly, and she was wearing a small amount of make-up, just enough to highlight her good features. Which happened to be all of them.

"Fantastic, honey. Let's knock 'em dead." They got out of the car and walked towards the building.

The appointment went well. Dr Baker was a charming gentleman and went through the same basics as Dr Ellis had done previously with Liam as they sipped freshly brewed coffee. All in all, it lasted about an hour, Liam asked very few questions, and Jen the same. Liam had passed on all his knowledge from the previous meeting, so this was a bit of a formality to bring Jen into the loop really.

Jen was suitably non-committal during the meeting—the real decision would be made between them in the next few days, no doubt.

After saying their goodbyes and thanks, the couple made their way out of the building and back into the car.

"Well, what do you think of that then, Jen?" Liam enquired as he started the engine and reversed the car out of the space.

"They seem to have a handle on what they're offering." Jen replied. "I'm keen to look into some of these case studies though. For such a new program, I'm not sure what data will actually exist. There must be some parents that have given testimony on how they have found the experience, because they've told us where to find it. But how do we know they are real? They could have made it up." Jen paused, allowing Liam to think about what she just said.

"I take your point Jen, but do we really think that such an upstanding medical company would mitigate their business by lying? You would bloody well hope not. Maybe we can research their case studies further once we've read them. Let's have a look later and see what we think. And hey, I'm still very open-minded about this whole thing. We don't have to do anything if we don't want to, we haven't committed to anything," he reminded her.

"Yeah you're right, I'm just being my normal paranoid self and thinking out loud," she replied. "Let's look later. Meanwhile let's get home and I'll whip us up something to eat, I'm starving."

Half an hour later they were at home with Jen buzzing around the kitchen while Liam checked his laptop. Jen was putting together a quick lunch of smoked salmon, eggs and rye bread. Once ready she put a couple of plates on the table. "OK big guy, let's eat."

After lunch, they started looking at the case studies from a link on the FMA website. The website was certainly secure enough, asking for passwords on entry and every time a link was followed, Liam observed. He was using his home laptop and they both huddled over the screen, chairs drawn together at the table.

"Look at this one," Jen said. The study detailed a successful couple in their late twenties that had embarked on the program when the pregnancy was confirmed, and they appeared to have written a paragraph on every step, right from the start up to a few years after the child was born. They both stared at the screen, engrossed, reading at roughly the same speedy rate.

"Well, they seem happy enough with it all," Liam remarked. "They haven't mentioned much about cost though. I can't see all this being cheap Jen." A frown crossed his brow briefly. Just how much *would* this all cost? Financials had not really been discussed at either consultation, but it was obvious you would need to be financially very stable to consider the program.

"I'm sure it isn't Liam. But what are we saving all our hard earned cash for anyway? We have the house of our dreams that's already mostly paid off, and our family will deserve the best." This was the first statement from Jen that was actually biased towards the twinning program since they had been considering it, and it didn't go unnoticed by Liam. He was encouraged by her positivity.

"Let's sleep on it, sweetheart. If we agree one way or the other in the next couple of days, then we can take it from there, no pressure." They looked at each other, and he smiled. "You're right about the money. I can't spend it all on guitars I can't play very well and fishing gear that sits in the garage because I never have time to go," he said light-heartedly. She leant over and pecked his cheek.

"You may have to sell some guitars instead of buying more, Liam—I've already earmarked your music room for a nursery regardless of what we do with FMA." He looked at her with an expression of mock horror on his face.

"Can we not convert the garage into a nursery, love? That way I get to keep my music room!"

"In your dreams, Liam. In your dreams." She responded, laughing. "Just don't forget who's boss around here, you're not at work now."

# Chapter Five

The obvious decision was agreed two days later, over dinner. They were both in favour of the idea, as they both knew that they would be, and Liam took the responsibility of booking a third appointment at FMA to finalise. The meeting was arranged yet again to see Dr Baker, but this time accompanied by a few colleagues—one of which was their friend, John Lee. General Consultant for FMA PLC. *Wow, this is going to be weird*, thought Liam. Last time he had seen John they were getting falling-down drunk on expensive cognac at Jen and Liam's place about two months ago. Next week they would be sat around in a very plush office discussing the details of the program, what had to be done and by when, the money involved, etc. It felt like a change of pace for Liam—all of a sudden, after months of his own deliberation, scurrying around having clandestine meetings in locations unbeknown to his wife, they were both about to commit to a potentially life changing program of huge proportions for their as yet unborn child. It felt strange and unnerving, but with an underlying flavour of relief—no more secrets or unknowns.

As per last time, the date came around quickly, almost jumping on top of them, and they were rushing around once more in nervous panic over minor clothing details. It was like Groundhog Day. Once this ritual had been performed, they were on their way to seal the deal.

In the space of half an hour, they were sat in Dr Baker's office, facing the office owner and their friend John. It was surreal to say the least. They had said their hellos in the most informal fashion that they all thought appropriate while Dr Baker looked on, waiting for his greeting. He was obviously more than aware of the connection between client and provider, and looked on with a slightly embarrassed yet curious expression on his face. He was the oldest in the room, and he almost had a fatherly look about him, accentuated by the significantly younger company.

"Pleased to meet you, Mr and Mrs Connelly. I'm Dr Baker." They sat down.

A lengthy ninety minutes later, they were done. Dr Baker had proved charming, intelligent and likeable. They had signed all manner of papers there and then, despite the offer to return later or have more time to consider—they had already decided that this was for them and their family. What better way to ensure the health and happiness of their son or daughter to be than this? Now began a period of co-ordination, organisation and timing. They must return once Jen had fallen pregnant for tests, monitoring, data collection, and a DNA sample of the growing foetus at six weeks. In the run-up to this follow-up appointment, bank debits would be set up, payments would be taken, and remaining documents drafted and subsequently signed. It was like any other formal process in that respect—all the boring stuff still needed doing.

A lot more was discussed between them on the way home than on the way there. There was an air of excitement in the car. Liam pulled onto the drive, waiting for the garage door to reach the end of its opening travel. "Well, it's been an eventful day, Jen," he said. "Lots to do for us now."

"Yeah, too right…best start thinking about my lifestyle, for starters. Early nights, less drinking, less stress and responsibility in work is on the cards I think," Jen commented. They got out of the car and entered the house through the side door in the garage.

"Me too—I need to start giving you more massages, running you more baths and cooking more," he half joked. Joking or not, he got the feeling he would be doing exactly that in the coming weeks. "In fact, why don't I cook tonight? That way you can put your feet up later and not worry." He looked at her and smiled as he turned the kitchen lights on. "Promise I won't burn anything."

"Well, if you insist—how about that Moroccan dish you do so well that we haven't had in six months?"

"OK, no problem. I'll have to pop out for some ingredients in a bit, I'm sure you'll survive without me while I'm gone."

"If you insist, my love," she replied.

The next few weeks went exactly according to plan. Plenty of indulgent lazy nights indoors, no visitors, less overtime for Liam and fewer trips away for Jen (she had spoken to her area Manager and explained that there were family priorities to be considered, and normal hours were fine, but no more if possible). Liam had backed off spending so much time at the office, and had upped his game in the kitchen, as well as in the bedroom. They needed no excuse to get intimate, and both revelled in the closeness and excitement of each other. Having a purpose rather than just self-fulfilling put a surprising edge on the proceedings, and they both felt differently about what their ultimate goal was. Liam was determined to perform at the drop of a hat (no real change there), and often multiple attempts were made in the same night (that had changed). Jen was accommodating and engaging as always, but perhaps more driven than usual. Either way, no one could accuse them of slacking—the carnal activity was at an all-time high. They both felt closer than ever. Life was good.

After a few weeks they had both pretty much settled into a slightly newer way of life, and Liam wondered why they hadn't been living like this all along. The changes weren't major, but all the tiny things added up to quite a different experience for them both. And they were both enjoying it. More exercise was happening—longer walks together in the early evening summer sunshine could be breezy at times, especially when they were coastal, but very invigorating. The kitchen duties were more evenly shared, but more joint efforts were happening, which made a surprising difference to evening meals. They were both keener than usual to cook and eat when all hands were at the pump.

There were differences around the home too—Jen was serious about Liam's music room undergoing a transformation. She had made him take all his gear out into the garage, while she cleaned skirting boards, scrubbed walls and carpets, and took down curtains to wash. The garage was dry, so Liam put up little, if no resistance; he could set up just fine out there, but he got the feeling that not much playing would be happening anyway. The priorities were shifting quickly.

Liam was returning from work one late afternoon (no overtime for him), and had been reflecting on their life choices and the change that had come about since their decision to try for a family and get on board with FMA. Largely, these changes were positive and good for both of them. He had tried to see a downside or any pitfalls, but came up at a loss when he thought along those lines. This was also good. He parked the car on the drive, as the garage was a work in progress. He would need to think about insulating it and also added security given the ten thousand pounds or so of gear now stashed in there, a lot more portable than a locked, alarmed car…he crunched across the wide gravel drive and opened the front door. Jen was in already as she finished marginally earlier than him.

"Hello honey! How's your day?" he called jovially. She was in the kitchen out of sight, but he could hear she had made a start on dinner.

"Hi big guy, yeah OK, what about you? I'm cooking steak for dinner, you can help once you're sorted if you like," she replied, equally upbeat.

"OK, give me five to get out of these clothes and I'll be right there." He kicked his shoes off and started upstairs. As he got to the bedroom, he started to undo his tie, and loosen his belt. As he made his way to his wardrobe (by far the smaller built-in wardrobe in the bedroom), he glanced at the bed and noticed something lying there—what was that? Some of Jen's make up, mascara maybe? He stopped and looked closer. It was a pregnancy test. Used. He picked it up carefully. *PREGNANT,* it declared in the little window. He stared at it uncomprehendingly. Pregnant…? Pregnant! His heart raced. She had obviously left it for him to find. He felt an exhilarated rush of excitement, quickly dumped his clothes, dragged on his jeans and a top, grabbed the test and scampered down the stairs. He went straight into the kitchen. Jen had her back towards him, she was at the fridge. He grabbed her, turned her around, and kissed her fiercely.

"You found it then?" she teased. "I thought you'd be smart enough to work it out on your own, Sherlock." She kissed him again. "Congratulations are in order, Daddy!"

"Woo-hoo! Yeah! This is just the best, love—I love you so much!" He hugged her tightly. "What happened?"

"Well, you took me upstairs, and then we kind of started kissing…" She continued to tease.

"You know what I mean—when did you know? When did you do the test? Why didn't you ring me? I could have finished early," he said, almost garbling his words. She brushed her hair behind her ear and pulled away from him, so she could look at him properly.

"Oh yeah, what could you have done for me? Directed my pee more accurately? Squeezed my bladder for a more effective delivery? Don't be daft. In any case, I've not long done it." She glanced at the clock. "I did it at five, so not even an hour ago." She smiled radiantly at him. "We knew it was going to happen sooner or later, and here we are. But it's as early as it gets, so let's keep our heads please, Mr Connelly." She was right, of course. It was a flying start, but it was the beginning of a long journey that may or may not be that straightforward.

"Yes, I know Jen, but this is the best news ever! But we can't tell anyone. Not yet. Maybe we wait until we get back from holiday. Apart from one phone call." *Bloody hell, I'd forgotten all about the holiday,* Jen thought. They had booked it earlier in the year, and now the date was looming in just two weeks, or thereabouts.

"No way, Liam. No one means no one. If I can't tell Mum then you can't tell anyone either," she said.

"I was talking about FMA, sweetheart," he replied in a slightly serious tone. "They told us to keep them informed of all developments or changes." He was right. They would want to know immediately. There was a strict programme to follow, starting from day one.

"Oh yeah, of course," she said, thoughtful. She had got so wrapped up in the moment that she had totally forgotten that there was a whole load of stuff to do with FMA once she tested positive. "I'll txt Kay tomorrow, and tell her I've got to take the day off. I'm going to need to take a trip to FMA I think."

"I'll do the same with Pete. We're doing it together." Liam said. "We can call the centre in the morning, there will only be night staff there now anyway. And they told us within forty-eight hours if possible. We're well inside that timescale if you only did it an hour ago."

"Well, it sounds like a date. You take me to all the nicest places, Liam." She teased him again. He laughed.

"If you behave yourself, we can stop for ice-cream on the way back. Low fat, no sugar ice-cream. Especially developed for pregnant women. Now, where's the champagne? We are celebrating whether the docs say it's OK or not!"

# Chapter Six

They both went to the FMA clinic the following morning, a crisp, autumnal feel in the air. The appointment was different than the previous consultations—Jen was subjected to a series of tests, bloods, eyes, ears, various physical checks, and she also had to provide a DNA sample. This was done relatively easily; a quick cheek swab appeared to give the doctor the material he required. He explained that they would start the twinning process immediately—if anything should happen during her pregnancy then they would decide the most appropriate course of action. The conversation took a darker turn when he told them that he was obliged by contract to explain that the twin would not serve as a replacement child for them should the worst happen and the pregnancy ended, for whatever reason. They both agreed solemnly that they understood the implications of what he was saying to them, exchanging slightly confused and almost scared glances.

Two and a half hours later, they were done. Jen felt a little frazzled after the whole experience, she had been poked and prodded quite a bit during their appointment. Liam also felt a little drained, but more emotionally than anything else. The tests they had run on him had been basic, like a standard GP health check. But it was done now, the first step taken. They both felt relieved in the car on the way back, as if a weight had been lifted. Liam stayed true to his word and stopped at a quaint little café just off the main route back and bought them an ice-cream and a coffee. They didn't have any low fat offerings, so Jen took advantage and had a full fat tutti-frutti. *Well, I'm eating for two now, I guess*, she thought, instantly justifying it to herself.

Once back home, they both settled in for a quiet night. Both had now taken a few days off work, so it was time for some rest, and if Jen had anything to do with it, baby shopping for absolutely everything they might need for the new arrival. They talked briefly about their impending holiday to the Caribbean, even considering whether to cancel or not, and both had decided that they wanted to go, especially given that they might not have another holiday abroad for a more extended period of time than usual.

They had decided to go to bed early, following about fifteen minutes of searching for something vaguely interesting on TV, to no avail. After a ten minute phone check, emails, social media, news and suchlike, they turned the lights out and went upstairs.

The usual routines applied—Jen, preening in the en-suite, make up removal, skin creams, hair lotions, and Liam generally pottering around tidying his laundry, arranging his bedside cabinet and rummaging through his tiny wardrobe. Once they both found themselves in bed, they took comfort from each other's warm bodies. One thing invariably led to another, and cuddles turned into more insistent, passionate caressing and fondling.

Liam had his head buried in Jen's neck and shoulder, kissing her passionately, making her tingle electrically all over. She responded by pushing her body into his, revelling in his attention, caressing his muscular upper body and cradling his head, running her hands through his thick, short cropped hair. She ran her nails over his scalp, making his head and upper body tingle—God, she knew how to press his buttons! She felt his insistence in her lower region, his gentle prodding becoming more urgent. Jen responded to his advances, moving subtly to allow him more access. She reached down between their bodies and caressed him, stroking him firmly. They adjusted positions to accommodate each other, both eager to experience each other's bodies fully. Liam pressed his hardness against her abdomen, pressing into her stomach. Jen sighed in pleasure, wanting more. He entered her, at first gently, and once inside her, deeper and more rhythmical movements took over. She shuddered with pleasure, running her hands over his back and neck.

She moved her body against his, tilting her hips to allow him full access, which he took immediate advantage of. His head was still buried in her neck, the kisses now wetter and harder on the top of her neck and shoulder. As he moved his lower body against hers, she felt a twinge of discomfort from deep inside her: *What is that...?* Was her first fleeting thought, quickly followed by: *it can't be anything to do with the pregnancy, it's too early...*momentarily distracted, she re-adjusted herself to relieve the strange sensation. Liam seemed oblivious, lost in their lovemaking. He grunted and moved her slightly to allow him more intimate contact. His hands felt sweaty and slightly pudgier than Jen was used to...almost like they belonged to someone else...almost feeling like they were leaving sticky handprints on her hips and buttocks. Then, there it was again: *Ouch, why is there pain there…? AHHH…feels sharp!* There was a bit more than discomfort this time. Jen reacted calmly, but all of a sudden, she was on high alert…the mix of intimate sexual pleasure mixed with unexpected pain was a first for her, and she did not like it much. She ever so gently pushed her hands against his body, as a defensive move. "Liam, stop, I feel something." She murmured, hoping he would relent. But Liam didn't relent—he was totally lost in the moment, kissing Jen's neck passionately and feverishly, slightly aggressively even. Jen was herself trapped, stuck between intimate pleasure and a nagging worry that something wasn't right…

"Liam…" she said in a low voice, but he either didn't hear her, or took no notice. She pressed against the back of his head: *He feels different,* she thought. Her hand wandered around his head and she felt a distinct lack of hair that she had felt moments earlier: *What is happening, this doesn't feel like Liam…?* Liam's thrusts became more energetic as he engaged with his carnal instinct, and then, all of a sudden, there was full pain for Jen…she felt a sharp, stabbing pain deep in her abdomen, again and again, in sync with the now piston-like movement into her pelvis, sending panic waves to her brain. *WHAT THE HELL IS THAT MY GOD IT HURTS*! Her stomach now started clenching along with her cervix and what felt like her womb, against the stabbing invasion into her lower body. It felt like someone was ramming a sharpened poker into her crotch. She tried to pull his head up from her neck, and as she gripped his head it felt like he had been wearing a wig that had slipped off—his head felt bald. *OH MY GOD WHAT IS THIS…WHO IS THIS…*raced through her mind. She looked down in shock and saw a glint in the dim light of what she thought was Liam's head—it had very little hair on it. And it also looked like it wasn't his. She withdrew her hand from his head, and started to writhe away from him, only to be stopped in her tracks by a huge wave of stabbing pain from her lower body: *AAGH WHAT IS HAPPENING TO ME? STOP HURTING ME!* She went into fright mode and let out a short scream.

"Aaagh, Liam, it hurts! Please stop, something's wrong!" she cried. Liam must have heard this, but continued his activity regardless. She grabbed his head with both hands and pulled it away from her upper body. She looked in horror as he looked up at her. It wasn't Liam's face that met her. It appeared to be Dr Nathan Ellis, features contorted into a macabre grimace, part ecstasy, part animal. She tried to scream again, but her lungs were incapacitated completely

44

by a huge wave of sharp pains emanating upwards through her body from her abdomen. She was rapidly going into shock. What was happening to her? Was it Liam or Nathan inside her? Where was the pain coming from? As she struggled against the Nathan/Liam thing that was copulating with her, all the time delivering agonising pains from feverish, now violent thrusts of his manhood, she looked down between their bodies—she saw dark blood everywhere, all over her body, all over the bed sheets, all over the thing that was still busy ramming his pelvis against hers, bruising, flowering, dull pain now adding to the intense sharp crippling stabs from within her.

"Get off! Stop…you're killing me! Stop, why are you doing this?" she managed to utter, no energy in her voice. She felt the strength sap out of her as the blood continued to pour out of her. Several deep, lacerating cuts had now appeared on the surface of her pelvis and stomach, from internal piercings that allowed the blood to flow out. The thing pulled away from her, its cock sliding out from her body: *Oh, thank God,* she thought. It must be over. But it wasn't. It leered at her as it reached down to hold itself—she looked and saw that its penis was very large, and the top half appeared to gleam in a metallic fashion. It was effectively a huge spike, and had been perforating her from the inside out. It took it in its hands, and pushed her down flat onto the bed, holding her by the throat. She was unable to make a sound—her jaw worked in a frenzy, but no sound came out. It manoeuvred the metallic spike towards her abdomen, and then proceeded to stab it into her, its face contorted with glee and a perverted masochism. This time her voice worked—Jen let out an ear splitting scream, as the spike pierced her skin. The stabbing continued, Jen screaming and thrashing all the while, until there was deep red everywhere. Her lower body was on fire with pain; her brain had gone into pain overload. She felt like she had gone insane and was living in a lunatic hell. The thing then reached forward and inserted its fingers into the holes it had just created, a disgusting leer on its face. A rough, powerful yanking motion made all the stab wounds stretch like elastic and join into one huge tear all the way across her stomach. It reached inside, and felt around inside her womb, searching…and finally, after a sideways rip of its hand, withdrew what it was searching for. Jen's unborn foetus nestled in its hand, still, bloody and dead. She looked at it in complete terror, and screamed again…and again…and again…

"Wake up Jen! Wake up darling, please, Jen… *STOP SCREAMING!"* Liam was panicking, and had to try desperately not to shake the living daylights out of her. God, what was wrong…? Jen continued to thrash and scream, tangling the bed sheets, her hair sticking to her sweaty brow, creased with disturbed frown lines. Her legs kicked out from underneath him (he was almost completely on top of her now, trying to control her erratic movements and bring her out of her sleeping hell), and Liam re-positioned himself so as not to hurt her and continued to try and wake her.

"NO! NO! Get off me!" Jen was screaming still and appeared to be directed at him…but he was the only other person there, apart from in her head, so he tried not to take it personally.

"Jen, wake up…you're having a bad dream, please wake up… WAKE UP!" Liam shouted. This seemed to do the trick—Jen fluttered her eyes momentarily, and then opened them fully. She looked dazed and exhausted as well as terrified, looking around crazily as if to try and identify an unseen assailant. Liam grabbed her shoulders and levelled his eyes with hers, forcing her to look at him head on.

"Shh, it's just a bad dream hon, you were having a nightmare." Jen looked at him with wild, terrified eyes, uncomprehending. She still appeared to be under the spell of the nightmare she had just been released from. "It's OK Jen, it's just me, you're safe." He drew her close and hugged her tightly. Her body was cold and clammy from the sweat of fear, and still every muscle tensed within her. Liam continued to try and bring her round, smoothing her hair away from her damp brow. "What did you dream? It's OK now Jen. It's just me and you. And the baby."

Jen moved away from him momentarily, only to compose herself. *What the fuck…oh God, that was horrible…what did it mean?* She consciously checked her stomach, looking down at herself, searching for any signs of damage. Of course, there were none—she exhaled a sigh of relief and exhaustion. Every bone and muscle in her body appeared to be affected by the trauma she had just been through. She felt battered all over. "It was just a bad dream," she said, almost to herself. "It's over now."

Liam pulled her close again, still determined to comfort her back to normality. "OK Jen, it's OK. Are you sure you feel alright now? You scared the shit out of me. What was it all about?" he asked, gently. "You haven't had a nightmare in ages." He stroked her arm to try and get her to open up to him. He thought it didn't really matter what she had dreamt, just that she was awake and safe now.

"Oh… I'm not sure," she lied. She knew damn well what it was all about, and could remember every shred of the nightmare in glorious detail. But she wasn't about to tell Liam that the dream consisted of rape and mutilation, in which he played a major part. "It was just a bad dream; I guess my body is changing rapidly. Probably to be expected, and perhaps not the last time it happens," she tried to rationalise it more for Liam's sake, than hers. He looked at her quizzically.

"Well, if what you're saying is that we have more in store, then I'll be carting you back to FMA for some tests, hon. Surely that can't be a normal part of being pregnant?" The thought of that becoming a regular occurrence throughout the pregnancy made him feel quite scared. *I've never read that anywhere, surely it's not normal…?* He thought to himself.

"I'm OK now Liam, so let's not get carried away. There's no need to involve the FMA over a nightmare for God's sake." Her tone was slightly sharp, and he noticed.

"No Jen, I'm not suggesting we do that. I'm just worried that's all, I've never seen you like that before and it scared me."

"Scared you? Try walking a mile in my shoes! I hope it never happens again!" She suddenly burst into tears and Liam pulled her towards him, holding her close, kissing her forehead again and again.

# Chapter Seven

Things slowly settled back down after the nightmare. Jen cross examined the content of it again and again over the next week or so—did it have any meaning? Why was Nathan in it? She had only met him twice and didn't know enough of him to form an unconscious opinion of him so why did he play such a vile part in her nightmare? She was perplexed, but over time the memory of the dream faded. She was glad; it wasn't something she wanted to carry around in her head really. Liam was suitably attentive, not overly pushy about it, but asking if she was OK at the right times. He was also freaked out by the episode—Jen had previously experienced bad dreams but never anything like that, so why now? He thought maybe it was hormones running wild, but she was only a few weeks gone, seven to be exact. Surely, hormone swings in pregnant women didn't happen with such ferocity? He hoped not, otherwise the rest of the pregnancy was going to be horrendous if this was anything to go by.

Jen had always suffered from very vivid dreams, ever since she had been a young girl. She never attached any importance to them, until she was eighteen or so. At that time, she started thinking a bit more in depth about her dreams and whether they held any significance in any way—she had done some research into the phenomena, and read a few books too, in a quest to try and understand if it was normal to experience such vivid and sometimes scary dreams. She thought about the timing of the dreams, and whether they were linked to any real-life events, but it was all too speculative for Jen's logical way of thinking. She just accepted the fact that she had them, and as she grew older they became less and less frequent…which in turn banished any probing questions about them to the back of her mind.

They both went about their daily lives as per normal in the run up to their holiday, trying to slowly forget about the whole thing. Which worked—time is a great healer, especially when you are actively trying to put something behind you and you're not alone. Neither had told anyone in their work circle about Jen being pregnant, or any of their family for that matter (although Liam had a sneaking suspicion that Jen had talked to her mum, Alison, about the fact she was expecting, early days or not). As it turned out, the holiday was a great idea. It allowed the couple to soak each other up as well as the blazing Caribbean sun. The ten days they were there were spent largely lying on sun drenched sands, cooling off in both the sea and pool, and long exploratory walks taking in the foreign fauna and flora. On the last evening of their break, they found themselves on the beach, walking hand in hand towards a group of locals gathered around a large beach fire. Neither Liam nor Jen had any intention of joining this group as they approached—as heads noticed their presence and turned towards them, the couple nodded amiably, and Jen gave a small wave to a young woman who was smiling at them. She waved back, and beckoned them to come over. She was sat on a driftwood tree trunk along with a few others, one of which was a much older woman, who appeared to be locked into an intense conversation with a middle aged man sat next to her. Jen and Liam exchanged quick glances, and after a shrug from Liam, they sauntered over towards the woman. She welcomed them warmly to their little evening gathering, and motioned for them to sit down, motioning to another man to bring some drinks over. The young woman introduced herself as Kadisha, and also introduced her grandmother, Cazembe. The old woman took an instant interest in Jen in particular, and after looking at her intently, turned to her granddaughter and proceeded to talk quietly but urgently to her in what Jen assumed was Portuguese. The young woman listened attentively, and then turned to Jen and Liam.

"My grandmother cannot speak English" she explained to them. "But she has asked me whether she can feel your hands—I know this sounds unusual, but she has a gift. Many from our town think she is able to to…well, predict certain things, I suppose." She paused, looking at the couple. "It's nothing to be scared of, honestly," she quickly added.

"What harm can it possibly do?" Liam said, looking at the old lady curiously. Her face was full of deep set wrinkles in her dark leathery skin, but they lent a kind expression to her. There were many laughter lines that had obviously been well exercised over the decades of her life. She was nodding enthusiastically in their direction. Jen shrugged and agreed also, so the two women swapped their perches so the old woman was sat next to Jen. She clasped both of her hands and drew them towards her lap, eyes half closed. After a few moments, she started babbling excitedly to Kadisha, whose eyes grew wide at first, and then a broad smile revealed her perfectly white teeth, lighting up her pretty, ebony face. Jen asked her what she had said, and Kadisha replied:

"She is very excited for you both! Let me ask you—do you have any children?" Jen looked at Liam.

"Well…not yet, but we hope to start a family soon," Jen told her, slightly taken aback at the enquiry. Kadisha's eyes lit up, and she turned and nodded to her grandmother.

"Well in that case, my grandmother brings good news—she says that you are with child!" Both Jen and Liam were taken aback at this statement—how did she know? How *could* she know?

"Oh my God, how did she know? Yes, I am in the first stages of pregnancy, just a few weeks in," Jen said, shell-shocked that this old woman could have predicted what she did. Kadisha quickly turned to the old woman and told her what had been said, at which she let out a peal of laughter and clasped her hands together in joy, before whispering something in Kadisha's ear. She turned to the couple once more.

"She says she knows what sex the child will be—do you wish to know what she thinks?" She asked, looking inquiringly at the couple. They looked at each other and Jen shrugged at Liam.

"Well, I'm game if you are, sweetheart," he said. Jen nodded at Kadisha in agreement.

"It's a boy!" She told them, smile wider than ever. *Wow… I'm going to have a son! That's if this woman knows her stuff,* Liam thought. And neither of them had any reason to disbelieve her—after all, she knew Jen was pregnant, so who were they to doubt she also knew the sex of the unborn child? Liam hugged his wife close, and she rested her head on his shoulder.

They stayed there for a short while longer and then made their excuses to leave, thanking both Cazembe and Kadisha for their kindness. There was a small table to one side with some locally made trinkets on, and Kadisha offered Jen a necklace from it, saying it would bring her good fortune in her maternity. Jen started by saying she couldn't possibly accept it, but Liam intervened with a reasonable sum of cash that he had in his pocket—it would be no use to them back home, so why not donate it to these kind people that had welcomed them so readily into their community? Jen let Liam put it around her neck, and they walked back along the beach, taking in the last of the sunset.

It was Friday the thirteenth of October, but Liam felt lucky as he pulled in on the drive. He had finished early, and Jen was already home. *The weekend starts here,* he thought cheerfully, and went inside. Jen was home, and sat at the kitchen table on her laptop. She looked up at the door as he opened it, and smiled. Liam looked good even after a full day at the office—his hair was still in place, tie still done up to the top button.

"Hey honey! It's the weekend…!" he called to her light-heartedly.

"Yep, you got it…how was your day?" She responded. She got up, unconsciously feeling her stomach—there wasn't any physical sign she was pregnant, but she did it anyway. "I deliberately haven't started tea…how about we go out for something to eat?" she said, almost hopefully. He detected the tone.

"Well, if you think being up the duff means no cooking ever, then you're mistaken, girl," he replied in mock seriousness as he kissed her on the cheek. "I guess that's OK as long as you pay."

"Bloody hell, I need to be a kept woman now I'm in the family way!" she exclaimed, pushing him away. "This is tantamount to abuse, Liam Connelly!" He laughed. She always managed to bring a little joy into his life whenever they shared these light-hearted moments together—it was as if their playful banter banished all the doom and gloom in the world for a short time.

"Well, OK but nothing too extravagant…how about Perry's?" Perry's Pizza was a fifteen minute walk from theirs, far enough out of the town centre to be suitably quiet on a Friday night. And they did a banging hot meat feast pizza. He started to warm to the idea as he thought about it, and he felt his stomach reacting accordingly. He nodded his approval.

"OK, it's a date, handsome. Get sorted then." Jen told him. Liam did as he was told. Fifteen minutes later, they were out walking together in the crisp October air. It was refreshing—and would help them work up an appetite. Jen looked up at him (Liam was a good ten inches taller than her at six foot two), and almost opened her mouth to speak, and then thought better of it. The nightmare was still on her mind, although faded, and she wanted to talk, but decided better of it. He looked back at her.

"What's on your mind sweetheart?" he inquired mildly. He had a feeling it may have been about the recent incident. Sometimes, it was like they had a sixth sense with each other. He remembered the time Jen had been dinged in her car while pulling out of a supermarket car park. She rang him once the incident was done and insurance details had been swapped. When his mobile went off he was on lunch at work, with some colleagues at a local greasy spoon. He made his excuses and went outside to take the call, and somehow just *knew* something was wrong. Sure enough, he was right. There were countless little incidents like this that had happened between them over the eight years they had been together. Mostly just little things, things that could be put down to coincidence or thoughts that maybe every close couple have about each other. But sometimes it felt like a stronger feeling.

"Oh, nothing much." She lied. She knew Liam would know this—but she didn't really feel like dragging it up right before they were due to have a dinner for two. She changed her tact. "I was wondering what my next appointment at FMA might hold in store," she said. This wasn't strictly a lie; she was curious, and a little scared maybe, of how things might progress.

"Yeah me too hon. I'm sure it will all go according to plan—we've done all the preliminary stuff so surely now the twinning process is in motion then the physical aspects will tail off at least," he replied. Liam also wondered what may lie ahead. All the exams had been done, and the samples and biopsies had all been gathered by the proficient FMA doctors and consultants. It was just a case of on-going monitoring through Jen's pregnancy. At least, that's what he hoped. It's what they both hoped. "We can ask when we're next there. I know we've got all the appointments in then calendar, but we can get more detail from them about what they want to do. That will make us both feel better, being in the know. I guess we're both suffering from a bit of the fear of the unknown…but at least we face it together." He pulled her closer as they walked, and ran his hand through his hair nervously.

"Yeah, let's do that. I still feel like a guinea-pig, even though it's tried and tested," Jen said. "I just can't help it—it seems so…*different* than anything I've ever read or known about being pregnant," she added. She was right there—it was hardly OK magazine's version of the blossoming fairy tale that is carrying a baby, having to attend quite formal medical appointments what felt like every day. In reality, it wasn't every day—more like once a fortnight. Jen was now nearly ten weeks gone, and they had attended a grand total of three appointments since she got pregnant.

As they turned the corner from relatively unspoilt countryside into a well-lit busy street, they both subconsciously attempted to re-join the human race. The conversation had taken a turn towards when they should next invite John and

Janet over—it had been a while since they had caught up and a social seemed overdue. The last time they had seen John was at FMA. Liam held the door open for her, and they went inside the quiet but homely pizza restaurant.

Within twenty minutes they were seated, drinks brought over, and pizzas were in the oven. They had a table for two in the far corner, a little tucked out of the way, which suited them both just fine. They were looking at their calendars on their respective mobiles, looking for a suitable date for a get-together.

"How about next Thursday?" Liam suggested. "I've got next Friday off, so I can get bladdered," he added, winking at her. He knew this was a tease, as she couldn't drink.

"Well, I have an appointment at FMA next Thursday afternoon at two," she responded, still scrolling through her calendar. "It may be a bit hectic trying to cook as well as going there in the day," she added. She looked at him with a slight tilt of her head. "It'll be the first one I've been to without you."

"Oh God, I totally forgot…shall I take the afternoon off? I can still come with you honey." He kicked himself mentally—normally he would never overlook something like that.

"No, it's OK honestly," she insisted. "I'll be fine. It's a bit unrealistic to think I would be attending every appointment there with you at my side, what with work and everything." She meant it sincerely, and even though she was apprehensive of going alone (especially for the first time); she also accepted that she needed to man up and get on with it. She could field this without disrupting her husband's work life—they still had bills to pay.

"Well, OK. If you're sure." He took her hand across the table, a slight look of concern and guilt in his eyes. "I know you've got this, but I don't want you to feel alone," he added.

"It's fine honestly. Why don't we get John and Janet round on the Friday? That way, we are both free." Jen had reduced her hours at work and gone down to a three day week. She had also shed her travelling responsibilities onto her protégé, Alice.

"OK, it's a date. Now, hadn't one of us better check that they actually want to see us…?" he joked. The waiter had arrived at their table with pizza.

The food was excellent as ever, and they had both cleared their plates. Liam paid by card, tipped his usual ten pounds, and asked the barman to thank the chef on his behalf. They made their way home, feeling fat and full. Jen had messaged Janet about the following Friday, and she had come back just before they left:

*"Oh that would be wonderful we were just talking about a get-together earlier! I'll tell John and be in touch in the week much love xx."*

"They're up for it, love—Janet's just replied," she commented to Liam as they meandered their way home. It was dark and chilly, but the walk was helping work the food off just fine.

"Great, it's been too long. And I'd like to get John's take on what how he thinks things will pan out with FMA—maybe get some inside info." Liam replied. Maybe John would be able to tell him what to expect in the latter stages of pregnancy for Jen, and beyond...

They arrived home at about nine, fairly tired. Food, drink and exercise did that. Liam was looking for another beer or wine (or whatever, for that matter), and Jen was looking for bed.

"I'm going up, hon," she said, and pecked him on the cheek.

"Night sweetheart, I'll lock up. I'm going to grab another drink, watch some mindless dross on TV, and then turn in myself. Don't stay awake on my account." She shuffled her shoes off and made her way upstairs. Liam made his way to the fridge. Within a few minutes he had poured a premium strength beer into a tall glass, and was settled in front of the TV.

# Chapter Eight

All had been quiet for Jen and Liam, apart from the odd work phone call here and there for Jen (when she was at home), and Liam getting the working week done, albeit a short one. It was Friday afternoon, and Jen was cooking Indian for their dinner guests—John's favourite. And she did a great job normally, so this should be no exception. The kitchen already smelled like a curry house, and she was flying around it stirring, washing, straining and adding as required.

"You sure I can't help, Jen?" he asked for the second time.

"Nope, forget it I've got it all under control," she replied. She liked to be in control, and was doing just that.

"Well, Ok. I'm off to the shop to get some nice Indian beer, and some other bits…do you want anything love?" He asked.

"Yes, can you pick me up some alcohol-free anything. How rock and roll," she replied, an edge of sarcasm in her voice. She missed drinking, but actually not as much as she thought she would. Her brain had switched into mother mode, and her sole priority was the growing bump inside her. She fancied she was showing a little now—at twelve weeks it was still early days, and she couldn't be sure it wasn't her imagination. She had posed in front of the bedroom full length mirror many times side on, either sucking her abdomen in or pushing it out, to see if she could see the tiny form inside her…was it visible yet, or was it just her imagination? Her due date was April 12$^{th}$. Surely she couldn't be showing at this early stage? But during her private mirror self-viewings, she had noticed changes in her body—her overall shape was changing ever so subtly.

"OK, no problem, see you in a bit," Liam said and picked his keys up on the way out. Jen carried on whizzing around like a demon, prepping everything to the extreme—she was looking forward to seeing their friends soon. She felt a little like they had been starved of company. Sure, they had contact with others— work friends and colleagues (but mostly in the office), and the FMA appointments, but this was a proper catch up with people that were close, and that felt nice. She hummed to the radio in the background as she worked, apron on and hair tied back loosely.

By the time Liam returned, she had it all prepared and dishes also cleaned and put away. She was just starting on the laying the table, well ahead of her game.

"I got you some fizzy fruit juice, hon. And a load of Kingfisher. And a bottle of Courvoisier for John and me later, once you ladies are out of the way." Normally John and Janet stayed over in the spare room—it was like an unsaid rule. That way everyone could quite happily have a skin full. Apart from Jen this time. "How's the food coming on? It smells lovely," he said as he loaded beers into the fridge.

"Yep, it's all good—should be on the table by seven," she replied.

Within half an hour, the doorbell rang. "Come in!" Liam called. The door swung open and their friends came in from the cold.

"Hey, boys and girls! We've missed you!" chimed Janet. She was a small woman, in her mid-fifties and her bushy, often uncontrollable, blonde hair fell to her shoulders. She ran into the kitchen and flung her arms around Jen. "Oh Jen, how are you doing? How's motherhood treating you? Have you been feeling OK or sick as a dog? Tell me everything!" she babbled excitedly. Jen hugged her back, and they proceeded to chirp away about motherhood, while Jen continued flitting around the kitchen.

John clasped Liam by the arm. "Good to see you buddy, it's been too long. I know you're both wrapped up in the baby thing, but we really need to get drunk together more often, mate." Liam looked at him and smiled warmly. John was small in stature, the same as his wife, a good six inches shorter than Liam. His eyes sparkled, giving hints not only to his personality, but also the well-defined intelligence that lay behind them. He'd missed his friend too, and they had plenty to catch up on.

"I couldn't agree more, I'm fighting a dry house alone here, brother! I need help!" They laughed together as Liam opened the fridge. It was going to be a good night.

The food came out about an hour later, time enough for Liam and John to get a little oiled, and Janet and Jen to catch up properly. They sat and ate, making mostly small talk over the table.

"Fabulous as ever, Jen. I've missed the food nearly as much as you," John teased. "Any more of that dhansak left? I've got some bread to mop it up." He stretched across the table and grabbed the dish, piling yet more curry on his plate. Janet smirked.

"Yeah that's it John, pile more into your gullet, 'cos you do look a little underweight. You're positively wasting away." She winked at Jen. John rose to the bait, as per usual.

"Well, I haven't worked the last forty years to skimp on good food, my love. And I didn't notice *that* much restraint from you either," he countered. His wife pulled a face at him as Liam placed another beer in front of him.

"Come on son, it won't drink itself," Liam said. They had already sunk a few; the recycling bin in the corner of the kitchen already looked like it was vomiting empty bottles. "I've got some nice brandy for later," he said, nodding imperceptibly towards the female contingent. "I assume you're staying?"

"Too right, the hospitality here is far better than at home," John commented as he glugged his beer. He got a titter out of the ladies, and the men toasted their bottles. The evening had started well, and appeared to be going from strength to strength. The atmosphere between the two couples was relaxed and cheerful— friends really were good for the soul.

After the table had been cleared away, more beer flowed (wine in Janet's case—she had brought a bottle with her), they moved into the living room. The TV chattered away in the background, but not loud enough to encroach on the conversation between the couples. Eventually Jen said "OK people, I'm done. See you all tomorrow." She kissed everyone in the room goodnight (John and Janet on the cheek, Liam on the lips), and wandered her way upstairs after explaining that the guest room was all made up, clean sheets, shower gel in the bathroom and if they needed anything just holler. They wouldn't need a thing. Shortly after, Janet also made her way upstairs and into the land of nod, leaving just the boys and their beers. Liam got up and opened the drinks cabinet, rummaged and clinked about for a minute or so, then produced an expensive cognac.

"This one came from France a little while ago...I've been waiting for a celebration with good friends, but this will have to do," he joked, setting two medium sized brandy glasses on the coffee table. "Drink that beer mate, we need to try this!" He set about fumbling with the cork.

"Okay, I'm on it...looks nice and expensive, wherever it came from," John said, as he drained the remainder of his beer and set the empty bottle down. Liam had managed to pour two sizeable glasses out and offered one to John as he raised his. "To old friends...and new arrivals," he toasted. They clinked glasses.

"Oh wow, that's lovely, Liam," John savoured the caramel burn on his palate. "Very nice indeed, you've done well, my friend."

"Yeah—bloody expensive, but worth it." Liam commented. "And no better time to try it. Thanks John. You know, for all the help with FMA and everything. I feel like we're making a wise decision, and it's kind of all down to you really. I can't imagine we would have looked into this without you putting me onto it." He paused to sip his drink.

"I didn't really do anything, mate... I just let you know what was on offer, that's all. But I'm really glad you and Jen are involved. And not because I work for them. This is a really good thing you're both onto here, Liam. Trust me, this will be the future." John swilled the brandy round and sipped.

"Yeah well, as I said, without you pointing me in the right direction, we wouldn't have known about it at all mate. It's not really the kind of thing you look for on the internet, is it? And they don't exactly have posters up in the hospital."

"No, I suppose not. The business is solid, but as no doubt you are aware, we don't shout it from the rooftops. It's not that kind of service. And it's new as well. How it will get advertised in the future is anyone's guess, but at the minute it's sort of a closed shop. The big guns at FMA like to keep it that way...at least for the time being." He paused, looking at Liam, his cheeks flushed from the brandy.

"Yeah I kind of get that, but it's a kosher product...so why so cagey?"

"Well, it's not all been plain sailing getting this far, truth be told. Far from it, in fact." Liam was looking at John intently, interested to hear more from his friend.

"OK, I'm sure it's taken a lot to develop the technology but now it's stable then surely they want to recoup development costs by getting it out there? Isn't that just good business sense?" he asked.

"Yes, that is a priority in order to keep business in order, but the other facets of the company have largely paid for this developmental service. That being said, it needs to make its own money sooner rather than later. Make no mistake, there's really not that many clients. You and Jen are part of a select few, relatively speaking. The directors are keen on what they call a 'soft roll out' of the service."

John paused to take a sip of brandy. "Due to a few earlier problems, they're a bit cagey."

Liam's interest was sparked. What problems? Was there something they didn't know about? Surely they hadn't just invested nearly eighty grand on a technology that wasn't proven? "What kind of problems, John? I assume that everything is resolved now. You know, the early teething problems all bottomed out?" he asked.

John finished his glass, and tipped it to Liam. He obliged by refilling, doing the same with his own. "Thanks mate. And we probably shouldn't be having this conversation, but I guess it's a bit late now…and we are friends after all, so no secrets." He paused. "Back in the early days, we actually paid potential clients to be involved in the trials. It was a different ball game back then—many more unknowns. The contracts were carefully drawn up by our lawyers to make them watertight, in the event of any mishaps. The risks were always deemed to be low, due to the technology being separate from the child in question. The program got off to a good start, with a few clients all happy. After all, they were being paid to trial innovative medical technology, so all was rosy in the garden. But, there were a few hiccups along the way, which resulted in some clients leaving the program. One twin didn't form correctly for some unknown reason, and the docs were baffled. It seemed physically and mentally impaired…the physical defects weren't obvious, but tests showed internal defects. The twin had to be terminated at the age of twelve months and the parents left the program. The docs still haven't got to the bottom of it to this day—the child's parents were perfectly healthy with no adverse medical history, and the child itself was perfectly normal. They performed a full autopsy on the twin, but found no clue as to what had gone wrong. It was a bit of a setback, and so no more clients were being taken on at that time." John sat back in his seat and drew a large mouthful of brandy. "Then there was the fire. It didn't affect the whole building, and was brought under control fairly quickly, but not before it had caused damage to some of the holding vessels for the twins in the laboratory. It resulted in one vessel cracking under the heat, even though the glass was supposed to be tempered against elevated temperature and is as thick as your arm. This one must have had a flaw, or some kind of inherent weakness—the encapsulating fluid leaked out very quickly, resulting in the death of the twin inside." John stopped for air. His face was flushed with brandy and also his heart was racing. The subject matter was a little too close to the bone, this was his livelihood and the contract was explicit about confidentiality. He was definitely in breach. "The heat had been so intense it had also resulted in the twin suffering multiple burn wounds. The docs didn't know if this was the cause of death, or suffocation. Seems weird—locked in a huge tube full of liquid, and you drown when it's not there." He paused again, and then resumed:

"The client whose twin was burnt had a terrible misfortune after the fire at FMA, she lost her kid. But, she got all strung out and obsessed with the idea that FMA were somehow responsible for her death…there were some strange circumstances surrounding the death of her daughter, and the coincidental timing of the fire just pushed her over the edge. She tried to blow the fucking place up shortly afterwards, with some kind of home-made bomb; luckily, she was caught before she could detonate it, God knows what damage it might have done." John reached for his glass and finished the contents in a hefty gulp.

"FMA covered all this business up very nicely. Naturally, they weren't keen on any negative publicity, so it all got swept under the carpet and kept out of the news."

Liam had been listening intently to all of this, his mind working overtime. Was this program going to fail him and Jen in some way? Were incidents like this likely to happen again? He told himself he was being paranoid, and that these were teething problems in the early days. John had certainly been loose lipped. The gaffers at FMA would not approve. Bang on cue, John said: "This is all confidential, Liam. I would come under fire if word got out that I had been talking to you or anyone else about this stuff. That means it has to stay between us. Don't even tell Jen. It will only serve to worry her anyway, and the program is stable now, I can assure you. We haven't had an incident in at least two and a half years." He looked at Liam for affirmation.

"Hey John, don't worry about that. What goes on tour stays on tour. And you're right—I don't want to panic Jen in any way. It's not relevant to us now, and the guys at FMA have been great up to this point—professional to the last detail. I've got no doubt the program will be a success, and result in peace of mind for us after our baby is born." He picked his glass up. "And talking of which, let's have a toast—to family. And friends. Past, present and future." John raised his glass and they clinked them together.

# Chapter Nine

In the run up to Christmas and New Year Jen had a further two appointments at FMA, mostly just monitoring and routine tests. All appeared to be going swimmingly with Jen and the baby, so life was good. They had both tailed off their working hours, Jen just doing two days a week and Liam backed off to a four day week. It would be chopped down to three once the baby was born. Jen would be officially on maternity in February, taken earlier than normal. Such were the privileges of their life. As the pregnancy matured, Liam became more aware of Jen's changes—the swelling breasts (this one particularly interested him), the growing belly, and the weight gain adding to her curves on her body. Her wardrobe changed accordingly. She shopped regularly for stretchy leggings and jeans, and baggy, disguising tops. Flat shoes were the order of the day, and even though she had plenty, she still felt the need to buy at least a couple of new pairs. *You can never have enough shoes if you're a woman, and pregnant,* she had told herself, by means of justification.

Christmas arrived quickly in the Connelly house. Liam put the tree and decorations up as per usual. Luckily, Jen had decided they didn't need any new ones so Liam dug the artificial tree out from the garage (which now looked like a junkyard full of expensive man toys since the nursery had come into existence) and set about the annual chore. Once done, the lights in the front garden were busy twinkling away and the living room looked just as sparkly. They were due to visit Jen's mum Alison on Christmas Eve, followed by Liam's folks on Boxing Day, standard Christmas activities for them. It would be the last time they did seasonal family visits as a couple. That meant they had Christmas Day to themselves, which suited them both just fine. At over six months pregnant, Jen was becoming increasingly less mobile, so they were both keen to keep travel to a minimum if possible. The arrangements over the festive season also meant that there was no massive Christmas dinner to be done. In previous years, they had entertained various family and friends on Christmas Day with a full turkey dinner and all the trimmings; not this year. It would be a tiny turkey crown for two.

The journey to Alison's house took a couple of hours—she lived in Wales, in a tiny village in the south. Alison was overjoyed to see her daughter blooming in her pregnancy, the last time they had seen each other was back in the summer, when she was barely showing. It was a different story now.

"Oh my God, look at the size of the bump!" Jen's mum exclaimed. "Let me feel! Has it been kicking? It's a boy, Jen. I can tell from the way your carrying." Jen and Liam exchanged knowing glances at this remark—maybe Alison had a touch of the sixth sense, as well as the old woman thousands of miles away on that sun drenched Caribbean beach. Alison continued to cluck for at least an hour after they arrived, Jen lapping the attention up from her mother, and Liam accepting that this was par for the course in his usual good-natured way. They exchanged gifts later that evening and the festivities wound up early. Alison was no drinker, and Liam and Jen retired to the guest room at about nine. After a hearty English breakfast the following morning, they made tracks back home. It wouldn't be long before they saw each other again, no doubt Alison would visit in January to keep tabs on her only child's condition and once more flap around her attending to her every whim and need.

After a quiet Christmas Day, Liam's mum Jessica got the annual Christmas visit too. They were lucky in the respect that both of their mothers approved of the choice of partner their offspring had made. This made things very easy at family weddings and get-togethers; rarely was there any bad feeling or friction between any of them. In the end it was one of the quietest Christmas and New Year holidays they had ever had, and they were both glad. Undoubtedly they would get more frenetic form this point onwards—children had a way of doing that.

As the New Year rolled in and the weather got considerably colder, Jen started spending even more time indoors. Liam was quite happy with that. "I don't want you out there skidding around on the ice, love. That would be a disaster, so let's play it safe and keep bump inside when it's frosty. Also, I don't want you driving in ice and snow, so you'd best let work know."

"Aren't you getting authoritative in your old age Liam? Since when have you been the boss of me? We both know it's the other way around," she joked. She liked the idea of him being so protective over her and the baby. "Don't worry I've already spoken to Alice and Sue in work. Alice will cover as and when needed." Jen was on track with her pregnancy. FMA were monitoring every three weeks, and were happy with her progress, but there was one appointment which they both felt a little apprehensive about. With all clients, FMA waited until absolutely sure there were no problems and then invited clients to observe the twin. The date for this was later this week, and there had been relatively little discussion on the subject. Both parents-to-be were unsure of how they felt, or how they would feel once they saw the twin. What would it look like? All they had seen of their unborn child so far were a couple of scans, one at twelve weeks back in late September and one at twenty weeks in the run up to Christmas. The scan quality was good, and FMA provided a service with all the expertise of the NHS or even any private health care organisation—because that's exactly what they were. But it would be different seeing a twin, a real, living thing, an identical unborn baby in a glass vessel filled with amniotic fluid…just like a massive, artificial womb. But outside of any mother's body. *I can't let on to Jen that I'm a bit freaked out by it,* Liam thought to himself on more than one occasion. Jen had her own concerns—how would she react? Would she be pleased, shocked, freaked out by the whole thing? She had no idea. They would just have to suck it and see.

The day came around soon enough—January 23rd, a cold frosty Thursday morning. They were in the car on the way to FMA.

"Is this going to be strange or what, Liam?" It was more of a statement than a question. He nodded with a quiet grunt in agreement.

"We have to see it, or should I say him, sooner or later Jen. How do we know they're not just conning us, and there is no twin? The proof is waiting for our approval I guess." he responded thoughtfully.

"It's going to be like seeing our own unborn son in a big jar, though… I just hope I don't faint or have a fit or something," she said, vocalising her concerns.

"It'll be fine love, don't worry. One thing's for sure—we know he will be perfect in every way. Just like his brother." He reached across and put his hand on her bump. His touch was greeted with the faintest of kicks—or was it an elbow? "Wow, did you feel that!" he exclaimed.

"Of course darling—it came from my womb. I'd be worried if I didn't feel it." She laughed at his initial dumb question. They were nearly there.

Once they had checked into reception, they were led to Nathan Ellis' office. He greeted them both warmly, exclaiming on the healthy glow and general radiance of Jen's appearance. She took this as a good sign—people had been gushing over her since she started showing and it was old hat now, but coming from Nathan it had more significance. After a short exchange of conversation regarding her health in general, any issues to report et cetera, Nathan cut to the chase and told them that their twins were held in a facility towards the back of the building, in the laboratory annex.

"You may be surprised at the size of the containment facility. It has a lower roof than the front of the building, so cannot easily be seen as you enter. The facility is constantly monitored by technicians and security is at a maximum. There is no entry without badges and door key-codes. Very few front-of-house staff have access. The technicians have no need to enter the containment areas unless there's an emergency—most of the monitoring and adjusting of parameters is done remotely from the lab that adjourns it. They can see in through the large glass walls at all times, and there are cameras on each vessel, so up close monitoring can be observed. Everything is recorded and date stamped so we can look at any events retrospectively, and document everything in detail. All records are backed up and stored in a secure, secret location. Again, all access rights are heavily restricted and monitored. All twin vessels have a code—yours is V29." Nathan paused for breath, and then walked round his desk to join them on the other side. "Shall we?"

The trio walked down a short corridor, got in the lift, went to floor-1. The lift doors opened onto a sterile environment, fluorescent tubes instead of soft glow lighting, medical notices, signs, and various pieces of equipment mounted on the whitewashed walls. Jen looked around in a kind of awe—this was nothing like the frontend of FMA. It looked very clinical, but not in a normal hospital way. More like what she would imagine a mental asylum to look like. There were no windows to the outside apart from skylights. They were partially underground, after all. It unsettled her, but she fought against it. She had known deep down before this meeting that she wouldn't like it much. Liam grabbed her hand, perhaps a little too tightly. He looked at her, trying to comfort her. In truth, he needed comforting as much as her—he was also nervous.

"Follow me—it's just a short walk, and then all will be revealed," Nathan said reassuringly. He glanced at them and smiled, as if he could feel the apprehension. "I know it seems a little strange, but we must take all measures to make sure the facility is not compromised. This means a certain level of…well, secrecy I suppose." he added with a raise of his eyebrows. Nathan looked a little flushed himself, as if in sympathy. Perhaps he was worried about their reaction to all of this—had they had clients in the past that had backed out at this stage due to the reality of what the program actually meant kicking in? They walked down the entrance from the lift to a large set of heavy armoured double doors, with keypads on the side. Nathan punched a five digit code in, and also waved his FMA badge that he withdrew from his pocket in front of a scanner. There was a beep and a heavy clunk as the doors' locking mechanisms disengaged and swung open. They entered, Nathan leading. The doors revealed a large space, mostly occupied by desks and equipment that neither Jen nor Liam were familiar with. There were a few people in lab coats bustling about, and a few more sat at desks, clacking away at computer keyboards. If any of them had noticed the three new arrivals, none made it obvious. They carried on doing whatever they happened to be doing without any acknowledgement.

"This is the monitoring lab. We have about ten technician staff employed here full-time to keep an eye on things. There are a further six security staff, also full-time; this place is monitored day and night. All unusual events or activity are reported live to a remote station, where the information is assessed, and any instructions are issued from there within minutes. It's a tight ship." Nathan looked at them both. "Please don't be apprehensive or scared. A facility of this nature has to be like this, in order to function correctly." Liam looked at Nathan.

"It feels a little sci-fi, Doc," he commented, trying to be light-hearted. Nothing could be further from the truth. He felt surreal. "Where are the twins kept, then?"

"Ah, yes—we are getting there. We need to go through this part of the lab to get there. Please be aware we won't be up close and personal—we will observe via cameras on a big screen. This is perfectly adequate for you to see what you want to see. We don't like to disrupt the environment too much by entering into the vessel containment area. Don't worry, you'll see." Nathan nodded to them both as if affirming his own words. They walked through the lab area, still no one taking any notice of them.

After another set of large security doors, they were in a vast area that was glass walled on one side. This allowed the viewer to see row upon row of containment vessels, each with contents that varied in size, colour and shape. Most were new-born sized or smaller—some appeared to have nothing in, and some had more advanced 'grown up' twins within their thick glass walls. Jen squeezed Liam's hand. He squeezed it back reassuringly, and asked Nathan "OK,

Doc—which one's ours?" He looked at the array of vessels in part wonder, part morbid fascination—he had never seen anything quite like this in his life.

"Yours is vessel V29. We do all of our observation through a camera monitoring system, but don't worry—we can move the camera around the vessel so you will be able to see your twin close up on the screen." Nathan indicated towards a large monitor on the wall to the right of the glass. He dragged a chair to the desk in front of them, and proceeded to log in to the PC there. "Once I'm in, you will be able to see clearly on the monitor." Two minutes later, the monitor flickered into life, and a close up image of vessel V29 was displayed on the screen. The twin within it was clearly visible, and Jen and Liam looked at the screen in awe. That was an identical version of their baby! It felt weird to both of them as they stared at the image. Nathan drove the camera around the vessel using a specialist mouse, so they could both see the twin clearly from many different vantage points.

"I know this is a strange experience for you both, but this is the pinnacle of medical science and technology with respect to your unborn child. He has the best safety net in the world now, and you're looking right at it." Nathan looked at them both. They were both still absorbed by the image of the twin. Nathan continued to move the camera around, so they could see it from behind and almost below, as well as above. Just as Jen felt her baby shift and give a little kick inside her womb, the twin also had a reflexive movement inside the vessel.

"Wow, did you see that?" Liam exclaimed. "The little fella moved!" Jen felt shocked: *Was that a coincidence? How come these two separate entities just moved in unison? No, it must be my imagination,* she thought. Her brow was furrowed, and as Liam glanced at her, he noticed her worried expression. "You OK, hon.?"

"Yeah, I'm fine, just a little weirded-out, I guess," she said, in a detached fashion.

"OK guys, have you seen enough of this little treasure?" Nathan enquired.

"Yes, thanks, Doc, it's been…enlightening," said Liam in response. Jen muttered her thanks as Nathan logged off, still troubled by the coincidence of movement between her baby and the twin.

After they had made their way back the way they had come, they ended up in Nathan's office for some paperwork bits and pieces, and to confirm the next appointments for Jen in the run up to the birth. Once done, Nathan asked if they had any questions.

"Just one—and it may seem a little silly, but I'd like to ask you anyway," said Jen. "Back there I noticed the twin had a little kick. When it did that, I also had some kicks of my own." She looked down at her belly. "And it happened at exactly the same time. How can that be, Doctor?" She looked at Nathan, feeling a little silly about what she'd just said.

Nathan looked at the pair of them momentarily, and then said, "Jen, that is pure coincidence, believe me. There is no physical or mental connection between the twin and your unborn child—there can't be." He paused. "I know that twins are often associated with psychic links and suchlike, like being able to predict one another's actions, thoughts, or words. But this is different. They are two separate entities, and although they carry the same genetic information as real twins do, they are completely detached from each other. What you are alluding to is impossible. But I understand your question. Please let this chat put your mind at ease—everything is fine with your baby, and also fine with the twin." Nathan sat back in his leather seat, allowing this statement to sink in and put the prospective parents at ease.

"So just coincidence and that's it?" Liam interjected. "You're sure?"

"Yes. Pure and simple." Nathan smiled at them. "Do you feel more reassured now, Jen?"

"Well, yes, I suppose so," Jen replied. "Thanks for putting me at ease, Doctor. But it was strange." Jen felt that Nathan's reassurance hadn't really been that comforting—she knew what she had felt inside her, and had seen the twin do the same.

"Yes, it sounds that way Jen. But nothing to concern yourself over. You concentrate on getting that little chap out on time, and in perfect condition—that's plenty for you to be thinking about, what do you say?" There was a light-hearted undertone to Nathan's comment. He wanted all qualms and fears to be put to bed.

"Yes Doctor, of course you're right." She stood up, Liam quickly following suit. "I'll see you in a fortnight, all being well. And thank you again for everything."

"My pleasure—see you folks soon, take care." Nathan shook both their hands and led them to the door.

# Chapter Ten

Things started changing slightly for Jen and Liam's routines as the pregnancy advanced. Liam had cut down to a three day week, and Jen had finished work completely. It was well into February, and with only eight or so weeks to go, she finished work with a bang—a large leaving party was thrown for her (not quite a complete surprise, as bigmouth Alice had let the cat out of the bag a few weeks ago), and she came home feeling wanted, loved and missed all at the same time. She had insisted to all of her colleagues that she would be back after maternity, but she questioned herself on this statement even as she was saying the words—would she return to work? Or would she be so consumed with being a new mum, that it just wouldn't be an option? She would have to wait and see.

Liam's work life quietened down with his three day week, and he usually spent one of his home days emailing and phoning colleagues to keep the ship afloat. Once that was done, he was able to spend more time with Jen, which they both relished. He had taken over cooking duties for at least three, sometimes four nights a week, and they enjoyed short trips into town for baby stuff and general browsing as well as some lovely, blood-pumping country walks in the surrounding frost covered fields and vales. Jen was getting bigger all the time now in the approach to the big day—her stomach seemed like it would pop, she often thought. Liam also filled his newfound time off pottering around the house, doing his own nest building of a different sort—DIY, decorating (it seemed never-ending), and sorting out his new man-cave (the garage).

This proved tricky as it had the BMW in it now, as Liam had bought a new 'more family-oriented' car. The new VW was supposed to replace the Beamer, but Liam had put little, if no effort into selling his baby—he loved it, and couldn't quite let go. What the hell, they didn't need the money, and had space for it in the garage while still being able to keep the VW and Jen's car on the drive. He still had space in the garage to sort out his music gear, and had mounted some guitars on the wall to save space. His DIY efforts included shelves in the nursery and garage, and other domestic chores such as cleaning the gutters (which were totally clogged with dead leaves and suchlike), repairing downpipes that had broken fixings, as well as fixing a jammed window upstairs. He also finally got around to looking at the extractor fan in the en-suite—Jen had been nagging him for months to get it sorted. All in all, life was quiet, low-key and good. They were both gearing up for the step change in their lives that was around the corner.

February came and went, and they found themselves in March before they knew it. Jen had been keeping fortnightly appointments at FMA, and all was good. She appeared to be in tip-top shape, and looking to be bang on with her due date according to the midwife there. She was a lovely lady called Claire, mid-forties, and very capable. Jen felt she knew her quite well, following all the meetings they had together over the last seven or eight months.

They had continued their country walks when the opportunity presented itself, the frost slowly dropping away and yielding to milder, drizzly afternoons instead for the main part. This did not stop them from wanting to get out—they both felt it was important to keep some low level of exercise up, and not just for Jen. Liam felt like he needed it too, now that he wasn't doing as much running around with work. Even though for the main part his job was office based, it did require him to get out and about on site at least once a week and that part was now missing. He still went to the local gym a couple of evenings a week, so he didn't feel too bad in himself and the walks definitely helped.

Jen was experiencing much more movement from her unborn child nowadays—kicks and punches were common-place, and she got Liam to feel as often as possible. He just sat there slack jawed in wonder, hand on her belly when they happened. As the weather got increasingly milder, Jen found she was more restless overnight, often getting up to get some fresh water, or even wander down to the fridge for a slice of cheese…solid blocks of sleep were becoming rarer nowadays. This resulted in her feeling drained and tired in the mornings, napping in the afternoons, and going to bed earlier in the hope of a decent sleep. This rarely happened, and more often than not she would find herself tossing and turning for hours, and then finally getting up. And the nightmares didn't help. After the first one (at least the first one in a long time), she had hoped that the experience wouldn't repeat itself—but it had. The subject of the terrifying dreams always altered slightly from each other, but they all had the same dreadful, ominous thread of meaning running through them, linking them together as if chapters from a book. She had had one just a few nights ago, and had managed to contain her fear on awakening from it from Liam, hand clasped over her mouth to avoid her crying out in terror, as she had done previously. This one had seen her wandering endlessly through the lab at FMA; everything appeared completely sanitised and unscrupulously clean. As she ran her hands along the white walls of the lab, her fingers gave resistance on the spotless painted surface. All the glass vessels were lined up, row after row of twins encapsulated within. As she walked slowly through the rows, she started to notice some odd things—one vessel she passed had what appeared to be a black mould growing on its base, slowly creeping up the glass sides of the chamber. As she stopped to look closer, her eyes came face to face with the twin within. A closer inspection led her to notice the mould wasn't just on the outside—it was growing on the twin also, its toes and fingers most affected with the black, slimy substance. A feeling of dread settled in her stomach like a coiled snake as she continued down the rows, sensing something was wrong. As she passed the vessels, eyes now wide with growing fear, she started to see things wrong with the vessels and the twins held within. As she passed another, she saw that the boy within had developed long, shiny, razor-like metallic nails on his fingers and toes—she could hear a faint 'whooshing' as the twin lashed out his arms and legs, the razors slicing through the fluid in the vessel, threatening to lacerate anything in their path. As she quickly moved on, the next vessel's twin had appeared to grow bulbous, weeping appendages from its head; the fluid around it turned a pinkish grey with the ooze. She heard a faint cry of anguish and pain from its ulcerated mouth. She looked at the next vessel—V29. Her eyes widened yet further with horror, her mouth now agape in a silent scream. The twin inside was motionless, but almost entirely scarlet red with blood, the whole vessel filled with red liquid. The cuts that covered its naked, tiny body were deep and slowly seeped blood so dark it appeared almost black, turning crimson on contact with the surrounding fluid. As she studied the subject, her stomach now knotted so tightly in fear she was gasping to breathe, she saw the two ugly, horn-like protrusions from its forehead, and as it opened its mouth to cry it revealed a row of razor sharp, blackened, filthy teeth, gnashing together in a grimace of hatred…the image had remained with Jen for a long time after she had awoken, laying there drenched in her own oily sweat, her breath hitching with fear, as Liam slept on peacefully beside her.

The weather continued to be relatively miserable, limiting activities outside the home to a minimum. They had a few trips out here and there, ate out a couple of times locally and continued to brave the elements daily for at least an hour, but as Jen got even bigger (if that was possible), they led a quiet life within the confines of the house for the main part. This suited them both, as they enjoyed each other's company, and had rarely spent so much time together in recent years apart from holidays away together.

Jen continued to keep her FMA appointments for monitoring and tests. Liam had accompanied her for the last three or four, if only to drive so she could be more comfortable on the journey there and back—he largely kept out of the poking and prodding once they were there, which suited them both just fine. The FMA team seemed happy that she was on track for a normal, healthy birth and on time too, by all accounts. This meant that the FMA appointments kept them both reassured with regards to the baby.

In the final week approaching the due date, they were both a little twitchy. Jen started being super careful about anything she might be doing, and the walks had diminished to thirty minutes at the most, in case anything happened. She had experienced a few bouts of preliminary contractions, and Liam reacted accordingly—*(do we need to leave now, lie down, shall I call FMA, etc.)*, but five minutes later they had passed, and it was back to routine—for the moment.

One such incident occurred two days before the due date, while Jen was doing the dishes following a light tea (meals were also less of a routine now, as Jen felt hungry at odd times, and ate sporadically).

She stopped washing up and exhaled while clutching her expansive middle. "Oh… I'm getting contractions," she said, almost to herself. Liam jumped up from the sofa immediately. He had offered to do the cleaning up in the kitchen, but she wanted to stay on her feet, insisting she felt more comfortable that way.

"Is everything OK honey?" he asked. He didn't bother to add "Shall I get the car out?" as he figured that would become obvious pretty soon, if that was the case. Jen continued to breathe out heavily, and was now supporting herself with her hand on the worktop. Her other hand moved to her lower back.

"It feels stronger than last time, Liam…maybe they'll pass." She paused, shifted position, and then decided to sit down. "Let's not panic just yet." Liam was pacing around her by this time, anxiously rubbing his stubbled chin. It felt like he had been preparing for the imminent birth for a lifetime, constantly on red alert, ready to spring into action at the drop of a hat.

"OK, OK. Just relax Jen, and let it happen." *Words from the wise!* Jen thought, not unkindly. Liam had no idea what it was like to carry a huge medicine ball around in his guts for nine months, but she knew he meant well.

Finally, after five minutes or so, Jen looked at him and said, "False alarm, my love—I think they're receding."

Liam, who had put his shoes on, identified the whereabouts of his car keys, got the baby bag from upstairs, and was in the process of populating his coat pockets, stopped what he was doing and went to her at the kitchen table.

"Are you sure? Shall I get your coat and shoes ready, just in case?" he asked. He was still in flight mode.

Jen looked less flushed than a few minutes ago, and more relaxed. "No Liam—they're going. Sorry, but it's another false alarm—but the biggest yet," she said, rubbing his arm. "In actual fact, they're all but gone now. I kind of feel relieved, but not, if you know what I mean? It's so close now. Maybe we should call FMA just to let them know what the state of play is." After a second or two she retracted this thought, and said, "Well, maybe not. They know that I'm due, and a call from us will only make them think I'm in labour, so let's not bother." Liam agreed with this. He also agreed to finish up in the kitchen, while Jen put her feet up and relaxed.

They both went to bed fairly early, as was the routine nowadays. Liam read for a little, while Jen aimlessly flicked through her phone, but forty-five minutes later the lights were out. It was nine thirty. Liam dropped off fairly quickly (Jen had always hated the fact that he could go to sleep what appeared to be instantly, while she spent hours tossing and turning restlessly), but Jen lay awake, in the dark and the quiet. She could hear Liam's slow rise and fall of his breathing but that was all, and eventually after about an hour she fell asleep too.

Jen awoke with a start—the baby was kicking again. She rolled over onto her left side, with much effort, and looked at her phone—three am. Liam was sound asleep beside her, in the same position that he was when he had fallen asleep. Then she felt the all too familiar constrictions on her bump—more contractions. But this felt more powerful than before. She struggled to sit upright, legs off the bed. Then came another—much stronger this time. A wave of panic, excitement and worry washed over her—maybe this was it, baby Joshua was coming! She felt a trickling sensation on the inside of her thigh and put her hand down there…it came back wet. Her waters had broken. Jen quickly gave Liam a push. "Liam, wake up…wake up! It's coming!" She whispered in an urgent fashion to him, although there was no one else there to wake, so no real need to whisper. Liam groaned, turned over, and then sprang into life, finally realising what Jen was saying.

"Jen—are you sure? It's the middle of the night!" he said, and instantly regretted his words. Like an unborn baby cares what time of day or night it is! Jen snapped at him: "Well, what do you think all this bloody wetness down here is, Einstein? My waters have just broken! Get your shit together, I need to get to the bathroom!" She got up from the bed, and quickly shuffled and waddled her way over to the en-suite. Now Liam's brain was engaged, he also got moving, turning the bedside lamp on as he did so. Jen was sat on the side of the bath, had taken her sopping wet bottoms off (light cotton PJs were the order of the day for the last two months). She was busy tentatively feeling around her lower area, examining her hands to check for blood. There was none, and the liquid felt viscous and slightly sticky. Most of it was either on the bed sheets or on her PJs. What should she do? Just quickly mop herself up, and get to the hospital as soon as possible? Or quickly douse herself with the showerhead? She decided on the latter, there was no time for dithering. Five minutes later she had cleaned herself up, got herself back in the bedroom, and was busy throwing some clothes on. There had been a set of clothes waiting specifically for this moment on the second shelf of her wardrobe now for a good while. During the time she had awoken, been in the bathroom and now out again, she hadn't had another contraction since the first one. Liam was now running on all four cylinders. He had quickly got dressed (the same clothes as he had unceremoniously dumped on the floor six hours earlier), and now swapped places with Jen. He peed, washed his face and didn't bother with his teeth. Back out, he asked Jen: "You OK there, big girl? This is it! I'll get the bag in the car. Is there anything else we need?"

"Yes—a towel for my seat. And I'll want to sort a spare skirt out, in case any more of this gunk leaks out on the way." She looked at him nervously. "It's going to be OK, right Liam?" He looked into her wide, beautiful brown eyes.

He hugged her briefly and gently. "Of course it is. I'll ring FMA now, looks like we're gonna be early. See you downstairs, be quick sweetheart. I love you." He kissed her and scuttled off downstairs. Jen checked herself in the mirror—massive, hair strewn everywhere, dark circles under her eyes, puffy skin: *Oh my God, I look terrible...but this isn't a fucking beauty contest, get your shit together, girl!* She told herself. She grabbed a hairbrush, skirt and her phone, had a quick look round desperately thinking she will forget something, and then went downstairs.

Liam was waiting, coat on, car keys in hand, her coat in the other. "The bag's in the car, Jen. You ready? I've called FMA. They said keep calm, and get here safely in our own time. They will be prepared and waiting. We need to go to the hospital block, on the right hand side. Any more contractions yet?"

"No, not yet—they're bound to wait till I'm in the car. Let's go."

They left the house as quickly as they could. Liam helped her into the passenger side, and she was careful to put the towel down first. "Good job you got leather, and not upholstered, Liam. I would hate to ruin the car seat." She still had her cynical, hard-edged humour to hand, he noted. A wry grin lit her face. He took her bits and pieces and put them in the bag with the rest of her 'pregnancy kit'. "Why don't you wrap the jokes in, and concentrate on keeping our little fella in there till we get there, hon.? Now is not really the time to brush up on your stand-up routine, is it?" he retorted. It was actually nice and stress relieving to have a bit of banter with her.

"Arrgh! AARGH! Oh *fuck,* that's painful…" Jen had kind of hunched over in the seat as her contractions kicked in. Liam wasted no time, and knowing there was precious little he could do to either console or help her, he got in the car and started the motor. "Let's go—hold on, hon. Just hold on." He squeezed her leg reassuringly, and then put the car into gear and drove off.

Forty minutes and two more rounds of contractions later, they were there. Jen had been trying to work out whether the contractions were getting closer, and of course they were. *That's what happens*, she reminded herself. Liam parked as close as he could to the patient entry doors, and set about getting Jen in there. She had a constantly furrowed brow now, and her hand hadn't left her bump for the whole journey. A short walk later, with much puffing and panting, they were met just inside by a friendly midwife (not Claire, her normal midwife—the name tag said 'Georgia'). Georgia briefly introduced herself while she got a wheelchair parked against the side of the lobby, and explained that Claire would be there too—she was in the delivery room, setting up and checking equipment. Jen manoeuvred herself into the wheelchair, and Georgia wheeled her down a short corridor leading off the lobby. Liam hurried along on one side as she pushed Jen through a set of double swing doors, and then into a room on the right hand side labelled 'Delivery suite 4'. Jen absent-mindedly wondered if there were three other women in the three other delivery suites, all in the same predicament. Once inside, Claire was waiting, along with another doctor whom they had both met before…*what's his name?* Liam thought. As if he read his mind the doctor introduced himself again as Dr Baker ("you may not remember me," he said). Liam confessed he had forgotten his name, but recognised his face. While this small talk went on, Claire had gotten Jen into the bed, and was busy hooking her up to various bits and pieces of medical monitoring equipment. There was an IV line waiting to the side, just in case, and a mask capable of delivering gas and air also. Jen took her surroundings in subconsciously as the nurses busied themselves around her.

"Okay Jen, just try and relax," Claire said. "Everything's going to be just fine. So, you take your time, Mum." She was a pretty brunette, and the beaming smile she gave Jen helped to relax her.

Jen looked at her gratefully, and then hunched over with pain again—*my God they're coming hard and fast now,* she thought. Liam had hold of her hand. She looked at him and said: "Here we go."

# Chapter Eleven

The labour took three hours in all. Everything went according to plan, and Joshua entered the word at six fifteen am on Thursday April 16<sup>th</sup> 2020. He weighed in at seven pounds and thirteen ounces, had a shock of dark brown hair (Liam's first thought was *my God, his head is like a small coconut!*), and made a considerable amount of noise when he opened his mouth for the first time. Jen was exhausted, and was quite happy to lie there with Joshua feeding for the first time, Liam at their side while the doctor and nurses flapped around monitoring, taking readings, making notes—doing all the usual things that they do.

Unknown to mother, father, doctors, and everyone else in existence, were the parallel activities happening in vessel V29 at the FMA laboratory. The vessels were monitored constantly, but the alarms only triggered with unusual activity. This was definitely just that, however it was too subtle to cause any system generated alarm. These were sensor-triggered generally by things like epileptic-type episodes, or violent unexpected movement within the chambers. None of that happened in V29. But, at the very same moment that Joshua was born and opened his eyes, so did his twin. The twin's tiny eyelids flicked open and stared vacantly through the amniotic fluid in the vessel. As Joshua opened his mouth and let out a *huge* wail, the twin's mouth also opened in a silent yawn. No noise emitted from it, silenced by its environment. No air was drawn in and expelled, as its lungs were already full of fluid. Small limb movements echoed exactly what little Joshua Connelly was doing in the outside world. Its mouth suckled on nothing as Joshua drew milk from his mother, mewling in satisfaction.

Joshua's twin had been born.

Jen finally slept once her baby had settled down and recovered from the trauma that was his birth. Liam dozed uncomfortably in a chair to one side, surrounded by medical clutter. Both Claire and Georgia were present, popping in and out of the delivery room and generally quietly going about their business. After a couple of hours, Claire disappeared completely (obviously needed for another birth in another delivery suite), but Georgia remained, keeping tabs on the family. When Liam awoke briefly, she commented that Joshua had adapted amazingly quickly to his new environment. Liam agreed with her, rubbing sleep from his eyes and yawning. He checked on his new son and wife before slipping out to grab a coffee. A short while later at about ten am, Nathan appeared.

"Congratulations Liam!" he whispered. He didn't want to disturb the new-born and mother. Liam thanked him, and they talked for about ten minutes about the birth, about what happens next with FMA and release times for the family. "If the results are all OK—and there's nothing to suggest they aren't at this stage—then you will be able to go home as soon as Jen feels up to it." This was music to Liam's ears. He wanted to get them both back to the family home as soon as possible, and get some proper rest. *Who am I kidding? No one brags about the amount of rest they've had since becoming a parent for the first time!* he thought.

Jen continued to sleep, shifting her and her baby every now and then. Joshua made a few complaints, but no major outbursts. He seemed contented. Once Jen finally came around, she had a drink of chilled water and cooed and clucked over her new addition. Liam took some photos and sent them to various family members and friends. He asked Jen when she thought she would be okay to travel back home. She debated this, and asked to rest for a short time. After about an hour, she told Liam she wanted to go home. He wandered off out of the delivery suite to find someone, and ended up talking to Georgia who was in the lobby area. She called Dr Ellis, and within five minutes he was having a final poke and prod at mother and son. Finally, he said: "Okay, boys and girls, I think you're ready to leave the building. Please gather your belongings in your own good time, and I'll see you in the lobby when you're ready." He gave Jen a reassuring pat on the arm and shook Liam's hand on the way out. Jen breathed a sigh of relief—the life changing event that is childbirth was over, and a new chapter awaited the young family.

Within half an hour, all three Connellys were in the car on their way home. Dr Ellis had gone through a few bits of paperwork with them, and given Jen a new schedule for her FMA visits now Joshua was born. The appointments were further apart now, and spanned the first year of Joshua's life. The first one was in a month's time, with a further three at longer intervals apart. Both new parents were excited, tired and nervous all at the same time—parenthood was upon them, finally! Liam would now be officially off work on paternity for at least eight weeks, something that both he and Jen were looking forward to. They could spend all day, every day, bonding as a family unit without work getting in the way for either of them. It was a luxury that they were both acutely aware wasn't the case for all families.

Liam pulled onto the drive thirty minutes later, and went around to Jen's side to help her out—she was in the back, with little Josh in the baby seat beside her. He had been remarkably quiet on the way back but now, as Jen fussed with the baby seat he started to cry—initially a kind of thin mewling, quickly escalating into something far more distressed and louder. There was nothing wrong with his little lungs, that was for certain.

"Oh, shh…shh, my beautiful boy, don't worry, we'll get you inside safe and sound," Jen said, wrapping the baby blanket around him and holding him close to her body. "Liam, let's get in."

He locked the car and opened the front door, flicking the hall lights on as he entered. "Josh—welcome to your home. I hope you like it, big guy. We do." He bent and kissed his son gently on the forehead. He closed the door behind them.

# Chapter Twelve

The Connellys had been blessed with a relatively straightforward birth with no complications, and a beautiful baby boy, perfectly healthy in every respect. This was not a surprise—FMA would have spotted anything untoward during the pregnancy. Both mother and baby were doing well—Jen and Liam's life pattern changed dramatically to accommodate little Josh and attend to his every need. This comprised mostly of feeding and changing, and Josh was calling all the shots when it came to the routine.

Within the first week of the birth, there were various visitors at the home to welcome the new addition. Both Jen's and Liam's respective mothers visited, and there was a cross-over on timings, so they actually spent some time with each other for a few hours. Despite them being very different people, they both loved their son and daughter, and now their grandson too. They clucked and fussed over Josh to the extreme—cuddly toys, baby clothes and useful baby gadgets appeared from the boots of cars, and now seemed to be everywhere inside. A few family, friends, and work colleagues also visited, bringing yet more baby gifts, until the house looked like an explosion in Mothercare. Liam was cajoled into wetting the baby's head on the coming Friday night—he asked Jen if it was OK, and was met with "Liam, I am perfectly capable of looking after our son on my own. In actual fact, I'm the only person on the planet that can do just that, so fill your boots, Daddy." He didn't need any more persuading—a few drinks were just what he needed.

"OK, OK, I'm only asking love—heaven forbid I should arrange to do something without her majesty's blessing," he retorted. "It will be local anyway, so if you need me for anything, just call."

Josh settled into a night-time routine fairly well, giving Jen opportunity to catch up on much needed sleep, usually four hour blocks at a time. She was breastfeeding him, so was also able to doze when he woke for feeding. ("I knew it, he's a tit man, just like his old man," Liam observed.)

Friday night came, and Liam was escorted by four of his work pals and a couple of old friends (John Lee included). He promised Jen he wouldn't get too drunk, and also asked if she was OK with John staying—Jen informed him that Janet was coming over anyway, so they would both be staying in the guest room. They were more likely to be disturbed than be a disturbance, and Janet and Jen could coo all evening over baby Josh, while Liam let it go with the boys—a perfect plan.

The seven of them were in the local brewery pub—The Bell—and were a few pints into the celebrations. The conversation ambled on; football, rugby, women, latest holidays, work. And, of course, parenting. At least half the men present were dads (not all full-time, the consequence of broken relationships).

"So how's fatherhood, Liam?" Jeff asked. Jeff was a draughtsman at work, and the two men were good friends after seeing each other every working day for the last five years.

"Well, it's helpful not having to worry about work while trying to get my head round the little man around the house," Liam replied. "He's good overnight—I rarely wake up when he stirs. Jen's breastfeeding, so no feeding duties for me. At least, for the moment. I guess that'll change once he gets weaned," Liam said.

"Well, Lucy never breastfed—I got feeding duty from day one," commented Liam's mate, Jay. "Damn near killed me with lack of sleep. Never really recovered, so you're lucky, mate. Enjoy it while you can, that's what I say," and raised his glass.

"My round boys—what are we having?" Said John, getting up and draining the remainder of his pint. "Let's get this show on the fucking road! We got a baby to celebrate!" This was met with much approval as he made his way to the bar with the empties.

The night went on, with much beer consumed. Eventually, they all went their separate ways "See you in work in two months, you lucky bastard!" Jay shouted, staggering off to the taxi rank.

Now alone, John and Liam decided to have a night cap at another bar at the end of the street, where they could talk quietly.

"FMA have been great John," said Liam. "The birth ran like clockwork and Nathan has been very good in all aspects—very professional." He sipped his whisky, savouring the burn.

"I'm glad you've had good service, Liam. Not that I would expect anything else. The company is at the top of its game. You'll never meet a more professional set of medical experts, my friend." John's round face had the stereotypical blush spots high on his cheeks from his indulgence.

"We saw the twin a little while back. It was a very…strange experience, I'm not gonna lie, John."

John looked at Liam, and paused before he responded. "Yes, I can imagine. Obviously, I've seen the twins and have an active role in their maintenance. But it's different for you than me, Liam. One of those twins is *yours*. So I'm not surprised you found it odd. Think of this though—if nothing ever occurs to facilitate the use of that twin, you'll never see it again. It's an invisible insurance policy like no other. Make sure you take solace in that. It might feel like you've paid a whole heap of money for nothing—and let's hope that you have, and you never need the full extent of FMA's services."

Liam raised his glass. "I'll drink to that, John."

The next morning greeted both John and Liam with hangovers, which were partially cured with coffee and bacon sandwiches (Liam struggled to keep his down—it was his first night drinking seriously for a good few months). Luckily for John, Janet was driving, and after about an hour or so they made a move home, leaving the Connellys to their day.

Jen was due a home visit in the afternoon from Claire to check on mother and baby, and once Liam had got rid of his hangover, he set about cleaning and tidying the house for Jen while she sat in the kitchen feeding Josh. He also got some daddy time, holding his son for a good hour before he grumbled about being fed and changed. Liam had done the changing honours a few times, and was getting the hang of it, much to Jen's delight. "It won't always be this non-offensive, you do know that don't you? Once he's on solids, then *wow*…you may not be so keen." Liam took this in his stride as per normal.

"Jen, I have committed to undertake all my fatherly duties, including unpleasant ones," he responded light-heartedly, as he fumbled in Josh's baby bag for lotion. "Our little fella has only been outside once, and that was on the way back from the birth. Should we take him to the park in a while? The weather seems OK out there, for once."

Jen debated this. She had resisted taking him out since getting home—the weather had been foul, five degrees at best, and squally, unpredictable showers all the time. She got up and looked out of the window. It was sunny, but she didn't know how cold it was. "What's the temperature out there?" She asked.

"About eight or nine degrees love, a bit warmer than it has been for the last few days," Liam answered. "We don't have to go for long. In actual fact, we don't have to go at all if you don't want to." he studied his wife as she weighed up the proposition, and again was struck by his depth of feeling for her. You would never guess she had given birth a scant few days ago—she looked as incredible as ever, her hair framing the dainty profile of her face perfectly.

"No, let's go. Get him sorted, and we can drive to the park." While Liam carried on with his changing duties, Jen went upstairs and got a few bits for Josh bundled into yet another baby bag. By the time she got back down Josh was changed, and within fifteen minutes they were all out of the door.

The walk was good for all of them—none of them had had much fresh air since the arrival. A few mums at the park with their young children stopped to coo over Josh: *Best get used to this,* Jen thought. After half an hour or so, they returned home in anticipation of the midwife visit, feeling invigorated by their walk.

Claire arrived prompt on two o'clock, and after about forty minutes of general questions concerning all three of them, some temperature reading and some form filling, she was satisfied everything was as it should be. Jen was relieved to hear this, although neither her nor Liam were overly worried anything was wrong—it was just professional reassurance.

Now they could all adapt to their new routine and responsibilities without fretting. It was the beginning of a new stage in all their lives, one which both new parents relished. They were at last the perfect family unit.

# Chapter Thirteen

Time flew past for Jen and Liam. They were completely wrapped up in parenthood, and everything for the first four or five months revolved totally around Josh. Liam decided to return to work for three days a week in mid—August. The truth of the matter was he was needed there, and remote working didn't always cut it. He and Jen discussed this move briefly, but she was largely in agreement. "I'm hoping to have Josh into nursery for three mornings a week in a months' time," she told Liam. "Once he's done the first few mornings, I'll be looking to get back to work at those times. I can drop him there, go to work for the morning and pick him up on the way back."

Josh was developing fast—he quite happily gurgled away to himself, playing with whatever toy was to hand and appeared to be quite independent already in the respect that he didn't always need Mum or Dad there all the time. This gave them both space, which was a welcome relief. They both adored Josh, but they also realised they have their own lives to sustain as well as his, even if it meant having time to shave, for Jen to do her hair properly instead of just tying it back, and other little things. Josh was now actively moving about—more rolling around on the carpet, rather than actual crawling, but he wasn't far off. Jen mitigated this by putting him in his cot and providing him with things to keep him occupied when she had things to do. Josh's favourite thing was the mobile that hung above his cot. It rotated and was brightly coloured. When wound up, it displayed lights and played chimes. Josh could be distracted with this for sometimes up to twenty minutes, which was great for Jen if she needed to put some washing on, or start prepping for tea. The cot was light and not too bulky, so Liam tended to place it around the house close to where they were. At present, it was in the kitchen while Jen folded some of his freshly dried baby clothes. She peered in on him, and he smiled at her. She beamed back at him and grabbed his hand, waggling it. He giggled, and she returned to the task in hand, making sure she wound the mobile first.

As Josh grabbed for the mobile and batted it playfully, the twin in V29 was having a similar experience. The twin's eyes were open, and he could see something bright, colourful, different shapes before his eyes. He extended his tiny arm to try and touch it, but there appeared to be nothing there. A tiny frown appeared on his brow. The twin could also hear something, but it was distant sounding and vague to him. All this was confusing for the tiny baby in vessel V29. He was developing at exactly the same rate as Josh, but in a very different environment. He didn't understand the noises he was hearing, or the bright colours and shapes he was seeing. He continued to try and touch them, reaching in front of him time and time again—nothing there. His frown remained.

Jen had been in touch with a local nursery on the phone. A very pleasant lady called Kathy spoke to her and suggested that they arrange a drop-in session for her and Josh, so they could get a feel for the place. It was only a twenty minute drive on the outskirts of town, so they arranged for the following morning. Liam would be at work, but that was fine. He didn't need to be there for this, she could assess the nursery and staff on her own. She arrived at ten the following morning and was greeted by Kathy, a short, well-rounded woman in her early thirties with a large mop of unruly, curly brown hair. She made them both a cup of tea, while Josh was set loose on all the wonderful, exciting things in the nursery. It was completely geared up for babies and toddlers, from Josh's age all the way up to three and four-year-olds, partitioned accordingly so the bigger children were all together and separated from the more delicate younger ones. Padded play mats covered the entire floor in the play areas. Jen liked what she saw, explained that she would try a couple of mornings with her in attendance to make sure he was happy, and then leave him there for three mornings a week. Kathy said that would be fine, and they could accommodate as soon as she liked. "New additions are always welcomed," she said, smiling warmly. After discussing the money side of things, Jen arranged two sessions, one on Monday, and one on Wednesday the following week. On her drive back home, she thought to herself *my God, the time is flying! He's six months old, nearly crawling, exclaiming the odd syllable and word here and there. Liam is back at work part-time, and so will I be very soon... I feel like if I blink, I'll miss it...*

The nursery try-out sessions went without a hitch, and Jen also revelled in the fact that Josh was interacting normally with the other babies and their respective mums—he had been relatively sheltered from outsiders up to this point, except occasional family and friends visiting. Before she knew it, she was walking back into the hotel chain's main office as if she'd never been away. Liam had settled straight back into his work life, relishing the challenges he'd thought he'd never miss, and this was all helped by the fact that Josh was exceptionally good overnight now. He woke normally once at about four for a feed, and now Liam was able to help. They were slowly but surely weaning Josh off breastfeeding and onto formula milk at night, with solids and purees coming into play in the day more frequently as time went by. Now Liam understood about the difference at changing time.

Jen also enjoyed reclaiming part of her former life back, safe in the knowledge that Josh was in good hands at the nursery. She had also made a new friend—their neighbours, Beth and Alex Gleeson, were a couple slightly younger than Liam and Jen. They had moved next door about eighteen months ago, and had largely kept themselves to themselves. Because the houses were so well-spaced, the two couples had had little interaction up to this point. The massive conifer hedge separating the houses lent itself to privacy, and this was part of the appeal of the house in the first place. Of course, they exchanged pleasantries when they encountered each other (Liam and Alex had talked about cars briefly when he had dropped a parcel over to Alex's about twelve months ago), but Jen wasn't aware that Beth had also been pregnant and had a baby recently—about six months earlier than hers. This demonstrated how isolated they were from their neighbours, as both women had given birth in the last twelve months and neither knew about the other. Beth's baby Alice was a regular at Little Tykes nursery and had been for the last six months. Jen recognised Beth immediately, and they began talking about the fact that neither had known about the other's babies. They soon became friends after a few encounters at the nursery (Jen found herself late for work on a couple of occasions as she had been talking to Beth before leaving). Both mums were keen that their babies met each other, and played with each other, too. This was an investment on all parts—childhood friendships often started with neighbouring families.

Jen talked to Liam about this new encounter over dinner, after she had spent some time with Beth earlier that day. She was also a good looking woman with short brown hair and a pretty, open face. She was slightly taller than Jen, and maybe a dress size larger, but had a great figure. The dads at the nursery were all too aware of the attractive mums chatting over a cup of tea when dropping their kids off, and many an appreciative glance was thrown their way. Jen had booked an extra morning and had stayed for the duration, and they forged a proper friendship following a morning of finding out about each other.

"She's lovely, Liam—I can't believe we haven't been friends with them before now. Bloody hell, I didn't even know she was pregnant! They didn't know about us either! How weird is that?" Josh was down for the night, upstairs asleep while the baby monitor blinked away. Jen and Liam had just finished eating, and they were tackling the kitchen together.

"Yeah, well that's great news hon. Alex is a nice chap, but as you know we've hardly seen each other since they moved next door. And if Josh gets a little playmate out of it, then that's a bonus," he said.

"Well, Beth mentioned that Alice is one next week, and on the Saturday they're going to have a party at their place. We simply have to go, and you'll have to get more acquainted with Alex. What do you think?"

"Yes, I'm up for that love. But it would be best if you chose a gift for Alice— I'm no good at that stuff."

"I wouldn't allow you to choose anything anyway—she'd end up with a cordless drill, or an electric guitar. I'll let Beth know we can make it during the week." She tidied away the last of the dishes and wiped the kitchen tops. "You can buy some kids food to take on your way back from work next week if you want to make yourself useful," she added.

Liam nodded in agreement and drank the remainder of his wine. "Yep, no problem—fifteen jars of pureed carrot and potato it is then!"

The week came and went without any major dramas for Jen and Liam, and before they knew it they were getting ready to go to the Gleesons. Jen had bought Alice a cuddly toy and a couple of pretty little dresses. *I love Josh so much, but for our next I'll be praying for a little girl,* she thought to herself as she wrapped the gifts up. Liam had bought some nice cakes from the local bakery, which should suit both adults and children alike—Jen was impressed with his choice.

At two in the afternoon, they wandered over to their neighbours' house with Josh in tow in his carry cot. He was wrapped up, as it was a little cold and Jen didn't want him getting a sniffle. He was happy enough, gurgling away and chatting his usual tirade of baby nonsense, bashing his little teddy all the while.

As they walked up the driveway, Beth came out from around the side of the house with little Alice clutching one hand. "Hello Jen! Hi Liam! Please, come around. If the weather holds then we can stay in the garden but if it turns, we can head inside," she said, beaming at Jen. She made a fuss of Josh, and they made a fuss of Alice ("Happy first birthday, special girl!") as they wandered around the side of the house. There were probably another ten or twelve parents there, all with their children of various ages running or crawling around. The Gleesons had no pets, and Alex had inspected the garden that morning for any rogue droppings—there was also a large play mat down on the lawn which covered most of the open space. Everyone seemed to be having a great time, and Jen and Liam were introduced to the others: *I'll never remember all these names,* Liam thought.

Jen let Josh loose on the play mat, and he started crawling around immediately. Alice soon was by his side doing similar, and they played together naturally. The two doting mothers looked on at their children, both smiling.

"These two are such good friends already," Beth said. "I hope they stay that way, Jen."

"Oh, so do I—it's so sweet! They'll probably grow up to be childhood sweethearts at this rate—look, Alice is captivated by him!" Jen replied, as Alice was offering Josh a lick of her ice-lolly. Josh obliged by slobbering all over it and laughing.

Liam was busy trying to find common ground with Alex, who had offered him a beer shortly after arriving. Liam accepted, and they both stood to one side of the patio doors talking about work and careers. Liam discovered that Alex was also into property, not civil engineering, but management. This gave them enough to keep them talking while they weighed each other up for friend material. Liam had plenty of friends already, but it wouldn't hurt to have another, especially as Beth and Jen got on so well, not to mention their kids.

At the FMA laboratory facility, the twin in V29 was active. Well, at least his brain was. His body has stopped mimicking Josh's every movement early on— he was aware of the movement, but no longer had the impulse reaction to replicate it. As Josh grew and developed, so did he. He didn't understand anything at all about his being, but what seven-month old does? Josh didn't know who *he* was, but he knew his mum and dad. He knew Alice. He knew most of his toys, and knew his favourites. He knew his favourite foods, and knew what pain and laughter was. The twin also knew these things by default—but could not experience them in the same way that Josh could. He was unaware that he was a twin, and Josh was living in the real world, while he was imprisoned in a vessel full of fluid, but he was aware of Josh's experiences. He knew the sensations of taste, smell, sight and hearing. He also knew touch, both nice and nasty, but experienced all of these sensory inputs differently to Josh. This was because Josh was having the real-life experience, the real deal, while the twin got a second hand, dumbed down version of events. When Alice offered her lolly to Josh, the twin also had his mouth flooded with the cold sensation of strawberry. When Josh looked at Alice and grabbed her hand, the twin saw her too, and felt her hand. His eyes were open, staring vacantly, as he soaked all these experiences in. The creased brow returned as he concentrated on what Josh's mind was feeding him. His tiny brain was like a sponge, absorbing a constant stream of sensory input from a remote source. He was learning about life, albeit second hand.

# Chapter Fourteen

As Christmas approached, both Liam and Jen realised how different this one was going to be. It was all about Josh. They debated whether he would even remember the slightest fragment of this event, his first Christmas, but not for long—they both agreed they couldn't remember much of anything prior to the age of four.

"That won't stop us from making this the best Christmas ever," Jen announced. "He will remember it—I'll have the photos to prove it." Both of their phone galleries were already brimming with literally hundreds of photos of their son, as well as the iPad and laptop.

"Of course it will be special, hon. He just won't remember any of it—a bit like my Saturday nights out with the lads," Liam observed. They had also both discussed the budget for Josh. Liam was keen not to spoil him from an early age. "Spoilt kids grow up to be wankers," he declared. "He doesn't need tons of money and gifts lavished upon him. Please, can we keep it reasonable?" he pleaded. There was no need—Jen was in total agreement. If anything, she had better financial skill than Liam.

They had both booked the holiday period from work. Liam noted that it felt like they had spent more time away from work this last year than actually working, and this was largely true. Jen was still on mornings, and had Josh in nursery four mornings a week—one of those she spent with Beth and their kids, talking about motherhood and husbands and all things girly. Liam had upped his game to four days a week, and this was good for his well-being—someone had to earn a crust for the family, after all. It also made him appreciate his time more with Jen and Josh. He put Josh to bed on his working days, and Jen did the other nights. Their routine appeared to be working just fine.

Jen's appointments with FMA had dwindled now that they were happy with mother and baby's progress. She went once in late September, and the next wasn't until early January. These were now just routine appointments for her to let them know if anything untoward was happening, or if she was unduly worried for whatever reason. She wasn't, so the meetings were normally brief.

At nine months, Josh's development seemed to be happening at an explosive rate. He was into everything, and now he was mobile (crawling quite fast and propping up on furniture, threatening to walk at any given moment), Jen really had to have her wits about her to stop him from getting into mischief. All plants had been re-arranged into more suitable, elevated homes. Technology such as DAB radios, phones, laptops and suchlike now all had new homes four feet above ground level. Everyday items that would normally be put down on sofas or coffee tables were now squirrelled away on a shelf somewhere, away from Josh's prying little fingers. The mishaps had been few and far between, but had still happened just as they do in any normal family home. A tube of hand cream had been unceremoniously opened and squirted all over the lower part of the sofa. Josh had tried to eat some, but luckily decided it wasn't for him. The shoe rack had been emptied of footwear, and then the rack pulled over on top of himself. Ten seconds of wailing later, and Jen was busy consoling him, kissing the small bruise flowering on his forehead. The downstairs toilet brush had been removed from its holder and Josh was busy whacking it against the sink: *Thwock, thwock*…until Liam this time intervened, and removed the offending article from Josh's tightly gripped fist, much to Josh's displeasure. This now lived on the cistern, and the toilet door was always kept closed.

His hair was now a thick brown thatch on his head—he definitely took after his dad for that. His eye colour had also settled on a stunning blue—a gift from both parents. He was a fairly stocky little boy, and they had no problem getting food into him. He liked most things that were on offer, and appeared to particularly love all fruits and vegetables (with the exception of avocado). All in all, he was the epitome of a baby boy just coming up to his first year—healthy, happy and content. This was reflected in his parents too. Their main concern now was their son, and if he was happy, then so were they.

Christmas was a resounding success in the Connelly household. Josh didn't really know what all the fuss was about, but seemed to have a great time anyway. The house looked like an explosion in a toy factory. They ventured out for a few excursions to visit family (both nanna and gran), but apart from that, it was a quiet holiday for all three of them. As the New Year came in, Liam and Jen mentally prepared themselves for the inevitable return to work, and also Josh's return to nursery. They had discussed what to do about nursery for Josh, and decided that they would try five mornings a week. He had made a few friends there (his favourite being Alice), and Jen needed to get back into work on a daily basis, if not full-time just yet. Jen made all the necessary arrangements with Kathy at the nursery, who was more than happy for Josh to spend more time there ("He's so adorable and absolutely no trouble—we'd be delighted, Jen!"). So, the New Year started with a bang—Liam was on a full working week again, Jen on five mornings a week and Josh in nursery when she was at work. It seemed like a whirlwind to Liam—it had all happened, and was happening, so quickly. Josh would be one in April, and he was back to work, as if nothing had happened.

Jen continued to see Beth at the nursery, although she no longer spent the whole of Thursday morning with her there, as she was working. In order to make up for this lack of time with her friend, she found herself and Liam having more socials on the weekends with them. Sometimes this would be at the Gleesons, others at the Connellys. They had also been out for Sunday lunch together, and the neighbours were fast becoming good friends. Alice and Liam now knew each other as well as small children can—Alice had the edge, as she was slightly older. She was walking now, and her vocabulary was also improving by the day.

"She's growing and learning so fast!" Jen exclaimed one Saturday afternoon. The Gleesons had come around to their house for some light lunch, and playtime for the kids.

"Yeah I know! She learns a new word every day, at least one." Beth was sat at the kitchen table with Jen while the men watched football in the living room. The kids were with their mums, Josh crawling around on the play mat and Alice tottering around the table with her favourite doll.

"It's so good for Josh to be around her, Beth. He's learning so much from her, you can see him trying to copy everything she says and does." Sure enough, Josh had lost interest in his puzzle toy and was crawling around behind Alice. She had noticed him and laughed as she tottered around the table trying to outrun him (and succeeding). "I'm so pleased they like each other so much. And they get to see each other all the time now."

"Oh, they're gonna be besties for sure, Jen—Alice talks about Josh, she was busy gabbling away about him the other night when I put her to bed—it's so sweet!" Beth said.

Liam was also happy the kids were friends—he had made himself a new mate, as well. It turned out that he and Alex actually had a fair bit in common, and their friendship was also developing fast. They had been out locally for a few drinks together, and this brought benefits—the girls were happy to stay at home babysitting together. Everyone was happy, and the fact that their respective wives and children were friends took considerable pressure off both of them when it came to going out for a few drinks.

As Josh's first birthday approached, he started to take his first steps. This was captured, more by luck than judgement, by Jen on her phone. When Liam came home from work she took great delight in showing him, and then she instantly felt guilty he hadn't been there to see it.

"Don't be silly Jen—we can't both expect to be there for every bit of progress he makes. I'm just glad you got it on your phone. He's bound to do it again before I put him down tonight." Sure enough, Liam got to see Josh staggering in all his glory for three whole steps, before tumbling to the floor. He was not fazed in the slightest; he just looked around, got up, and was trying to do it again before you could blink. Naturally, both parents were flooded with pride and love at this simple act from their son.

As Josh's first birthday approached, Jen and Liam were busy preparing for his big day. They intended to have a party for him at home—there seemed little point in hiring a venue, when their house was more than accommodating. Their judgement was also swayed by the resounding success of Alice's party next door. Jen intended to do a similar affair to Beth and Alex, and in the weeks prior to the party she sent out all the invites. It would be the first time some of their respective families had been brought together—Liam's sister Jane and her husband David had never met Jen's mother Alison and her father Geoff. They were going to have the party on the Saturday following Josh's birthday, in the hope that most invitees would be able to make it.

The theory paid off. Almost all of their family and friends were in attendance, and the weather remained fairly clear and rain-free all day. Josh was the centre of attention of course, and loved every minute of it. He was clucked and fussed over constantly throughout the day. Liam regretted not firing the barbeque up. "It's a perfect day for it—why didn't I get the food in for a barbeque?" he grumbled, more to himself than Jen.

"Don't beat yourself up about it, Liam. If you had gone to all that trouble and expense, then you can guarantee that it would be raining. Besides, all the food has been lovely." Jen said. She was right—it was Sod's Law. As the festivities wound up to a natural conclusion, people started to make their way back to their respective homes. John and Janet were staying at the Connellys, and Liam was looking forward to sinking a few cold ones later with John. He had been on his best behaviour all day but felt like he could use a drink shortly. Sure enough, once everyone had left, the beers started flowing and the two couples meandered their way through the evening once Josh was asleep.

During the day, the twin's mind had been active. There were images of different faces and people beamed directly into his brain. All this information was carefully stored in the memory of the twin. He knew a lot about Josh now. He knew what his mum and dad looked and sounded like. He knew about the place his mum dropped Josh off to every morning. He knew the faces of the other children there. He knew what Kathy looked and sounded like. He knew about food and drink. He knew what bananas tasted like, although he had never eaten one, and never would. The twins were fed nutrient-based solutions directly into their stomachs, with the excrement being carried away from the bowel and bladder in a similar fashion. The twin's mind was developing just as Josh's was, and it was storing and hoarding information, just as Josh was. His mind was completely dependent on Josh's learning and experiences, although he was too young to make that connection. But as long as Josh carried on learning and developing, so would his twin. And at the moment, Josh's learning was on an exponential scale, as all young children's are.

# Chapter Fifteen

Jen had trouble containing her screams from the nightmare she had just experienced. She sat on the edge of the bed, drenched in cold sweat, shaking from the terror. In her slumber, she had heard Josh crying in his cot and had gone to him, knowing he wanted feeding. It was dark, and although Josh was eating solids during the day, she was still breastfeeding him overnight, as well as feeding with bottles of formula milk. As she picked him up, she felt the tense anxiety of his little limbs struggling against her body as she undid her top to give him access to what he wanted. Her mind still fuzzy with sleep, she was operating the tried and tested routine of night-time feeding on auto-pilot, and was vaguely aware of Josh clamping on to her right nipple, making contented suckling noises all the while. As she continued to doze, she thought he felt a little colder than usual. She pulled the duvet up over her upper body in order to keep the chill at bay, even though it was nice and warm in the bedroom. *That's odd,* she thought hazily, *he feels almost clammy…*as her hand stroked his tiny head, she was sure she detected moisture—was he *wet?* Puzzled, her hand continued to feel his tiny form. As she did so, trying to work out whether she was still half-asleep and imagining it all, her baby started to suckle her breast a little more enthusiastically than normal, the sucking and slurping noises getting louder as Josh's cheeks sucked in with quite a considerable force compared to his normal feeding behaviour.

As Jen began to leave her sleepy world behind and gradually wake up, she felt a cold wetness on Josh's all-in-one pyjamas. She drew her hand away from his body, and rubbed her fingers together—they were wet and cold, and ever so slightly slimy. Her brow creased in confusion: *Has he wet himself, and it's leaked through his nappy?* Her logical mind tried to make sense of what she was feeling, and at that moment she felt a sharp stab of discomfort on her breast. *Ow! What's he doing down there…not* biting *me, surely…* As she looked down at her child, his face looked almost greyish-blue and wrinkled, like your fingers looked like after being too long in the bath. Her eyes widened in alarm, and as she undid his poppers on his nightclothes, she saw his back was the same—and he *was* wet and slippery all over. A small grunt, almost like a growl, came from Josh as he moved his head frantically to one side, so as to gain a better purchase on his mother's nipple. She felt sharp stabs as he did so, like teeth on her delicate flesh, causing her to take a sharp intake of breath as she felt shooting, sharp needles of pain course up from her chest. *What's happening! He can't be biting me, he hasn't got any teeth!* She was confused, and Josh gnashed away, head moving erratically from side to side. Her mind went into shock, and as she looked down she saw rivulets of dark blood coursing down the swell of her chest. As Josh re-asserted his position, more aggressively this time, she again felt an agonising, sharp pain from where their bodies met. Panicking, she tried to lift Josh away from her, but as she moved him she realised that he was more than just suckling on her breast—he was fully biting down on her flesh, piercing it with what felt like little needle-like teeth. Her mind reeled: *This isn't happening,* she told herself, but the pain she was experiencing told her otherwise. As she struggled with the tiny body attached to her, she looked in horror at what she thought to be her son. His head and exposed body was completely drenched in a glistening wetness, the ooze dripping from him like rendered fat, his dark hair now plastered to the top of his wrinkled skull. She pulled him harder away from her, his body slipping in her hands. As she continued to try and wrench him away, her breast stretched out of shape as his vice-like clamp refused to let go. The pain exploded in her head, sending a wave of shock induced nausea through her. She felt like passing out and throwing up all at once, her mind reeling with disgust and terror. She looked down and saw that the baby-thing did indeed have teeth— as it moved its head to the side in a biting motion, she saw a row of blood covered, thin, razor sharp teeth sinking into her nipple. As its jaws clamped even harder onto her nipple, she felt the flesh tear there. She tried pulling away from it in panic, and as she did, one final jerk of its alien looking, slimy head was enough to bite her nipple off completely, severing it from her body. Jen recoiled in absolute terror, mouth and eyes wide, as she realised what had happened to her body. Her jaw worked soundlessly as blood now coursed down her torso in thick spurts from the newly created wound. There was a ragged, round hole where her nipple used to be, almost black with blood that had now filled the hole and ran freely. She gagged with revulsion as she saw the thing—that a few minutes ago was her son—chewing on the remains of her severed nipple, the

95

tough exterior skin being flayed and shredded by the row of dagger like teeth as it gnashed them together. As the flesh became more and more lacerated, lumps of the decimated skin and tissue dribbled down its chin, dripping from its blood filled mouth, as it looked at her with a demonic grin on its face...

As Jen came to terms with the fact it was another nightmare, she looked over at Josh—he was sleeping peacefully on his side, his tiny body rising and falling rhythmically. Though relieved, Jen was still in shock. She didn't want to wake Liam, and sat silently on the end of the bed, breathing as heavily as if she had just run a marathon. Her slick, oily sweat was now drying, and left her feeling chilled as her mind tried to process the nightmare: *Why do I keep having them?* She asked herself, desperately trying to make sense of it all. She got up and wandered into the bathroom. As she washed her face, desperately trying to erase the memory of the hellish dream, she realised that all of the dreams she'd had to date were connected—they were all about Josh, FMA, the twin...a nervous pang of anxiety squirmed in her stomach, tightening it into a knot. What if there was some kind of sinister meaning behind them? Were they trying to warn her somehow of something bad? Of something she didn't yet know about? As she made her way back to bed, the frown stayed on her face. She may have gone back to bed, but she didn't go back to sleep for the remainder of the night.

# Chapter Sixteen

Josh's formative years went quickly, and for the main part, without issue. Jen and Liam gradually reclaimed their previous lives back in one form or another—nothing was quite the same as before Josh was born, but normal life had resumed. Some of their weekend time was eaten into by other children's parties and nursery related fund raising events, and there were also regular trips to the local swimming pool with Josh, as well as trips to see family and friends. As Josh's first year rolled out behind him and his second year embraced him, he became more of a force to be reckoned with. By the time he had turned two, he had quite an impressive vocabulary, and could now get himself quite easily into mischief if not monitored. His climbing was as good, as his walking and running. He had a keen interest in books, which both parents were keen to encourage. "I know it's the age of technology and all that, but I don't want him to spend his life glued to a smart TV or phone," Liam declared.

"Yeah, well good luck with that, Sir Isaac Newton. That's the age he's growing up in, and there's not a lot you or I can do about it. All we can do is encourage the lost arts of reading and writing," Jen had responded. Of course, she was right. They looked to limit his time on devices (Liam's tablet was as much a favourite as the television), and vary his input so he didn't become locked completely in the digital world. He was an active little boy, and the way to do this was to get him out and about. He loved rambling around the countryside on weekend walks with his mum and dad. He also loved all living things, from bugs to cows. Books were a big part of Josh's life, everything from standard children's books to picture books of animals and plants. Jen had also taken to reading to him at every given opportunity. She was old-school, and the favourite at the moment was Aesop's fables. Although the fables themselves were beyond little Josh's capacity, the hardback he had also contained finely drawn pictures to accompany the classic short stories within, and Josh spent ages poring over them with wonder.

His friendships outside of the home developed, too. He was now firm friends with Alice next door, and they spent quite a few afternoons a week together, either at their home or next door. Swimming and adventure play parks were also regular venues. Jen had negotiated two afternoons off a week, in order to ensure that she had as much input into her son's life as possible. Her company were accommodating to her request, and were quite satisfied that Jen would be able to do all her usual tasks on a reduced working week. During these times, Beth and Jen had become the very best of friends. They talked about everything from marriage to motherhood, family to politics and religion. They discovered that they had a lot in common, and they both relished each other's company. Evening soirées occurred between them as well, when the kids were tucked up in bed. Alex and Liam had also become friends, although maybe not quite as close as their wives had become—perhaps this was a 'man thing'. That being said, the two guys also got together, sometimes in the absence of their respective wives, for beers, football matches and other social gatherings. All in all, both couples felt privileged to have such good neighbours and friends—the Gleesons had experienced issues at their old house with bad neighbours, to the point that this had been one of the primary reasons that they had moved house in the end. This made them all the more appreciative of the Connellys.

Both Alice and Josh were still attending Little Tykes nursery, but the time was rapidly approaching when Alice would be starting at the local primary school. Beth and Jen had discussed this at length, with both mothers apprehensive about the imminent change. Beth was obviously nervous about how Alice would settle into her new school environment, and Jen was a little nervy about how Josh would react to not having his best buddy there anymore. There was still a few months left to go, it was May now, and Alice didn't leave the nursery until September. Beth had been trying to instil in Alice that it wouldn't be long before Josh was there with her too when they talked about her going to 'big school'. It seemed to be sinking in, slowly but surely, that her life was going to change. Beth was determined to make the transition as smooth as possible for her little girl. Jen was doing a similar thing with Josh, trying to explain why Alice wouldn't be at nursery anymore, but he would be with her again soon in a little while at a different, bigger school. Josh seemed upset at first that Alice was going away, but cheered up about the whole thing once his mum explained it wouldn't be for long. Conceptually it was all a little beyond Josh anyway—Alice was a bit more difficult to appease, as she was that little bit older and therefore had a slightly more advanced grasp on concepts such as time and change.

The summer came and went in what felt like a blink of an eye to both Jen and Beth alike. Before she knew it, Beth was having a few glasses of wine with Jen at the Gleeson house one Saturday late afternoon, saying to Jen that Alice started primary school on Monday. Naturally this led to a sprawling conversation about all the things both women were apprehensive about. They both concluded that of course everything would be fine, and made arrangements for the kids to play together later in the week. Beth could then tell Jen all about Alice's new adventure.

As expected, Alice settled into her new school with next to no teething problems at all. When Beth relayed this to Jen during the week, both mums were relieved—Josh had also accepted that he wouldn't be seeing Alice every day, and constantly nagged his mother as to when he would see his friend. As long as Jen reassured him it would be soon, he seemed satisfied. After all, he had other friends in nursery, and it would be less than a year now before he would be at primary school with his best friend. A year for Josh would seem like a lifetime, but for Jen it would fly by, she was sure.

# Part II

# Chapter One

"Hurry up, Josh; we need to get Beth and Alice." Jen was busy giving Josh's walking boots a quick clean. *He takes after his dad for bringing mess and mud into the house,* she thought, as she brushed them off in the back garden. She heard a muffled, distant reply from her son—he was upstairs still messing around with his hair, no doubt. He always seemed to put a bit more effort into his appearance when Alice was involved…or was she just imagining it? Maybe all seven-year old boys did the same and were like that nowadays. Jen couldn't remember being that fussed over the way she looked at such a young age. Maybe that was because she was the prettiest little girl anyone had ever seen, regardless.

Liam was working a rare Saturday morning in the office, and Beth and Jen had taken the opportunity to get out with the kids for a ramble in the countryside, decided the previous night after a few glasses of wine and a catch up. Alex was on a lad's weekend in Cornwall, and wasn't due back until Sunday. He had wisely pre-empted the sorry state he would be in, and booked the Monday off work in anticipation of the hangover. Jen checked her phone—they were already fifteen minutes later than she had told Beth. She quickly messaged her saying they were running late, and then came inside with a considerably cleaner set of boots. Another quick shout up the stairs resulted in a similar reply from Josh, so she made her way up there to see if she could 'assist' him.

On entering his room, the first thing that struck her was the mess: *Surely this isn't supposed to happen until the teen years…?* She thought. Josh wasn't there—he was in the bathroom. She picked up a few bits of dirty washing along with some of Josh's toys, tidying as she headed back out. Football cards were picked up and put on his chest of drawers, along with a half-finished Lego kit and the various bricks lying around it. She picked his bedside lamp up off the floor and put it back in its rightful home by the side of the bed, deftly giving the duvet a quick shake at the same time, an action that transformed the previously rather grubby looking pit into something that resembled a little boy's bed again.

Jen never got bored nowadays—Josh put paid to that. Probably three quarters of her day (every day, when not at work) was consumed by activities that either involved, or were a direct result, of her boy.

Liam also pulled his weight, especially with sport (swimming and football were his domain, although Jen did make appearances at both on occasions), but the household tasks generally fell to her. And for the main part, she relished them. Josh was happy, healthy and contented. This meant in turn that so were they, and they never took their fortunate lives for granted. Both parents always looked to instil a sense of gratefulness into Josh's thoughts whenever they could. Now he was old enough to see, and perhaps understand to a certain degree, other kids and the fact that they maybe did not have lives as nice as his own, the concept of being lucky had been introduced and was slowly sinking in.

Josh was busy preening himself. He had his dad's looks in the main. You could see the strong jawline was forming even now, and his hair had the same thick, wavy quality to it. It was this that Josh was desperately trying to sort out, by the looks of it. As Jen came in, she noticed it looked like he had put half a tub of styling gel on his head and then rubbed it in with a scrubbing brush. Tufts jutted out here and there as Josh patted, twisted, smoothed and dabbed away at his mop. A frown creased his normally smooth brow.

"What have you done, Josh? It's too much. Let me sort it out for you, we are late already." She manoeuvred him closer to the sink despite his whiny protests, and turned the tap on until it ran warm. She ducked his head under the stream, explaining to him that she would make sure his hair looked cool before they leave. Josh was for the main part compliant in this process, with only the odd grumble and protest being uttered as Jen rinsed the gel out of his hair. Once done, she roughly towel dried his hair and applied a more reasonable amount of styling gel. Within a few short minutes, Josh looked every bit the good looking cute boy next door—just as nature intended (with a little help from some extra-firm hold styling gel). He appraised himself in the mirror and nodded his approval as Jen scurried out of the bathroom, calling for him to follow her and get himself ready. One last look and he was on his mother's heels, asking where his boots were, and whether they were taking a picnic. Jen answered his questions as she put on a light jacket and handed him his from the coat rack. Once his boots were on (he was able to tie his own laces after Liam had spent a painful evening a few months ago endlessly showing him two different ways of doing it), she grabbed her keys and they left the house. Jen was driving, but it was only a short journey—if you went towards town but then took a left onto an A road before the main street, it took you up to a higher area of land that gradually became less and less populated with houses and shops. She and Beth had been there with the children many times over the last three or so years, once the kids were more independent and able to run around on their own. After the twenty minute drive, there was a small gravel car park (normally a few other cars there, never full) that relied on a donation from drivers parking there. There were several country walks that branched out from the clearing, and the kids had their favourite—one path led to a wooded area that had a good sized pond in it, fed by a small stream. This provided endless hours of fun looking for frogs, toads, and tadpoles, along with a plethora of other critters for the curious children. It normally resulted in copious amounts of mud being transferred into the mothers' cars, but nothing that wouldn't wash off.

Josh was not big enough to travel without a booster seat in the car, but the days of a full child car seat were over. Jen started the car and made the short trip from her drive to Beth's, beeping her horn as she pulled in. Within a few moments, Beth and Alice appeared. Josh's face lit up as he saw his best friend run over to the car. Beth had a booster seat for Alice, and after a little bit of messing around, had her all buckled up in the back along with Josh. They instantly started jabbering to each other, each battling with the other to get their sentences out first. Alice was a pretty girl. Her blonde hair was halfway down her back, and Beth had put French plaits in for her. This took her hair away from her dainty features and showed her beauty to the full. She was a dead ringer for her mum, and Beth got comments to this effect all the time, from schoolteachers commenting on the similarity in the playground to old ladies crooning over them at the supermarket.

The two mothers kissed each other on the cheek as they said their hellos, and they set off on their morning woodland adventure. The short trip was easily long enough for both kids and mums to catch up with each other. Jen and Beth talked about the school, their husbands, work and whether Beth wanted to come over later for a barbeque. Jen knew Alex was away, and Liam wouldn't mind—he would have a few late afternoon beers, cook them some food in the garden and once Josh went up, he would probably retire to the garage to crank some music up and butcher it with his half-cut guitar improvisation over the top. This would leave Jen and Beth to drink as much wine as they liked and put what they wanted on the TV or radio. Beth jumped at the chance—not before reminding Jen that she wouldn't be able to leave Alice. Jen assured her that it wasn't an issue—Beth could bring her over and they could both stay in the guest room for the night, or alternatively carry her back home at the end of the night. Once the evening plan was settled, Jen thought she had best message Liam and let him know. He could get supplies on his way back from work, or she could take a detour into Cleedon on the way back.

As Jen brought the car to a halt, the kids were unbuckling themselves in the back, desperate to get out. After a few words about not running too far ahead, they were gone. The women followed their lead at a brisk pace, in order to keep them in sight. This was easier said than done—both children were active and full of energy, trying to outrun each other along the shaded woody path. The strong, warm sun glimmered through the leaf canopy giving a glittery, mottled look to the path they walked. It had been consistently dry over the last three or four days, which was not always a given in the summer—often the path they now walked was a quagmire of mud, leaves and puddles. Today it was firm underfoot, with mud only present in the deepest darkest corners and edges of the path where the sun's rays had not penetrated and been able to dry it. As they wound along the path, Beth shouted to both children to wait—they were near the pond, and both parents wanted to have a firm eye on what their offspring were doing. Neither Beth nor Jen really knew how deep the pond actually was, but it seemed large enough to be at least three feet deep in the middle. It was oval in shape and its length had to be at least fifteen feet by a width of ten. They allowed the kids to go to the edge of the pond to look for critters, and even take their boots and socks off to paddle if it was nice enough. On the wetter days, they insisted Alice and Josh keep their boots on as the edge of the pond was a belt of sloppy mud. This meant for messier cars, but kept them from going in too far. On drier days such as this one, the edge of the pond appeared much cleaner, with a small, dry bank around it allowing an easier entry to the shallow water. The water in the pond always appeared much cleaner under these circumstances, and automatically made it more inviting to the children, the water sparkling and glinting in the filtered sun. There was a favourite log that the mothers liked to sit on while the kids splashed and played, and they took up their normal residence. Josh asked if he could take his boots and socks off from the edge of the pond and Jen briefly considered this before replying okay, but don't go in too far. Alice took this as a yes from her mum too, and both children stripped off boots and socks, eager to feel the cold water on their feet. Josh rolled up his jeans in order to get a bit further out without getting them wet—Alice had no such worries, as her pretty blue dress came to just about knee height, requiring no clothing adjustments.

Jen took off her backpack and brought out a few items of food in preparation for the kids once they decided they were hungry. Both mothers chatted away easily and relaxed, always with one eye on the paddling children, who were also chattering away to each other while examining the contents of the pool. They were talking about school, and in particular a boy called Adam Winters. Adam was a bit of a bully, and had teased Alice about her lunch bag in school last week. Alice had taken it in her stride, but was now grumbling to Josh about him.

"Don't take any notice of him, he's a bully and he's nasty," Josh advised Alice solemnly. "I don't like him anyway. And neither does Benny." Alice looked at him, momentarily pausing her frog hunt.

"Who's Benny?" She looked at him quizzically. She didn't know anyone in their class called Benny. In fact, she didn't know anyone in the whole school called Benny.

"If I tell you, you have to promise not to tell anyone Alice, not even your mum and dad." He looked at her sternly, as if to re-enforce the point. She lowered her voice to a whisper and promised she wouldn't tell.

"Benny is my special friend. He only knows me; I'm his only friend in the world. And he can't talk out loud. But he talks to me in my head, and I can talk back to him." He hunkered back down to further inspect the water. Alice's quizzical expression stayed on her face for a few moments, as she tried to make sense of what Josh had told her. Then she bent down and re-joined him in his quest to explore.

# Chapter Two

The vast array of vessels housed within the FMA laboratory area were all reporting a status of normal function. This could be seen by the blinking of the small green LEDs that accompanied each vessel. The perfect lines of glass houses were all supported on sturdy metal frames that also facilitated electronic monitoring and administering devices. This enabled the subjects to receive all that they needed in order to function and grow normally. At least, as normally as they could. Their environments were sterile and devoid of all input from the outside world, apart from the regulated nutrient supplies going in and the waste matter being removed via timer-controlled tubes. The walls of the laboratory were a cold, clinical white along with the floor and ceiling. There were glaring fluorescent strip lights also in neat rows mounted on the ceiling above the vessels, also electronically controlled. The timers ensured the lights provided an as close to natural daylight frequency of light for a period of ten hours every day. They faded over a period of an hour every evening until no more light emitted, and the reverse happened every morning. Such was the importance of re-creating an as close to normal living environment for the nearly two hundred twins housed there.

The FMA laboratory only had five regular workers, all technicians with some form of medical background—both experienced and qualified. There were doctors and specialists that also spent time in the lab monitoring, studying and recording the twins and their feedback from the vessels. Their presence was naturally more prolific when there was an event that was deemed to be out of the ordinary. This only happened on rare occasions—the electronic monitoring and feedback systems were designed to correct any anomalies before they could get out of hand and cause problems for any of the twins. The pressure and liquid levels within the vessels were all controlled with valves and sensors, which would auto-correct when a drop or increase in either parameter was detected. The events were all recorded, and the small team of technicians were trained to go through the logs of each and every vessel daily, to spot any unusual events. A complex front-end software package allowed everything to be observed, monitored, and adjusted accordingly. The technicians spent most of their working day (or night) looking at long lists of status codes, and making the call on whether anything needed to be adjusted or kept an eye on. Anything too far off the norm would be reported, and generally resulted in the experts coming in for a visit to analyse the problem and the subject in question.

The twin in V29 had learnt to keep himself quiet. He wasn't able to see much outside of his own vessel, but was aware that the rows of blurry shapes he could actually make out were more than likely similar to his own living quarters. During its lifespan, the twin in V29 had caused the technicians some concern. Jez Poole had worked in the lab for many years, and had not seen too much out of the ordinary in his time there, but he had noticed movement in V29. Motion activity was monitored in the vessels, and this one had more than usual. Jez had let it go the first time it occurred—the status warnings were low importance, in other words not an emergency. He switched to camera V29 on the PC and looked at the screen with interest. The little guy was having a right old party in there by himself—kicking out with one leg one minute, the next trying to rotate within his confines. It looked like he was almost struggling to get out: *Completely impossible and ridiculous,* Jez thought, as he watched the twin on the screen. From what Jez understood, there was no consciousness as such associated with the subjects. Their awareness of anything was minimal. This in turn meant that if the subject was to be used for its brain, then it could only be used in a limited capacity as there was no consciousness, there was no learning. No learning, no experience, no memory. This meant that the brain was the only organ that couldn't be used as the other organs could—a complete replacement for its human counterpart. It also meant that the twins were invariably quiet in their little glass houses—their brain stimulus was so low that it rarely resulted in a physical reaction like he was now seeing, for the second time in as many days.

Jez decided that even though the event had low risk written all over it (what was the little dude going to do—kick his way out of there...?), that he would submit a UAR—an Unusual Activity Report. This took all of five minutes, and then it was sent. Jez didn't know who looked at these in the first instance, but he did know that response time was immediate. Sure enough, five minutes later, there were two doctors asking him in more depth questions about what was happening in V29. After some discussion and observation, the two doctors decided that it was an anomaly not worth too much concern. The doctors talked to Jez for a few minutes to explain the reasons why this sort of thing may happen (motor neurone over-activity, subconscious stimulus and suchlike, none of which really made a lot of sense to him). When he enquired as to why this didn't happen to all of the twins, their response was that it probably *does,* but just doesn't result in such a noticeable physical reaction in all subjects. Jez accepted this explanation easily enough; although he still felt it strange that V29 had the symptoms and none of the rest: *I don't completely understand the science behind it; I'm just paid to monitor them. So how would I know what's normal and what isn't...?* He thought. The doctors made their exit through the large steel double doors and left Jez alone again.

What Jez (and the doctors for that matter) didn't know was that the twin in V29 had more stimulus than the other subjects. This input came in the form of what felt like remote experiences seen through someone else's eyes...in this case, Josh. The twin knew a lot about Josh. In actual fact, the twin probably knew as much about Josh as Josh did himself. Josh was also aware of the twin—he didn't know where he was, or what he looked like, or what his life consisted of, but Josh knew he existed. He *had* to exist, because the twin talked to him. Not out loud, like a normal person would, but almost like the twin was sending him thoughts.

At first, when Josh was four or so, he didn't know what the seemingly random thoughts that popped into his head were. They didn't worry him, just confused him a little. As the thoughts became more frequent, Josh started trying to send his own thoughts back. He didn't know who or what was sending the thoughts, and wasn't sure if his own thoughts *were* going anywhere for a while, and he didn't dwell on it too much—after all, four-year-old boys have other, much more important things to think about. As Josh grew older, his relationship with this other 'person' developed. It developed to the point that Josh gave him (he was sure it was a 'him') a name—Benny. Josh and Benny started communicating with each other more frequently as time went on, and neither twin nor boy fully understood the nature of what they were actually doing with each other. The nature of their exchanges were largely innocuous—Benny would often *suggest* things to Josh—like *ask your mum to take you swimming,* or *see if you're allowed some ice-cream.* And he also asked a lot of questions. Questions like *who's that boy you're playing with, what's his name, does he live near you, do you like him?* And Benny was very curious about Josh's best friend, Alice.

110

He asked Josh about her all the time, as if trying to understand why Josh liked her so much more than his other friends from school. He was also curious about the family pet—a very cute, furry little hamster called Ginger (for obvious reasons). It was the closest Benny could get to another living thing that wasn't a human, and he asked Josh to get him out of his cage regularly and stroke him. The sensation of the soft, warm fur on Josh's palms resulted in a sensory experience for Benny, one that he had never experienced before, and it filled his mind full of wonder.

Josh realised quickly that when he talked out loud to Benny when his mum was around, she took notice. Josh had gotten into the habit of talking to Benny as if he was in the room. Some part of his subconscious knew that he was talking to him inside his head, but he talked out loud to all of his other friends, so why not with Benny? He was the same as a 'real' friend, apart from he couldn't see him, and that's why they have to talk to each other in their heads. But Benny *felt* more real if Josh spoke out loud to him. After the first such incident, Jen talked to Josh about it in that oh-so-subtle way that mums have—not accusatory or disapproving in any way. She asked him who he was talking to, and when Josh explained about Benny she instantly thought: *He isn't the first kid to have an imaginary friend, and he won't be the last.* Given this, she decided that it was not a major issue, and she should handle it in an appropriately low-key fashion. During that afternoon, she asked Josh a further couple of times about his friend, and once she was happy he had nothing more than a vivid imagination, she let it go. Obviously, she would mention to Liam her discovery and instruct him to approach with caution if he felt the need, and to just monitor events. As time went on, Josh talked to Benny more and more…to the point that one particular afternoon, Jen decided to talk to him about Benny again. Josh had been chattering away in the back garden for hours—to himself. Tactfully, she explained to Josh that, because no one else could see or hear Benny, then maybe he should talk to him *silently* instead. Little did she know that actually that was how they were communicating anyway. Josh was accepting of this, and agreed to do just that. From his perspective, it made no difference—they were still talking to each other, so nothing changes. Jen was satisfied she had tackled the subject well, and was pleased (if not slightly relieved) to notice Josh not talking to himself quite as much over the coming few days. The last thing she wanted was for Josh to be bullied or teased for being strange and different at school.

And so, Josh and Benny developed their alien friendship inside their heads, and the world was blissfully unaware of how close they were both getting to each other. Barely a minute went by without some form of communication between them, Benny eager to glean experience and learning from Josh, and Josh only too willing to impart his every thought and act with his silent, distant friend.

# Chapter Three

Josh was in his room looking at Ginger. The little furry bundle was busy scurrying around in his cage, nibbling seeds from his dish in between stretching up on the bars of his cage, sniffing the air enthusiastically. Josh put his finger up to the cage and scratched his head through the thin chrome bars. Earlier in the day he had rummaged around in the coffee table drawers in the living room, looking for a suitable implement.

Josh and Benny had been having a lot of discussions about Ginger recently. Benny appeared to be a bit obsessed with the concept of having a pet, and this obsession had kind of turned into some form of bizarre jealousy on his part. Josh had explained to him that Ginger was just a stupid dumb animal that lived in a cage in his bedroom and didn't really do much apart from eat, sleep and go around endlessly on his little squeaky wheel. Josh told Benny that this annoyed him sometimes, as it either woke him up when he was asleep or stopped him from getting to sleep in the first place. Josh frequently told Ginger: *Shut up, I'm trying to sleep* or *stop running, it's noisy*. Benny grabbed hold of this information, and suggested to Josh that maybe he should do something to stop him. Then, he would be able to sleep without being disturbed.

Josh was confused by this—how could he stop him? He had always done it, virtually from the day they got him from the pet shop. Josh had moaned to him mum about it, and they had talked about it. Jen explained to her son that hamsters were nocturnal, which means they are awake when we are asleep, and asleep when we are awake. After Josh said that it was the wheel squeaking that was the problem, his dad had a look and applied a small squirt of oil onto the offending article while Josh watched, holding Ginger and stroking him. Once done, the wheel was much quieter for a while. But it didn't last for more than a few nights, and then it was back to the incessant high-pitched, penetrating sound that it always was. Josh complained to his dad again, and Liam promised to oil it again.

*But it doesn't work, Dad,* Josh had said dejectedly. He suggested taking the wheel away to his dad, and Liam had then explained to his son that it probably wasn't a good idea to do that. Hamsters in a cage needed to be able to exercise, and without the wheel he would get fat and unhealthy. His dad said that if Josh wanted Ginger to have a happy, long life, then the wheel should stay. He promised him he would get another wheel, and hopefully it wouldn't squeak— but that was ages ago, and the wheel had not yet been replaced. Josh reminded him a couple of times about it, but his dad appeared to be constantly busy, or distracted with some other, more important task. The second time Josh pestered him, he oiled the wheel again to try and get his son off his back. He made a mental note to pop into the pet shop the next time he was in town. *Josh appears to be overly concerned with his little furry bundle of joy, lately,* he thought.

The oil didn't work, of course. Josh found himself annoyed at Ginger. What he was actually feeling was resentment towards his pet, but he didn't know what resentment was. When he talked to Benny about this, he was only too happy to try and resolve the problem for him: *You could do something to get rid of it, no one would have to know,* he suggested. Josh didn't like the idea of this—he could get into trouble with Mum and Dad. And even though Ginger was annoying him lately, he didn't *really* want to do anything nasty to him—he loved animals. He was always looking to find wild animals whenever he was anywhere in the countryside or in the garden, everything from worms and bugs to looking at sheep and cows in fields. Benny didn't appear to share his enthusiasm—he said that because he couldn't touch them or pick them up that they were boring.

Josh opened the cage door and put his hand in to stroke his pet. Ginger sniffed his fingers, nose twitching eagerly. Josh stroked him and Ginger appeared to like it, raising his head and looking at Josh. The darning needle that Josh had taken from the sewing kit was on his bedside table, just within arm's reach of Ginger's cage. He curled his hand around the little creature, and carefully brought him through the tiny barred door of the cage. Ginger was still sniffing his hand and the air avidly, whiskers twitching while he raised his nose in different directions.

Benny was watching Josh's actions from afar, and started to communicate with him: *You need to push the needle into his body, and then the noise will stop forever.* Josh frowned. He knew what he was doing when he stole the needle earlier and what it was going to be used for, but now he was actually on the brink of acting, he felt a little differently. Ginger was lovely and cute, after all—he was harmless. Did he really deserve to be hurt because of his stupid squeaky wheel?

It wasn't his fault. If anything, it was his dad's fault for not replacing it—but he definitely didn't want to hurt his dad, and Benny had not suggested that he do so. Anyway, how exactly could he hurt his dad? He was big and strong, not to mention clever. And he loved his dad—he didn't want to think bad thoughts about him, so he stopped thinking about him and turned his attention back to Ginger. The warm, furry animal was now getting adventurous, looking to climb up Josh's arm. His tiny claws tickled his skin as he scrabbled to climb upwards from his hand, and Josh juggled him back into his palm again when he looked to scamper away. *Get a proper hold of him, don't let him run away!* Benny urged Josh. *I don't want to hurt him, he's cute and I don't want to be nasty to him,* Josh told Benny. He was having mixed feelings now, as opposed to last night when they were talking. Last night Josh was in bed, and the stupid thing was endlessly running around and around, the squeaking driving him mad. He was angry then, and wanted to make Ginger stop somehow. He was willing to do anything to make him stop then—but not so much now. It was different when he wasn't keeping him awake and annoying him. He was just a harmless little animal that liked to be stroked. *You might think that now, but just wait until later! You will hate him again! It's not fair to keep hating him and then liking him again. It would be best to get rid of him.* Josh reached for the needle—Benny had gotten his way, and the frown had melted away from Josh's brow. His face now had a determined, cold look on it.

Needle in one hand and Ginger in the other, Josh moved towards his bedroom door, which was slightly ajar. He craned his neck to one side, listening for clues as to where his mum was. His dad was working, so he only needed to know that his mum would not disturb him. God knows how much trouble he would find himself in if he were to be caught. What would she think of him? *Stop thinking about getting caught, just make sure she's busy,* Benny told him. Josh stopped his train of thought from wandering, and listened with renewed purpose. It sounded like she was talking; she must be on the phone (probably to Alice's mum). She also sounded far away—maybe in the back garden…? Josh moved to the window and peered out. Sure enough, his mum was sat at the patio table talking into her phone. Good—she was busy. Josh positioned the needle between his thumb and forefinger. It was quite big—the biggest one in the kit he had searched. Compared to Ginger, it looked like a lance. He manoeuvred the hamster in his hand, making his grip a little tighter in order to keep him in position. Ginger felt this rougher handling, and started to wriggle. *He's quite strong for something so tiny,* Josh thought. Benny heard this too. Josh put down the needle and used his other hand to get Ginger into the position that he wanted him in—upside down, with his legs pointing upwards. The hamster struggled even more, but Josh's hands were far too strong for Ginger's resistance. His claws scratched Josh's hand, and he had a sharp intake of breath through his teeth—it hurt! With renewed vigour, Josh clamped his left hand tightly around his pet now he had him on his back. *Hurry up! Before your mum calls you!* Benny urged. Josh picked the needle back up. Ginger was now making squealing noises in protest. He had to be quick; if he got any louder, his mum might hear. He quickly positioned the needle between the hamster's front legs. *DO IT!* Benny shouted inside his mind. Josh pushed the needle into Ginger's fur and skin, and was met with resistance. He pushed a little harder. Ginger's mewling suddenly escalated in volume to a very loud, high-pitched screeching: *Oh no, stop, be quiet, Mum will hear...*he pushed harder, and the shaft of the needle started to grow smaller. Ginger appeared to become momentarily stiff in his hand as the sharp point penetrated its tiny body. The survival instinct kicked in, and it began to squirm and screech with a desperate fervour. *PUSH IT IN ALL THE WAY! HE'S MAKING TOO MUCH NOISE!* Josh's mind was reeling. Benny was in there screaming at him, he was very nervous his mum would burst in at any given moment, and he was trying to stab his pet hamster with a darning needle while it fought for its life in his hand. He pushed the needle, with more force this time. The needle disappeared almost completely, and Josh could feel Ginger's fur on his thumb and forefinger. The struggling stopped, and a small bloom of crimson appeared around the base of the needle. The noise stopped, too. Relief flooded through Josh, only to be quickly replaced by the adrenaline that had been flowing previously. Ginger wasn't moving. He pulled the needle out, surprised at the effort it took to do so. It was as difficult to remove as it had been to put in. It slid out, no longer shiny and metallic, but now stained a deep red. The bloom remained on Ginger's lightly coloured fur. It was a small mark, but very noticeable due to the contrast in colour. On Benny's advice to try and hide it a bit better, Josh licked his fingertip and rubbed the affected area. There was no resistance from Ginger—he was gone. The mark smudged a little, which appeared to make it larger if anything. Josh repeated the action, not worried about the blood on his fingertip as he licked it again. After a second rubbing, the mark was definitely faded. Josh was nervous, worried about being found out. He quickly placed Ginger back into his cage, putting him behind the wheel at the back. He moved some straw bedding and wood shavings from the bottom of the cage around and over the motionless little pile of fur until it was nearly covered, but not quite. He assessed the cage—that would do. He quickly closed the door and breathed a sigh of relief. It was done now, no more deliberation or questioning. Benny had receded from the forefront of his mind for the time being, and Josh was glad. At that moment, he heard his mum calling him from downstairs. He picked up the blood-stained needle and placed it in the bottom of the drawer in his bedside cabinet. He would have to sort it out later.

"Coming, Mum," he shouted, closing the bedroom door behind him.

# Chapter Four

It had been a normal Wednesday so far for Josh. The routine of up out of bed, breakfast, ready for school, and dropped off had happened with no dramas (these were usually about appearance, namely hair). The morning had gone quite quickly. Class had been a little heavy on maths for Josh's liking, but this was compensated by a science class in which his teacher, Mr Buckingham, had shown the wonders of what Sodium did with water. Josh's inquisitive mind lent itself to all of the science disciplines, and he found himself wrapped up in the various class activities during these lessons. This earned him praise and encouragement from his tutors, as they could see the interest and natural ability to learn in these fields.

Before he knew it, it was lunch time and he was sat out on the grass verge to the side of the playground with a couple of classmates, eating his packed lunch. Alice was skipping on the tarmac of the playground with a few of her school friends. They had a large skipping rope held at both ends by two girls, while two others skipped in the middle. The girls were singing some silly rhyme to accompany their playing. Often Alice and Josh spent at least some of their lunch time together, but such was the nature of boys and girls at that tender age, they were content to be apart and with their own peer groups, which were inevitably of the same sex. What also often drove them to spend time with their other friends was the fact that when they were together around other children, either his or her friends, then some form of teasing occurred. They both found this irritating, but rather than cause a scene it was easier just to be with other friends. They spent plenty of time outside of school together, so neither child minded particularly.

As Josh ate and exchanged light-hearted banter with his mates, he occasionally glanced over at the group of skipping girls. They were blissfully unaware of everything around them, except maybe Alice, who caught Josh's glances from time to time, giving him a sly smile back. Alice and her friends didn't notice the group of lads standing at the corner of the main building, casually observing the girls as they played. One of them was Alex Winter. Alex was the ring-leader of his little group of chums, most of which had an unpleasant streak running through them, just like Alex. But Alex's mean streak was a little fatter than the others', which meant he was the one who had the 'naughty' ideas for the main part. He eyed the girls with a mean-spirited, squinting look. He especially didn't like the pretty, blonde-haired one, Alice.

He had already had a couple of nasty encounters with her in school. Last week, he decided to squirt his orange drink in her hair—the little bitch had to wash it out in the toilets, and spend all afternoon with damp hair, which in turn had made her blouse damp too. She didn't cry though. Alex had hoped she would, but she had appeared tougher than he first thought. He hadn't managed to make her cry yet, and it wasn't for the lack of trying, he had played a few little pranks on her over the last few months. The truth of the matter, of course, was that Alex actually *liked* her, as in so many boy-girl playground spats. Alex didn't want to admit that, oh no. He didn't want to think that he thought she was pretty, and that he would like her to be his girlfriend, and kiss her on the lips around the back of the canteen building, oh no—that wouldn't do to think like that *at all*.

Alex was not really a very good looking kid, with a pug nose, big flappy ears and a head of hair that looked like dirty steel wool. It didn't help that his uniform was tatty at best; grey trousers frayed at the bottoms, with the knees either very worn or completely ripped, and school shirts and jumpers in a similar state. His mum didn't really have much money (there was even less when his dad had been around), and what money she did have seemed to get sucked away by her scruffy, selfish boyfriend. He was one in a long line since dad had disappeared a few years earlier. Alex largely went overlooked in his miserable home life, and this meant his clothes were often dirty and unwashed, just like him. With no one that actually cared whether he had a bath or shower, he often went many days without a proper wash.

A girl as pretty as Alice would laugh in Alex's face if he so much as suggested being her boyfriend to her. Besides, that jerk Josh was her boyfriend, everybody knew that. Even if he wasn't, he was going to be, for sure. This angered Alex even more—that little weird kid had been seen talking to himself a few times in the playground and at the back of class, when he thought no one was looking. What was the deal with that? Did he have a pretend friend inside his head, like a little four-year-old freak? Admittedly, he had only been seen by Alex doing it a few times, and hadn't done it for ages now…but that wasn't the point. He was still a little weirdo in Alex's view. But he wasn't as interested in making Josh's life a misery as he was Alice. He was busy trying to think of what nasty trick to pull on her next, without getting into trouble of course.

As the group of three eyed the girls, the bell rang, signifying the end of lunch. The girls stopped skipping and started gathering the rope up between them, one of them taking it once done. They started to make their way towards the school main building doors, walking past Alex and his cohorts. None of the girls took any notice, especially Alice—she didn't want anything to do with Alex and his horrible friends. That would just be asking for more of the same trouble that had already happened to her from him. Alice didn't really understand why Alex was so nasty. She had never done anything to upset or annoy him, so why was he so horrible to her? She decided it was just that he was an asshole (as her dad would say). Best to steer clear of him and his unpleasant group of friends whenever possible.

Josh was also making his way back inside with his friends. He was chattering away to them still, but now had a watchful eye on Alice and her group as they passed Alex. He watched Alice as she gave him a wide berth, and then continued on her way. It was then that he saw Alex make his move. He quickly broke away from his mates and moved swiftly towards Alice, who was blissfully unaware. When he was close enough, he stuck his foot out and managed to hook it around her shins from behind. Alice immediately stumbled forward, desperately trying to keep her balance, but it was in vain. She crashed to the ground onto the hard tarmac, her friends scattering away, not knowing what was happening. Alex had shrunk back into the throng of kids behind her by now, seeking anonymity, as Alice's friends gathered around her and started to help her up. Alice was desperately trying to keep her composure during all of this—even though she hadn't seen directly who had tripped her, she instinctively knew. She would not cry. She would not show that horrible kid any weakness.

As her friends clucked around her asking whether she was okay, did she want to go to Miss, it needs a plaster and to be washed, she looked over her shoulder and saw him. Alex quickly looked down, and shuffled with the rest of his friends past her and into the school. Alice looked at her knee—it was bleeding and was very sore, but she would live. And she would not cry.

Josh watched all of this, his anger slowly rising. His friends had also seen the incident, and were chattering in his ear about it—*did you see that Josh, Alex Winter did it, I saw him, he hates Alice, he keeps picking on her, he's nasty*, but

Josh had zoned out from this. Benny was piping up too. His message appeared much clearer inside Josh's mind. *We need to stop him from doing this. For good. Once and for all.*

# Chapter Five

The afternoon crawled by for Josh. During classes he simply sat there, stewing in his own mounting fury and hatred for the kid that was making Alice's school life a misery. He was completely detached from what was going on around him in the classroom, including the odd glance that was shot his way from Alex across the heads of the other pupils in the classroom. Alex was more than aware of Josh's liking for Alice, and wondered idly whether the little bastard kid would try and do something in revenge for what had happened during lunch. He wasn't overly concerned about this concept—not only was he considerably bigger than Josh, he had his little clan of thug buddies that pretty much did whatever he said, and if need be he could rally them around for protection if Josh tried anything.

Josh had spoken to Alice briefly after the incident, asking if she was okay. She had seemed a bit shaken, but otherwise fine. Josh had reminded her not to worry about that kid—he would get what was coming to him. Alice had scurried off to get her knee cleaned up (she hadn't gotten any teachers involved, as although her knee and ankle were hurting, it seemed to be just a scrape and a bit of blood). Benny was being very vocal to Josh about the whole thing, and Josh was busy engaging with him as to what should, or could, be done. *We need to teach him a lesson. He will stop bullying Alice if we do, and that's what you want isn't it?* Josh considered this. It would be easy to try and fight him, but he had all his bully mates around him most of the time. He would be outnumbered and come off worse, no doubt.

*How can I teach him a lesson? He's always got his friends around him, and they will beat me senseless if I try and do anything to him,* Josh told him. *I need him to be on his own, so I've at least got a chance of giving him a thrashing…and even then, he's not tiny, so I may lose the fight anyway. I couldn't bear it if he beat me up. What would Alice think of me? That I was stupid and weak. I would hate myself.* All the time Josh was talking to Benny, the classroom ticked on blissfully unaware of his telepathic conversations with his distant twin. He had become very adept at holding in depth discussions with Benny during every day ordinary scenarios, and hiding this from others.

It was a form of multi-tasking—being able to talk to others, his parents, friends and suchlike, while doing normal things and also maintaining a full dialogue in his head with Benny. He was doing it now, busy writing a paragraph about the different continents of the world with his geography book open for reference, on auto-pilot, while discussing how to deal with Alex Winter with Benny simultaneously. In many ways, his psychic link with his remote friend was strengthening certain aspects of his mind and thought processes; and this was in turn strengthening Benny's growing mind too.

*We need a weapon. A knife or something, so we can really do some damage to him, hurt him real bad.* As Josh mulled this over, he was also trying to think of the right opportunity to strike. School was not the right place—too many other kids, too many teachers. But he never saw Alex outside of school. It would require a plan of some kind. *I haven't got a knife. And besides, it may go wrong and I might end up killing him. That would be bad for us both…we don't want that. Maybe something else…a stick or a bat of some sort?* As Josh thought this over, another idea came to him. Maybe he could follow Alex home part of the way and ambush him then?

He normally had to wait between five and ten minutes after school anyway (with Alice more often than not, the mothers shared the school run when possible), and instead of being stood outside of the front gates, he could tell Alice something, and slip off to follow Alex…he grew a little excited at this thought, and the two emotions of anger and excitement mingled in his mind. Benny experienced this too, and then had an epiphany of his own. *Forget a stick or bat, it will be too big, and people will notice it. It has to be tiny. What about your compass?* Josh's eyes widened at the thought. It was in his bag right now, with the rest of his maths stuff. No messing around looking for a weapon—it was right there. He quickly bent down and rummaged in his school bag, locating his maths set. He opened it and gazed at the silver implement, now considering it in a whole different light. It was perfect. He could carry it in his pocket unnoticed, and the sharp spike could no doubt cause considerable damage if used aggressively. The plan had started to formulate.

After what appeared to be an eternity, the final bell rang. The classroom erupted into the hustle and bustle of schoolchildren packing their stuff away and talking animatedly to their classmates now the school day was done. Alice was in another class away from Josh for about half of her school day on most days—they always met outside the school gates to wait for their chauffeur for the day to take them both home. Josh already had his compass in his trouser pocket, and as he made his way out to the front of the school, he switched it into his coat pocket. Up ahead of him, that asshole Alex was walking with a couple of his mates out of the main building. A worrying thought crossed Josh's mind—*what if his friends walk all the way home with him? I'll be outnumbered, and get a kicking for my troubles.* Benny placated him. *Don't worry about that now—just don't get seen following him. If his mates are with him, then we will have to think of something else.*

He met Alice at the front of the school, as per usual. She looked dejected, but tried desperately to make an effort to be cheerful. Josh asked her how she was, all the time aware that Alex was horsing around with his friends a little way down the road. Good—he didn't want him to hurry. He needed to keep a certain distance away to keep cover, but not too far behind.

"I'm okay thanks. My knee is a bit sore, and I think I've twisted my ankle a bit. But I can walk alright, and I haven't got a hole in my skirt, so Mum won't be mad." Alice touched the plaster that had been put on by her English teacher that afternoon (she told her teacher she had fallen), and winced when her fingers brushed against the scrapes she had suffered either side.

"I'm glad you're okay Alice. Look, can you wait here by yourself for five minutes? I've just remembered Chris has got my geography book and I need it for homework, I'm just going to try and catch him up and get it back," he lied convincingly. All the while he had one eye on his potential victim, who had stopped messing about with his friends pulling each other's coats. One of his friends was waving goodbye and walking off in the opposite direction back towards the school, but Alex and his remaining friend started walking off together. *Shit! I wish they had both walked away, then he would be alone!* Josh thought, anxiously. Again, Benny stepped in. *Don't worry about that now; just get following them to see what route they take. If we don't do anything today, then there will be other chances.* Josh re-composed himself, told Alice he wouldn't be long, and left his bag at her feet. He walked quite briskly in the same direction, trying to gain some ground on his foes and still maintain a safe distance from them.

"That bitch took quite a good fall at lunchtime, Alex. Stupid cow, she deserves it." Alex looked at his friend John approvingly. It was always nice to get praise for his actions. It proved that he was the boss, capable of leading his thug mates into meanness towards their school companions when they needed a thrill. He had used his friends a few times to escape trouble, and they had carried the can for him. They rarely moaned at doing this, as they all desperately wanted to keep on the right side of him. They had seen him turn nasty on former mates, and none of them fancied being on the receiving end of his cruel temper if crossed.

"Yeah, that fucking little whore got what she was asking for alright," he responded. "I hate her guts." The two friends walked along the pavement side by side for a minute or so, blissfully unaware of Josh tracking them from a short distance behind. He was shielding himself by means of another couple of school kids walking the same route, and besides, they didn't appear to be looking behind them anyway. When the two children in front of Josh crossed the road he decided to stay on the same side, despite there being less cover. *Just stay this distance away for the minute, use the bushes for cover now they're gone,* Benny advised. Josh's right hand had been curled around the compass in his pocket so tightly the metal was now the same temperature as his blood. Then, up ahead, Alex's thug mate appeared to be saying goodbye. He couldn't quite hear what they were saying, but when his hand rose up to wave goodbye, he knew they were about to go their separate ways. This was the moment he had been hoping for! His heart rate increased, leading to him feeling slightly hotter than normal. His cheeks had a slight flush to them now, partially from the brisk walking, and partly from the adrenaline now pumping around his body, creating butterflies in his stomach and tingles at his nerve endings. Sure enough, Alex's friend crossed the road and took a right turn down a neighbouring street, very quickly disappearing out of sight. *Stay calm; don't do anything hasty just yet. We have to pick the right moment, when no one else is around.* Josh quickly glanced in as many directions as he could, trying to see who, or what, was around. There were a few parked cars, and one moving car coming towards him. A few school kids were behind him, but quite a distance away. *Too many kids around,* he thought. And then, a divine intervention—Alex turned off the main street into a small alleyway. *Perfect! He's taking a shortcut! Let's hope the alley is empty, get a move on, hurry up!* Benny urged. Josh stepped up his pace, and very quickly turned into the narrow lane. He could see instantly that no one else was up ahead, so he glanced behind to make sure no one else had turned into the lane. They hadn't. Alex was busy kicking clumps of weeds and the odd stone up ahead, and had not looked over his shoulder the whole time he had been walking home. Josh stepped his pace up a gear. Benny was now very animated and vocal, almost barking instructions at Josh: *Now is the time! Get the compass ready! Keep it down by your side—check behind you! Speed up, hurry up… DO IT! DO IT NOW! IN HIS FUCKING SCRAWNY DIRTY NECK!* Josh's head was now pounding with anxious excitement. He had never done anything like this before—he was not a violent person by nature, but this was giving him the thrill of his life. He was actually high on adrenaline, but didn't understand this concept. All he knew was that he felt dizzy, excited, and almost superhuman. All the time, Benny added to this with his constant dialogue in his head, racking the tension and anticipation with every step he took. He was now only a few steps away from Alex. He raised his hand, compass handle poking out of his clenched fist. As he closed in on his quarry from behind, he brought his fist down quickly, the arc of his arm bringing the compass spike down directly to the back of his enemy's neck.

Alex suddenly felt a hard thump and a very sharp pain in the back of his neck. "OWW, WHAT THE FUCK IS THAT!" he shouted, in pain. His hand immediately shot up to the site of the pain, but Josh was quick. He grabbed his wrist from behind him and twisted it cruelly and sharply. Alex's legs buckled. *KICK HIM! KICK HIM TO THE FLOOR!* Benny shouted. Josh did exactly that, his foot connecting squarely in the side of his knee. Alex then buckled completely and collapsed on the floor, wailing in pain. His hand finally had found its way to the source of pain in his neck, and as he brought it back around into his field of vision, his eyes goggled at the sight of his own crimson, smeared blood covering his palm. He looked up in horror to see Josh stood above him, bringing his fist down again. This time he wasn't aiming at any feature in particular. The compass pierced Alex's cheek and the force of the downward motion dragged the sharp point down, creating a jagged wound. Blood sprang from it immediately, coursing down the boys' face. He had stopped howling now, having gone into shock in a matter of seconds since the first blow. This was good news for Josh, as so far there were no witnesses to all of this—the lane remained empty apart from the two of them. Benny was still urging him to do more, and Josh obeyed. He felt like he was almost outside of his body looking down on the scene, as if watching someone else. The adrenalin was still coursing through his veins and he struck again several times in succession in a tight, stabbing motion. He wasn't even looking at where the blows were landing, such was the fervour he was gripped in. He continued to rain the stabbing blows down on his adversary, his mouth twisted into a grimace, teeth clamped tightly together, his breath pushed out in short bursts due to the exertion.

It was all over in under a minute. *That's enough, should teach the little cunt good and proper. Let's get out of here before we get seen,* Benny urged. Josh obeyed. He discovered that his former rage and excitement had now taken a greasy twist into fear and worry. He felt sick, and needed to get out of there, and fast. He turned away from Alex, who was crumpled on the ground whimpering, still in shock, his face and head covered in what appeared to be a huge amount of blood, and ran. As he turned out of the lane back onto the street, he looked anxiously around. A few kids on the other side, no one close by. A car passed him as he walked quickly back towards the school. He had returned the compass to his pocket out of sight and inspected his hand for blood. Just a few specks and a smear on his palm were present, so he licked his hand and rubbed it on his trousers as he half-walked, half-ran back to Alice. He hoped his mum hadn't arrived yet—how long had he been? He had lost track of time in all the excitement and rage. As he rounded the bend in the road, he saw Alice stood where he had left her, with a few others dotted around waiting for lifts too. No car—thank God! *You're in the clear, now calm down Josh. We did it!* He tried to compose himself as best he could as he approached Alice. She was looking at him in a quizzical fashion.

"Did you see Chris? Where's your book?" she asked him, looking at him curiously. He was very red in the face, and almost panting. His eyes looked a little bit wild, rolling around in their sockets as if looking for something that wasn't there.

"No, I didn't," he said, still breathless from his ordeal. He tried to compose himself. "What I mean is, I did see him, but he didn't have my book. I made a mistake, it was in my bag all along," he lied again, stammering in his speech slightly. His heart rate started to return to normal, and the redness in his cheeks slowly started to fade. "Mum not here yet, then?"

"Here she comes now," Alice pointed towards the car. She picked up his bag and handed it to him. "Don't say anything about lunch time, Josh?" she half-told, half-asked him. She looked at him pleadingly with her achingly pretty blue eyes.

"I won't tell if you don't," he replied. He had lost most of the high colour in his face now, and his breathing was now more regular than before. As Jen brought the car to a halt, they walked towards the car.

"Had a good day, kids?" Jen asked cheerfully through the window. They both replied in unison that yes, it had indeed been a good day.

# Chapter Six

"Josh, take this food upstairs for Ginger—you must be running out. Fill his dish up and check he's got a drink in there—we wouldn't want him to go hungry or thirsty, would we?" Jen had popped out for a few bits of shopping, and had returned with Ginger's normal supplies. Liam was in the garage re-stringing his guitar; she had poked her head in and told him to keep an eye on Josh while she was gone. By the time she had returned, Liam was still in the garage, tuning up the newly strung Les Paul. As she packed the groceries into cupboards, drawers and bread bins, she wondered where her son was. She absent-mindedly called him again while bustling about the kitchen, but a few minutes later there was still no response. *Maybe he's engrossed in his game with his headphones on,* she thought. After the last of the goods were put away, she grabbed the pet supplies and headed upstairs.

As she entered his bedroom, she saw he was sullenly laid on his bed. He had been a little off in the car on the way home from school, unusually quiet and a little sombre for the normally chirpy Josh. Alice had seemed fine, so she had dropped her off next door, scuttled Josh inside, and headed out. She walked over to his single bed and sat down next to him. He looked at her with a slight frown on his forehead. She asked him if he was okay, and he mumbled that he was fine.

"Look, supplies for Ginge. He must be out, do you wanna feed him?" she enquired, trying to lighten his obviously morose state. Who knew what went on inside the head of a seven-year old? It could be anything making him miserable. Usually it was his hair, and Jen had a hard time sympathising—if all you have to worry about is your hair, then that's not a bad place to be, seven or not. Maybe something had happened at school. She squeezed his leg affectionately, imparting all her love for him in one simple gesture, as only a mother can. She glanced at the cage.

"Come on, let's give him his dinner. Kind of smells like he needs his bedding changed too, don't you think?" She encouraged him off the bed, and he took the food. She was stood in front of the cage, stooped over to look in through the bars. *All quiet in there...but I guess they are nocturnal,* she thought. Josh was stood to her side.

"He's been really quiet over the past few days Mum. I haven't heard a peep." She gently opened the cage and put her hand in, fingers moving and rustling the straw bedding. Still no sign...maybe he was asleep at the back? As she moved more bedding, she noticed a clump of bedding at the back corner. This was not unusual—Ginger liked to curl up and bury himself at the back. She pulled lightly at the straw, revealing the trademark ochre-coloured fur. She didn't want to wake him, but as her finger brushed the small animal's body she noticed there was no heat coming from it. She frowned and said, "When was the last time you said you saw him, Josh?" He looked at her with a strange expression on his face— almost pained, Jen thought.

"I don't know mum—a few days ago I think," he said dejectedly. God, he really was miserable today, she thought. Something must have happened. Jen resolved to quiz him later and find out what was troubling him. She turned her attention back to his pet. Jen touched the little furry body again, this time with a couple of fingers, prodding gently. Ginger was stone cold and stiff under her touch. Her heart sank. She would now have to break the news of a death in the family to an already morose young lad.

"Josh. It looks like Ginger is no longer with us." She drew him close to her and hugged him. His reaction was not as she had expected. She thought tears would be a given, but there were none. Josh remained still, his body a little stiff as she cuddled him and showered his head with kisses. They both sat back down on the bed and Jen brushed a lock of his thick, brown hair away from his eyes. She explained that hamsters hibernate, and often when they go into hibernation, they don't come out of it. She told him that they could look to get another one, if he wanted. It wouldn't be Ginge, but it would be just as cute and loveable. She also suggested that he may like a hamster instead, and that they could look in the pet shop to see what different animals they had. Josh remained silent through his mother's monologue, staring vacantly at his lap. She tried to cheer him up by changing the subject—she was cooking his favourite for tea, macaroni cheese. Jen suggested he help her. *Hopefully it will take his mind off Ginger...and whatever else seems to be bothering him,* she thought.

Jen gave Josh some more cuddles, and then persuaded him to go with her into the kitchen to help with tea. He still remained largely unresponsive, but maybe some practical activity would distract him from Ginger. *Although it's not really that that's on his mind...need to get to the bottom of what's wrong later,* she thought to herself, while setting Josh up to do some prep. Liam was still messing around in the garage, judging by the faint twangs that reached her in the kitchen from the garage. Instead of going out there and disturbing him, she fired him a quick text instead: *Ginger has died...Josh is upset, could do with talking to him later xx.*

Josh remained in a largely depressive state throughout tea into early evening. Liam had tried to cheer him up a little, suggesting, as Jen had, that they could look on Saturday for a new addition to the family: *But no dogs or cats, big guy, not at the moment. Maybe next year, if you do well at school,* came the promise from his dad. This did spark a little hope in Josh's eyes as he looked at his dad, a little smile threatening to creep onto his sullen little face. Jen had sat him in-between them on the sofa, and was busy quizzing him gently about what was bothering him. She did most of the talking, with Liam chipping in occasionally from the sidelines. He was quite happy for Jen to hold the reins—she was great at all this stuff, far better than his clumsy, blundering approach. She was sympathetic, inquisitive, compassionate, and understanding all rolled into one— by far the best choice for these types of talks. But, despite all of her best intentions and soft approach, Josh was a closed book. He just continued saying very little and mostly staring down at his lap, head drooped in a black cloud of depression. Occasionally Jen would look at Liam with a kind of desperate expression of frustration on her pretty face, as if to say: *I can't get him to open up, I need a way in...* All Liam could do was stay in the background, murmuring agreement or approval to what Jen was saying to their son as and when he felt it appropriate—in truth, he felt like a spare part.

All the while, as his mum was talking to him, Benny was reminding Josh not to say anything about the incident on the way home from school. This, in part, was why Josh was sealed up like a clam. He didn't really need Benny to tell him to keep quiet about it, that was obvious to Josh without any advice. Once he was at home and the violent episode was over, along with all the adrenaline seeped out of him and Benny's feverish encouragement gone, he had started to feel bad. Not just *I took another ice-cream cone from the freezer without Mum knowing, even though I've already had one* bad, but *really* bad. And worried, too. His stomach was all tied up in nervous, crampy knots and his mind was cluttered with remorse. Sure, Alex was an asshole, but did he really deserve that? Josh re-ran over and over the compass coming down, the feel of the resistance as it dug its sharp spike into Alex's cheek, the effort he had to make in order to drag his hand downwards, creating the red, open gash down the side of his face and it immediately filling and spilling over with dark crimson blood. The stark look of shock and horror on Alex's face as he tried to comprehend what was happening…and who was doing it. Alex had not made much noise during the episode, but Benny sure had. He had been screaming in his head the whole time from start to finish, in a complete frenzy. But it hadn't been Benny that had actually carried out the act. It had been Josh, and now he felt bad. Josh didn't think that Benny felt bad about it—he just seemed concerned with keeping it a secret from Mum and Dad.

As Josh sat wallowing in what felt like a mixture of grief, regret and worry, the doorbell rang. His mum looked at Liam and he nodded and got up. They weren't expecting company, but it could be Adam fishing for an evening beer, as they often did on a Thursday night. Jen continued fussing and quietly questioning Josh about why he was so troubled, as Liam answered the door.

A minute later, after some muffled conversation through the living room door, Liam came back in. He looked at Jen, and then at Josh.

"It's the police. They want to come in."

# Chapter Seven

They were sat round the kitchen table, which was easily big enough for the three Connellys and the two police officers. Both officers were in their thirties by the looks of it, one male and one female. *They probably sent the policewoman because of the sensitive nature of the call,* Liam thought distractedly. The police had briefly explained the reason for their unannounced visit on the doorstep. There had been a violent incident on the way home from school, for a lad in Josh's class. Very violent—he was in the nearest major hospital. This was Dartmouth, about fifteen miles away. *It must be serious if they've taken him there, otherwise he would be looked at locally,* Liam thought. They had not given him too much detail on the door, just that they believed a compass, or similar sharp object, had been used to inflict facial wounding, and the boy had said that Josh had done it on the way home from school. That was more than enough detail for Liam. What was Jen going to make of all this? He looked worriedly across the table at her. She looked shocked and dumbfounded. Josh was the same as he had been all night—silent and upset.

The police were very professional, and dealt with the details of the incident with tact and diplomacy, the female taking the lead when talking to Josh. As the details emerged, the look on Jen's face went from concern, to worry, to horror at what Josh had done. Josh didn't deny any of it—he knew the game was up. Benny was being very quiet. *Too* quiet. When asked why he had done it by the policewoman (while she did the talking, the other officer took all the notes), Josh quietly answered:

"He is a horrid bully. He makes my friend Alice cry, and upsets her all the time. I just wanted to teach him a lesson!" As he approached the end of his sentence, which was the most he had said all evening, his voice rose and cracked. Then came the tears, rolling down his flushed cheeks in fat, hot drops. Jen was torn as she put her arm around his shoulders, on one hand she was furious Josh had actually done something so horrible and damaging to another human being, but on the other flooded with sympathy for her little boy. The four adults at the table shot each other glances—they had all known it was going to get emotional before the job was done. The police still had their work cut out. They had to decide the outcome of all of this. Alex's mother had been hysterical when she put the call in, and things did not get any better when the police arrived at the hospital. The ambulance had already picked Alex up and drove him and his distraught mother there, and the interviewing had happened at Alex's bedside on the paediatric ward, with the flimsy curtains drawn. This stopped other children and adults alike gawping at the scene, but did not stop their ears from waggling. Alex would need stitches on his cheek and neck. The doctor advised both wounds would scar heavily, and this was not well received by Alex's mother, Abbie. She shouted and cursed loudly in the ward, and was told by both the doctor and the police to calm down, as she was agitating the other child patients on the ward.

"That little bastard needs to pay for what he's done to my boy! Unprovoked attack, he's a fucking psycho! I demand to know exactly what you intend to do about it!" she said, her outbursts aimed at the officers. Her mousy coloured hair was shoulder length, and resembled a bird's nest. She wore denim cut off shorts (a little *too* short), and her blouse was sufficiently undone in order to display what cleavage she had. She looked underfed, and a little grubby—relatively little effort had been made on all fronts. The officers looked at each other before the policewoman explained they would be going to pay them a visit immediately after they were finished at the hospital getting Alex's statement. This appeared to settle Abbie down a little, which was a relief to hospital staff, patients and police alike. After another half an hour or so of more questioning, scribbling, iPad tapping and general police documentation, the officers assured Abbie they would ensure that the child's parents would be made fully aware of the severity of the situation. Abbie bombarded them with a string of questions, all punctuated with expletives, about what was going to happen to the child and his parents. The policeman, P. C. Read, did his best to pacify her yet again, and assure her the correct procedure would be followed, and yes, this was a serious matter. She was still ranting as they left the ward.

Josh sat sobbing at the table, while the officers outlined the potential outcomes to his parents. It appeared that the school would have to have a say in the matter, and the police would be visiting on Monday morning, first thing.

"I would imagine that they will enforce an expulsion immediately, but the term will largely depend on the headmaster's judgement," P. C. Read explained.

"As Josh is a minor, we rarely would oppose what the head decides. Can we talk to you and Mr Connelly alone for a few minutes before we wrap this up please?" Jen looked at Liam, her face drawn with worry and shock.

"Yeah, sure. Josh, why don't you go up to your room for the time being. We can talk about this once the police are gone, it's not over son." His dad employed a firm tone of voice with him. Josh got up from his chair, hitching breath after breath, tears still running. Once they heard his footfalls on the stairs, they resumed their conversation. The police explained that they often deal with misdemeanours for minors, but this seemed an unusually brutal attack—has Josh been acting out of character lately? Is he normally quick to get upset or angry, does he lose his temper and do things of a destructive or violent nature? Does he enjoy school, has he got lots of friends, is he bullied, does he bully others…? The questions seemed never-ending to Jen and Liam, and what started as answers that were explained in more detail quickly descended into tired, monosyllabic yes or no responses. They were both tired, upset, angry, and confused. Josh was a very friendly, well-balanced young boy, and they had never had the experience of dealing with this sort of issue.

Eventually, it looked like the police were winding up their investigations. Again, they advised the bewildered parents that the school would have a big hand in things and to expect a fairly lengthy expulsion, probably four to six weeks. This news got Liam's mind whirring—this would affect the day to day dynamic of their family life, for sure. Jen would have to take time off, and he would have to consider how to help also—this was likely to eat into their annual leave in a big way. Once the final case notes were made, the officers thanked them for their time and offered some words of sympathy and understanding: we often see this sort of thing, it doesn't matter about the family background, it happens across the board, etc. etc., but it was again mentioned about the savage nature of the attack. This was obviously not common fare for the police. Once they had left the Connelly house, Jen and Liam both resumed their places at the table, Liam pouring two large glasses of scotch. They both agreed to leave Josh for tonight— he had been through enough grilling, and he also needed time to calm down so that a proper talking to would sink in.

"I just can't believe he would do such a thing," Jen said morosely, looking into her glass. "It's just awful." Liam took her hand across the table, and thought *God, she looks tired, and an emotional wreck. Bet I'm no better.*

"Let's see what the school says on Monday. I'm going to take the day off, you should too, hon. We will have a lot to deal with, and we always work better as a team. We'll get over this, I promise." She looked at him, tears squeezing from the corners of her already red and puffy eyes. He got up and went to her, embracing her tightly.

"Don't worry Jen. We will get through this. Sure, Josh will be punished for this, and just thank fuck he didn't do any more damage than he did—it could have been so much worse. I'm thinking we need to consider getting him some help. Some professional help, to make sure he's going to be okay."

Jen cried quietly into his shirt.

# Chapter Eight

*Don't worry, nothing will happen. You'll just get some time off school. And we showed that bastard good, Josh. Real good. Alice will love you for this.* Josh was not quite so sure and was still very upset. The police had left, and his parents had gone to bed. He had been lying in bed for hours, talking to Benny. Well, it was Benny doing most of the talking, busy trying to persuade Josh that everything was OK…which was proving difficult. Josh was still confused and distraught by the high mix of emotions he was feeling. One minute he was remorseful and full of regret, the other he was sad and a little disgusted with himself. Running through all of these feelings, like a dark ribbon of sinister sickness, was the worry. His mum and dad were *very* upset, and had not reacted the way he thought they might. Instead of anger and fury quickly followed by punishment (which he guessed could be anything from grounding, no pocket money, no PlayStation or TV, no friends round, early bedtimes, the list went on), they were simply shell-shocked and upset. He discovered that he hated seeing his mum cry—this was the first time he had ever seen it. Of course, what made this infinitely worse was the fact that he was the cause of it.

*Everything is horrid now…all because of what I did to Alex. And now I can't undo it, and my mum is crying all the time. And I'm in trouble with the police. Why did you make me do it, Benny?* This was not what Benny wanted to hear, and they were as close to arguing as they ever had been. It had been a joint effort! They had *both* wanted to do it. In actual fact, Josh said that he had wanted to teach him a lesson in the first place—Benny had just suggested how they may want to do it. So, they were both to blame, Josh just as much as him. Eventually, they left each other's heads alone and Josh fell into a troubled, restless sleep, the tears still slowly rolling down his face from the corners of his closed eyes, keeping his cheeks hot and damp throughout the night. Josh's last thought before he fell asleep was that he really didn't want to wake up in the morning.

Liam had wasted no time in trying to do something to help the situation that Jen and he found themselves in with Josh. When Jen had dropped off to sleep (another troubled slumber in the Connelly household), he had spent some time texting John. After briefly explaining what had happened, John asked him to call in the morning so they could talk properly, friend to friend. This made Liam feel a little better—he could do with talking to a mate about this, rather than just Jen. He was dreading the inevitable show down that they were bound to have with their son in the morning, and how they were going to try and make him realise the severity of his actions. He would have to discuss the punishment options with Jen before they decided on anything. He was actually hoping she had ideas on how to approach it, and he would then just agree—most things between them were a joint decision, but he was happy for her to field this one. He felt too erratic emotionally to come up with anything meaningful. But for all he knew, Jen may feel the same way. They would have to deal with it as it came, he guessed. But first, he would talk to John. He set his alarm (early for a Saturday, seven thirty), and turned the lamp off.

Jen was in the shower. It was early, Liam was still asleep, and she had shed a few tears when she woke but had stopped now. She had to get her shit together; there was a lot to deal with today. She had cocked an ear to pick up any sounds from Josh's room down the hall, but it all appeared quiet in there for the minute. She would wake Liam once done in the bathroom, and if Josh was still asleep, then they could discuss how to approach him before he woke. When she got out of the shower, she heard Liam stirring and went from the en-suite to talk to him. He was sat upright, scrolling and tapping on his phone. She sat on his side of the bed next to him and kissed him good morning, her damp hair brushing his shoulder. Ordinarily, Liam may well have taken advantage of this situation by removing her towel and coercing her back into bed, but neither of them had that in mind today. Liam quickly relayed the string of texts he had exchanged with John.

"I'm going to call him as soon as I get out of the shower, he may well offer us some sound advice. maybe someone at FMA can help. Have you told Janet anything?" Jen said she had sent her a text last night, which was good—John would have only told her about their conversation anyway. By the time Liam was downstairs, Jen had coffee and toast waiting. There was no sign of Josh.

"He's still asleep, I checked on the way down. Looks like he's had a rough night of it, his face is all red and blotchy," Jen informed him. Liam took his coffee into the living room and called John. After five minutes of talking (mostly Liam), John told him about a colleague of his, Jason Ireland. John had known him for a little while, a child psychiatrist by trade.

"He's a really good guy, mate. Knows his shit inside out. He's not particularly cheap, and does NHS work as well as private, and the private comes at a premium. I can tip him off, if you like? Get you to see him sooner rather than later, what do you think? Sounds like you want to deal with this ASAP, Liam." Liam jumped at the chance, telling John to call him, give him a brief lowdown, and then send his number once he's done. John agreed, and they said their goodbyes. Normally they would make plans to hook up, but now was not the time. *Maybe next weekend*, Liam thought. He relayed the conversation to Jen, and she seemed relieved that they were actually doing something pro-active to help the situation, given that there was some unpleasant, upsetting talks to be had with Josh (who was actually awake upstairs, but had kept the noise down deliberately—he too was apprehensive).

Within fifteen minutes, Liam had a text from John. Jason's number was at the bottom (*Let me know how you get on good luck buddy*). Liam didn't waste any time, and called the number straight away after thanking John for his help (and mentioning about next weekend). After a few rings, Jason Ireland picked up. Once Liam had briefly explained who he was and how he got Jason's number, they got down to brass tacks.

"Children can be just as volatile as adults, sometimes even more so. In their world, things that would be minor to a grown up can seem huge and insurmountable from a child's perspective. And peer groups are far more important to the young than they are to the older generation. This is true across almost all spectrums—rich, poor, creed, colour, et cetera," Jason explained to Liam. He took all this on board. It would be nice to try and find out whether there was anything deep-rooted in all of this, or whether it was, as they hoped, just a one-off incident that had gotten out of hand. They talked for a little while longer about the incident, with Liam furnishing Jason with the details as and when necessary, and then discussed an appointment. Jason suggested they both attend with Josh, and the session would consist of partly all three of them together, and partly with Josh on his own. He said this was standard, so the parents didn't influence the child's behaviours and reactions, and he would be able to (hopefully) get a true picture of what was going on. They agreed on Monday morning. Liam didn't need to check with Jen—Josh would not be going to school, and they both had the week off work. Liam expressed his preference for the afternoon, as they would no doubt have to get in touch with the school in the morning, and they booked for two-thirty.

Liam went back into the kitchen once they had said their farewells, and told Jen the plan.

"He seemed like a really down to earth guy, and John was right, he knew what he was talking about. Maybe he can shed some light on this mess. Has he stirred yet?" He nodded upwards towards Josh's room. Jen said she heard some movement a few minutes ago, and they both sat at the kitchen table, brooding on the scene that was about to unfold once he came downstairs. Within five minutes Josh shuffled his way down, in his pyjamas and dressing gown. He hung his head low, and looked dejected to say the least.

"You'd best come and get a seat with me and your father, young man. I think we have some talking to do, don't you?" Jen's cheeks were flushed, and there wasn't an awful lot of sympathy in her voice.

Josh's face cracked, and tears sprung immediately from his eyes. He looked at his parents in distress.

"I'm so sorry, Mum and Dad. I didn't mean to do it. It was Benny," he wailed, and ran into his mother's arms.

# Chapter Nine

This revelation came as a shock to Jen and Liam. Josh had not mentioned Benny for months (or was it years?) now. It threw a spanner in works with regards to their approach to the situation, and Liam wasted no time—his patience had run out with his son. As parents, neither of them had had to deal with any major crises with regards to their son, he had been almost a model child from day one. They were firmly out of their comfort zone with this new twist in the tale.

"What the hell do you mean exactly, Josh? JUST WHAT EXACTLY ARE YOU SAYING?" Liam's tone rose from a loud exclamation to a shout. He was working on auto-pilot, and whatever came out of his mouth now was coming out, regardless of who thought what about it. "Benny? Your imaginary friend from years ago? What has *he* got to do with it? Did he just appear miraculously and stab that little boy while you stood there and watched? I cannot believe you are bringing bloody *Benny* into this. It's about time you did some growing up, and take responsibility for your own actions. You're nearly eight Josh, and it's time to let this invisible friend idea go. No one believes it, and I for one am NOT IMPRESSED!" Liam had got up and was pacing the kitchen furiously, adding to the tension in the room. Josh was still cowered in his mum's arms, not looking at his dad. He was sobbing uncontrollably, and Jen felt helpless and torn. She wanted to comfort him, but was also shocked and upset that Josh had pulled Benny as his ace get-out-of-jail free card. *Where the hell has this come from?* She thought. *He hasn't talked about this for ages…it must be just the first excuse that came to hand, he's scared.*

"Regardless, we still need to deal with this, Josh. What you did was very serious. You could have killed him! As it is, he will be left with scars on his face for the rest of his life! How would you feel if someone gave you those scars?" Jen had broken their embrace and moved Josh onto his own chair. He sat there looking at his lap, which had been the default position for the last day or so. "It doesn't look like you will be going to school this week, for sure. And it may even be longer than that. It will depend on Mr Matthew's rules for things like this. And don't think it will be fun and games at home while you are suspended. You will have to be punished for this, Josh." She looked at Liam to see if he appeared calmer than a few minutes ago. Liam sighed and took his seat again, across from the boy and his mum.

"We will have to call the school on Monday. That's if they don't call us first. In the meantime, you are grounded to your room until your mother and I can figure out how exactly we should punish you for this, Josh. To be honest, no punishment we can give you is worthy of what you've done. I can't believe you did something so horrid and violent to another human being. You certainly have *never* been taught by us that violence is acceptable. It's wrong, and you know it, so you need to do a lot of thinking about how to make things right. You will need to apologise to Alex when you next see him in school. And *mean it.*" Liam paused. "And you really need to forget about Benny and grow up. I can't believe you tried to use that as an excuse, Josh. You should be ashamed of yourself, you're not four anymore. Now, you'd best go back to your room for the minute, while we try and sort out what to do with you." He looked to Jen for affirmation that he was now dealing with their son in a calmer and more appropriate manner. She also had red eyes as well as Josh, and looked on the brink of more tears. It was becoming more of a familiar, upsetting sight since the police had visited last night. Josh got up from his chair and shuffled off towards the stairs, hitching back sobs as he went. Once he had gone up, Liam hugged his wife tightly, kissing her hot, furrowed forehead. *What the fuck do we do with him now?* He thought, aimlessly.

It was a strange morning for all concerned in the Connelly house. They had tentative plans to hook up with Beth, Adam and Alice that afternoon, and go and do something—that wouldn't be happening now. Jen had messaged Beth and cancelled without giving too much away, and said she would pop around to theirs for a chat later that day. *I have to tell her that the reason for Josh doing what he did was because of Alice,* she thought. She told Liam she'd cancelled their arrangements, and her plan was to go around to talk to Beth.

"Well, you may as well tell her what's happened in all its glory. They will find out on Monday, anyway. That lad's friends are bound to know, and the gossip will be rife in the playground I would imagine," Liam said dejectedly. "Let's just hope they don't decide that our son is a violent child psychopath and not talk to us again." Even though he uttered this last statement with an air of sarcasm, it planted a seed in both their minds about how this would affect not just Josh, but all three of them in the future. Other parents would hear of it—how would they react to Jen and Liam at parents' evenings and school functions? *Look, there's the parents of that nutcase kid… I blame poor parenting, lack of discipline…it wouldn't have happened in* our *family…* Liam could hear the whispered chatter and gossip now. And what about Josh? What had Jason said on the phone? *Peer groups are more important to the young…*he would come under fire for sure. His life would no doubt take at least an initial turn for the worst once he got back to school—kids could be cruel. *Very* cruel. The repercussions of Josh's actions could affect them all for quite some time to come, something that Josh no doubt did not consider in his moment of madness. He would have plenty of time to reflect on it, that was a given. After an hour or so of moping around downstairs, dinking more coffee and absent-mindedly doing chores, Jen decided she would lay down at least *some* punishments for Josh. She may as well let him know where he stood, and then he could start to come to terms with it. And so could they. She agreed a PlayStation ban and bed-time at seven for the foreseeable future with Liam. Normally he would go to bed at eight thirty on weekdays, and sometimes much later at weekends, so seven would be quite a blow. She went up to find Josh on his bed. The PlayStation wasn't even on—normally he would have been gaming for at least a few hours by now. She told him what they had decided, and he took it in the same fashion he had taken everything else. His limited reaction and sullen expression said it all about how he might be feeling. There had been time for things to sink in for him, and Jen guessed that the real punishment here would be his own conscience. He had always been a good, kind boy up to this point. *We will all get through this, and things will return to normal,* she told herself. Her mind kept returning to what her son had said about Benny. Josh had not spoken about Benny for some time, and both she and Liam had assumed that he had simply grown out of his 'imaginary friend' stage. Both parents were glad about this, as it signified that their son was growing up normally—growing out of more childish things and growing into behaviours more suited to his age, making Benny redundant in his own mind, in order to accommodate a more mature way of thinking. *He must have been just clutching at straws, looking for a scapegoat,* Jen told herself. But she couldn't shake the feeling that there was more to it than that. Why mention Benny after all this time? Something seemed a little odd about the whole thing, and the back of Jen's mind remained troubled.

After a light lunch (she took Josh's up to him), Jen told Liam she was off to see Beth next door. Liam was busy occupying himself in the back garden, happy to lose himself in a normal weekend task of repotting herbs and weeding borders in order to distract himself from recent events. Jen grabbed a bottle of wine from the rack on her way out—God knows she needed it. Beth answered the door before Jen had chance to ring. She could see Jen was upset straight away, so she hugged her on the doorstep before asking her to tell her what was wrong. Adam was out for the afternoon with Alice since the plans with the Connellys had been canned, so they were home alone. Jen started telling Beth about the recent events while she poured two large glasses of wine. Beth listened to her friend unravel the tale in her own way, without interrupting.

"He said the reason for the attack was because this kid Alex was bullying Alice in school, and Josh wanted to teach him a lesson. Well, he taught him a lesson alright! Nearly fucking stabbed the poor kid to death with a compass! Jesus, Beth! I am absolutely mortified at what he's done, I'm gutted." Jen looked exasperated as well as tired and upset, but so far she had managed to hold her tears back.

"My God Jen, how *awful*. This is so shocking—I never would have believed lovely Josh was capable of such a thing! You poor thing, you are obviously devastated. What's going to happen next, hon.? How's Liam taking all this? Adam would have gone ballistic, I know that much." Her facial expression at this comment indicated she would never want to deal with the scenario her friend was going through. Jen explained that Josh would be off school for the foreseeable future, and the school had yet to be in touch. Liam had taken it okay…although lost his temper when Benny was mentioned. This opened up a whole new direction of conversation between the two women. Jen had never mentioned Josh's 'friend' before. There was simply no need, and they hadn't gone around broadcasting it when Josh had been going through the imaginary friend stage. Jen explained to Beth that Josh hadn't mentioned Benny for some time, and both she and Liam thought it was an excuse for what he had done. Beth agreed that this was a likely explanation. They quickly moved on to talking about what to tell Alice. If Beth and Adam didn't tell her before Monday morning, she would find out in the playground, and they both agreed that this was not the best way for her to find out about Josh's recent exploits.

"Are you happy we talk to her tonight about it, Jen? They're due back at tea-time. We won't go into detail… I mean, about the compass and everything. We can just say that he had a nasty fight with the lad that's been bullying her. What do you think?"

"Yes, that sounds like the best plan. Thanks for being so understanding and not thinking that Josh is a monster, Beth. This is so out of character for him, it has hit us like a ton of bricks. And I wouldn't want it to affect their friendship; he thinks the world of Alice. If it wasn't so fucking horrible and callous, his actions are almost chivalrous. I don't know what drove him to it, he must have just lost the plot momentarily." Beth took her hand and squeezed.

"I'll text you later to let you know how it goes with Alice. The main thing is she will hear it from us before Monday morning. And if I can help at all, just shout," Beth reassured her friend. Jen thanked her and made her way back home.

# Chapter Ten

Monday morning had eventually crawled around and before Jen had gotten around to phoning the school, they had called her. She had been dreading the conversation, and had known it would be her that took it rather than Liam. It was just the natural order of things. Mr Matthews was straight to the point—he would be suspending Josh for two weeks following the attack on Alex. He explained quite matter-of-factly that this was the policy with such an incident, and made a point of also telling her he had not experienced such a violent attack from one of his pupils on another in his time as a headmaster, which was fifteen years. Jen apologised profusely for her son's actions several times during the course of the uncomfortable conversation, and as the head knew the family, he softened towards the end, telling Jen that he empathised with their position. Josh had always been a good boy in school, and yes, the staff at the school were all aware of his good upbringing. He closed the exchange by saying he would call on the Friday before Josh was due back to confirm his return, and that they had their sympathy—*this must be a very upsetting time for you all. Please ask Josh to think about his actions before he returns, and that he understands the severity of the situation.* Jen assured Mr Matthews that they had been enforcing that mind-set since the beginning, and that Josh was suitably remorseful of his actions. She didn't mention Benny, or the appointment they had this afternoon with Dr Ireland. She felt that this was their business, and keeping these gems of information close to her chest was for the best at the moment. Once the phone call was done, she went up to tell Josh the news. Liam had been eavesdropping, and had already grasped the bare bones of the conversation. Josh had not been eavesdropping however, and the news of a two week suspension came as a shock. He had been expecting a week, not two, and was suitably upset by the news. He had discovered very quickly that being off school when under punishment was a royal pain in the ass. And he still felt terrible about the whole thing. Benny was not helping much at all, and every time he raised his voice in Josh's head, Josh

145

just wanted to make him go away—but couldn't. He was there, like a persistent fly buzzing around his head that no amount of swatting could get rid of. Once Jen had spoken to him, she tackled Liam.

"We can't keep treating him like a leper banished to his room, it's just not healthy, Liam. I know he deserves and needs punishment, but this feels counter-productive. We have to try and get back to normal, for all our sakes. And my own fucking sanity." This last statement was no exaggeration. Her nerves were more than frayed, and her head had felt like a flock of blackbirds had been pecking at her brain since this had all started. Liam reluctantly agreed with the sentiment of Jen's thoughts.

"I don't want him prancing around without a care in the world like nothing has happened, because it *has.* As long as he is fully aware that this is a serious matter, then we can think about how we relax the rules. Let's see how this afternoon goes first. Did you tell him we have an appointment?" Jen told him she had said they were going to see a child doctor, to make sure everything was okay and that there wasn't anything else to worry about.

"One thing's for sure Liam—he's so goddamn miserable he definitely regrets it. Let's just hope we can all move on, and that nothing like this ever happens to us again. Ever."

"It won't. I promise you both it won't." Josh was stood by the living room door. Jen went to her son and hugged him fiercely as he collapsed into wracking sobs and tears yet again.

Dr Ireland's private practice consultancy business was run out of a small office space in a town called Horbury, about fifteen miles away from the Connelly's. They had calmed Josh down, reassured him they were going to see a friendly doctor to make sure everything was okay with him, and bundled him into the car. Twenty minutes later they were there just ahead of time, quietly sat in a tiny reception area. Josh didn't seem fazed at all—in actual fact he had been distinctly un-fazed by anything since Friday night. It was almost as if he were detached from the real world, living his own misery and regret while the rest of the big old world rolled on around him.

A tall, handsome man in his late thirties came in from the side door and introduced himself as Dr Ireland. He was dressed casually in a shirt and jeans: *He doesn't look like a doctor to me,* Jen thought. He was softly spoken as they made their introductions, and stooped to shake Josh's hand gently.

"Don't worry little fella, I don't bite—it's just a few easy questions for you to answer, do you think you can do that for me? There's a bag of gummies in it for you if you can!" he said to Josh. Even though the premise of what he said sounded patronising, the way he delivered it just came across as friendly and well meaning. This was duly noted by both Jen and Liam. They followed him into his office, which was minimalist. A small desk with precious little on it apart from a few papers, a small family photo, desk tidy, and phone. A bookcase against the side wall was full of medical tomes apart from the bottom shelf, which housed children's books, both fiction and non-fiction. They each took a seat; the receptionist had followed them in with an additional chair to make three, and then disappeared again. Jason had insisted they all call him by his Christian name, and started off by asking for a recounting of the incident with Josh. Josh said precious little during this, and it was Liam that did most of the talking while Jen took a back seat. Once the facts were out, Jason asked a few general questions about past history, and then asked the parents to wait for five minutes in reception while he spoke to Josh alone briefly.

"So, do you think Alex deserved it? He wasn't very nice to your friend, was he?" Jason mused. "It's never nice when someone is nasty to you, or someone you like, so I understand why you did it, Josh. But tell me, did you mean to hurt him more or less than you actually did?" Josh had come out of himself a little, and thought about this. No one had asked him anything like this, not even the police.

"Well… I wanted to teach him a lesson, for sure," Josh said thoughtfully. What Jason didn't know was that Benny was busy shouting inside Josh's skull. He had been fairly quiet over the last day as conversations between them had not been great, but he was alive and kicking now. *Don't tell him about me! He doesn't need to know about us at all! KEEP YOUR MOUTH SHUT!* Josh was annoyed and upset with Benny. It felt like he was doing what Benny asked for, and getting all the blame for everything while Benny got off scot-free. It didn't seem fair to Josh. "It was mostly Benny that wanted to do it so bad." Josh looked at Jason, knowing what was coming next. *YOU BASTARD! I TOLD YOU NOT TO SAY ANYTHING! IT'S NONE OF HIS BUSINESS!* Benny screamed from the confines of Josh's head.

"Who's Benny, Josh? Another friend from school?" Jason enquired.

"He's a friend…but not from school," Josh said slowly, deliberating over his words. "He's kind of in my head." Jason's eyebrows rose slightly at this statement.

Jason asked a few more questions, and then called the Connellys in. He got his receptionist, Sally, to take Josh out, and instructed her to 'dig the goodies out' for Josh, while he talked quickly to Mum and Dad. Once they were gone, he talked to them about Josh's friend. Liam got a little hot under the collar: *I've already told him that you have to take responsibility for your own actions, and he needs to stop this imaginary friend business and grow up.* Jason said that this was an area that definitely needed exploring, especially as Josh was associating his friend with the attack. He recommended a series of sessions to talk about Benny, both with and without parents present, in order to ascertain there was 'nothing untoward' going on with Josh psychologically, to which they both agreed.

The journey home was mostly silent. It felt like a cold blanket of doom and despair was settling over the family, with no one sure on how long it was going to be there for and how to get rid of it.

# Chapter Eleven

Both Jen and Liam had mixed feelings about their meeting with Jason, and this resulted in a largely unsettled atmosphere in the house. They had agreed to be a little more flexible with Josh, and he was now allowed in both front and back gardens during the day. Both were fairly spacious, and had things for him to keep himself occupied in them—a football with a goal, a swing ball and his bike (not that there was much scope for riding, the gardens were big, but not *that* big). Josh took advantage of this slackening of the punishment, but when Jen checked on him late that afternoon, he was sat sullenly under the willow at the bottom of the back garden. Her heart ached for her little boy in that instant, and she was nearly overcome with emotion yet again, yearning to rewind the clock back to before all this awful time. It had only been a few days, but it felt like a lifetime already. When would things get back to normal? She had this dreadful feeling that had crept into the back of her mind—*what if it* never *went back to normal? What if this* was *the new normal?* She quickly pushed the thought back to where it came from. She resolved to strive for a return to how things used to be at all costs. She would *not* let this ruin their lives, or family. Jen decided to talk to Liam about this approach too—she was concerned that he was losing patience very quickly with Josh, and was threatening to go into a spiral of rage and anger about the whole thing. The idea of Benny re-surfacing after all this time appeared to be the root of his discontent. Liam had made his feelings very clear on the subject to both Jen and Josh, and a few times they had nearly come to verbal blows about it. Jen was aware that most fathers are not as sympathetic or understanding as their female counterparts, their approach often blunt and more direct, their views and solutions to problems often black and white, with no blurred lines. *Liam would just have to see reason on this,* she thought.

In a bid to get back to some normality, plans had been made with John and Janet for Friday and Saturday. Both parents thought it would be a welcome distraction from recent events. No doubt they would end up talking about Josh at some point, but still, some adult company and some nice food and drink would be a welcome change. Liam had decided he was going stir crazy at home, and had made plans to go to work for the rest of the week. This wasn't an issue—Jen felt they were a bit scratchy with each other anyway, given the premise of their recent circumstances. Now they knew what they were dealing with when it came to Josh, the school, and punishment, it only required one of them at home, really.

Jen had made plans to see Beth over the phone. She asked Beth whether she would like to come over with Alice once she had picked her up from school, and Beth had readily agreed. Alice had a dentist's appointment that afternoon anyway, so they would be over at about three. This was ideal, as it would give the two girlfriends chance to catch up with neither Liam nor Adam around—and the kids could see each other too. This was deemed a good idea by both mums, especially Jen. Josh could see his friend and have some normal child interaction. He had only been under punishment for nearly a week in reality, but in a child's world that seemed like forever. Maybe it would help bring him out of his morose state a little. She told Josh about the get-together, and his reaction was pleasing. He smiled (the first time in at least a week), and said he would like to play with Alice. He asked his mum whether she would set up the badminton net in the back garden so they could play when she got there, to which Jen said she thought this was a good idea. Half an hour later, Jen had set the net up and they were batting around the plastic shuttlecock back and forth, when she heard the doorbell chime. After getting them in, Alice scuttled off into the back garden to see Josh.

"Hey Josh! You've not been in school, I've missed you! Yesterday George Brown threw a rubber in class, and it hit Miss Tierney in the boob by accident! He got detention." She finished her quick school news report with a serious expression. "He regretted that. I could tell 'cos he went bright red." Alice was the epitome of an eight-year-old girl, full of bounce and enthusiasm. She wore a pretty blouse and flowery leggings, and her blonde hair flounced around her shoulders as she animatedly told her story, while Josh listened attentively. The two mums looked on in a doting fashion.

"Alice has really missed him this week, Jen. She's been asking questions, but I've been playing it down… I didn't know how much to tell her to be honest. And I don't know whether any other kids in school know much. You would like to think not much, but you know what they're like," Beth said. "I've told her that Josh had a fight with the kid that's nasty to her in school, but that's about it."

They sat down at the patio table. "It's been an absolute fucking nightmare Beth, I swear. I'm not exaggerating; this has been one of the most depressing times of my life. I just wish it had never happened." Jen explained in detail what had happened from start to finish. She obviously needed to offload, and Beth was the best person in the world to help her with that. Jen had debated calling her mum, and then thought better of it. Family sometimes had opinions that weren't needed, or particularly helpful. Beth listened and made the occasional comment as Jen spilled her guts. The kids were busy batting the shuttlecock over the net at each other, spending more time recovering it from the lawn than keeping it in the air. Both were laughing, and it lit Jen's heart up to see joy on her boy's face. Once Jen had told her tale of woe, Beth started with the questions—*do you think he really meant to be so aggressive? What happened to Alex in hospital, did he need stitches, how long did he stay in for? What did the police say? Are there any follow ups from them?* Jen answered them as best she could, and discovered that not even she knew all the outcomes. After she imparted that Josh had brought his imaginary friend into the situation, Beth had wanted to know more. Jen told her all about Benny, about how Josh had first talked about him when he was about four years old; he continued this for about a year, maybe a year and a half after that. She talked about how they subtly tried to convince Josh to stop talking aloud about him, and slowly introduced the idea to him that Benny wasn't real. All perfectly normal. But then he had mentioned him again, and implicated him in his attack on Alex.

"I'm not going to lie, it's worrying. At first I thought that Josh was clutching at straws looking for a scapegoat, but now I'm not so sure, Beth. He hasn't mentioned him in years. And now he pops up out of the blue, for fuck's sake. We saw a child psychologist yesterday; he's a friend of a friend. He wants to see us for a series of appointments to see if there's anything in it or not." She paused and sighed. "I could do without another complication to all of this, if I'm being honest."

"The whole thing is awful, and so out of character for Josh—he's the sweetest lad. Alice thinks the world of him. All I hope is that this mess is over and done with sooner rather than later, and you can all move on and forget about the whole bloody thing. You know I'm here for you, hon. Anytime you need a shoulder to cry on, or just someone to offload onto, then call. Promise?" Jen thanked her and kissed her cheek.

As the women talked, the kids had moved on from the badminton and now were under the willow at the end of the garden, presumably looking for wildlife.

"When are you coming back to school? Jake Smith told me that you really hurt Alex with a compass. What did you do to him?" Alice asked Josh, her eyes wide. Josh was quiet for a moment, and then replied:

"He deserved it. I did it because he is always so mean to you, and I don't like that. Nor does Benny. He had that solemn look on his face again. *Benny doesn't seem to mind when I talk about him to Alice,* he thought."

"I know he's mean and all, but I wish you didn't hurt him so much, Josh. I think you hurt him *too* much," Alice said. "Maybe you should have just punched him, or something." Josh looked at her, frowning.

"I did it for you, Alice. You're not being very grateful, are you? I've got into a lot of trouble for you. The police have been here and everything." Josh continued to rummage around at the base of the tree and the garden fence, head bowed. He didn't want to look at her, and didn't want her to see that his face had grown hot and red with frustration at her reaction.

"Hey! That's not fair to say that. I didn't *ask* for you to hurt him. Anyway, I can look after myself, okay?" Alice replied indignantly. Josh was becoming annoyed with her, and Benny was fuelling this. *She doesn't even care that you got in all this trouble just for her! What a fucking bitch!* Josh was hard pushed not to agree with Benny's view.

"I think it's best we stop talking about asshole Alex now, Alice. I don't want to get angry again." He looked at her grimly. "I'm in enough trouble as it is." *And it's your fault,* he thought.

# Chapter Twelve

John and Janet had been discussing the ins and outs of the Connelly's latest saga in the car on the way over there. Between the pair of them they had most of the facts, but both were still keen to see their friends and their son, hoping that they were all okay and getting through what was obviously a tough time. They arrived early evening, but Josh had already gone to bed as per punishment schedule. Both Jen and Liam looked tired and a bit washed out to their friends when they greeted them at the door—hardly surprising. Liam had suggested to Jen they get take-out, but Jen was keen to keep herself busy, so had decided to cook. She enlisted Josh's help with the prep to keep him occupied in the afternoon. It had been a very long week for the boy, and as time ticked on Jen felt herself softening more and more to her son and his predicament. Liam was a little more hard-edged than her, but truth be known he also felt similar, for almost selfish reasons. He just wanted all this horrible shit to be over. What was done could not be undone, and they needed to move on. The real goal was to get Josh back to school and settled back into a normal routine—then he and Jen could return to theirs. He had gone back to work, but found his thoughts increasingly drifting off topic, thinking about his home life and his son. He also found himself thinking about the other lad a lot, too. How would he feel if the boot had been on the other foot, and it was Josh that was scarred for life? His anger simmered at this thought. Josh had not been brought up to be a violent thug, and he would make sure his son understood that, one way or the other.

The company was welcome for Jen and Liam, and worked as a distraction despite the subject matter being largely dominated by their son and the recent events. Janet went upstairs to see the lad with his mum, partly to make Jen feel better, and partly to reassure Josh that they didn't think he was a monster, despite what had happened. Josh was unresponsive at first, but came around to Janet in the end. Jen thanked her friend for being so kind and understanding on their way back down, and the foursome settled around the table eating and drinking. The conversation didn't stay Josh related all evening, and as different topics of conversation threaded their way in, the Connellys relaxed more than they had all week.

In true fashion, the evening wore onto the late hours and the boys were now well oiled and the girls were tired. As they made their way to bed, Liam and John remained around the table, radio on quietly in the background. The conversation came around to work, and Liam said he was trying to keep things as normal as possible by keeping full-time hours in the office while Jen held the fort. John said that things at FMA were busier than ever, with new client opportunities appearing by the week.

"This thing with Josh has highlighted how beneficial being with FMA really is to us," Liam commented. "Imagine if something happened to Josh, like what he did to that other kid, but more serious." Both men mused on this thought for a minute.

"Yeah, it's an insurance policy for sure…sitting in the background, waiting for the unexpected to happen, which, of course, we hope never happens." John replied.

"I'll drink to that, my friend." They raised their glasses.

The women were up early, and both wives had let their respective husbands continue their alcohol fuelled slumber. Josh was also still asleep, so they had the peace and quiet they wanted to catch up on 'girl talk' without interruptions. As they sat at the table with coffee and toast, their conversation meandered from this to that, but settled on John's work. Janet was worried that he was under too much pressure at FMA, and continually working long hours day after day, week after week, wasn't good for him. Jen had not thought about FMA for some time. It wasn't like the early days when she was pregnant for Josh—she and Liam were constantly discussing FMA, and there were appointments at the FMA centre all the time, so it was very much at the forefront of her mind. Nowadays, FMA just sent a monthly correspondence to them, but this was largely a reassurance that everything was on track with Josh's twin, and a sales plug for other products.

"It's not that he's not home until late and I don't see much of him in the week—I can cope with that. It's just that there's so much going on in there at the minute. John tells me more than he should about what goes on there, and although the business side of it is good, he is also dealing with complaints more and more," Janet said. Jen's interest spiked at this comment, and she asked what kind of complaints. "Well, for example, John told me last week that they had a new client, and everything was going fine up until the first scan on this woman. There's a problem with her baby and they're not sure what it is—they think it's a brain deficiency of some kind; it's not developing at a normal rate. So, they send her home while they try and sort out what's going on. A few days later there's an emergency in the twin lab. When the docs get down there, one of the twins has entered this kind of vegetative state in its vessel. None of them know what to do about trying to resuscitate it. After a few minutes John said that all the monitors went flat line, and that was that. It turns out that the twin belonged to the young lady that was in the other day—the one with the problem with her child. Everyone was panicking and no one knew what to do at this point, they were all worried about what to tell the girl and her husband. They are only a young couple, but well-to-do, inherited a shit load of money, I would imagine. Anyway, this awful thing happened next. The FMA got a call from a hospital saying they needed to talk to Dr Ellis urgently. He took the call, and they explained that they had a young woman in their care, and she had lost her baby. Some kind of trauma inside the womb, and then gone. Same woman." Janet paused and cocked her head to detect if there was any movement from upstairs. She didn't want to get caught telling her mate all this confidential stuff by John, he'd have a fit.

Jen had been sitting across from Janet, staring at her wide-eyed. She was both shocked and enthralled by her friends' story. *You would never imagine that this type of thing happens in real life, it's more like science fiction,* she thought. But although she found this secret revelation fascinating, it also sowed a seed of nagging doubt in her. They had a twin for Josh floating around in the lab at FMA, too. What if something happened to his twin? All of a sudden there appeared to be a million questions generated by a million thoughts on the subject.

"Oh my God, that's shocking! What does it mean? The twin and baby *both* died? What's that all about? Do they think the deaths are linked in some way?" Jen exclaimed.

"They're not saying, Jen. But there's heat from the woman's local hospital and GP. They want a full investigation on what the fuck is going on at FMA. They are pissed for starters, as they feel that FMA are cutting them out of the picture when it comes to patients and patient care. As you know yourself, you sign it all over to them when you sign up. And that's just one recent incident. There have been other weird things that have happened over the years." Janet looked at Jen, realising she might be inadvertently worrying her friend. "I'm sure it's all coincidence," she hastily added.

"Like what, Jan.? Other incidents connecting twins to their counterparts? You're starting to worry me, hon.!" She laughed nervously. Janet reassured her that these were one offs, and nothing to worry about. Besides they were isolated incidents. These things happened all the time at general hospitals, you just never got to hear about them really. They're just stats at the end of the day. Jen pressed her for another example, not entirely sure that Jan would spill any more gossip, or that she even wanted to hear it if she did. But she did.

"A few years ago, there was another strange thing that happened with a single mum and her kid. Her daughter was eight or so, and perfectly normal. The lab encountered some electrical problems and a fire broke out in there. Turns out that the guy on nights was having a kip on duty, and was woken by the alarms. But, by the time he got his shit together, significant damage had been done to some of the vessels—the fire had managed to get in the holding area through the cables or something, I'm not quite sure how. One vessel got damaged so bad by the flames that the twin had started to literally boil in the fucking thing. At least, that's what John told me. Sounds awful, doesn't it? But if that wasn't bad enough, it's what happened to the kid that's truly terrible. According to the mother, when she rang it in to the emergency services, her daughter had suffered some kind of spontaneous combustion in her sleep. When she went into her room after hearing the smoke alarm, she found her little girl thrashing around on the floor, trying to put out the flames. She was completely on fire. She didn't know what to do, and by the time the emergency services got there, she was dead. When they asked the mother what happened, she said she didn't know how the fire had started. She then had to go through an arduous investigation to try and get to the bottom of it all the while trying to deal with the death of her child." Jan stopped talking. *Fuck, John will kill me if he finds out I'm telling Jen all this,* she thought nervously. *Enough is enough, time to shut up.* "Jen, swear to me this will go no further? I really shouldn't be telling you this, it's classified. John will definitely lose his job, and may not work again if you even breathe this to another living soul. That includes Liam. Promise me." She looked pleadingly at Jen. Little did both women know that their husbands had discussed this very incident, many moons ago, and Liam had also agreed not to speak to his wife concerning the matter.

156

"I promise hon, I won't breathe a word. I swear." Jen's mind was now swimming with all kinds of thoughts about the twin and FMA, the majority of which were not good ones. These revelations were worrying, to say the least. Linking twins with kids? What if something were to happen to Josh's twin? What would, or could, happen to Josh? She consciously decided to stop thinking about it. The chaps and Josh would be up soon, and this needed to stay firmly brushed under the carpet.

But now she found that thoughts about FMA that had been tucked away at the back of her mind had come to the surface in light of Jan's revelations. And that the thoughts were dark and foreboding, like a thunderous sky laden with black storm clouds, waiting to unleash merry hell.

# Part III

# Chapter One

"Josh, come down and help me in the garden, I could do with an extra set of hands with these pots," Jen called up. They were approaching the end of his first week at home, and Jen was concerned she couldn't get him to engage in pretty much anything. He constantly stayed in his room, looking sad and worried. This in turn affected Jen, and she was determined to try and get things back to normal for all of them. When she heard the mumbled, unenthusiastic reply she knew she would need to go and get him. She put on a bright, happy face and cuddled him once she'd entered his room. He responded faintly, and she got him moving. Before long, they were out in the back garden messing around with plants and compost, Jen making small talk with her son to try and coax him out of his clam-like shell. It was an arduous task, but she persevered nonetheless.

"Well, it will be back to school next week, Josh. We need to have a fresh start really, for all of us. We need to make sure you go back there with a new attitude." She paused and brushed the compost from her fingers as she spoke. She had tied her hair back with a brightly coloured scarf to keep it out of her eyes, and her face was make-up free, allowing her natural beauty to shine. Josh appeared to be listening, despite his lack of response. "I expect you've missed your friends. Maybe they will help cheer you up. But there may be other kids that give you a hard time, Josh. And you will just have to accept that and take it on the chin—you did a bad thing, and there are always consequences for your actions, no matter who you are. On saying that, you still need to make sure they don't get *too* nasty towards you. Two wrongs don't make a right, do you understand what that means?" she asked. She looked down at her son as he fumbled with a pot and its new seedling inhabitants.

"Yeah. It means that just because I did something bad, it doesn't mean it's okay for anyone else to do something bad too." He was busy transferring big trowels of compost into the large pot with some bamboo shoots in. He looked up at his mother, who was stood trying to make sense of assorted pots and what plants they might house. "I just hope Benny doesn't decide he doesn't like someone else in school." Jen froze what she was doing, her brow instantly creasing with worry. There it was again! Josh hadn't really talked much about his friend, but he hadn't really talked much about anything, so that wasn't unusual…but here he was again, raising his ugly head. *Thank God Liam isn't hearing this, he would lose the plot like last time,* Jen thought. She hunkered down on her haunches to Josh's level.

"Josh, how come your friend is tied up in all of this? I thought you'd moved on from Benny a long time ago. You haven't talked about him for years, and now all of a sudden he's back and appears to be in the middle of all this mess we're in," she said, careful to keep her tone gentle and even. She needed to get him to open up about this so she could work out how to make sense of it—if she even *could* make sense of it. Going off half-cocked like her husband would not achieve results. Josh continued dumping compost into the pot in front of him, a frown creasing his brow now, a pensive, dark expression on his small face.

"He's always been there Mum. He never went away. I just thought you and dad didn't want me to talk to him or anything because you thought it was weird, so I stopped." He reflected on this briefly and then said: "Some kids at school thought it was weird too, so I stopped it. But I can't stop Benny being there."

"But don't you think Benny is just…well, just your own imagination? Like, you made him up. Like a cartoon character or something, but only you know about him because *you* made him up. In which case, you may be able to…*unmake* him up, if you see what I mean." Jen was in unchartered territory here. Truth be known, they had never really spoken about Benny in depth, not even when he first came to light. Both her and Liam had taken it completely in their stride, and if anything downplayed the whole thing. "Josh hon, I think it would be better for everyone if you could kind of *get rid* of Benny, especially for you. I'm not sure he's helping much at the moment, is he?" She moved his fringe away from his eyes and cradled his face, angling it towards her so they could look at each other.

As Josh looked at his mother's beautiful, wholesome face, he wondered why Benny was being so quiet through all of this. Normally, at the mention of his presence or name, he became very vocal inside Josh's mind. Often, *too* vocal. Josh knew Benny didn't like being discussed by other people at all, and it normally triggered some kind of outburst from him—but not this time. *He will be angry with me later,* Josh thought. "I don't know if I *can* make him go away, Mum. I didn't make him up, he's always been there. It's like he's my twin

162

brother, or something." For the second time, Jen froze. But this time she felt genuinely scared. Her heart rate had picked up and was banging away in her chest, as the realisation of what her son had just said sank in. *WHAT DID HE JUST SAY?* She tried to mask her shock, quickly composing herself. The word 'twin' was making an unwelcome appearance in too many conversations of late for her liking. *Far* too many. Josh was now lost in thought, after being guided down a path by his mum—a path that held just as many, if not more, questions for Josh than his mum or dad. "He might get angry if he thinks…well, that I don't like him and want to get rid of him. It was Benny's idea about the compass mum, honest it was. I wanted to stop Alex from being mean, but I didn't know how. Benny came up with the whole thing. But no one will believe that, because imaginary friends aren't real. Which means it's all my fault, and I get all the blame." He was reddening in his face, and looked about to cry. "What if he has any other ideas about being nasty, mum? I won't be able to stop him, and he might get me into even more trouble," he said dejectedly, as if accepting the fact that Benny was calling all the shots, and controlled what he did. *Jason needs to hear this,* Jen thought.

"Now listen to me, Josh. We need to get all this straightened out, once and for all. Benny is definitely *not* your twin brother, or anything of the sort. He's just a childhood imaginary friend. Children have them all the time, and they all grow out of it sooner or later. They are just a natural part of a kid's active imagination. Your mind and your brain is a very powerful thing, Josh. It can make things that aren't real seem real, and things that are real seem not real. Kids have very strong imaginations, and that's why they have things like imaginary friends, and adults don't. It's because their imaginations are more vivid, stronger. Maybe Dr Ireland can help with all this. We have another appointment in the week, so let's see what he makes of it. But you must promise me you will tell him the truth, like as if you were talking to me. That's very important Josh, so he can work out what's going on. Do you understand?" She took his face in her hands again, drew him close and hugged him. He wasn't crying yet, but not far off. As she hugged her son, her mind raced with her own thoughts. It was all a bit overwhelming for her—first Jan with her explosive confessional about FMA, and the sinister problems that others had experienced, making her wonder whether she and her family would ever have to endure something equally as unpleasant and unsettling, and now Josh with Benny. As an afterthought, she said to her son: "Best not talk about Benny when your dad's around, Josh. It makes him…upset. Promise me you won't? Let's keep it between us for the minute is best, I think. And we should try and concentrate on getting you in shape for school next week. There will be a meeting we have to have on Monday with Mr Matthews, but I will be there sweetheart, so don't worry. Let's just try and get through this together. I love you more than anything in the whole world Josh."

"I love you too, Mum," Josh said, as he tightened his little arms around her waist. *She doesn't love me though, does she Josh?* It was the first thing Benny had said all morning. Josh hugged his mum even tighter, hoping Benny would recede to the back of his mind. *She doesn't love me much at all, now you've told her all about me. It might be best if you stop talking about me for a bit, Josh. Just…shut…the…fuck…up.* Josh squeezed his eyes tightly shut at this, as if it would help shut Benny's voice out of his head. But he knew that it wouldn't.

The week appeared to move quicker than the previous one, which was a blessing for all of them. Liam was in work, so that left Jen and Josh to their own devices, and she did her best to include and involve him in activities to try and keep his mind off recent events and keep it all positive before the inevitable return to school. Before she knew it, it was Wednesday morning and they were getting ready to leave to see Dr Ireland. Once they arrived, Jen asked to leave Josh in reception with Sally as before. Sally had taken a shine to Josh after their last meeting, and was more than happy to set about dragging a few bits out of the cupboard at the back of the room to keep him occupied. As they cleared the small coffee table to start a jigsaw, Jen went in with Jason. She wasted no time in relaying what Josh had said to her the previous morning, and gave him a brief rundown of the history with Benny. Jason took notes on his PC and was happy to let Jen talk freely without interruption. She paused, and asked him what he thought of it all—was this anything to worry about? She had omitted anything to do with FMA. Even though she was gradually becoming more and more doubtful about FMA and the twin after Jan's revelations, she still felt it had nothing to do with Josh. Or Benny. Jason tried to reassure Jen that this was all still within the realms of normality for a seven to ten year old child. He referred to a couple of case studies of older children with a dependence on their imaginary friends. One such case involved a twelve year old girl that had blamed her fictional friend (in this case, not human, but a bear called Boris) for spitting in a kid's lunch box repeatedly until caught. She had done it every day for nearly three weeks by that time. Jason used this case study as an example of how children will look to push blame onto others when they feel they are going to get into trouble for something. "Most kids will look blame other kids around them once their back is up against the wall, but there are a handful that will turn to imaginary friends and suchlike to pass the buck onto," he explained. "There's no real pattern to this. All that can be said is that twelve is unusually old for a child to still have connections with a past imaginary friend. Josh is not even eight, so I'm not overly concerned that Benny is still coming to the fore. Especially given the circumstances. I expect he was nearly frightened to death, and Benny was a fitting scapegoat for him." He paused, gauging Jen's reaction. She sat opposite him, with a slight frown on her forehead, as she digested his synopsis. "But on saying that, I think it would be best to try and talk to Josh about what might lie ahead for his friend. He is old enough to understand the concepts of real and not real, and we may well be able to make progress towards getting him to leave this part of his life behind. To leave it in the past, where it should remain."

# Chapter Two

Monday morning came around quickly, and there was tension in the Connelly house. Josh was nervous about going back to school, and Jen was nervous about taking him. She had spoken to Beth, and explained she would need to take Josh herself today, as they had a meeting with the head. Beth was supportive as ever, and told her as soon as she wanted to ease back into the routine of sharing the school run, give her the nod.

The walk through the playground to the main entrance of the school was okay. A few looks and whispers from a couple of groups of kids, but nothing more than that. Mr Matthews was reasonable too, considering what it must look like to a relative outsider to the situation. From his perspective, this was a callous attack by one pupil on another, but he was a little more 'human' about it than Jen had expected. The headmaster knew both boys—the school had about four hundred pupils in total, and although this sounded a lot, Mr Matthews was a diligent school master. He made it his business to know as much as he could about his pupils. He knew more of Alex than he did of Josh, as Alex was a troublemaker and his name was often on detention lists. This gave Jen and Josh a little bit of a leg-up, as Josh had kept his nose clean to date…apart from the obvious recent escapade. The meeting lasted no longer than fifteen minutes, and in that time Mr Matthews made it crystal clear to Josh about what should and shouldn't happen in school from this point onwards. He also told him that if there were instances of bullying from others due to what had happened, then he should report this to a teacher immediately, to prevent any situation from escalating.

"What you've done is very serious, Josh. Alex may not be back at school for a month while he recovers. And when he *has* recovered, he will be left with some nasty scarring on his face. However, I believe that you are essentially a good kid from a good home, so I'm allowing you to return here because of that. I think that what you did was unforgivable, but I don't believe that you intended it to be so vicious, I just think that…well, that it got out of hand. You best make sure there are no more incidents like this, or I will expel you without hesitation. You need to keep your head down, young man." He delivered this speech to Josh with a stern look on his face, forehead furrowed so his grey bushy eyebrows almost met in the middle. He looked at Jen. "Mrs Connelly, I appreciate that this is a difficult time for you and your family, but let's hope we can all move on. There's no saying Ms Winters will want her son to return here once he's recovered. If there's anything you want to talk to me about, please don't hesitate to get in touch. We are here to support all of our children that attend Hartwood School." Jen thanked him for his understanding, and they left his office. Jen reassured Josh everything was going to be okay, as long as he behaved himself. She kissed him goodbye and made her way out of the main entrance, glancing back to see her son walking down the corridor. His head was hung low as he shuffled towards the classroom and again she felt a pang of anguish. He had a hard day ahead of him.

It felt a little strange to be alone at home for Jen. She had gotten used to Josh being there over the last two weeks, even though he had spent a lot of that time holed away in his room. She decided that she would take it easy today, she had earnt it. There were a hundred and one things to do around the house, but there always was. Such was the nature of a busy family home—it could wait, she needed some downtime. After an hour or so with a coffee and morning television to keep her company, her mind turned to what Jan had told her the other night. Specifically, about the incident with the mother and her little girl. Intertwined with this, she kept returning to what Josh had said about Benny yesterday—*he's like my twin brother*...she couldn't shake the idea that the twin at FMA had something to do with all of this—but how was that possible? Her logical mind couldn't rationalise that train of thought but she still kept going back to it, trying to unpick her thoughts, as if teasing a pulled thread on a piece of cloth. She picked up her laptop and fired up the internet. At first, she just stared at the open explorer window, unsure of what she even wanted to do. Then she started typing into the search engine. She started with Future Medical Advancements, and that threw up the website and not much else. The website itself was pretty sparse on information, as she knew from the early days. If you were really interested in what they do, or taking up one of their products or services, you had to make an appointment. It was a fairly closed shop. She tried FMA accident in the search bar. Again, this led her largely to the website, as the word 'accident' appeared in their text. She scanned a few random results for anything of relevance or interest,

167

but nothing appeared to be what she wanted. *What exactly* do *I want?* She thought, running her fingers through her hair as she stared at the screen. But she knew what she wanted. She wanted to find out about the fire at FMA. But more importantly, she wanted to find out more about the alleged 'victim'—the girl and her mum. She wanted to know what the mother thought about the death of her child—and what she thought FMA had to do with it. She tried a different approach, and typed in "girl dies in fire tragedy cause unknown." This threw up a whole plethora of results, so Jen started wading through them, clicking the links when she thought they might be related to the case Jan had told her about. After about half an hour of searching and dismissing webpages and articles, she finally came across something that could have some relevance. "Girl, 8, dies in tragic unexplained fire accident," the link said. It was from a newspaper local to the Southampton area called 'The Marchwood Herald'. Jen clicked the link, and it took her to the newspaper's website archive. The third entry down was the same line that had been thrown up in the search—dated nearly four years ago. She clicked it, and it opened an archived article—she had found it! She avidly read the report, which was about half a page. She skimmed it at first for the key facts, and then re-read it more thoroughly, absorbing all the detail in the text. She opened up Word on the laptop, and created a new document, unassumingly titled Jens Stuff. She copied the names of the mother and daughter into it: Naomi Goodman, aged forty-three, Sammi Goodman, aged seven. She copied the date of the article in, thirteenth of August 2018. The date of Sammi's death was three days earlier, she copied this too. She opened another browser and searched for Marchwood. Google maps told her it was about a hundred miles away—*not too far,* she thought. But what was she planning? Was she really going to try and hunt this poor woman down and hound her for information about her daughter's tragic death? She sat back from the laptop and drew a deep breath. She needed a break from this, so she saved her document, left the browser windows open, and made herself some lunch.

She returned to her laptop about an hour later, feeling less tense after spending some time in the garden away from the screen. She now had some key information in order to continue her research, and typed 'Naomi Goodman' into the search bar. Within seconds she realised this would need narrowing down—who knew there were that many Naomi Goodmans in the world? She added Marchwood, and hit enter. There was a link to social media halfway down, the links above that all had the word 'Marchwood' struck through, and the results below got less and less relevant. Jen switched tactics and brought social media up in another window. She searched for the name, and unsurprisingly got a whole ton of results. She began clicking on each one, quickly dismissing profiles that were obviously not what she was looking for. There appeared to be no way of filtering her search results by age or area, or if there was she gave up looking for it within a few minutes, so Jen just ploughed on clicking every profile in the order they appeared. She clicked on one that looked hopeful—it hadn't been used in a long time, maybe five years. *That makes sense, why would you be bothered about social media after going through the loss of your child?* Jen thought. She scrolled through the profile details. The profile photo showed an attractive brunette that looked like she was in her forties—that all stacked up. The Marchwood Herald had cited her age at forty-three. There had been a photo, but it had been small, black and white, and blurry. Jen copied the profile photo into her document. As she sifted through the information on the screen, she saw a name under the "worked at" section—Razzle Dazzle Hair and Beauty. It stated Naomi was the owner, and gave the address as Sixteen Alden Street. There was also a phone number. Jen copied all of this into her document. She sat back, thinking about what to do, and where she was going with all this. She didn't want to call the beauty salon—even if Naomi was there, she would undoubtedly be unwilling to discuss what Jen wanted to talk about while at work. She would probably be unwilling to discuss it at all, no matter where she was. After all, she was a complete stranger to the woman in question.

After thinking about it for a few minutes, Jen opened another browser window and searched for the local business register in Southampton. Once she had accessed this, she realised there was no specific search function on the webpage; however, she was able to sort alphabetically, and quickly found the salon. She clicked, and the information sprang onto her screen. She scanned it, looking for details of Naomi's address or a contact number. And halfway down the page, there it was. The telephone number appeared to be associated with Naomi's home address, both of which were different to the salon. Jen pasted the details into her document and then saved it. She stared at the number for a few minutes, trying to decide what to do. Eventually, she picked up her mobile and tapped the number in. *It's probably disconnected anyway,* she thought, but at that instant it began to ring. Jen's heart rate increased and she all of a sudden felt nervous. She also felt a bit sneaky—she had spent the last hour or so investigating a complete stranger and collating all their details, something that she had not had any reason to do previously. Someone picked up at the other end of the line. A cracked, hoarse voice came through to Jen.

"Hello?" Jen felt like her heart rate had jumped another notch on hearing the voice at the other end. Her mouth had gone dry, and she licked her lips desperately trying to conjure some moisture from somewhere that would enable her to talk.

"Oh, hello…is that Naomi? Naomi Goodman?" she asked politely. God, why was she so nervous? It was only a phone call for Gods' sake!

"Speaking." The voice seemed a little more normal now. "Who's speaking please?" Her tone was abrupt and direct.

"Hello Naomi. My name is Jenny Connelly. You don't know me…and I don't know you, but I really would like to talk to you about something important to me…and to you too, I think. I would be very grateful if you could spare me a few minutes of your time?" Jen waited with bated breath for a response. There was silence for a few moments, and then:

"Look, I haven't got time for this sales cold-calling bullshit, or any insurance scam crap either, so stop wasting my fucking time." Jen responded quickly, sensing Naomi was on the brink of hanging up.

"Please don't hang up, Miss Goodman. It's not any of those things…it's about my son. And a place called FMA." Jen waited for the disconnect tone for what seemed like an age. But it never came. Instead she at last heard a weary sigh from the other end of the phone.

"I might have known that I would never be able to forget FMA," Naomi said hopelessly. "Not only haunting my nightmares, but now when I'm awake. Fucking great." Again, Jen responded quickly, hoping desperately that she could keep the woman's interest and keep her on the line. Not the easiest of tasks when the subject matter was of obvious distaste to Naomi, and they were complete strangers to each other.

"Is now a good time, Miss Goodman? I can call you back at a more convenient time if you like…?" Jen mentally crossed her fingers. She was unconsciously pacing nervously back and forth in the living room.

"Well, there's never a good time, lady. Never a good time to talk about anything these days it seems, so whatever it is, you may as well get it off your chest." She still sounded abrupt, but Jen thought there was a *slight* softening to her tone.

"Okay, well firstly thanks for talking to me. I'm aware that I'm a total stranger to you, and I appreciate your time. You may well be wondering how I came to call you, so let me explain. I have a friend whose husband works for Future Medical Advancements, and she told me about you and your daughter. I am so very sorry for your loss, Miss Goodman. I cannot imagine the pain you must have been through. And I guess the pain is still there. It must be horrible." She paused. The rattling of Naomi's breath was at the other end of her mobile.

"Yeah, I miss her every second of every day. The hurt is just as hard now as it was when it happened all those years ago. Nearly four years of misery and heartache every…fucking…day. And you know the worst thing? I can't get any closure. None at all." Jen could hear the bitterness in her voice.

"You have my deepest sympathy, Naomi. I can't imagine the hell you're in. And I'm desperate to understand what happened from your perspective—I'm worried about my own son, but I can't work out why. I know that sounds stupid, but it's like there's some pieces to the puzzle missing, and you may be able to help me work out why I feel so worried. And the more I think about it, the more I think FMA have something to do with it, but I don't know what." There—she had said it out loud. She was worried about Josh and the twin at FMA. She proceeded to tell Naomi all about Josh, the imaginary friend that had re-surfaced in a sinister fashion recently, and her making what felt like an ambiguous connection with the twin. Naomi listened intently (Jen heard the flick of a lighter at the other end, and the draw of a cigarette quickly followed). Once Jen had relayed the bare bones of her situation, Naomi reflected on her words for a moment, and then said:

"Look, this isn't the type of thing you talk about over the phone really, Jenny. Why don't we arrange to meet or something? Then we can talk face to face. Where do you live? I'm in Southampton." Jen neglected to mention she knew exactly where she lived, but jumped at the chance to meet, offering to meet her somewhere local to where she lived. Naomi suggested she come to her home, and gave her address. Again, Jen made out that this was new information to her. After arranging for Thursday, they said their goodbyes and hung up. Jen felt a mix of emotions, from anxiety to almost excitement. This meeting may put all her fears to bed—she may be worrying about nothing, just a victim of her own over-active imagination. There may be no reason to suspect FMA had anything to do with Sammi's death, it may just be paranoia from a devastated, bereaved mother. Jen hoped with all her heart that this would turn out to be the case.

# Chapter Three

Josh's return to school had been relatively straightforward so far. He had been back a few days now, and he was happy to see his friends again—although some of them reacted differently to others, he was discovering. One of Alex's cohorts actually approached him during break and told him he thought Alex deserved it—this came as a shock to Josh, as he was expecting trouble. *See? Not everyone thinks it's bad that we hurt that asshole. I told you he deserved it!* Benny had piped up, obviously pleased that someone else was on their side. Josh considered this, and agreed that Alex had needed to be taught a lesson, but it was alright for everyone else. They had not had to go through all the horrible police interviews, punishments and see his mum and dad so upset. And it was especially alright for Benny—there were no consequences whatsoever for him. This made Josh resent him a little. Things had been a bit out of sorts between them since the attack, and Benny was keen to resolve this—but Josh was still hurting from it all, it had been quite traumatic for him, and he still blamed Benny for the whole thing. Benny countered this during their constant exchanges, reminding Josh that it was *both* of them that had decided to attack Alex. It also didn't make Josh feel any better the fact that he and Alice were a bit scratchy with each other. They were supposed to be best friends, but things had definitely cooled off a little since their exchange of words after the incident. Benny wasn't bothered either way—in fact, he sort of revelled in the idea that Josh wasn't Alice's flavour of the month at the moment. There was certainly a little jealousy at work there. Josh hoped that he and Alice would be back to normal soon, and he made several attempts to rekindle the friendship in school. She was definitely still a bit distanced, but was slowly but surely coming around, and that made Josh happy.

But it wasn't all a bed of roses for Josh getting back to normality in school. He had already received some snide comments from other kids in the corridor between lessons, and he had also noticed a couple of instances where small groups of pupils were obviously talking about him—probably not in a complimentary way. He had convinced himself that a few of the teachers were reacting to him differently too, nothing blatant but maybe the odd hint of distain in the tones of their voices when talking to him—but he couldn't be sure. Maybe he was being over-sensitive about the whole thing. It was all over now, and he wanted to move on. He was sat with his normal friends out on the grass bank overlooking the playground eating his sandwiches when he noticed Rich Avery looking at him from where he was stood by the benches. He was alone, and that was normal for a kid like Rich—he was bigger than most of the other kids, and nastier too. He wasn't part of Alex's little band of merry men—in actual fact, his merry men consisted of just him. He was a loner, and sported a constant frown of disapproval on his already pock-marked face. He was one of the oldest in the school, being in the final year, and being old for that year added to his overall intimidating look. Rich had heard about Josh's antics from one of Alex's henchmen last week, and was fascinated by the fact that this little upstart had the balls to carry out such a vicious attack on a kid that was not only bigger than him, but also with a relatively fearsome reputation. When he asked Alex's friend, Will, why he had done it, he couldn't quite believe that it was apparently all driven from the fact that Alex had been a bit nasty to his girlfriend. It seemed a bit of an extreme reaction, for sure. Rich was of a mind he wanted to goad the little fucker. It was an easy win—no one would be overly bothered if he gave him a couple of knocks, just to remind him who was boss. There would be leniency from teachers, as they all knew what he had done, and they would all think *well, he deserves it after what he's done…* Rich continued to eye Josh, who had stopped concerning himself with Rich, and was busy fooling around with his mates—another little bit of normality for Josh.

After the ringing of the bell, Josh and his friends were filing in through the main doors and into the corridor for their afternoon sessions. Rich had purposely hung back in order to be behind the group of boys, and as they walked down the corridor Rich picked up his pace until he was right behind Josh. The group in front were blissfully unaware of Rich behind them, or of his intentions. As the boys jostled with each other, a natural gap appeared between Josh and his other three friends—Rich saw his opportunity. He closed in on Josh from behind, put his right leg in front of Josh's and shoved him hard. Josh sprawled onto the hard, slick floor, and the side of his head connected hard with it. He momentarily saw stars blooming in front of his eyes, as his brain tried to decipher what had happened to him. His friends had backed away, and were now all looking at Rich, stood over Josh, as he tried to recover and get back on his feet. He had only managed to get to his knees, rubbing his temple and checking his hand for blood, when Rich decided to give him a kick in the ribs for good measure. This took all of Josh's wind out of him as the sharp pain exploded in his left side of his torso. He yelped out in pain and held his hand up, open palm, in defence.

"Oww! Stop hurting me, you bastard!" he yelled at his aggressor. Rich grinned back at him, revealing dirty, yellow teeth. He almost looked as if he was snarling, like a rabid dog.

"Why should I? You seem alright to dish it out to others, but can't take it yourself can you, you fucking faggot?" He spat the words out between clenched teeth. His fists were also clenched—his blood was up and he felt like carrying on, battering the fucker's brains out until he was spent, but had already decided he would have to stop and be satisfied with the damage already inflicted. Any more and he would definitely run the risk of trouble, in the form of a teacher.

"Just leave me alone! I haven't done anything to you, you fucking bully!" Josh exclaimed, his hand still outstretched in a vain attempt to ward off any more blows that may rain down on him. His mates had now clustered to the side of the corridor, far enough away to not come under fire from Rich themselves, gawping at the two boys. Josh managed to get to his feet, head spinning and his temple now throbbing with every pulse. It felt hot and sore, and was already starting to swell into what would no doubt be a nasty bruise. His ribs also hurt, but in a different way to his head—the pain was sharper by his left ribs, and all the immediate area around them had developed an ominous dull ache. He immediately backed away from Rich, ready to run if it came to it. He didn't want any more pain in the form of kicks and punches from the much larger and heavier opponent, but he sensed that the attack was over.

"You call me a bully? You little cunt—next time I'll stab the fuck out of *you* with a compass, and see how you like it. Give you a taste of your own medicine." Rich walked away, spitting at Josh as he did so. His friends immediately crowded around him, asking if he was okay. He nodded as he wiped the spit from his jumper with his sleeve, and the boys made their way to their next class. Josh sat through his lessons with his head and torso becoming increasingly painful during the course of the afternoon. He was unable to concentrate on anything apart from his encounter with Rich. He hadn't bothered to talk to a teacher about any of it—again, he just wished it would all go away, and wanted to forget about the whole thing. *It's still going on—I just wish it would end,* he said to Benny.

*Don't worry—it will, Josh. I'm sure that asshole will get his come-uppance for what he just did.* Even though Benny was upset and angry at the unprovoked attack on Josh, he was at the same time pleased that he was confiding in him once more. Their arguing days were over—long live the reunion. Whatever it might bring.

# Chapter Four

Jen was apprehensive about her meeting with Naomi, and a few things had added to her already mounting worry. She was aware that Josh was having a little bit of a bumpy ride since his return to school—he wouldn't talk to her about the specifics, but as a mum, she just knew. She had tried to gently coax information about what may or may not have been going on at school, but he wouldn't divulge anything to her. Jen felt desperately sorry for him, even though what he had done was awful. She couldn't help it. He was her son, and she only ever wanted the best for him. This nasty little episode had opened up a whole world of hell for all of them. Liam was fairly tight-lipped about the whole thing, and subsequently they had not had many conversations about it. The few brief times that they had actually ventured into talking about it had threatened very quickly to turn into an argument, so they had both (wisely) decided that maybe it was best they just let it be and let the whole sordid affair become a thing to forget.

Jen decided she didn't need much for the journey and put a bottle of water and some mints in her handbag on her way out of the door. Hopefully the journey wouldn't take too long, the sat nav in the car told her two and a quarter hours, depending on traffic. It was a clear, crisp day, with the sun's morning warmth quickly taking the cold away. As she got on her way, she called Naomi to let her know she'd be with her in a couple of hours. They had a brief conversation, and Jen told her she would call nearer the time of arrival to let her know where she was. Naomi seemed okay on the phone. Jen couldn't work out if she was in a permanent state of shock and depression, and thought that there may be some medication contributing to her seemingly lacklustre demeanour. All sorts of thoughts were cluttering Jens mind as she drove, all to do with FMA. She hoped Naomi may be able to put her mind at rest that she was just being paranoid and ridiculous, but somehow she knew that hope was remote, given their initial conversations. She hadn't mentioned anything to Liam about her liaising with Naomi, and she wasn't used to keeping secrets. It seemed like there were more and more secrets creeping into their family by the day, and it didn't feel good. It felt like there was a slow, crawling worm of doubt and mistrust deviously slithering its way into their family that put everyone on edge and on the defensive. *Once I've got the lowdown from Naomi I will tell him all about it,* she resolved. *Let's see what she has to say first.*

Jen was lucky—the traffic was nowhere near as bad as it could have been, and she made good time in just over two hours. She had called Naomi a few minutes ago, and told her she was nearby. Naomi asked for a street name or something she could identify her whereabouts, and once Jen had described where she was, Naomi told her she was literally ten minutes away. Sure enough, ten minutes later Jen was pulling her car up to the kerb outside Naomi's house. The street was average looking, with some houses looking nicer than others, and some gardens more unkempt than others—a standard council estate street that had a few trees planted alongside the pavements here and there, and looked distinctly rougher at one end than the other. Luckily for Jen, Naomi appeared to live in the middle ground, if anything a little more embedded into the nicer end of the street. She had a cursory look around, and spotted a few young kids playing football further up the road. She didn't really relish the idea of leaving her car parked on the street unattended, and hoped she would be able to keep an eye on it once inside Naomi's place. She looked at the house in front of her. It was tired and in need of a bit of care and attention, but apart from that it seemed okay. She had assumed Naomi lived alone, and the outside of the house and the garden confirmed this to Jen as she walked up to the door. The curtain twitched in the window to her left, and she caught a glimpse of Naomi through the grubby glass just before she knocked on the door. Naomi answered straight away, opening the front door to reveal a sad looking, tired, and despondent woman in her late forties (although the lines etched into her face around her eyes and mouth suggested much older). Her hair was dark and unbrushed, falling just past her shoulders. She had a "just got out of bed" or "rolled off the sofa" look, and her clothes added to the illusion. A baggy top was accompanied by greyish, grimy looking jogging bottoms, and her feet adorned a seemingly ancient pair of pink slippers. Her frame appeared skeletal beneath her disguising, baggy attire, given away at the shoulders and hips, where clavicles and pelvic bones poked into the fabric in an angular fashion. There appeared to be little or no cleavage below the neckline, and whatever may have existed certainly wasn't supported in any way. Her eyes were a lifeless, grey colour sunk into darkened hollows, framed by deep running crow's lines, and her mouth echoed this at its corners at the end of her thin, tightly drawn lips. Jen looked at her, part pleadingly, part sympathetically—the woman looked dishevelled, and her eyes portrayed a feeling of constant dismay and complete loss of any kind of happiness or positivity.

"You must be Jen. Glad you got here okay. You'd best come in, you'll have to excuse the state of the place... I haven't had the energy to keep on top of things lately," she said in a soft, cracked voice. She sounded like she would collapse in a fit of wracking sobs at any second.

Jen cleared her throat. "Nice to meet you Naomi, and let's not worry about the housework, eh? My place is the same," she lied unconvincingly. The Connelly house was a palace in comparison, and as the two women stood face to face on the doorstep it was apparent that they were poles apart. *I hope I never end up like her,* Jen thought, and instantly felt mean and spiteful for thinking it. She knew only the faintest bit of what this woman had been through, and you wouldn't wish it on your worst enemy—no wonder she looked under the weather. Naomi stood aside and motioned her inside, and as Jen stepped in she smelt stale cigarettes, alcohol, damp, and dirt. The greenish brown carpet felt kind of sticky under her feet as she followed Naomi through the narrow hallway into the living room off to the right. The curtains were half drawn, and the weak sunlight that filtered through the almost brown glass of the window cast a sickly yellow over the parts of the room it could penetrate. The coffee table in the middle of the room was cluttered with dirty glasses, empty wine bottles, and an ashtray that was almost overflowing, brimming with cigarette ends. Ash was spilt all around it, and had been subsequently soaked up into little pools of slowly evaporating, sticky pools of spilt liquid. A television flickered away in the corner on mute; the unit that it sat on was in a similar predicament to the table. The carpet had various items scattered over it—remote controls, empty or half empty cider cans, discarded letters and envelopes, a few books seemingly thrown into one corner along with a few DVD cases and discs. Naomi had sat down on a very old, tired looking sofa. It was difficult to work out what colour it had started life as, but it appeared a dull brown now. She made an effort to pick up some empty food wrappers and cigarette packs in order to make some room for Jen.

"I'm really sorry about the state of it in here. Please have a seat." Jen carefully perched herself on the corner of the sofa, actively trying not to contact too much of it. Naomi smiled wryly as she noticed this. "Haven't really been in the mood for cleaning lately. Not for the last four years to be precise," she drawled.

She looked at Jen squarely, her face resolved in a near grimace. "Shall we get started, honey?"

# Chapter Five

Jen and Naomi talked for about an hour in total, with Naomi doing most of the talking while Jen prompted her with leading questions to keep her in her flow. Jen felt as if Naomi had been bottling a lot of this up for some time, and was even keen to have someone listen to her ramblings. *Who knows if she's even ever given an account like this,* Jen thought. *The police interviews wouldn't have been like this.* After a while, Jen checked her watch. She had purposely put her phone on silent while at Naomi's house, so as to not interrupt the proceedings, and discovered she had lost track of time a little—she needed to leave, in order to be home for Josh. It was well planned that Beth was picking the kids up today, as she would certainly have been late.

"Oh Jeez, I've got to go, Naomi. I need to be back for Josh. But look, thanks so much for your time. I'm not sure what to do from here, but hearing your story has certainly helped me make at least *some* sense of it all." She looked at Naomi, who was busy finishing her second large gin of the afternoon. She had offered Jen a drink and Jen politely declined, sticking to her bottled water. She wasn't sure she even wanted to touch anything in there, let alone put anything to her mouth, and had purposely stopped in a service station in order to have a bathroom break before arriving.

"Well, now you know what happened to me and my lovely Sammi…you probably think I'm an alcoholic madwoman, but there it is. Maybe I'm just that." She looked at Jen with her darkened, hollowed eyes. "If you want my advice, then get FMA out of your lives for good. Or, like me, you may live to regret it Jen. I hope I've helped you." There was genuine sincerity in her voice, and Jen all of a sudden felt a pang of sorrow for the ruined woman stood before her— and resolved to have a painful conversation with her husband just as soon as the opportunity arose.

They said their goodbyes and hugged each other on the doorstep, both women knowing they would never see each other again. It was a bittersweet moment, and Jen found herself close to tears. She actively choked them back. Naomi just looked plain sad. It was an expression of sorrow she had obviously grown into. Jen looked back briefly and waved as she opened her car door, only to discover Naomi had retreated back inside her home already. She lowered her hand and got in, feeling decidedly deflated, worried, and confused all at the same time. As Jen drove, she slipped into auto-pilot and began digesting her encounter. Naomi had started by outlining her beautiful daughter—tall for her age, slim, pretty, with waist length auburn hair. Lively and fun loving, she wasn't short of friends both in and out of school. It transpired that they never lived together in the house Jen had visited. Naomi was a successful businesswoman, and her salon was going from strength to strength. She had always been a single mum, her pregnancy an accident from a drunken night away on business promoting the salon. A charming gentleman had won her affections during the evening and they retired for a night of passion, throwing pretty much all caution to the wind. Naomi discovered two months later that she was pregnant—and that she had also neglected to keep the gentleman's number. Being the strong, independent character that she was, she decided to keep the baby—and Sammi had changed her world. Naomi had shown Jen some photos of the early days, and Jen had to disguise her look of shock at the transformation of the woman that now sat beside her. Naomi had been truly stunning, and obviously took great pride in her appearance before all this had happened.

As Naomi was relatively well off due to her business ventures and the salon going from a small one-woman show into something much more lucrative, she decided to invest wisely for her daughter—a friend of a friend had mentioned FMA to her, and she had done her research and decided to pay them a visit. The rest was history, almost a carbon copy of what Liam and Jen had gone through themselves in the early days, before Josh was born. Naomi could remember Dr Ellis (*that fucking murdering bastard*), but none of the other names rang a bell with her when Jen ran them past her. *Hardly surprising, given what she's been through,* Jen thought. All had gone well with the birth and FMA, and life ticked on merrily, just the two of them living their lives with Naomi basking in her newfound motherhood, watching her tiny baby grow into a beautiful young girl. *So far so good,* Jen had thought. *But I know there isn't a happy ending.* Naomi had dwelt on these early days of motherhood for quite a while, using photos to punctuate her retelling of Sammi's childhood. Jen couldn't help but notice the dreamy, wistful look in the woman's eyes as she flicked through her old photos.

It was all she had left of her daughter. As she retold the early years, the tone got darker as Sammi got older. Naomi outlined the first time she had an idea that all was not well in the Goodman household. She detailed how she had caught Sammi muttering to herself several times, and eventually decided to talk to her daughter about it. Sammi got flustered, and refused to talk about it again no matter how much her mum pushed her. She had then found a diary of sorts hidden in Sammi's room. As Sammi was only six, she didn't see the harm in having a little look at the contents, but quickly discovered she didn't like what she saw one bit. There were some sketches on some pages and writing on others, and Naomi had a hard time making sense of it—one of the drawings seemed to be of herself, but locked in some kind of transparent cylinder with the words 'Let me OUT' written underneath it. Jen asked Naomi about Sammi's behaviour—did she talk about an imaginary friend? Did the friend tell her to do things? Nasty things? Naomi furrowed her brow at these questions, trying to recall any specific incidents. She told Jen there was nothing to speak of, although Sammi had been subject to some very vivid nightmares, in which she said she was trapped in some kind of container and couldn't get out. This tied in with the sketches that Naomi had discovered, and she had started making the connection between the drawings, nightmares, and the clone held in the FMA laboratory. Apart from that, Sammi's behaviour in general was normal for a girl of her age. *Not like Josh's recent change,* Jen thought resentfully. She spent every day now wishing that things would return to normal for her and her family, and daydreamed about being able to rewind the clock to before when all of these horrible things had started happening.

Naomi had retold Sammi's ultimate demise in a very emotional, heart-wrenching fashion, her sentences punctuated by wracking sobs of misery, her words hitched by small wails of sorrow. Tears flowed down her face the whole while as she unfolded the last chapter of her daughter's life. Jen found it all very upsetting, and comforted the distraught woman with an arm around her shoulders. She repeatedly said to Naomi that she didn't have to tell her, and she didn't want to upset her—if it was too distressing to re-tell the tale then please stop…but Naomi struggled on, regardless. It was almost as though she *needed* to tell the story in its entirety, and doggedly stuck to her narrative despite the upheaval of emotion that it was causing her to do so. Jen was also close to tears for most of this monologue from a woman that was a complete stranger to her. She empathised with her and felt her anguish, as she struggled on with her heart

182

breaking tale. Naomi recalled how it had been a normal Saturday—she had taken Sammi out in the afternoon to an outdoor play area with a few of her friends, and after dropping them home they had a takeaway together in front of the television. At about eight o'clock, Sammi had gone up to bed. Her mum said she could play on her tablet for half an hour, then lights out. Naomi had gone up to Sammi's room a short while after and kissed her goodnight, the same as any other night. *I didn't know then, but actually that was the worst night of my life. It has ruined my life, from that night onwards nothing matters to me anymore. I feel like an empty shell, a huge space inside me that was filled with my beautiful girl is now filled with nothing. I miss her so much every second of every day.* Jen tried to comfort her as much as she possibly could, but how do you console a grieving mother that has lost her baby? She found her words of comfort sounding trivial and inconsequential, so in the end she just rubbed her shoulders in consolation. Naomi re-composed herself for what felt like the hundredth time since she had started talking about the demise of her daughter and doggedly continued, determined to purge herself of the tale.

Naomi had finished her glass of wine and gone up to bed herself after a couple of hours. She fell asleep almost immediately after the busy day. As she slept, at some point during the night she became aware of a commotion. *It sounded like distant wails of pain and screaming, but was all blended into my sleep... I was sure I could smell burning. It was the smoke alarm that then awoke me with a start, all of a sudden I was in total panic mode... I sat bolt upright in bed, and within seconds was running to Sammi's room. I didn't know at that point where the smoke was coming from, but instinct took me there. I kicked the door open and the black some billowed out—I had to step back from that and the heat, my heart was pounding, I was sweating, shaking, terrified and totally panicked by the whole thing. I didn't know what was happening, or what had happened, but I had to get in there. I put my arm over my face and went in, only to see my girl thrashing around on the floor desperately trying to put the flames out—they were all over her. Her bed and bedding was ablaze, she had obviously got onto the floor to escape the fire. I didn't know what to do; I had started screaming by then, as well as Sammi. I grabbed the pile of clothes on the chair next to the dresser and just jumped on her with them. I didn't think about getting them wet or anything, there was just no time to think. Everything went in horrible slow motion, but it was probably all over in seconds.* Jen listened with wide-eyed horror as Naomi unfolded the last chapter of her tale, still clinging to her shoulders. It was like Naomi had gone back in time, and was reliving every second of anguish. Her expression was glazed and completely wracked with sorrow and misery, her face blotchy from a constant stream of hot tears, her lips trembling with the pain of her memories. *Christ, this is awful for me, God knows how painful it must be for her,* Jen thought.

Naomi shrugged Jen's arms off, and stood up. "Do you want a drink hon.? I'm sure as hell having another one." Jen declined, her trip home a convenient excuse to avoid alcohol. Naomi poured herself a large gin and tonic into a distinctly grubby tall glass.

When she returned to her story, the mood was slightly different—she appeared to be more melancholy than in actual pain. *Maybe the telling had done her some good,* Jen thought to herself. Naomi told how she battled with the flames that had set Sammi on fire for a short, frenzied period of time, until the movement underneath her and the screams of pain had stopped. Then came her own screams. She said she couldn't remember how long she had knelt by her daughter's smouldering body, with a tee-shirt pressed to her mouth while the bed continued to slowly burn, filling the room and house with yet more filthy black smoke. She remembered the blue lights flashing through the window and the sirens wailing, although the smoke alarm was far louder, and still sounding. There was a vague pounding downstairs, and then a rush of cold air hit her as the front door was forced. Firemen were shouting and coming closer up the stairs, and she just sat there, her body now wracked with huge sobs that heaved her whole body.

She told Jen that the rest was just a blur. Before she knew it, she was at the local hospital and couldn't even remember getting there. She remembered screaming as a fireman picked up Sammi and carried her downstairs, and having to be restrained by another of his colleagues. The rest after that was just a series of doctors and nurses poking, prodding, undressing, injecting, the list went on. Naomi said she had no clear recollection of any of the rest of that night. *I must have been sedated quite heavily. Once I came around, I was confused and disoriented—until I realised what had happened. Then the screaming started again.*

As Jen drove, she let her mind pore over the details of Naomi's story. She knew it was horrific, but actually she had been completely unprepared for the onslaught of her encounter. And as with every good story, Naomi was saving the best till last. As she recounted the aftermath of Sammi's death, a dark, foreboding sense of dread settled inside Jen's mind. As she listened to her go through the last motions of the tale, she felt more and more a feeling of uneasy panic growing in her mind. The cause of death verdict was misadventure. The police were asking Naomi questions morning, noon and night about Sammi, her home, of any recent incidents involving matches or lighters, any recent incidents *full stop.* Naomi was shattered, distraught, and felt like she was in a living nightmare. She answered and co-operated with the police and their questioning in a zombie like haze over the next few days. After she was released from hospital, she realised the magnitude of what she needed to sort out now Sammi was dead. The funeral. Informing relatives and friends. She hadn't spoken to anybody but hospital staff and police for days. Her salon. She had countless missed calls from her staff asking where she was, was she OK, when was she coming into the salon. FMA. There would be no need to continue with her contract now. When she got back home, she didn't want to go inside. She stood on the doorstep for what felt like forever before going in. The front door had been secured, but was unlocked, the marks from the battering it had taken a dark reminder of recent events. *Another thing to sort out,* she had thought, grimly. It smelt foul in there, a horrid mixture of burnt fabric, wood, and dampness. There was a sickly sweet undertone to the stench that Naomi didn't want to think about. She wandered around aimlessly downstairs with the front door still ajar for about fifteen minutes, her brain still desperately trying to process what had actually happened. Eventually, she faced her demons and went upstairs to Sammi's room. The bed had been taken away for examination along with a few other things. There was a large, black scorch mark on the pink carpet next to where the bed once was. She simply sat down on the floor and started crying. Again.

The next few days were a blur, same as the previous few. She managed to sort a few things out, but for the purposes of Jen she left these details out and jumped straight to her discovery of the accident that had happened at the FMA laboratories. She had tried to call FMA, but had got a garbled answerphone message saying that their helpline was temporarily not operating due to 'unforeseen circumstances'. Her curiosity was spiked, and a few online searches later she was reading the article in a newspaper local to the area about the fire in the lab. Instantly her mind made a connection, despite the relative lack of detail in the report. That would be all the detail she would discover, too. When she did finally manage to get hold of someone at FMA, they were very tight-lipped about the whole incident. Naomi was clever during the conversation, and did not actually let on that anything had happened to Sammi, and let the customer services representative dig himself a hole. He told her they were still "analysing the effects of the accident" after Naomi pressed him on what had happened in the lab, and whether her daughter's insurance policy was affected. The conversation ended with Naomi being told that she would be informed if her policy was invalidated or affected in any way due to the accident within the next week. She mentioned nothing of her own circumstance, and decided just to wait for answers from FMA.

As things transpired, the answer did come in the end. Naomi's policy was terminated, and she was issued full insurance based compensation, stating that the twin was 'biologically damaged' in an unprecedented accident at the laboratory facility. Naomi knew what damage. Fire damage. The same damage that had happened to her daughter. This cemented her belief more than ever before—the twin and Sammi were somehow linked. What happened to the twin had happened to Sammi. Even though the concept sounded fantastically, outrageously science fiction-like, there was no other explanation, rational or otherwise. She was a non-smoker, hated candles (the waxy smoke from them always made her wheezy), and the only access to any naked flame in the house was the gas cooker. She had never caught Sammi with matches or a lighter, and had never smelt cigarette smoke on her. At twelve, she was a bit too young for that, anyway. So, Naomi spent her life from that moment onwards up until now getting more and more embroiled in a conspiracy theory type mind-set which had ultimately led to her demise. Her business went downhill fairly rapidly, and eventually she closed the salon. Her friends and employees from the salon had been worried about her for a while, and tried their best to rally around and support her. But all to no avail. Naomi appeared to have taken Sammi's death so hard that her life was quickly spiralling out of control. Contact with anyone became more and more limited as time went on, and alcohol and anti-depressants played a more prominent role over anything else in her life. And then there was the stint in prison for trying to blow up the lab. She had been caught red-handed, and received a twelve month prison sentence. This was much less than she had expected, but her lawyer successfully argued that she was not of fit mind as she was traumatised over the death of her daughter. FMA's representation seemed relatively unconcerned with this seemingly light punishment—they were more concerned with bad publicity for the business. They had taken extensive measures to keep the incident under wraps, out of the local papers and online news websites. And they had been successful; money talks, and it had found its way into all the right pockets.

Jen reflected on all of this, trying to make sense of the link with the twin at FMA. *Could this be what's happening to Josh? The twin somehow influencing what he does?* She was only thinking what she had been tempted to think over the past few weeks, but every time her mind had wandered into that territory she had dismissed the line of thinking as ridiculous. How could that ever be possible? Now that she had met Naomi and heard her tale, she was quickly convincing herself that FMA and the twin may well have been playing a sinister role in Josh's recent behaviour. Naomi's story would seem crazy if being told to anyone else, that was for sure…but Jen had her own dark suspicions bubbling away. An imaginary friend telling Josh to do bad things…? Her mind was running away with her as she drove homewards. *I need to speak to Liam about this and tell him about Sammi and Naomi,* she thought. *He's going to think I'm nuts, but I have to tell him and see what he thinks. And see how he feels about pulling out of the FMA policy.* She made up her mind to talk to her husband as soon as possible about her feelings on the matter. And see if he would agree to get rid of this fucking twin.

# Chapter Six

Jen arrived back home with half an hour to spare before Josh came home from school. Liam was normally a little later again, so the timing was good—she would approach Liam later and tell him everything. The time for secrets and worrying on her own were over. They never had secrets from each other, and now was not the time to start, she thought. She tried to put it all to the back of her mind as she started preparing tea—there would be plenty of time to discuss it all later.

As she heard Beth's car pull up, she left the kitchen to say hello and welcome Josh home—she discovered her recent resentment for her son and his horrible actions was melting away, as she now increasingly associated the misdemeanours with something else apart from wild behaviour on his part. *We need to help him, and soon—before anything else happens,* she thought. Beth was amiable as ever, and they chatted on the drive as Josh bundled out of her car and scampered indoors. He looked worried and preoccupied, as per usual. Who knew what was going on inside his head? After some small talk about the kids and their respective families, the women made tentative arrangements to get together on the weekend at some point—*Let me check with Alex, details to follow!* Beth had said as she pulled away. Jen waved goodbye and returned to the house, calling Josh as she entered the hall. No response greeted her, and his shoes and bag were in the hall. She went upstairs to see him. Josh was sat on the end of his bed looking miserable—*an all too familiar sight nowadays,* Jen thought. She sat beside him and tried to engage him.

"Was everything okay at school today, sweetheart? I've missed you." Josh looked at her and replied that it was okay, but he was glad to be home. She ruffled his hair and told him it was chicken for tea, cooked just how he liked it, and he could forget about school for the minute, at least until tomorrow. Jen managed to coerce him into helping her with tea, and they both went downstairs together. She felt happier that he was at her side at least, and not upstairs in his room on his own, wallowing in his own obvious misery. *This* has *to change,* she thought. Liam came in just as she was about to serve up, and they ate at the table making conversation with Josh about school. They were both anxious to make sure that nothing untoward was happening without their knowledge, but Josh, as per usual, gave nothing away, saying that everything was 'okay'. Part of that was due to Benny telling him to keep quiet about Rich Avery and the bullying that had taken place. Josh needed no persuasion from Benny—he had already resolved to keep that little gem of information to himself. He would deal with Rich as and when the time was right. Benny settled back into the background of Josh's mind, satisfied that their potential plans for revenge were kept from Josh's parents.

After Josh had gone up to bed, Jen asked Liam if he wanted a drink. He gladly agreed, and she returned from the kitchen with a bottle of wine and two glasses. As he poured, she said:

"Liam, I've really got to tell you what I did today. I don't quite know what you'll make of it—shit, I don't know what *I* make of it even, so here goes." Jen proceeded to tell Liam about the day's events in as much detail as she could remember. Liam sat quietly through the relaying of the story, letting Jen tell it as it came. As she drew it to a conclusion, she looked at Liam.

"I hope you don't think I'm going crazy, but I really think that something has been affecting Josh. In a bad way. And that's why the horrid thing happened with that kid. And his friend Benny—I know it sounds batshit crazy, but we can't deny this imaginary friend is all tied up with this somehow. For fuck's sake, Josh *told* us he was part of it!" she exclaimed. Liam remained silent for a minute, and then cleared his throat.

"Look Jen, we can't jump to any conclusions here. We just can't. We don't know if this Naomi woman is for real or not. You said yourself she's a washed-up alcoholic. And there's no concrete proof, either. She sounds like a very unfortunate mother who has lost her daughter in a slightly unusual and mysterious way, and is now looking for a rational explanation for it." He reflected for a moment and then continued: "Well, not even rational by the sounds of it. It's a completely out there conspiracy theory straight out of a science-fiction movie, let's be honest." He drained his glass and poured another. Jen looked dejected at her husband's reaction—she was hoping he would be at least open to the idea that the twin at FMA *could* be a contributing factor to what was at play with their son. But she wasn't getting a warm feeling from Liam. She

189

decided to press on, regardless of the flat response to her worries about FMA from her husband.

"I know we've invested a lot of money in FMA, and all for the right reasons, Liam. But the more I think about it, the more I get this horrible feeling that something's not right. If you had seen Naomi today and heard her awful story, you may be more convinced. She showed me pictures in a notebook that Sammi had drawn—they looked a lot like the vessels at the lab. And I mean *a lot*."

She searched Liam's face, looking for some kind of softening of the hard set frown and downturned mouth. He didn't appear to be warming to the idea at all—quite the opposite in fact.

"Jen, I want to sympathise with your newfound friend, or however you want to describe her, but I'm struggling to identify Josh's behaviour with FMA. Seriously, listen to yourself hon! It's a bit hard to swallow, you must admit." Liam looked torn between his logical thought process and his normally level-headed wife. The last thing he wanted was some kind of divide opening up between them—they needed to be a team and stay resolute while they weathered the storm with Josh. They already had their differences of opinion on Josh since the attack. "I tell you what; I'll take Josh to his next appointment with Jason and see what he says. I promise I won't blow it up to sound like something out of a science-fiction film, but Josh may have said something to him during his sessions there. Maybe he will have a rational opinion on what you say Naomi has been through, and it may help us both put things into perspective. What do you think?" He looked at her hopefully, desperate to reach some common ground with her on the issue. She sighed and put her head on his shoulder, seeking comfort from him.

"Okay Liam. But don't make out like I'm unhinged or anything, I don't want him thinking I'm a neurotic mum with an over-active imagination. I'm just really worried there may be something going on that we don't fully understand. And if there is, how do we resolve matters with our son? This is just one big horrible fucking *mess.*"

# Chapter Seven

Josh was in afternoon class, and his mind was wandering. This was often the case nowadays. He was too young to recognise the change in himself—the poor results in school, no engagement in lessons, minimal participation in just about everything. He was constantly in a different place, mentally. He had been engaging more and more with Benny, especially after the incident with that bastard Rich Avery last week. Benny had worked himself up into a right old frenzy, encouraging Josh to wreak his revenge on him. Josh was reluctant about agreeing to anything, as he knew what the repercussions had been from last time with Alex. Shit, he was still dealing with the consequences of that episode, and he wasn't keen to repeat the experience quite so soon, if at all. He was still seeing that doctor guy Jason, and he was nice enough. But he didn't like the way he kept asking him about Benny. And neither did Benny, that's for sure. Benny did nothing but scream at him: *Don't tell him anything about us! It's nothing to do with him, it's our secret! He just wants to interfere and cause trouble! DON'T SAY ANYTHING ABOUT US!* Josh had only had a few sessions with Dr Ireland, and he liked him good enough, but he always asked about Benny and that caused other problems for Josh, so things had not really advanced much during their sessions together. But his dad had said he would take Josh next time. This was unusual—normally both parents took him, and when he asked why he was taking him without Mum, his dad just said that he wanted to talk to Dr Ireland on his own. Josh didn't really make much of this, but Benny didn't like it much. He said that now his dad was going to start interfering more, and he didn't like that idea at all. He started to say some nasty things about his dad: *He's always working and you never see him. Are you sure he loves you? I mean really love you, like your mum? I bet he doesn't. I bet he doesn't care at all about you.* Josh had nipped this in the bud, and Benny had backed off, aware he had touched a raw nerve. He didn't want their friendship to deteriorate now, especially as they had not long got back on track. They had work to do with that asshole Rich, and

191

they needed to work as one for that. Benny was busy dreaming up unpleasant scenarios on the matter, but largely kept them to himself, waiting for the right time to pitch them to Josh. He had already suggested they keep an eye out on what he does in break times and after school: *Which way does he go home? Does he walk home or get picked up? Does he have friends with him at break times or is he on his own?* Benny was laying the foundations for a revenge strike, that much was certain. And Josh was aware of this too, and was doing his best to try and avoid any scenario that would get him into more trouble.

Josh was thinking about Alice. They had definitely grown a bit distant from each other since she had expressed her opinion on the compass-stabbing fiasco, and Josh was sad about this. He was constantly trying to think of ways to make things *proper* again with his best friend, but there was still a cold undertone to their relationship. He knew that their mums had plans to meet up this weekend, so maybe he would get chance to make it better then, he thought. This cheered him up a little, and he daydreamed of games they could play together to fix their friendship up. Maybe they could play table-tennis in the garage—he knew she liked to play that with him, so he resolved to mention it when he saw her at the end of the day. It was his mum's turn to pick them up today. The car journeys to and from school had been very dull lately, with Alice not hardly saying a word to him and just grunting in response when he tried to talk to her. He made his mind up to try and put it right this weekend.

He came out of his little reverie to realise that he had not only missed nearly all of his science lesson, but it was also nearly time to go home. He glanced across the classroom to his right, and caught sight of Rich Avery. He was busy with his index finger up his nose, inspecting the goods once withdrawn. Benny seized the moment—*look at that fucking pig! We will make him pay for what he did, Josh! He won't know what fucking hit him!* It worked—Josh felt a wave of anger wash through him as he stared. Benny was satisfied his well-timed interjection had achieved its purpose and sank back into obscurity, letting Josh feel his own rage unaided. Josh looked away to avoid being caught staring at Rich, and as he did so, the bell rang. The day was over. He packed his books and pencil case into his bag, and got up from his desk, thinking about how to approach Alice about the weekend rather than wait in stony silence for his mum to turn up, which is what had been happening lately.

As he walked to the school gates (being conscious to avoid that Avery twat), he saw Alice stood there looking down at her feet. He braced himself, put on a bright expression and stopped beside her.

"Hi, Alice! How was your day? Mine was pretty boring." he said, as cheerfully as he could muster. She looked at him and he gave her a small, almost humble smile.

"It was okay, I guess," she replied. The conversation was faltering already, and they had barely said two words to each other. Josh ploughed on doggedly regardless:

"I think our mums are meeting up this weekend, maybe on Saturday. If it's at mine, would you like to play table-tennis? I promise to let you win!" he nudged her playfully with his elbow at this little dig, and was rewarded with a smile. This filled him with new hope that re-kindling their friendship was not beyond limits.

"You won't have to let me win—I'll do that anyway, dumbass," she said, and nudged him back. The smile on her face lit up her pretty little features. Josh's heart flooded with warmth and relief at this tiny, but significant gesture— progress at last! Now all he had to do was keep things on an even keel, and he would have his best friend back. Things were definitely looking up. Benny smouldered away in the back of his mind and wisely decided to keep himself to himself—let Josh be happy for the minute. It wasn't that he didn't want Josh to be happy or have other friends—it was just…well…*he* needed to be his best friend, not Alice. But now was not the time to address this rejuvenated friendship. Not now. There were other things to address rather than Alice. *All in good time,* Benny thought. *All in good time.*

The journey home was much better than of late—Alice and Josh chattered away in the back, and Jen noticed the pair seemed to be getting on bit better than they had recently. She was pleased at this. Just a little bit of normality could make all the difference when every day appeared to bring inexplicable problems and issues, she thought. Josh asked her about Saturday, and his mum agreed that as long as Beth was okay with it then they could play at theirs while their mums caught up on the week's events. Both children were pleased at this, and banter began immediately on how many games they would play, who would serve first, who would win and suchlike. Jen enjoyed their babble, and actually relaxed for the first time in what felt like forever as she pulled into Beth's drive to drop a decidedly more bubbly than usual Alice off. As Beth came out to meet her, it was obvious that she noticed the difference in her little girl straight away, and a happy, slightly surprised smile lit her face. She gave her a kiss, and Alice waved to Jen and Josh before running inside. Beth had a quick chat with her friend, and they cemented plans in for Saturday at the Connelly residence before saying their goodbyes. Josh felt happier than he had for what felt like an eternity, and started wishing the weekend to arrive, already thinking about whether they had a spare ball or not, where were the bats, and had they put the net down or left it up? Benny stayed quiet, just as he had since the end of school. He would just have to grin and bear Alice for the minute; he didn't want to upset Josh. They had things to do. Bad things.

# Chapter Eight

Liam's mind was full of different fragments of thought as he drove Josh to Dr Ireland's clinic. Josh had appeared continuously depressed to Liam for what seemed like forever, but in reality it was a couple of months since all this had started with his son and his unruly behaviour. He was far less patient than his mother, and so rather than lose his temper with Josh all the time, he simply detached himself from the situation and threw himself into his work. He had no issues with this, as his job was demanding, regardless of what was going on elsewhere in his life. He had been well-practised in the art of detachment since he'd been doing the job, so it became easy to simply not think about any of it—which is exactly what he had been doing. He realised that this was not a long term solution to dealing with the issues—*perhaps this little outing is a baby step in taking a different approach to it all,* he thought. He had tried to make some light conversation with his son, but this had fallen at the first hurdle. Josh was moody, worried and sulky all rolled into one. He quickly gave up, and thanked God it wasn't a long trek to get to the clinic.

Jason came out of his office, and motioned for Liam to go in. He told Josh he wouldn't be a minute and left him in reception. Sally instantly took him under her wing, and after Jason had closed the office door they had a quick chat about how the session was going to work. Jason suggested that he talk to Josh alone in order to get as much background as possible and then talk to Liam, also alone. Liam agreed—he was happy to go with what Jason thought was best. He left the office, and Josh went in. Jason asked him to sit down and make himself comfortable, and wasted no time in trying to pick the young boy's brain. First he asked him about school, and what was different between before and after the incident with Alex, if anything. Josh wasn't overly communicative about this subject, and had to be prompted all along by Jason. In response, he got mostly grunts and murmurs. Jason persisted, and after a few minutes he started to make progress. This came after talking to him about his friends, and Josh and brightened a little as he talked to the doctor about Alice, about how things weren't right but had got better only yesterday, and he was seeing her tomorrow. Jason grabbed hold of this line of conversation, and slowly but surely, Josh began talking more freely about school in general. Occasionally Jason tapped away at his keyboard, but his style was that he didn't want perfect note-taking to interrupt the flow he had struggled to establish. Carefully, he shifted his topic of conversation onto peripheral areas, to Josh's behaviour, and of course, inevitably—Benny. Jason was hoping and praying that Josh wouldn't clam up on this—he was keen to delve into their special friendship now more than ever. Initially, Josh appeared to retreat away from the subject of Benny, but Jason's calculated, experienced approach enabled him to engage his subject. He asked Josh whether Benny felt any sadness at what had happened. Josh replied that he didn't think so, because he didn't like Alex. He asked him whether *he* felt any remorse, and Josh said that he did—it had caused a lot of problems and upset his parents, and he didn't like that. Jason paused his questioning to think. In order to create a natural break in proceedings, he offered Josh some juice from a small fridge in the corner of the office, and asked him to come and choose what he wanted. It gave Jason time to come to the conclusion that Josh didn't really care about what had actually happened to Alex, he cared about the fact he had upset his mum and dad. He thought that if there was an option to do the same action but with no fallout, then Josh would still have done what he did. This unsettled him slightly, as it drew a parallel with Benny's feelings on the matter, from what Josh had said earlier. He couldn't shake the feeling that there was more to Benny than met the eye, he just couldn't put his finger on it. Was he more of an entity in his own right, or was Josh using him merely as a scapegoat for his own ends?

Dr Ireland finished his session with Josh on a lighter note, asking about what he and Alice were going to do on Saturday when they saw each other. Josh got more animated and even almost excited as he relayed their plans, and Jason was pleased he had managed to wrap things up in a positive way. This meant that Josh would leave hopefully with good thoughts on the session, rather than feeling negative and reluctant to return next time. As Josh left, his dad entered, giving his son a brief hug as he did so. It occurred to Liam that physical contact with his son had been limited to a goodnight kiss for ages. He felt a significant pang of guilt at this thought as he settled into Jason's office. The two men talked around the background of the subject for a while, and Jason made more computer notes than when he was with Josh. This was mostly due to the fact that Liam was easy work compared to Josh, and he didn't need to work as hard on controlling the direction of conversation. They were both coming from the same angle, and wanted to shed some light on what was going on and how to fix it.

"One thing is for sure, Liam—his 'friend' is definitely playing a major part in his behaviour. At least, the behaviour that's causing the problems. He is adamant that Benny is behind most, if not all, of it. I also think that there's not an awful lot of remorse being experienced by your son. He doesn't like the idea of being punished, or causing you and his mother upset, but I get the impression he would quite happily do any given action prompted by his imaginary companion if there were no real consequences for him. This worries me a great deal, Liam. The reason being is that regret and remorse are very real, powerful emotions that are felt by *all* humans that have a rational, normal thought process. The absence of these base emotions indicates a leaning towards a few mental health dysfunctions, such as narcissism for example. Or sociopathy. A general lack of empathy for one's fellow man." Jason paused, reflecting on what he had just said, allowing Liam time to process the implications of the doctor's opinion. Liam had a feeling that he wouldn't like what Dr Ireland may tell him during this session, and this confirmed it. *Great, my eight-year-old son has all the makings of a fucking serial killer or something. That's all I need.*

"Well, I can't say I'm overly happy to hear your prognosis, Jason. I was kind of hoping that this was just a stage or phase he's going through, and that it would even out in time—but from what you've just said, this doesn't sound likely. Maybe I've been a little too optimistic about the problems we are facing with Josh. It's probably about time Jen and me came out of denial and look at our options to try and rectify the situation." Liam paused and then added "That's assuming that this type of behaviour *can* actually be rectified?" He looked at Jason with more than a little hopefulness to his voice and expression. No doubt the child psychologist had seen this adorn the faces of desperate, worried parents many times before, and he measured his response accordingly:

"We need to formally assess Josh before jumping to too many conclusions Liam, so if I've scared or alarmed you by what I said, then I didn't mean to. Josh is very young, and not all problems that are either inherent or develop in children are automatically carried forward into adulthood where they have to bear that particular cross for the rest of their lives. There are a great many techniques in our arsenal to try and combat such conditions getting a foothold on someone's life. One thing we have on our side here is the fact that Josh is very young. This means that whatever's going on inside his mind, it hasn't been festering in there for decades." He looked at Liam straight in the eyes, and hoped he could convey a sense of hope to the father on the other side of his desk. He had grown to like Josh and his parents during the course of their sessions, even though this was the first real time he had spoken to Liam on a one to one basis—both Jen and Liam were with Josh every time they had come here since the initial consultation.

"Okay, first steps—let me collate all of my notes from our previous sessions with Josh into a more concise report. Once that's done, I can make a recommendation based on my findings and report conclusions. In nearly all cases such as this, the initial recommendation will be intensive therapy sessions. Probably twice, maybe even three times as often as what we have been doing with Josh to date." Liam looked relieved at this—he had been envisaging strait-jackets and padded cells. He gave his agreement to Jason, asking him whether the therapy would differ in approach to what he had already been doing in his previous sessions with Josh. He couldn't help but wonder if Jason had been dealing with many other kids with similar issues, and a small part of him wished this to be the case. This thought somehow normalised what they were going through with their son to him. Jason drew their meeting to a close by saying he would email him and Jen summarising what had taken place today, and his initial action plan. He told Liam there would be more detail in the mail as to what the therapy sessions would entail, whether they should be present during these times, and an outline timescale for the treatment. When Liam asked him what other courses of action may be available if therapy proved non-productive, Jason answered him carefully.

"There *are* other options if therapy proves ineffective, Liam. But let's not jump the gun, here. Most conditions are able to be managed by therapy, and almost completely eradicated in some cases. This is what we need to focus on, as the alternative almost always involves drug treatment. Even though the available drugs are very effective in most instances, it's not a path I would choose to go down in the first instance with any patient. Especially such a young child like Josh." Liam nodded in acknowledgement at what Jason had said. He didn't want to go down that path either if he could help it, and was fairly sure Jen would be horrified at any such thought. *Let's hope this child shrink can untangle my son's mind before it gets knotted up beyond repair,* he thought pensively. The frown stayed on his face for the entirely of their return journey home as he contemplated the best way to relay what had been said at the clinic to his wife, who was already working herself out of her own mind with relentless worry.

# Chapter Nine

Jen was keen to hear all about the session with Jason, and pounced on Liam as soon as he stepped through the door. After Josh had sorted himself a drink of milk, he asked whether he could go into the garage—he wanted to check the table-tennis stuff in anticipation of Alice's visit tomorrow, and make sure they had everything to hand. This was good timing for Jen and Liam, as they would be able to discuss the ins and outs of Jason's plans for Josh.

Once Liam had told Jen the suggested route of therapy and the reasons behind it, she remained quiet and thoughtful for a moment. Her expression on her pretty, normally bright and breezy face was a little troubled. She obviously didn't like the idea that her beautiful, perfect son actually needed *therapy*. It just felt all wrong to her. She was still being nagged by the feeling that this stupid twin at FMA was somehow involved with all this business with Josh, the behaviour, the violent episode and all the little things that had happened with Josh over the last few months. Even though his imaginary friend was not new on the scene, she still felt that it was kind of coming to the fore and affecting Josh. Finally she met her husband's eyes and said:

"Well, I just can't believe our lovely boy is having to go through this. But if Jason says it's the best option for him and us, then let's do it. And hope he can straighten our son's head out before anything else happens or goes wrong." She sighed, resigned to the mess they were in, and the unenviable task ahead for all concerned to try and make things better. *But it won't get any better... I know it won't...because we need to get rid of this fucking twin, it's at the bottom of all this shit,* she thought. She wisely decided not to vocalise her thoughts on the matter—Liam was already on the verge of thinking she was a nutcase for having this opinion about FMA and the twin. At least, that's what she thought. In reality, Liam didn't think this at all—he thought that his wife was looking for a reason to explain it all, as is often the case for people who are in denial about things. She needed something tangible to pin the blame on, and FMA came out conveniently on top, especially since her clandestine visit to see that psycho-alcoholic woman. *She's definitely a victim of paranoia, looking for an excuse for her own child's death, and now has managed to infect my wife with her crazy, obsessive reasoning too,* he thought. He wisely decided not to go there with Jen, not now anyway. It was best to let sleeping dogs lie for the moment, and get the therapy underway. He told Jen that he thought they should both attend the sessions, even if only to sit in the waiting room. She agreed, and volunteered to ring Jason to have a chat with him and book their first appointment. Liam took this as a positive, and so they let the conversation finish on a high. Jen told Liam that Josh and Alice seemed to be on a better footing after the other day, and this may be a good thing—perhaps it would take his mind off things a little bit. Liam was pleased about this as well, and they both were looking forward to seeing their friends over the weekend as it had been a little while since they'd had an evening together.

Josh wandered in from the garage. "It's all set, for the greatest table-tennis match the world has ever known!" he announced dramatically. "Alice doesn't stand a chance against my skill," he added confidently. His parents engaged him in this, glad to have some level of normal interaction with their son instead of doom, gloom, frowns, and awkward conversations about what went on inside his head. In the next instant, there was more boasting of prowess, and smiles and laughs graced the Connelly household for the first time in what felt like forever. The simple banter worked its magic, and for Jen it felt like a looming grey cloud had been lifted from her family. She basked in it, and it served to remind her just how much she had taken their ordinary 'old' life for granted. She vowed never to take *anything* for granted again.

Saturday was busy at the Connelly's, in preparation for their neighbours. Jen bustled in the kitchen for most of the morning while Liam went out for supplies, taking Josh with him so Jen could crack on unhampered. By the time they returned, the house smelt divine due to Jen's efforts of putting tray after tray of home-made party food in the oven. Both father and son immediately began picking at what was on offer, with Jen scolding them mildly and encouraging them to leave some for their guests. Liam was busy loading the fridge with wine and beers when the doorbell rang. Jen hollered for them to come in, and they bustled in through the door. Alex and Beth had brought some of their own supplies and had their arms full, while Alice immediately rushed ahead of them looking for Josh. No sooner she had found him in the kitchen, Josh announced they were going into the garage to play "the greatest table-tennis battle known to man." Both women were pleased that their kids were kind of getting back to normal with each other, and this was the topic for the first ten minutes between them, while the men wasted little time in depleting the fridge. The fact that the beers had not had time to chill didn't appear to stop them, and Liam chose two that had come from the supermarket fridge, so at least it wasn't warm. The garage door was slightly ajar, which allowed the grown-ups to hear the muffled, excited voices drift through to the kitchen. In the garage, Josh was busy telling Alice how many games they should play, and whose bat was whose. He explained to Alice they only had two balls, so they must be careful not to squash or lose them, a solemn, serious expression on his face. As they took their positions at each end of the table, Josh thought about who should serve first. Benny seized the opportunity to have an input: *Don't let her go first, you idiot! She will have the best chance of winning if you do!* Josh thought about this, while Alice at the other end of the table picked a loose piece of rubber from her bat. He hit the ball over the net to her.

"Ladies first—you can serve, Alice. You're gonna need all the help you can get anyway!" he joked. Alice caught the ball neatly. *You fucking idiot! You should have served! I hope she beats you now, you fucking loser!* Benny was blatantly not happy about Josh's decision. *Just shut up Benny, and stop ruining my fun for once.* Josh actively pushed his twin to the back of his mind, which only served to incense Benny further. *Have your fucking fun! Ignore me if that's what you want! Have it your way. You'll come running to me when you need me, loser. And when you do, I might not be here. That will fucking teach you, won't it?* Josh did his best to ignore him as they played. He could make amends with Benny later, but at the moment, he wanted to play with Alice. And he didn't want Benny to interfere for once. Just once. And secretly, Josh was pleased he was able to contain him to the back of his mind and thoughts. Benny was not so pleased about this. Not pleased at all.

In the living room of the Connelly's, Adam and Liam were busy chewing the fat about work over a couple of chilled beers. The two men were good friends, and this was reflected in the easy manner in which they spoke with one another— free and easy, and able to speak their minds without double checking they won't offend. They were similar in many ways, which contributed to their friendship. They both had relatively good careers and lovely homes and families. This common ground helped cement their friendship in the first instance. As the beer went down, the topic of conversation moved to Josh, and the recent problems Jen and Liam were facing. Liam told Adam about the psychotherapy sessions that he was engaging in with Josh, and about how this was the first time he had truly been engaged with the problem.

"It's not that I haven't wanted to get more hands on with Josh and try and resolve things," Liam explained. "It's just…well…mums usually deal with this kind of shit. I think I'm a bit heavy handed when it comes to this sort of thing." He paused, arranging his thoughts. The only other people he talked to about it was Jen and Jason, and he felt he was on new territory talking to Adam about it, despite them being good mates. "So, what I mean is, if Alice does something that requires some kind of parental input, who does it generally? I bet it's Beth." He looked at Adam for confirmation and Adam nodded in agreement, taking another gulp of beer.

"Yup, you got that right, mate. She deals almost exclusively with Alice and any tackling of issues." He drained the last of his beer. "And we've talked about it openly too—she's the best one to deal with it, end of. I'm sure it's the same for you and Jen," he added. Liam grabbed Adam's empty can and went to the kitchen to get more refreshments. When he returned, Adam was tapping away on his phone. He set the beer down in front of him and sat down again. After a short silence between the two, Liam continued to talk to Adam about the situation. He explained that he was hopeful that Jason may well be able to resolve their issues by getting Josh's imaginary friend to recede sufficiently into the background, so they can focus on getting Josh back to normal. He went on to tell his friend that Josh had implied that the imaginary friend had been in some way responsible for his behaviour, in particular the vicious attack on the other school kid.

"Liam, it's not unusual for some kids to have an imaginary friend, is it? You hear about it all the time, and it's been well documented for decades, if not centuries. It sounds like Josh is just using his friend as an excuse for what's happened. Kids lie and look to blame others for things all the time," Adam said. *Thank fuck it's not Alice,* he thought, and then instantly felt guilty for it. He wanted to support his neighbours as best he could and not bring anything negative to the party—there was already way too much of that as it was.

"Agreed, mate—but there's another development." Liam took a hefty gulp of his beer and then proceeded to tell Adam about the recent episode with Jen and Naomi. He paused periodically and leant towards the door while relaying the tale in a lowered voice, to check none of the girls had come out of the kitchen. He didn't want Jen to catch him telling Adam this part, really. It was still a sore point between them, and he didn't want to exacerbate the issue. Adam listened intently without interrupting his friend—he obviously needed to get it off his chest. Liam continued, telling Adam about Jen's erratic thoughts once they had discussed it and she had told him where she had been that day.

"I can't help but feel she's looking for answers to Josh's behaviour in all the wrong places, Adam. I mean, come on—it sounds like something out of a fucking science-fiction movie. She's really clutching at straws here, and to be honest I'm really worried about her. This isn't like her at all to act so impulsively and be so irrational." He sighed, an exasperated expression creasing his brow. "Need to be a bit careful I don't end up falling out with her over it, mate." Adam raised his eyebrows at his friend.

"Surely it won't come to that Liam? She's just looking for a reason for Josh's actions. That's normal for a mum. Must be difficult for her to accept her little angel is misbehaving," he said, trying to convince his friend that his wife's departure down this particular rabbit hole was a temporary, desperate search for an answer.

"Well, I'm not having any of it Adam. So it's best she doesn't mention it to me again." He drew another mouthful of beer. "I've never heard her say anything so ridiculous in all my life, to be honest. And I don't think it's helping the situation. Let's just hope Jason can cast Josh's imaginary friend out, and then we can start to untangle this whole sorry mess." Adam raised his glass.

"Here's to that, buddy." The friends clinked glasses and got back to the serious business of Saturday afternoon drinking.

# Chapter Ten

Alice had ended up beating Josh 11–10 at the end of their mammoth table-tennis tournament, and to Josh's surprise, he felt glad she had won. *It's more important we are friends,* he told himself. He had finished up the weekend feeling happy for the first time in ages, and he realised he missed that feeling a lot. Things had been far from normal for the boy of late. Alice felt happy too—she was also glad to have her friend back, and acting a little more like the Josh she used to know. Even his mum and dad seemed more relaxed after seeing their neighbour friends. There was no talk at all about Dr Ireland and the clinic (although he knew there would be another appointment soon), or Benny either. He had been quiet all weekend, even after Alice had left, but Josh knew it was only a matter of time before he piped up in the forefront of his mind, like a recurring dream. And not always a nice dream, at that.

And sure enough, right on cue as Josh lay in bed waiting to succumb to sleep, there he was. *I let you have this weekend with Alice and didn't interfere, Josh. It's obvious you like her more than me, so I hope you're very fucking happy together. She won't be there to help you when you need it—I will. So you think about that, and about who you like the most.* Josh had been dreading this encounter with Benny, but knew it was only a matter of time before it happened. Benny had always been there, in the back of his mind, and it didn't appear he was going away anytime soon. This thought prompted Josh to think about whether he actually *wanted* him to go away—normally, they were fine together. Benny offered Josh an escape from the real world, and this was often a welcome reprieve from the drudgery of school, homework, and the countless other activities that Josh found to be a chore. He stopped his life from being boring as he always had someone to talk to, even when he was alone. *It's not that I like Alice more than you, Benny. It's just I wanted to have a nice time with her, that's all. I would feel better about things if you didn't get mad at me for that. She's nice. Why don't you like her?* Josh responded, but Benny had gone quiet—as quickly as he had voiced his opinion, he had disappeared again. Josh turned over in his bed and tried to put him to the back of his mind and fall asleep. As he did so, Benny had one last thing to say on the matter. *I don't think she's good for you, Josh. She can't help you and protect you like I can. She can't get even with that cunt Avery can she? But I can help there. And you know I can.*

Josh had a restless nights' sleep following his exchange with Benny, and woke up feeling a little groggy and tired. He felt a little better once he'd had a bowl of cereal and some orange juice for breakfast, and he got dressed quickly after—he didn't want his mum getting upset that he was making them late, especially as the weekend had seemed so nice with his mum and dad. It was Jen's turn to take him and Alice to school and he was looking forward to seeing her, even if it was inevitable she would boast about her table-tennis win. Sure enough, when Alice clambered into the car the first thing she said (after saying good morning to Jen) was how she beat Josh hands down on Saturday. Josh engaged in some light-hearted banter with her on this matter, vowing to teach her a lesson next time. He asked his mother when they could do it again, and Jen responded she would talk to his dad and Alice's mum and dad about another get-together soon: *Let's get this week out of the way first, it's half term soon so let's see what we can do then,* she responded. This satisfied both children for the time being, and they settled into some school chatter in the back as Jen drove. She didn't want to feel too hopeful that things may be getting back on an even keel with her son, but couldn't help but bask in some of the pleasure of hearing them both in the back of the car sounding like two perfectly normal school-mates. *Maybe we can get this thing under control now. And get back to living a normal life,* she thought. As she dropped them both off at the gates she couldn't help but think that this may well be the beginning of the end of the worst chapter in her life.

The week went without anything too eventful happening, both at school for Josh and at home for the Connelly's (and the Gleeson's for that matter). This was fine with both families, but especially fine for the Connelly's, for obvious reasons. Things seemed less fraught between Liam and Jen—it was almost as if the totally normal activity of getting together with their friends had somehow reset their boy into being normal again. Neither parent dared utter this out loud to the other (probably for an illogical superstitious reason of jinxing it), but both were quietly happier than they had been in months. Liam had made another appointment for Josh the following week, and had gained Jen's approval by doing so—she had not had to prompt her husband into doing it.

The phone call came on Friday afternoon, not long after Jen had returned from shopping. Her Fridays were sacred as she no longer worked on that day, and she had been looking forward to actually putting her feet up for an hour with a glass of wine after her busy morning of housework and grocery shopping. But as she looked at her mobile screen, her heart filled with dread—it was the school. She answered it, and was greeted by the deep tone of the headmaster, Mr Matthews. The feeling of dread intensified, and she felt worry creep inside her head like a slimy sewer rat.

Mr Matthews didn't waste any time. "Mrs Connelly, unfortunately we've had another incident here at the school involving your son. If you're available, I'd strongly suggest you come down here so we can discuss the matter. It's serious, and I have placed Josh in supervised detention until such time you can get here." Jen's stomach did a slow queasy roll. *I knew it was too good to be true—this is a fucking never-ending living hell,* she thought. She responded by saying she had a day off and would be at the school as soon as possible, probably about half an hour. They said their goodbyes and Jen quickly hurried upstairs to brush her hair, her mind whirling with all kinds of dark thoughts about what Josh had done now. Mr Matthews had declined to give any details, so the sooner she got to the school and found out, the better. Within five minutes she was in the car and on her way, chewing her bottom lip unconsciously while driving on auto-pilot. Twenty minutes later she was sat in the headmaster's office, facing him across the desk. Mr Matthews had a stern, worried expression on his face that made his already bushy grey eyebrows look even bigger. He was a large man, in both weight and height and his face was suitably proportioned—ruddy jowls framed his mouth and nose and his forehead was creased with frown lines—years of disapproving looks aimed at pupils had cemented the expression Jen faced. Even though his appearance seemed formidable and stern, Mr Matthews was actually a very fair headmaster, and he was generally well liked by staff, pupils, and parents alike. Jen was no exception to this—at parent's evenings and school events she had also found him pleasant. The trouble was, she seemed to be seeing him for all the wrong reasons lately. Her stomach was still knotted with worry, and her head still reeling and whirling with the impending dread of the conversation she was about to have. Mr Matthews had asked Jen if she wanted tea or coffee—she politely declined, and as a nervous afterthought, said that maybe a brandy would be more appropriate, in a vain attempt to bring some levity to the situation—it failed.

"Josh has got himself into bother again, Mrs Connelly. Another episode of violence towards another pupil, another boy." Jen asked him what had happened, and the headmaster explained that earlier at lunchtime, he had attacked a boy called Rich Avery. Josh had hit him repeatedly in the side of the head with a stone. The stone wasn't very big, but big enough to inflict considerable injury—the boy had been taken to hospital.

"Hopefully his skull isn't fractured, and head wounds have a habit of looking worse than they actually are due to bleeding. But it's the second serious attack on another pupil in a relatively short period of time, Mrs Connelly. We at the school are all worried about the welfare of all of our pupils, Josh included. We are concerned about his sudden shift into erratic, violent behaviour. Have you any thoughts as to what may have triggered this?" The question was direct, and Mr Matthews sat back in his chair as Jen processed what may or may not be being implicated here. Jen's head was spinning with a hundred and one different thoughts and worries, and she just stared at him, at a complete loss for words. The headmaster obviously was expecting some kind of shock reaction from this type of news, and remained impassively sat across from the poor woman in his office. He had a base knowledge of Josh and his parents and knew they were good people. God knew he had dealt with far worse parents in his time. He was glad that Jen and her husband were reasonable people. Eventually, Jen found her tongue.

"I really don't know what to say, Mr Matthews. Josh's behaviour recently has been awful, and it's completely baffled Liam and myself. We don't know what's gotten into him lately." She paused. "We are taking him to see a child psychologist. He's had a few sessions already, and we are now undergoing a formal assessment program—it starts this week." The headmaster was looking at her intently, but with an air of sympathy. He rubbed his ample chin thoughtfully. When the incident had been reported to him by Mrs Cotter, he immediately knew what the sequence of events would have to be for the troubled young man. Mrs Cotter herself had been visibly shaken up, and was trembling as she relayed the incident to him. She had been in the playground—there was a loose rota for teachers to keep an eye on things at breaks and lunchtimes. As long as there was an adult presence there in one form or another, no one got too hung up on who it was, whether it was someone else's turn, or whatever. Some teachers relished it more than others, and Mrs Cotter, a thin, stick-like lady in her mid-thirties, was happier out in the fresh air than in the staff room. She did more than her fair share of playground patrolling, and was happy to do so. She loved the children—part of this was to do with the fact she couldn't have any of her own. She and her husband had discussed adoption in the early days of their marriage once they found out she was infertile, but had never followed it up. She found she could get her fix from her profession, and they had settled for that. As she had strolled around the corner of the main building, a highly excited George Davis had run up to her, panting and out of breath.

"Miss...there's a fight! Josh Connelly hitting Rich Avery's head with a stone! He's hitting him *hard!*" he stammered, turning his head and pointing. George's face had been red with excitement and nervous energy. She wasted no time, and ran over to the far side of the playground. Here, there was now a small gathering of children. She couldn't see anything due to the cluster of small bodies. As she approached, she could hear guttural grunts entwined with wails of pain. As she pushed the children out of the way, the scene unfolded in front of her, sending shock waves through her mind. *Jesus...what the fuck...he's going to kill him!* She thought, panicked by the situation. Josh was sat on top of Rich Avery, on his chest. His right hand was raised, and she could just make the stone out in his clenched fist as he brought it down on the side of the boy's head. She heard the crunch of the impact, and for a split-second felt sick to her stomach. She instinctively cried out:

"Josh! Stop that...what are you doing, you're going to kill him!" She was within arm's length of the boy, and grabbed his arm by the wrist as he drew it back for another downward swipe. Josh seemed in a daze. He looked up almost in surprise at the source of the unexpected force that was stopping his fist from crashing down again. Rich was pretty much motionless, and couldn't have moved much anyway with Josh sat astride his chest with his body weight on him. He was moaning in pain though—*Thank God he's conscious...and alive,* she thought. Her instinct kicked in and she applied upward force to his arm, dragging him off the other boy's body. She then used her other hand to prise the stone out of his grasp, and threw it away towards the perimeter fence. Blood from the makeshift weapon smeared across her palm and again a nauseous wave flooded into her stomach. Looking down at Rich, he was now moving his upper body in small, twisting motions. There was blood on the grass beside him, and all over the left side of his head and face. She looked around her at the five or so stunned faces and found George's.

"Go and find another teacher—anyone—and get them to call an ambulance, straight away!" She told him. George immediately scuttled off. "Josh, don't you dare move—I need to check Richard," she looked at him with a mixture of anger and upset. She taught Josh English and drama, and he had always been one of her top pupils. She had heard about the previous incident a few months back, and remembered thinking how out of character such a vicious attack was for the normally mild mannered boy. Yet here she was, dealing with another violent episode from him. Josh still seemed slightly dazed, as if it had been him taking the blows to the head, rather than delivering them—he looked detached from the whole thing, and said nothing in response to her instruction. She knelt down to the boy with the bloody head laid on the grass before her. His eyes fluttered open and his brow creased at her.

"Don't move, Richard. Help is coming. Can you speak?" She brushed his hair off his forehead in order to try and get a better look at the damage inflicted to his head. It was on one side only, but it looked nasty. Very nasty. There was a lot of blood that had plastered his hair to his head and face, some of it soaked into the white collar of his school shirt. Mrs Cotter didn't regard herself as being particularly squeamish—Saturday nights often consisted of horror movies—but real life was different, and her stomach did an uneasy, slow flip as if in confirmation of this fact. She didn't need to check his pulse as he was conscious, and his eyes open.

"Owww, my head... I feel sick," Rich stuttered, in a low groan. He instinctively tried to move his hand to his head, but the teacher knelt over him placed her hand on his, resisting his movement. "Shhhh...just try to keep calm and still until help gets here," she told him soothingly. She tried to get a better look at his wound. His hair was matted around his left temple, the blood clotting fast and turning everything into a dark crimson mat. There was fresh un-clotted blood there too, but there appeared to be no large amounts of blood coming directly from the wound. *Maybe it's not as bad as it looks,* she thought hopefully. There was now a bigger circle of school children around her, their morbid curiosity drawing them to the scene. More kids were wandering their way, too. She didn't bother telling them to go away, but instructed them to stay back. She didn't want them going home to Mum and Dad full of horror stories from the playground. She looked up, and through the throng of littler bodies she saw Mr Matthews approaching, bustling his large form across the playground in large strides. He had less patience with the pupils of his school, and ushered them all away as he got closer, shooing them as if they were troublesome cats under his feet. They didn't need to be told twice—the show was over. He knelt beside Mrs Cotter and the boy, out of breath.

"Oh Jesus," he said, as he looked at the head wound. "Ambulance will be about five minutes. What the hell happened?" he asked. Mrs Cotter explained what she had seen, but was mindful of Josh still stood nearby. As she relayed the story, Mr Matthews looked over at Josh. After a minute he got up and approached a motionless Josh. After a few words, they walked off together, headed for his office.

"Mrs Connelly, as you're more than aware, this is the second violent outburst in a relatively short period of time. Both incidents are very serious with regards to the damage inflicted on other pupils, first Alex, and now Richard. I have no choice but to expel your child from the school." He looked at her gravely. Jen's hand was covering her mouth and her eyes had sprung leaks. She wanted to say something, but no words came. "I wish you all the luck with his treatment. The school will stay in touch with you and your husband, certainly for the next few months as there are reports and follow-up actions to be done—we will keep you informed of the formal decisions that are made, and all documentation that you have a right to be privy to. In the meantime, I think it's best you take young Josh home straight away." He stood up, signalling the end of their meeting. Jen struggled with her emotions. She had managed to stop the deluge of tears that threatened to release from escaping, but her emotions were running high. Her nightmare had just gotten worse—and after being given hope at the weekend that things may be on the up, this blow hit her twice as hard. A small whimper escaped her, and she nodded to the headmaster in acknowledgement of his request. He picked up his desk phone and pressed a button. He spoke, telling the other end of the line that she would collect her son from reception in a minute. They said their goodbyes and Jen left the office, her tears running freely now.

# Chapter Eleven

Jen couldn't call Liam in the car to tell him what had happened—she didn't want Josh hearing that particular conversation, and felt it was too serious a topic for a text message, so she waited until they were both home. She sent Josh to his room—this was always going to be the case—and phoned Liam once she was happy Josh was in his room with his door closed. He picked up straight away, and Jen wasted no time in telling him what had happened. She cried through it all. She hadn't really stopped since being at the school, and her eyes and face were red and puffy with emotion. On the way home in the car, she thought about the times before all this horrid stuff with Josh had started—he had been the perfect son. No problems at home, none in school, always cheerful, bright, inquisitive and generally a joy to be around—he was the apple of both their eyes. Her heart felt like it was actively aching to be back there, instead of this living hell that she ploughed through every day for what seemed like an eternity now. Life had appeared to throw her and Liam the cruellest of curve balls, and she was having trouble dealing with it. She needed Liam's support.

"WHAT? Yet *another* kid beat up? Jesus, when will this end? Fuck's sake! Well, he will be getting it both barrels from me, Jen. This all absolutely has to stop. I've had a gut load of it. I'm on my way in twenty minutes—got a few bits to do before I leave, I'll see you soon. We can tackle him then. Love you." Jen listened to his outburst, not surprised at his reaction. They both were at the end of their tether with their son, and the frayed ends were well and truly showing in both of them. Their lives had been thrown into turmoil—Liam was finding it increasingly more difficult to concentrate in work, and was generally morose when at home. His interaction with Josh was at an all-time low. There were no longer any Saturday afternoon kick-abouts in the garden with a football. No more trips to the local pool, or even the park. A similar effect was happening with Jen. She found herself detaching from her husband and son in a way that that worried her. Was it a bizarre self-coping mechanism? This was all alien to her, which added to her fretting and worry. Her marriage seemed to be just rolling on in the background, completely overshadowed by Josh and his issues. God, when was the last time they cuddled each other, let alone anything else? They hadn't made love to each other in what felt like an eternity—and what's more, she didn't really want to either. Jen had the distinct impression that Liam felt the same way. They were both just so consumed by recent events, she supposed. *Nothing feels right any more,* she thought. *What if Naomi was right? About the twin…could it really be at the bottom of all this…? Surely not…? But she had said her daughter was affected before her death…oh God, what if Josh ended up the same way…* She was giving herself the creeps, and tried to stop thinking about it, actively pushing it to the back of her mind. She simply had to talk to Liam about this FMA thing again, and try and make him understand. Even though it had been discussed previously between them, she didn't feel he quite understood the potential implications of this twinning program. He hadn't seen Naomi, and the devastation she had been through with Sammi. If he had, then he might well feel differently. She knew it sounded like half-baked hocus-pocus, straight out of an eighties sci-fi film, and Liam had made it clear that's how he viewed it last time. But she couldn't shake it. She kept re-visiting her encounter with Naomi, the emptiness that she had seen in her sunken eyes, her life devastated by her loss. It scared her when her train of thought tried to parallel her experience with Naomi's…she couldn't even begin to think what a bleak future like that might be like.

Liam pulled onto the drive with a face like thunder. Instantly, Jen's heart sank even lower than it already was—there was going to be fireworks for sure. She would have to make sure he didn't get too carried away. He came in and said "Where is he?" She looked upstairs. As he started to climb them, she caught his arm. He looked at her, his face full of angry colour and his expression resolute. He didn't look like a man to be messed with at this particular moment in time, that was for certain.

"Please Liam—go as easy as you can. We don't know what's going on inside his head, but it's not good. Let's not make it any worse than it already is." She looked at him pleadingly, and his expression softened. He was also aware that things weren't good between them—not good full stop, in fact. Even through his simmering anger, he didn't want to make things any worse than they already were. He squeezed her arm.

"We can talk to him together, hon. But he has to learn that there are consequences—when will it end? We can't allow him to go on doing these things." He exhaled and rubbed his forehead. He didn't even know what he intended to say or do to his son. So many emotions were exhausting him—worry, anger, self-pity. Jen nodded, and they went upstairs. Josh was laid on his bed, face down. Quiet sobs were coming from him, muffled by the bedding. Instantly, Jen's heart melted. *My darling boy is so dreadfully unhappy…and now we, his Mum and Dad, want to make it worse for him…and us, too.* Liam also softened, and stayed stood by the door while Jen sat on the bed and gently nudged her son. He turned slightly to look at his mother, both of their faces red and blotchy from too many tears.

"Oh Josh—what are we going to do?" she murmured, her voice cracking with sadness. Josh sat up, his chest still hitching with sobs. He looked incapable of inflicting any damage onto anyone at that moment; he was just a scared, upset little boy that needed his parents.

"I don't know mum! It's just that… I… I just can't stop him from making me do it! I wish he would leave me alone!" he exclaimed, his face pulled into an exasperated, frightened mask of misery. She looked at Liam, who also wore a mask of exasperation. *How can I punish him?* What *can I punish him with, anyway? He's punishing himself more than we ever could,* he thought.

They stayed with Josh in his room for about half an hour. Jen did most of the talking—even though Liam had been fired up to let Josh know exactly how he felt about violence, his son's behaviour, and the downward spiral of events, the actual sight of his distraught son had taken the fire from his belly. He just felt desperately sad and upset, just like Jen. He was not a stupid man; he was watching the disintegration of the very thing he held the most dear—his family. He vowed to himself that he would do everything in his power to resolve this mess. He would talk to Jen later about the clinic, and the trials. About how they can set about mending this horrible mess and get back on an even footing with their lives. Jen, on the other hand, was also keen to talk to her husband—but her agenda would involve FMA, and how exactly they were going to terminate their involvement with them before things got out of hand. *Fuck, things are* already *well out of hand,* she thought. During their exchanges with Josh, no real punishment was laid down. Jen explained that he would have to stay at home for the foreseeable future, and didn't have to explain to him why. Josh remained quiet for most of it, with just a morose sob being emitted every now and then.

Both parents left their son's room feeling awful. They remained fairly quiet downstairs, as did Josh upstairs. It was like a huge black cloud of misery had settled directly over their house, leaving the rest of the world unaffected and unaware of the suffering going on under its roof. Both were apprehensive about the evening's agenda of discussing what their next move should be, and getting a plan to try and resolve the world of shit they had been unceremoniously plunged into. After a light tea (they ate together in the kitchen, mostly in silence), Josh was yet again told to go to his room, under the premise that "Mum and Dad need to talk." Liam ploughed straight in with his thoughts about the clinic, trials, and Dr Ireland. He was obviously pinning all his hopes that they would be able to get treatment for their son via this route, and he went back over all the things Jason has said about the trials and potential outcomes. Jen listened patiently, although she had heard most of this before—they had talked immediately after the appointment with the clinic, two weeks ago. At that point, Jen was as hopeful as Liam for a real result. Josh was definitely in the right hands. Now, her view was a little jaded and cloudy on the subject, due to her ever increasing thoughts about FMA and the twin. She let her husband talk himself out as she quietly listened, sipping her glass of wine intermittently. *Best I let him vent it all, then I've got the best chance of getting him on side with what we need to do with FMA,* she thought, as Liam continued. Once done, he looked at her expectantly, awaiting her response. He was sure that Jen's response would be positive—after all, what other hope did they have? She paused and looked at her husband.

"Of course, I think the trials are a good idea, Liam. There's no doubt of that, and I'm 100% behind the whole thing, as you obviously are. But I can't help thinking about something else that I think is affecting our boy. It's this whole imaginary friend thing. And I can't help constantly thinking about Naomi, and what she told me about her daughter… I'm worried sick that there's something weird going on and we don't know what it is, Liam." She paused, trying to gauge Liam's reaction to this. They had already touched on the same subject when she had returned from her excursion to see Naomi, and he had been largely dismissive, as she recalled. She hoped that she wouldn't get the same closed-door reaction now. Liam's brow was furrowed following Jen's response to his dialogue. *Here we go again…we've been here before. But I can't just brush her thoughts under the carpet this time,* he thought. He took her hands in his. She looked at him almost desperately, willing him to be open-minded about the whole thing, but scared of what may come out of his mouth next at the same time. He sighed and squeezed her hands with his.

"Jen, I really wish there was a sure-fire explanation for all this with Josh, I really do…but just listen to yourself, just for a second. Please—just think about what you're saying is the cause of our son's problems. Are you really telling me that you believe—and I mean *really* believe that the twin at FMA, which we invested in for his well-being, is behind all this? How? How on earth can FMA have anything to do with all this?" He looked at her, desperate for her to see sense.

"I just can't shake it, Liam. If you had been there and seen that poor woman… I know it sounds crazy, fuck, there's not a moment goes by that I don't think the same, but it's stuck in my mind and I can't shake it. I am just so petrified that things are going to get worse! Oh God, I just don't know what to do Liam! I'm so scared!" She cracked, and hot, salty tears made their way down her flushed cheeks yet again. She wiped them away almost absent-mindedly with the back of her hand: *It seems like I'm always fucking crying nowadays,* she thought. Liam moved closer to his wife and held her in an attempt to comfort her. It worked to an extent, but Jen was now getting towards the distraught, frayed ends of her emotions. Liam's brain was now doing overtime. *She found out about this crazy bitch from Janet,* he thought, back tracking to their initial conversation about her day trip to the south coast. *Janet made her swear not to tell anyone…but she had to tell me. Why would she want to keep it a secret if there was nothing in it?* He pondered this as he hugged his wife, stroking her forehead thoughtfully. *Maybe John knows more,* he thought. He suddenly realised that he was actually considering the validity of what Jen was saying for the first time since her liaison with Naomi. He thought long and hard before opening his mouth, and finally said:

"Well, how about I talk to John about this? Maybe he can shed more light on the matter. But don't be too hopeful—he works for FMA, so I doubt he will say anything too detrimental about them," he said softly to Jen. She pulled away from him in order to see his face. She touched his cheek gently.

"Thank you Liam. I mean, I really don't know…it may all be a load of horse-shit, for all I know…but I think after Naomi's experience, I don't think we should take any chances. I mean…she was absolutely *convinced* that Sammi's twin was the cause of her death. She tied the fire at the lab and her own daughter burning to death on the same night—*the same fucking night*—together, and I can see why." She paused, wiping her cheeks again. She was still very upset, but the fact that she had somehow managed to get her husband to at least *consider* that all this may be a factor gave her hope. "Let's just hope to God Naomi was wrong, Liam. Because if she wasn't, then what the fuck are we going to do?" Liam didn't answer, and they remained sat together, locked in an embrace of despair.

Upstairs, Benny was talking to Josh. Well, he was actually talking *at* Josh—the conversation was, up to this point, one sided. *See...? I told you! Your mum and dad haven't even punished you this time! It's because they don't really care! THEY DON'T GIVE A SHIT! You should be grateful Josh! We've got away with it! Little bastard, he was lucky you didn't kill him! I'm surprised his grey brains weren't leaked out all over the floor! Shame we got stopped when we did, if you ask me.* Josh wasn't asking Benny. He just kind of wished he would shut up, but it was easier just to listen to his ranting for the minute. And yes, Rich had deserved it—he fucking started it! Josh had done nothing to the motherfucker, and he had hurt him for no reason, right out of the blue. So, what was he supposed to do? Just take it? Just let him beat his fucking head in, just lie down and take a kicking from anyone in the world that felt like doing it? It may not have felt right after it had been done, when sitting in the reception area while his mum was in with the headmaster, but there had to be some justice, surely? Perhaps Benny was right—if someone does something bad to you, then they should pay. And just like that, before he even really knew it, he was mentally agreeing with his friend on the matter. Benny sensed this change of direction in Josh's thoughts, and pounced on it straight away. *No one has the right to hurt us, Josh! I'm here to help you! And make sure these cunts don't get away with it! They will get what's coming to them, whether they like it or not! Together we have proved to each other that we can defend ourselves! That we can SURVIVE!*

# Chapter Twelve

Liam had called John towards the end of the working week. After a quick catch up, Liam asked his friend if he wanted to get together at some point at the weekend for some drinks and a proper social, to which John eagerly agreed...*where to? Mine...? Yours? Do we want to get the wives on board, or is it strictly lads, mate?* Liam thought about this briefly. He wanted to see John and talk crap about football and suchlike, but he also wanted to talk to him about FMA. It would have to be without their respective wives this time. He messaged John back saying he was up for lads only, and they could do it at his. He would see if Jen wanted to spend the night with Janet at her place, a boy and girl swap. They had done this before—last time it was instigated by the women. It worked out nicely for all concerned. He didn't quite know *what* exactly he was going to say to John about FMA...but he knew he would have to broach the subject with his friend, after the recent discussions with Jen. Even if it didn't help make things any clearer for him, it may help his and Jen's alignment on the matter. At least, that was the hope.

When he got in from the office, Jen was in an okay kind of mood. Liam couldn't really expect her to be jumping through hoops in ecstasy really, could he? He didn't exactly feel over the moon, either. It was all getting a little on top—now that Josh was permanently expelled, they needed to think about his education, and potentially consider private tuition, at least for the foreseeable future. Him and Jen bordering on squabbling and worrying about FMA and the twin that resided there in its glass vessel, its cold unseeing fish eyes gazing vacantly outwards. He had been thinking about the twin more often lately...it really was quite a creepy concept, when you took it on face value. A carbon copy of your own offspring housed in a giant test tube, waiting to be butchered in the unfortunate event of an accident, or suchlike. A shiver crept over Liam as the thought bounced around inside his head. He tried to push it all to the back of his mind as he approached Jen about his plans with John. She readily agreed, and immediately began messaging Jane to cement her own plans in. Liam thought she should get out of the house for the night, and said so to Jen. She agreed—she needed some downtime and someone to offload onto, besides Liam.

"How's he been?" Liam asked, raising his eyes upwards towards his son's bedroom. Jen gave a small sigh and told him he'd been okay...but quiet and withdrawn. "I'm going to pop up there and see him for ten minutes or so, love. I really feel that I'm becoming detached from him with all this shit going on all the time, and it's not a nice feeling." He paused, his brow furrowed, as he digested his own words. No, it wasn't a nice feeling. Not nice *at all*. It's always a common belief that dads don't have the same bond with their kids as mums do, but Liam had always been close to his lad, and it felt wrong to have that closeness disrupted in any way. He headed upstairs and left Jen to it. After a quarter of an hour or so, he returned looking more worried than when he went up there. Josh was definitely in the doldrums, and he had had trouble getting any words out of his son. He had tried different subjects, deliberately avoiding the elephant in the room, but still not much came from Josh. Eventually he had put his arm around the small, desperate looking boy and cuddled him. He felt like crying, but the man in him absolutely refused to do so, especially in front of Josh. He was able to maintain his composure, but it was a fine line he was treading with it, for sure. Josh was called down for tea, and his stomach told him to obey—he didn't need telling twice. The three of them sat at the table and ate together, yet again mostly in silence. It seemed false to try and instigate conversation when no one felt like talking, so they didn't. Once finished, Josh looked to go back to his room, but Jen intervened and asked him to come into the lounge and watch some television. Josh agreed, albeit reluctantly, but once he settled in there he was soon absorbed by the cartoon channel. It came as a subconscious relief to both parents—it may have been a simple thing, but this at least was a normal activity in their new living nightmare world.

Saturday evening came around quickly enough, and Jen had said her goodbyes to both her son and husband before backing the car off the drive and making her way to Jane's, armed with wine and snacks. John had already messaged Liam to say he would be there at six, so the timing was perfect. Josh has skulked off to his room once he realised his parents had their own respective plans, and Liam didn't try to stop him. The subject matter he had in mind to discuss with his friend wasn't for Josh's ears, anyway. The doorbell rang, and Liam welcomed his friend into his house. It had been a little while since they had caught up properly, and there was plenty of fat to be chewed as they sat at the dining room table with beer and nuts. Jen had messaged to say she was at Jane's, so all was well with the world.

As time ticked on and the two men slowly exhausted their more trivial topics, the conversation naturally turned to Josh and his recent problems. Liam gave John the lowdown on the latest unpleasant development and outlined the plan with Dr Ireland, which was due to start next week. He also talked about the schooling issue, and the associated problems with Josh not being in school like a normal kid—this subject particularly worried Liam, as he and Jen had no firm plan of attack. He decided to take the bull by the horns (after having a quick check on Josh and telling him it was time for bed), and see what John may have to offer on the subject of the twin. He started by telling his friend about Jen's little trip to see Naomi.

John sat thoughtfully through Liam's retelling, stroking his beard, a light frown on his face. John knew about Naomi. His mind quickly transported him back to when the incident had happened. Quite a few people at FMA had been talking about it—the death of the young girl was front page news, and most top tier employees (the ones like John, that were privy to the client base and records) had the wherewithal to identify the mother as an FMA client. And everybody there had known about the fire. At the time, John, like most of his co-workers, had instantly dismissed any link to the fire at the FMA laboratory and the unfortunate accident that had befallen the young girl. The press had been saying the cause was "a household fire of which the source was unknown." They certainly hadn't been saying "spontaneous combustion associated with a psychically linked clone in an experimental medical facility." But John had thought it was an uncanny coincidence. Enough to talk to his wife about it.

And it was now apparent his wife had been talking to his friend's wife—despite knowing that John had signed a confidentiality agreement at the point of contract with FMA. This stuck in John's throat a little; his fucking bigmouth wife Janet blabbing away, fuck the consequences! Thank God he had the foresight not to tell her about the nutcase woman trying to blow the fucking place up, as no doubt she would have blabbed about that, too. Although that was a moot point now—Naomi had already told Jen all about it. And now he was busy listening to his mate relay it all back to him. But more worrying than all of this was that John had his own thoughts and opinions on this very subject. In actual fact, part of his key development tasks at FMA was an on-going project concerning the investigation and determining whether the twins they had created had any psychic capacity. Namely, with their counterparts in the outside world.

"So—what are your thoughts on all this, John? Jen is convinced that the twin at FMA is somehow linked to Josh's behaviour. Is that even possible?" He took a long slug on his beer. He felt like he could probably do with something stronger, but that would have to wait until he'd had this particular conversation with John. His friend's large, rounded face still had a frown on it, and John ran his fingers repeatedly through his thinning hair.

"Fucking hell, Liam. What a mess. An absolute shit-show. I know you and Jen must be going out of your minds with worry. I can't possibly imagine what it's like, so I'm not even going to pretend I can empathise with what you're going through. I remember the fire at the lab. It was fucking horrendous. FMA were lucky no employees were hurt—and also lucky only one twin was killed. But even that was one too many. Could have been a whole lot worse though." He paused, wrestling with how the rest of this chat should go. *It's already gone further than I'd like, so may as well let it run its course,* he thought.

"Look, I can't tell you that the twin is making Josh do bad things, Liam. How can I possibly say that? They'll have me carted off to the fucking nuthouse, mate. Once they've sacked me, of course. But…in the interests of being straight with you… If I had a kid, I wouldn't invest in a twin." John paused, obviously thinking about the nature of the conversation he was having with his friend. He was bordering on saying things he really shouldn't be saying—hell, it was all but too late to worry about that now, though.

He looked directly at Liam, his eyes fixing on his. "It's all a bit beyond my comprehension to be honest, Liam. Even though I work there, I've helped develop the processes surrounding the technology, I've conducted the tests required to make it all viable—I still can't buy into it. Call me superstitious, but it just feels like we are meddling with Mother Nature just a little bit *too* much. And we all know, she can be an absolute bitch when you fuck with her." He drained the remainder of his now flat beer. "Any more of this on hand, mate? I'm a bit dry after all this chinwagging." He shook his empty can as proof he needed a refill. Liam got up and brought two more chilled ones from the fridge. He was keen to keep the momentum on the conversation though—he felt he needed as many facts (and non-facts, for that matter) as he could get. On his way back into the living room he paused at the foot of the stairs, cocking his head to one side, listening for any signs of activity from Josh's room. All was quiet. It was gone ten, so Josh would be well asleep by now, he thought.

As he sat back down across from John on the sofa, he said, "Well, what if Jen and I decided we didn't want to continue with the twin programme? What happens then? Can I just terminate the contract as if it were home insurance, or something?" He popped the ring on his can and took a slug. John did likewise, before replying:

"Well… I don't think it's that simple, Liam. If you read the contract, you'll find you're tied in until Josh turns eighteen. Once he does, you can effectively pass the contract over to him if you so wish, as he will be an adult in his own right. But even if you do that, and Josh doesn't wish to uphold the agreement, there are still caveats." Liam considered this. He had read (at least he thought he had) the contract at the point of entry, but he guessed that Jen and he had been so caught up in getting it all signed and sealed, that his subconscious had glossed over all these details that John was now citing.

"Eighteen doesn't help us at all, John. Not one fucking bit. The problem is right here, and right now. And I've got to try something—*anything*—to fix it. At this rate, it's gonna blow my family apart. I hate the idea that I am slowly but surely distancing myself from my own son. God, we were so close before all this." He drank, taking large gulps. His mind was now working overtime, chewing over what they had already discussed and new blooms of thought popping up all the time, the alcohol fuelling the haphazard thought process whirling away in his mind. "Or am I just approaching this all wrong? There's no proof that the twin is having any effect on Josh at all. Not a scrap. This batshit crazy woman and her daughter—the whole thing has convinced Jen there's some bizarre link with the twin. And now she's got me thinking it, too. John—there's nothing that's happened previously that you can think of with twins? Apart from Naomi and her daughter?" he looked questioningly at his friend. John was blatantly wrestling with his own conscience, his face a picture of worry, desperately wanting to console his mate, and at the same time acutely aware that he was treading on thin ground with confidentiality. He wrung his hands over and over in his lap, unconsciously.

"None really, Liam. No cases like the Goodman woman, anyway." He took a deep breath and continued. "We did, and continue to do, significant research into this field at FMA. It's an on-going project to be able to fully understand the science of what we are doing there as much as possible. A large amount of funding goes into it, and it forms a major part of my role there. Tests are conducted, results obtained and logged. It's the same as any other medical facility in that respect. Certain test programmes result in nothing of particular interest, and are then put to bed. That avenue is documented, and no further investigative work is undertaken. Other avenues are pursued over longer periods of time, in order to try and understand better the nature of the clones. One of these projects involves brain-wave activity of the twins. We have seen that some are more active than others." He paused to drink. "*Way* more active." He looked at Liam, who was fiddling nervously with the ring pull on his can as he absorbed this.

"What about Josh's twin, John? Is there any extra brain-wave activity, or whatever the fuck it is, with that one? How can I find out?" His mind was racing. "If it did have a super active brain or brain-waves or whatever, does that link to any kind of... I don't fucking know...psychic ability?" he could barely believe what he had just said. The words sounded ridiculous, and he felt ridiculous saying them. But the question was anything but—it was deadly serious. John's mind was also racing. It was all a big mix of emotions for John, talking to his friend in this way—sympathy, concern, worry...and the fact he was breaching confidential information about his place of work. Yet more worry.

"Fucking hell, Liam, I'm on shaky ground here, mate. We shouldn't even be having this conversation. FMA would fire me in an instant if they knew what we were talking about." He exhaled, looking at his feet, shaking his head ever so slightly. "But...what the fuck. Me and Janet love you guys—and Josh too, obviously. And we want to help. So, if talking about this shit helps, then let's do it. But do me a favour—keep all this to yourself, Liam. FMA are hot on secrecy, and confidential leaks are really *not* well received. I could lose my livelihood." The two men's eyes met; no more needed to be said on the matter. It was unspoken between them, but they both knew what the look meant. "Off the top of my head, I don't know if Josh's twin has been exhibiting any signs of extracurricular brain activity. I'd have to check the records. I'll have a look next week for you. I look at records all the time, looking for trends and analysing results, so that's no biggie. But be clear on this Liam—if there *are* any signs of unusual activity, this doesn't mean that your son is somehow being controlled by an evil clone by means of telepathic thought."

Liam's mouth opened and the words were out before he could stop them: "They're your words, not mine, John." John looked down at his restless hands for what felt like a long time.

# Chapter Thirteen

*Now it's just you and me, we can become proper friends again, Josh. Without anyone interfering. No school. No Alice. No anyone. Just you and me, like in the beginning.* Josh was listening to Benny in his room. His room felt like a prison cell, and even though he had free rein over the rest of the house and garden, he found himself spending eighty per cent of his time up there. During these long periods of isolation, he was re-connecting with his twin. Or rather, his twin was re-connecting with him. Benny was keen to worm his way to the forefront of Josh's mind and thoughts, now that other distracting factors were out of the way—and he was doing a good job of it, too. Josh was vulnerable now. He was expelled from school, and had little interaction with anyone else apart from mostly his mum and occasionally his dad, and was alone for the majority of the time with just his own thoughts. And Benny knew this. And he was taking full advantage of the situation. He was treading gently at the moment—he didn't want to go planting any bad seeds in Josh's mind just yet. It wasn't the right time, anyway. Josh was here, stuck in his room for most of the time, and that was no good. So, he would make the most of their time together by regaining the trust that he felt had been lost, or at least compromised, over the last few weeks. The trouble was, every time Josh and he did something bad together, Josh pushed him away. This meant Benny was constantly trying to get back in the good books with him. That was no good—he needed to be in the good books all the time.

*It's better with no school, Josh. So bashing that little bastard with the rock was a good thing. It means you don't have to go there and endure all those little twats every day. No bullies. No nasty looks in the corridors. No whispering when you know they're whispering about you…just us.* Josh contemplated this. Benny was right—he didn't really miss school. His mum had talked to him about what she called 'home teaching', so he didn't get behind with his learning. When she asked what he thought, he had agreed morosely that he was okay with it. His mum seemed a little pleased at this, and said they would start next week. He had overheard her on her mobile talking to someone saying she needed to talk about her hours for her job. That meant she would be home a lot more to teach him. Josh didn't mind this—he loved his mum. Benny accepted this, even though *he* didn't love Josh's mum. Far from it. He was downright jealous that Josh had such loving parents. No one loved Benny, did they? No one took care of him, did they? Apart from the men in white coats at the lab, checking the settings on his vessel. Changing the fluid once every three weeks (this coincided with his hair and nails being cut, as well as a once over body check for any anomalies). Benny tried not to think about these things. It generally made him uncontrollably angry, and that led to maybe saying things to Josh that he didn't necessarily mean to. Now was not the time to be angry; he had bridges to build with his friend. And that was exactly what he intended to do, now that he had the perfect opportunity to do so. Josh was receptive again, and he needed to take advantage of that.

Josh heard someone coming upstairs. A small knock at the door preceded his mother coming into the room. She sat down on the bed asking him how he was, was he OK? He replied: Yeah, he was fine, just bored. Jen made a mental note to get a list of stuff to do with Josh to keep him occupied. Gardening, maybe helping cook, and God, she also needed to get him out of this house; it wasn't healthy staying in this room all the time, a visit to the park wouldn't hurt. He could feed the ducks and use the climbing stuff there—this would get him some well needed fresh air and exercise, too. She would have to get some kind of rota together to follow, so she could be sure her son was getting the right mix of work and play. She had never had to consider it before really—the general structure of the school week sorted it out automatically for her, pretty much. But it was all different now. Much different.

"Your dad is going to see nanny later today," she told him. "He's staying overnight, as he hasn't seen her in a little while. I'm staying here with you, so we will have to find a good film to watch after tea, maybe?" She clasped his hand. Her heart was breaking with love for her troubled young man. Every time she thought of Josh (which was pretty much all the time), she felt the same, like her emotions were tattered and ripped to shreds. It felt like a physical hurt, it was so strong. She hated the feeling with all her soul. Josh nodded imperceptibly in agreement, and accepted a brief cuddle from his mum. He was also distraught inside. One thing that had remained a common thread through all of the incidents that had happened recently was that he absolutely hated upsetting his mum. And his dad too, of course, but it wasn't on the same level. Not quite. Jen left her son, telling him to come down and say goodbye to his dad in about ten minutes, she would shout up to him to let him know when he was leaving. She told him that his dad also loved him very much, and was very worried about him. They both were.

Liam was packing an overnight bag when his wife came into the bedroom and put her arms around him from behind. She missed the closeness they had shared for many years—it had seemed to become diluted over the last six months, since the trouble had begun. He paused his rummaging around in the wardrobe to embrace her in return, and they stayed that way for a minute or so, not saying anything.

"Give my love to Jessica when you get there. And from Josh, too. Please try not to tell her too many gory details of what's been happening. What have you told her already?" She enquired. She was close to her mother in law. Jessica had been a widow for many years; Liam's dad had died of cancer way before Josh was born. She had other family to support her and look after her (she was well into her seventies but still sprightly), and Liam visited her a few times a year. Jessica had also spent a good few weekends at their house too, where she was waited on hand and foot and spoilt rotten. It was a joy for the couple to see Josh spending time with his nanny; it was almost the last bastion of the innocence of childhood.

"Hardly anything, don't panic hon. I didn't want her to worry, so I've told her that Josh has been having some issues at school with some other kids, and that's it. I thought it best to play this one close to my chest." This was true, and he knew this response would appease Jen. He could see the mild relief that crossed her face. As he put his bits and pieces into the holdall, she went to shout Josh—he was leaving in five. Downstairs in the hall, Liam hugged and kissed his son and wife goodbye, making sure he told Josh to behave for his mum. He mumbled that he would in return. They waved him off the driveway, and then returned into the house.

Jessica lived in a small town called Longdown, about fifty miles from Cleedon. The distance was short enough to be easily commuted, and long enough to just have that little bit of separation that is often needed within families. Just to make sure you're not wearing each other out by living in each other's pockets. The drive seemed to pass in a blink of an eye for Liam. This was due to the fact his mind was cluttered with all sorts of thoughts, following his evening with John the other night. John had definitely given him food for thought. He hadn't shared any of their conversation with Jen, and probably didn't intend to. As he pulled up onto his mother's driveway he saw the twitch of the living room curtain, followed by the front door opening. His mother was a small woman (age helped this impression), but you could still see that in her youth she had been a strong-looking, beautiful woman. Her hair was still worn long, back in a tail, grey having now taken over from the fiery red locks that used to cascade over her shoulders. Her weathered face cracked into a beaming smile at the sight of her one and only son, revealing a full set of her own teeth. She was bearing up well for her age, for sure. Liam grabbed his bag and walked up to her, throwing his arms around her and hugged her as hard as he dared, and his mother hugged him back surprisingly fiercely. The family resemblance wasn't strong; he took after his father for his looks and stature, but he was very much like his mother in personality. They were two peas in a pod when it came to their strong characters and opinions on life. They said their hellos and went inside, where Jessica poured him a cup of freshly brewed coffee. They sat at the table talking pleasantries for a short while, generally catching up with each other—how long had it been? Last time was earlier in the year, maybe February, when she had come down to their house (well, Liam had gone and picked her up at any rate—she didn't own a car, and couldn't drive even if she did). The conversation inevitably drifted onto how things were at home: *How's Jen and that beautiful grandson of mine? Is he getting on any better in school nowadays? All that trouble disappeared now?* Liam tried to keep the frown off his face, and didn't quite succeed.

"Well Mum, it's not great if I'm being perfectly honest. He's been expelled, and Jen is worrying herself into an early grave about him. But I don't want you to worry about him, Mum. Please. It's just a school-boy phase he's going through—all kids go through it. I did! Remember when I got into a fight with that horrible kid—what was he called...? Ben Goodman, I think? I was about Josh's age then, and I whopped him so bad he had to go to A and E, and got expelled for a week! And I turned out okay, didn't I?" He looked at his mother with an impish grin, trying to inject a light-hearted element into the chat they were having. He didn't want to get too bogged down with Josh and his recent issues; in a way, the trip to his mum's had been partly to try and forget all that for a bit and get some downtime from it. Maybe he would start to think a little clearer after spending a weekend away from it. A little more objectively, maybe.

"Well, there's little point in telling me not to worry is there, Liam? I'm bound to be concerned about Josh, he's the light of my life. I can't bear the idea that he's gotten lost and is off the beaten track, the poor lamb. Oh, I wish it would all just stop for him! Is there anything you and Jen can do to help?" She was wringing her hands in frustration. *I keep seeing people around me doing that,* Liam thought absent-mindedly.

"Well, we are engaging in a child psychology assessment program next week. The doctor involved is a top guy, and very clued up on this stuff. He thinks he can help, so we're approaching it with an open mind. Also, Josh has seen him before, so he's familiar with him already." He looked at his mother expectantly, trying to gauge her reaction to this. He didn't want her 'out-of-touch' way of thinking to lead her to believe that they were committing her grandson to a nuthouse, or something. "He thinks it's all tied up with this imaginary friend of his. Benny, he calls him." He sighed and held his head in his hands for a moment. "I don't know if there's anything in it or not Mum, but it's got to be worth a try. At this point, I'm willing to run down the bloody high street butt-naked covered in custard if I thought it would help."

She picked up on his attempt to lighten the conversation: "I doubt that will help, Liam. But let's hope the doctor can help him. But I can't help but think there's something you're not telling me about all of this." She looked at her son in that questioning way only a mother can master, accusing, enquiring, and guilt-tripping all rolled into one. "He wouldn't be going to a child psychologist for a few bullying issues in the playground would he, Liam?" *She may be old, but there's no doubting where I get my grey matter from,* Liam thought, slightly irritated at his mum's astute take on things. He would have to give her a bit more in order to satisfy the fact she thinks he's withholding information from her.

"No, he wouldn't Mum. And it's been a little more than bullying." There. Too late. The cat was out of the fucking bag now, wasn't it? *Well done, bigmouth. I'll have to explain it all in glorious Technicolor detail to my mum now.* "There's been a couple of quite…well, dangerous incidents where he's put other pupils into hospital." As he looked at her, he saw the kind wrinkles and laughter lines on her face contort into something much more morose. He didn't like it much— he knew his mum was instantly filled with dread at the news her beloved grandson was actively hurting other kids. And badly hurting them, at that. "Look Mum, it's just a phase, like I said. Hopefully Dr Ireland will help sort all this out. It might involve some medication of some kind, but if it helps, then so be it. And it's therapy sessions first. I really don't want you to worry about this—we will deal with it, I promise. But in return, please, *please* promise me you won't worry? And don't say a word to Aunt Gillian, Mum. Or Jen. She didn't want me to tell you because she didn't want you to worry."

Jessica sighed and shook her head, as if to clear it of this new knowledge she had just been made party to, like trying to clear the fog of a hangover the morning after. She promised her son she wouldn't worry or say anything about it, and Liam tried to move the conversation on, somewhat successfully, by engaging her in her recent gardening activities—*it's looking great out there Mum, let's go and have a look...*but all the time, while they were looking at newly planted ferns and rose bushes in the borders of Jessica's very well-kept garden, they both had other things on their minds.

Liam, in particular, had something on his mind. Something that had lodged itself there since his chat with John—or had he been thinking about it before that? Something that Jen didn't know about. Something that *no one* knew about. He didn't just want to visit his mum for a brief retreat, for a catch up and top make sure she was okay; he had another agenda. A secret one. A dangerous one. He had come to get something that may just change things. Hopefully, for the better.

# Chapter Fourteen

John had kissed his wife goodbye and set off for work, just the same as any other working day. Except there was something a little different about today's trip to FMA for John. He had agreed to look into the records for twin V29—Josh's twin. He had managed to contain his mouth and his anger with Janet; after his initial annoyance, he had time to reflect on the situation. Of course Janet was going to talk to Jen—they were the best of friends, and friends talk to each other. As his anger subsided over the next twenty-four hours after talking with Liam, he softened to this fact and decided not to bring the subject up with his wife. Why make waves? What's done is done, and there seemed little point in having any kind of falling out with Janet over something that couldn't be changed, even if the principle of it stuck in his throat a little.

He said all his usual morning greetings to his colleagues on the way to his office. *Business as usual,* he thought. Although the extracurricular activity he had planned was making him feel a little edgy. He kept telling himself that the records for the twins were analysed all the time by him and a few others also, so it was no big deal—they paid him to look for trends in the statistics produced by their sophisticated monitoring equipment, and that was all he would do. But…the fact that he had another agenda kept nagging his conscience. *Just get it bloody well done—there won't be anything out of the ordinary anyway, and then it will be over,* he told himself as he logged onto his PC. It didn't take him long to bring the file for V29 up and start poring over what appeared to be endless data files, all spanning back to the day of conception—nearly nine years' worth all in all. John wasn't really interested in anything older than the last six months. After all, the trouble with Josh hadn't been going on for that long, had it? He quickly narrowed down his field of search, and started with the mental activity files for the twin. After briefly manipulating the spread sheet to give him the most recent timeframe results, he started looking in earnest at the data, his eyes narrowing to inquisitive slits as he scanned row after row of what looked to be thousands of numbers and associated graphs to the untrained eye. As he absorbed the information, his eyes started to widen a little—it seemed there *had* been some 'unusual' activity going on with V29. Not wanting to jump to any conclusions, he checked the notes file, which contained entries by various laboratory technicians. A quick scan of the notes confirmed for John what he had already gleaned from the data. Abnormal brain activity at various times over the last six months. Very frequent bursts of high level activity. John frowned. *Looks like I'm having an awkward conversation with Liam soon,* he thought. He sat back and stretched, his already large form seeming to expand even more in his chair. Then he decided to have a quick look in the archive files—for V13s records. V13 was Sammi Goodman's twin. As he accessed the data, he subconsciously hoped there would be little correlation between the two datasets. He was disappointed. And more than slightly alarmed. They were very similar. *Too* similar for his liking. Spikes of over-activity, just like V29. Overall elevated level of consciousness, just like V29. He checked the notes and they were also all of a similar nature. He exhaled deeply. John's mind was working overtime. Did this mean that there was conclusively a psychic link between the twins in question and their counterparts on the outside world? No. Did it mean that the children involved had any interaction whatsoever with their twins? No. Did these records prove anything at all? No. But did the similarities worry him at all? Fuck, yes. They worried him *a lot.*

While Jen and her son were busy rearranging his room into a new configuration (Jen was determined to do something constructive with him, and make the most of her one-on-one time with him), Liam was busy treating his mum to dinner at a local Italian restaurant. During the course of their meal, Liam had asked her what she wanted, or needed, doing around the house. There were a few bits and pieces that she would like help with—one of them was she wanted to wash the curtains in the bedrooms. Liam tried not to show the spark of excitement in him. This may well give him the ideal opportunity he had hoped for. He readily agreed, and told his mother he would get the steps out from the garage and set to straight away: *The nets can stay up tonight while you wash the curtains, and we can do the nets tomorrow—I'll re-hang them before I make a move.* He felt guilty—he didn't generally keep secrets from his mum (or his wife for that matter), but unfortunately this had to be kept under wraps. When they got back to the house, Liam started straight away.

"I won't be more than ten minutes Mum, you just relax while I sort them out and I'll bring them down," he said, as he manoeuvred his way up the stairs with her small step ladder. She turned the television on and advised him to be careful. Liam entered his mother's bedroom and placed the steps by the window, ready to take the curtains off the rail. He looked at the bed—two bedside cabinets. It was obvious which one was his mothers, and he went to the other one. The one that used to be his fathers. He quietly opened the bottom drawer and moved a few things onto the floor beside it. He had a glimpse of the dullish-grey metal in the bottom drawer, and his heartbeat quickened. It was still there. His father had served in the army for many years; he was never decorated, but had a solid career record with the services, and had climbed his way up to Second Lieutenant followed by Lieutenant. On leaving the army after seventeen years, he took his service issue pistol with him. He unconsciously held his breath as he picked the Browning semi-automatic service gun up, giving a quick glance over his shoulder as he did so: *Oh, trying to steal your dead fathers' service gun are we, Liam? That's fine, you carry on son! It's not like he'll be needing it now, is it?* A stab of guilt accompanied his adrenaline. He laid the gun under the rest of the contents of the cabinet on the floor and had a better look into the back of the drawer. There was a box of bullets and a spare clip there; he took them and put them with the gun. Another guilty glance over his shoulder confirmed his activities were going unmonitored. He left his mother's bedroom and called down the stairs.

"Ok down there, mum? I'm just taking them down now. Won't be long." She replied that was fine, take your time: *Just be careful!* He quickly took the gun, bullet and clip into the guest room and bundled them into his bag, shuffling some clothes over the top, and zipped it shut. His heart was pounding like a hammer on a blacksmith's anvil—he wasn't used to stealing. Even if it was from his mother: *possibly the worst kind of theft possible,* he thought, uneasily. A real baptism of fire into the world of deceit. The deed done, he returned to the decidedly mundane task of his mother's curtains, his heart rate slowly returning to somewhere near normal. Once the bedroom curtains were down, he took them downstairs and helped his mum load them into the washing machine before settling in front of the television. The usual chit-chat went on between them as his mum asked about the family, work and suchlike. Liam gave her all the latest news, omitting the details of the horrible events happening with Josh. He actually found it quite difficult to achieve this, as it seemed that Josh's misfortunes had bled into every corner of Jen and his lives. As he trod through the conversational minefield of his life with his mother, slowly his guilt melted away. He was quite sure he had done the right thing by taking the gun. It sure would come in handy.

"Well, what do you think, Josh? Better than before?" Jen stood with her hands on her hips, surveying the new bedroom layout with her son. She looked down at him, and felt such a pang of hurt, anger and love all rolled into one that it nearly overwhelmed her. She felt the slight pricking of tears in her eyes and fought determinedly against it. *Why does absolutely nothing feel normal anymore? Will it ever go back to what it was?* Josh nodded in slight approval and grunted. She ruffled his hair and suggested they have ice-cream, as a reward for their hard work. She had refrained from talking to him about recent events while they pottered around his room moving and rearranging stuff—it just seemed like it would make him retreat into that lonely place that he so often frequented nowadays, and she didn't want to encourage that. But she did want to talk to him about the home schooling that was going to have to happen now he had been expelled from school. *It'll keep till later,* she thought. Jen had spent some time earlier on the phone to Beth, and had been offloading to her (luckily without succumbing to tears while she did so). Beth was supportive as ever. The two women were pretty tight. Once Beth learnt that Liam was out of town, she suggested what Jen was hoping she would—a girls' night with the kids packed off with a movie in the lounge, while they drank wine in the kitchen. Jen jumped at the chance. She had casually mentioned to Josh that Beth and Alice were coming over that evening, and she was slightly puzzled by the response she got— a brief lighting up of his face in anticipation of seeing his friend, followed by a dark frown.

"What's wrong, hon? I thought you'd want to see Alice and watch a movie, or something," she said. Josh still wore his frown.

"Yes, I do Mum." He responded. But his face said otherwise. Little did she know that Josh *was* keen to see Alice; he had not had any interaction with anyone his own age for nearly a week, since he got expelled, and there was only so much 'adult' you could do. But Benny wasn't so keen. Not so keen at all. *Great. We've got golden girl Alice coming over. Well, isn't that just lovely for us... I can just lay quiet while you two play boyfriend and girlfriend. I can't fucking wait.* Josh was not surprised at Benny's reaction. Benny had never liked her from day one. When exactly *was* day one? To Josh it felt like forever. Maybe it *had* been forever. Come to think of it, he couldn't remember when Benny hadn't been there. Josh didn't bother responding to Benny—hopefully he would just fade away into the background and let him and Alice have a good time later.

"Hmm. Okay, well you'd best jump in the shower before they get here. In fact, we're both a bit grubby so I'll do the same, what do you say big guy?" Jen ushered him along into the en-suite bathroom of the guest room and went into her room to do the same. As she washed the dust off herself from the days rearranging, her own frown crept onto her face. She had expected Josh to be happy to see Alice, and he had to begin with—but she couldn't help but wonder why he looked concerned afterwards. *He's got a lot on his mind at the moment. It's just all a bit much for him so it's no surprise he's acting a little out of character. A little out of character? Fuck, he's been busy smashing people's heads in with rocks and cutting them up with sharp implements!* She thought, and immediately felt bad. She decided to stop thinking about it, over analysing it, and just try and focus on having some downtime from it all tonight.

The women had decided to have tea at their respective homes, so that it was all done and out of the way with. When Beth and Alice knocked it was just getting dusky outside, and she was armed with two bottles of wine. Alice had her mousey blonde hair done in a French plait, and was wearing denim dungarees. She looked the epitome of the pretty little girl next door—which was exactly what she was. Jen called Josh down from his room, and he came down looking happy enough. Straight away the children started talking to each other as they sat on the sofa, their mothers deciding to leave them to it and retiring to the kitchen. Alice was busy telling Josh about the week's events at school. Hartwood was a tiny school, which meant that most kids knew each other in some form. This in turn meant that school gossip was always rife. George Beam had been given detention for refusing to dispose of his chewing gum in Mr John's history class. Kevin Blackwood had asked Isla Farringdon to go out with him, and she said yes. Johnny Tressdale had thrown up during football, and had to be collected by his mum and taken home. Josh sat and listened while Alice rattled off all the news titbits, feeling a bit detached from it all—he wished he was back in school, even though he used to moan about it all the time before. As usual, the old adage was true: *You don't know what you've got till it's gone.* There was no mention of Josh's recent misdemeanour from Alice. *I bet her mum has told her not to say anything,* Josh thought sullenly. But that was OK—he didn't really want to talk about it anyway. That would just give Benny an excuse to pipe up and interfere, and he didn't want that at the moment. Their mums were busy chattering away in the kitchen, and Josh briefly tuned out of Alice's tirade of school events (which were getting increasingly less significant), and strained to catch a thread of their conversation. *I bet they're talking about me, and what's been happening,* he thought. This time Benny *did* surface. *I don't think they will be talking about us, so stop worrying about it! They don't care what you've been up to, Josh. If they did, your mum and dad wouldn't be sending you to a nuthouse.* This upset Josh: *I'm not going to a nuthouse! I'm not crazy! He's a doctor that will help me! Now LEAVE ME ALONE!* Benny had managed to get under his skin very quickly and effectively, evoking the reaction he wanted: Anger. *Well, we will see what happens! You'll be locked up soon enough, and I won't be there! It's because they want to get rid of me! You'll be all on your own! Good luck!* Benny was right—the two women weren't talking about him, from the little snippets he had managed to hear. He zoned back in to hear Alice talking about how Ben Redding was going to leave at the beginning of summer, because his mum and dad were moving away. He nodded in acknowledgement to indicate he was listening, and had been all along. He offered to get him and Alice a drink, and wandered out to the kitchen while Alice scrolled through the apps on the TV looking for something good to watch. As he approached the kitchen, he noticed the door was only just ajar and the conversation between the two mums was hushed. Just as he pushed the door open a little, Jen caught him out of the corner of her eye and quickly shot Beth a glance that was easy to interpret: *Shut up, he's right there!* So, they *were* talking about him after all. Josh wasn't surprised, but still felt a pang of bitterness. His mum asked him what he wanted, and quickly poured a couple of glasses of squash for the kids while Beth talked about Alex's boss, who was apparently having an affair with someone in the office. But Josh knew it was just a cover up. He knew what the subject really was, and left them to it. When he went back into the living room, he was careful to push the door so it was almost closed.

"Do you know if Rich Avery is OK? Is he in hospital? I guess he is." Alice looked at him warily. She had been told to try and avoid talking about it by Beth (*It might upset Josh, so don't mention it*), but now Josh had brought the subject up himself.

"Yes, he's in hospital still I think. But I think he's going to be OK," she answered cautiously and in a lowered tone, glancing at the door. She didn't want her mum to hear them talking—she had been asked (well, pretty much told) not to, and would undoubtedly get into trouble for disobeying her mum. "You hit him pretty hard, Josh. It was lucky he's not dead. Why did you do it to him?" She asked. Josh fell silent. Why *did* he do it? Well, because he had bullied him, of course. But…why didn't he tell a teacher instead? *Because he needed to be taught a lesson,* Benny chirped up.

"He needed to be taught a lesson," Josh said, directly echoing Benny's words. He looked at Alice, and she was staring at him, wide-eyed in a mixture of fascination, awe and just a touch of fear.

"But now you're not in school any more. I miss you in there. I wish you could come back, somehow. Do you think you'll be allowed back, or will you never come back at all?" Alice asked him. His brow furrowed at this question. Truthfully, he didn't really know. He hadn't really thought that far ahead. Now that he had been prompted, his mind raced with the possibilities of what the future may hold for him—no school? What, *ever…?* Josh wasn't sure he liked that outcome. Maybe he would have to go to a different school; that would mean he wouldn't get to see his friends. He didn't like that outcome either. Now that he had started thinking about it, it all seemed a bit bleak and depressing.

"I don't know what will happen, Alice. I may not be allowed to come back. Because of what I did. I've hurt two people at school now." He looked down at his hands dejectedly, and then brightened a little: "But, I'll still be able to see you, because you live next door! So, it doesn't matter if I go back to school or not, does it?" He looked at her small, pretty face and saw traces of doubt there, flickering behind her pale blue eyes, just dancing below the surface. She paused before answering, and lowered her voiced even further:

"That's if my mum and dad let me, Josh. I guess they're a bit worried…well…you know…that something might happen to me." She looked at him levelly. Alice was now talking about things that were definitely forbidden. She had heard her parents talking last night, her dad's voice elevated to easy hearing volume, and her mum telling him: K*eep your bloody voice down, I don't want Alice to hear this!* And her dad responding, albeit in a lower tone: *What if Josh decides he's annoyed with her for whatever reason, and tries to hurt her? You'd never forgive yourself, Beth!* Her mum countered this by saying that the two kids were so close that it would never happen: *Josh wouldn't hurt a hair on her head! Those other kids had done some nasty shit to him, Alex. Alice has never done anything to Josh.* Alice felt guilty for eavesdropping and once she had gleaned her fill, she slunk back to her bedroom from the landing as silently as a cloud slipping over the moon. Josh found himself confused by this last statement from his friend. He would never hurt Alice! But, her parents were worried he might. What did they think he was, some kind of ghoul that just went round inflicting huge amounts of pain on kids for no reason? He felt himself getting angry at the thought, and quickly tried to control it as he answered Alice.

"I wouldn't hurt you, Alice. Never in a million years. And I'll make sure Benny doesn't hurt you either." This time it was Alice frowning as she digested his last remark.

# Chapter Fifteen

Liam rang Jen when he was on the road back home from his mother's. All seemed OK at home according to Jen, and he breathed an internal sigh of relief at this. It felt like every corner of their lives was cluttered with some kind of drama or unpleasant incident that normally involved Josh. It had been going on for so long now, that he struggled to remember what it was like before all the troubles began. In reality, Jen and Liam had only been dealing with issues with their son for six months or so, but it certainly felt like a lot longer than that. This was their new normal—trying to deal with constant issues and battles concerning Josh and his strangely violent outbursts, which had manifested seemingly out of bloody nowhere.

And Liam had also received a text from John over the weekend—asking whether he fancied a night on the beer. John had not given too much away about Liam's request for information on V29, and had simply said: *got some stats you may be interested in.* Liam thought that John wouldn't want to commit too much information in a text, so even though he found this 'teaser' frustrating, he was loathe to get too pissed off with his mate—he had done what Liam had asked him, by the look of it. Still, the fact that John had obviously found *something* during his investigations troubled Liam. If there had been nothing of consequence, then why even mention it? John had obviously found some correlation between the clone's data record and Josh's behaviour. As Liam mulled all this over, he mentally checked himself—*Christ, I'm as bad as Jen. There's no reason to think that this is linked to this fucking clone, surely? I'm paranoid; it's rubbing off on me from Jen. Need to keep a level head.* He had messaged John back, and once he got home he could firm up his plans to see him. He decided Jen didn't need to know about what he had asked his friend to do at FMA—she had enough on her plate, and he also didn't like the idea of feeding her already growing conspiracy theory about FMA. It didn't feel great keeping secrets from his wife; they normally shared every last detail with each other and trusted each other implicitly, but this felt like it may be wiser (and safer) to keep it close to his chest. At least until he had chance to get the full lowdown from John. His mind wandered on to the upcoming assessment for Josh with Dr Ireland. He had taken some time off work so he could take Josh, and Jen wanted to go too—*nice little family outing,* he thought cynically. But they both trusted Jason, and they both hoped he could make a difference with their son. He had said a lot of things that made sense so far, so it may be a real opportunity to get over this seemingly impossible hurdle with his professional help. It was a lifeline, for sure.

Once Liam had got home, he felt a little more positive about things, and put on a brave face to his wife. He was fed up of feeling worried, depressed and anxious all the time (and was sure Jen felt the same way). She also appeared a little more upbeat than usual, and told him all about the weekends' activities with Beth and Alice. She made sure to hammer home the point that Josh had been a little more like the old Josh they all loved. Josh made a brief appearance to greet his dad, and then scuttled back off to his room. Liam suggested they coax him into staying downstairs with them after tea: *Let's see if we can lighten his load with some normal family time, maybe forget about the bad shit for a few hours.* Jen agreed, and that's exactly what ended up happening. Liam gently reminded Josh of the appointment with Dr Ireland in the coming week before he went up to bed, and he nodded in acknowledgement, a look of resignation on his face. Jen reassured him it was no big deal—he just wants to help. Josh agreed and went up to bed.

*Good job you're not in school at the moment isn't it, Josh? They would all be calling you a nutcase! They call those doctors 'shrinks'. They try and help mental patients in old, dark hospitals. The people in there are insane, and walk around dribbling all the time, and shitting in their white hospital dresses. They talk to themselves and eat flies! And even their own shit sometimes! That's what the shrink thinks you'll end up like—and your mum and dad! A fucking nutcase, shambling around in a cold, dirty hospital with all the other mental people! We don't want to end up like that, Josh—so you make sure you don't fall into that fucking shrinks' trap. He wants me to go away, and wants you in a mental hospital. Don't forget that.* Josh laid in his bed in the dark, listening to Benny's words bounce around inside his head, a gradual feeling of dread creeping over him like a cold, black shroud. His eyes were wide open and staring blankly at the ceiling as Benny continued his tirade. *But I guess you'd like me to go away too, wouldn't you Josh? That way you and your girlfriend can be together without me, isn't that what you want? Well, I'd be careful of her if I were you. She thinks you're crazy, too. Why do you think she said what she did about you doing bad things?* Josh pondered this. Up until now he had kept silent, allowing Benny to rant on and on. Often it was a good tactic to employ if he wanted Benny to shut up—it's not as much fun having a one way conversation, so not engaging with him was effective at times. But not this time. He had a real bee in his bonnet, and was determined not only to get it off his chest, but draw Josh into the debacle. And it had worked.

*She doesn't think I'm crazy! She's still my friend, and there's nothing that can stop that, not even you! She only said it because of what her mum said to her about me. She still likes me—she's not scared of me!* Josh knew his reasoning with Benny would probably end up being futile, but he fought his and Alice's corner anyway. *Dr Ireland won't make you go away, Benny. He just wants to make sure I don't carry on doing bad things; you'll see tomorrow when we go there.* Josh didn't know if this approach would work or not, but it was worth a shot to keep Benny happy—things had a nasty habit of going very wrong when he wasn't.

*That's bullshit and you know it...he wants me gone from your head! He's already told your mum and dad, we heard him say as much last time we were there. And as for Alice—she DOES think you're nuts. She's a little bitch, just messing with your mind. She only comes around to your house because her mum wants to, it's not because she likes you anymore. Stop lying to yourself and face the truth, Josh. Otherwise I will be gone...forever.* There was an element of finality to this last statement—what would it be like without Benny? Josh had always had him there. And in Benny's defence, he had always stood up for him. Not like the others at school and his other friends; Benny was different. It didn't matter what Josh did or didn't do, Benny was always there for him. He always supported him, even when everyone else seemed against him, including his mum and dad. His teachers. Dr Ireland. Alice. At least Benny was consistent, unlike everyone else. His parents were angry one minute, then sad the next. Then they were worried, and then they were upset. His teachers and Dr Ireland were a similar story—they keep saying they want to help, but do they *really* want to help? They just seemed to be making things worse, by expelling him from school and then forcing him to see this shrink to try and brainwash him. Then there was Alice. She used to be super cool, and his best friend. Now she was busy saying that she's worried he might hurt her. What kind of person thinks that about their so-called best friend? What were her exact words the other night? *They're worried…something might happen to me.* What she meant was *she* was worried something might happen to her. She didn't trust him. How can you have a best friend when they don't trust you? Josh reflected on his thoughts for a moment. Benny had recessed himself to the back of Josh's mind for the minute; Josh seemed to be doing a good job of coming around to his way of thinking without further intervention from himself.

Finally, Josh fell into an uncomfortable sleep, with all those recent thoughts lingering in his subconscious. At some point during the night, he whimpered to himself as he dreamt. He was dreaming he was with Benny—but Benny was real, just like him. In actual fact, he looked identical. They were even wearing the same clothes. They were on a huge see-saw, in the middle of a large park. Because they were the same size and weight, the see-saw kept continuously going up and down in a perfectly even movement, never losing momentum. They were looking at each other across the large wooden platform of the see-saw, laughing at each other as it went up and down. Josh looked around—there was no one else in the park apart from the two identical boys, laughing as they ascended and descended again and again. Benny's laughter steadily got louder and more raucous as they flew up and down opposite each other, each boy being lifted by force at the height of their travel. Josh felt the slightly queasy, excited feeling in his stomach as he left the wooden seat and floated in mid-air. As he came back down, he glanced around him again. This time the park was no longer empty—there were people there. But they were all laid down and not moving. Josh frowned and looked closer. They were all dead. He recognised them, and his eyes widened in horror as he looked at the familiar faces staring blankly back at him—his mum, his dad… Dr Ireland… Beth and Alex…he looked around to the other side, catching Benny's face contorted into a rictus of hilarity and madness all at the same time. Huge bellows and peals of laughter came out of his mouth, which appeared to be unnaturally wide open. His teeth looked much sharper than Josh's own. There he saw Alex Winter, motionless, face covered in dried blood. It had formed a black crust around his hairline. A large, fat-bodied black fly crawled sluggishly out of the corner of his twisted mouth. A little way away, Rich Avery sat propped against a bench leg, his head twisted grotesquely to one side—so much so, he was almost looking backwards. But he wasn't looking at anything at all…he was also still, the angle of his head allowing Josh to see the gaping black hole by his temple. As Josh's eyes bulged with terror, he spotted a few of his teachers similarly motionless. Mr Matthews, who was laid on his side, with one of his arms jutting out at an impossible angle, Mrs Cotter nearby with her neck obviously broken, her head lolling lifelessly to one side. Until her head moved, her broken neck craning towards Josh, who was still crashing up and down on the see-saw, Benny's laughter now nearly splitting his head with the volume. His eyes were now bulging with horror as he stared at the dead Mrs Cotter, her head lying impossibly on her right shoulder with her lifeless, bloodshot eyes staring accusingly back at him: *You did this, Josh... ARE YOU FUCKING HAPPY NOW, YOU VILE LITTLE MURDERING BASTARD?*

Josh awoke from this nightmare with a jolt, and only just managed to stop himself from screaming out loud. He was clammy with an oily sheen of sweat, and lay gasping in his bed, trying to shake the horrible images from his fuzzy mind. Slowly, he came to terms with the fact it was only a dream, and was able to shake the gory images off, but one lingered. It was Benny, howling with laughter, head thrown back in hysterical and manic ecstasy.

# Chapter Sixteen

Jen and Liam sat in the reception area of the clinic, not talking much. Liam was scrolling on his phone, a permanent frown glued to his forehead, while Jen aimlessly flipped through a six-month old copy of Good Living magazine. She wasn't even really looking at the photos, let alone reading any of the text. They had both been in with Dr Ireland and Josh for the previous forty minutes or so, and were both still shell-shocked as to the unfolding of events with their son—had it really come to this? Psychoanalysis of their precious eight-year-old boy? It still felt surreal to both parents.

Dr Ireland had asked for there to be an open discussion from all three family members, and started the ball rolling by asking some direct questions relating to Josh and his recent misdemeanours. *Were the attacks on the other boys linked? Was Josh punishing them both in the same way for similar reasons? Was the violence due to losing his temper, or was it pre-meditated?* Josh had sat sullenly in his chair, reluctant to engage at first, but once Jen and Liam started vocalising their thoughts and feelings he became more animated as he got drawn into the conversation. Jason made notes throughout it all on his laptop. Eventually he asked the parents to leave in order to talk to Josh alone. Jen and Liam knew his agenda—he wanted to draw Josh into talking about Benny. They had avoided mentioning him when they were talking earlier, and because of that, Josh had been reluctant to mention him as well. He got no resistance from Benny either; he was quite happy to nestle in the back of Josh's mind for the minute.

Jason hadn't gotten anything new from Josh during their chat with his parents—it was all stuff they had already heard before: *I wanted to teach them a lesson, they deserved it, I didn't mean to hurt them so badly but I was angry,* etcetera. Now, Jason was alone with him, he was hoping to extract some information about his invisible friend and ascertain whether this really had anything at all to do with what had been happening. He was pretty sure it did, but not quite sure in what capacity…and it was this he was hoping to uncover.

After a few innocuous leading questions from the doctor, Josh began engaging with him a little more than earlier, which was what Jason had been hoping for. Once he had him properly engaged talking about school, he steered the conversation in the direction he needed it to go.

"You must miss school—do you think your friends there are missing you, Josh? It must be kind of lonely being away from there all the time, don't you think?" Josh paused before responding, considering his answer.

"Well, yes, it can get a bit lonely, I guess…but there's Alice next door, I get to see her sometimes on weekends." Jason took the opportunity.

"And what about Benny? Does he still talk to you? And do you still talk to him, or has he gone away?" Josh's eyes remained cast down, brow furrowing slightly. He didn't really like talking about Benny (well, *Benny* didn't really like talking about Benny), but he knew it was inevitable. That was part of the reason he was even here. He hoped and prayed Benny would stay squirrelled away at the back of his mind while this chat was happening.

"Yeah, I guess so," Josh ventured reluctantly, nervously trying to twist his brown curls of hair behind his ears with his twitchy fingers. "Sometimes when I'm alone, he talks to me…but usually he's quiet." Josh wondered if the doctor would realise that this was a white lie to play Benny down, and maybe move off the topic. Benny wasn't usually quiet—he was always there in one form or another, waiting to surface and have his input into whatever Josh was thinking or doing at any given moment. Now was no exception to this; although he was quiet (for the minute), he was still there. Josh could sense him at all times. Jason pursued the subject.

"Does Benny *just* talk to you, Josh? Or does he ask you to do things? And if so…does he ask you, or does he *tell* you?" The words were out before Jason had time to cross examine his choice of dialogue: A *bit heavy handed, but too late now,* he thought retrospectively. As he studied the little boy in the chair opposite him, he felt a pang of sorrow for the lad. He had grown to quite like Josh over the few meetings that they'd had, despite the fact that Josh was obviously more withdrawn than usual during these encounters. He could see that the nature of these latest questions made him uncomfortable. The hair twisting had developed into a nervous scratching of his neck and shoulder, Josh worming his hand underneath his tee-shirt collar. He squirmed a little in his chair, and finally looked up at the friendly doctor.

"I don't really like talking about it, Dr Ireland. Maybe because I think people will think I'm stupid for having an invisible friend. They might even think I'm crazy, and I'm not!" His voice rose, almost cracking on this final exclamation. Jason interjected:

"No one thinks you're crazy, Josh. That's not what this is about." He said solemnly. "We just want to try and help you. And Benny, if need be."

"He's the only one that understands me properly! We're like brothers, and he loves me. But he gets angry when things go wrong," Josh responded. The doctor sensed an opportunity to drag some more information from his subject.

"When was the last time he was angry, Josh? And what did he say to you about it?" he probed. Josh paused thoughtfully. Benny would not like the way this conversation was going. It wouldn't be long before he would be chipping in on the sidelines of Josh's mind at this rate. This made Josh even more anxious than he already was. But he continued regardless:

"Well…he didn't like Alice coming over to my house the other weekend. I think he gets jealous," Josh ventured cautiously. Jason asked him what Benny does when he's jealous: *Does he get angry? Does he shout and scream? Does he ask you to do anything to them?* Josh contemplated this before answering.

"He mostly shouts at me, and says some nasty things, maybe. I try not to argue with him, because it makes him angrier. So I try to ignore him until he calms down." Josh's hands had settled in his lap, and his fingers were squirming around each other, interlocking and releasing on an endless cycle. His palms were sweaty and he kind of felt clammy all over. And Benny was still ominously quiet—a bit *too* quiet for Josh's liking.

"Did Benny have anything to do with Alex, the boy in school? And what about the other lad?" Jason reasoned that this blunt line of questioning was as effective as any other method of drawing information form the boy. It had worked up until now.

"They were bullies! They were nasty in the first place, not me! They asked for it…and Benny helped me," Josh blurted out. "We weren't the ones in the wrong! They are horrid boys, and they'll think twice before hurting Alice or me again!" Jason was not surprised at this outburst. He had been expecting a colourful reaction to his direct questioning, and now he was getting it. But, the important thing to note for him was the inclusion of Benny in his responses— and his friend Alice. He took the opportunity to change his tack slightly:

"Does Benny like Alice then…? He must do, if he wanted to teach Alex a lesson for hurting her in school. But, didn't you say he was jealous of her? Surely, if he was jealous of her then he wouldn't have helped you get revenge." Jason could see instantly that the line of questioning he had employed had confused Josh. His brow became more furrowed and an obstinate expression had settled on his face like a dark, rain-laden cloud. This was a bit of a curve ball for Josh; the doctor had a good point—a *very* good point. It didn't make sense that Benny wanted to help protect or avenge Alice in the first instance, but then said horrible things about her later. As Josh struggled with these thoughts, Benny finally stepped in:

*Don't listen to him! He just wants to cause trouble! You know why we hurt those bastards—they deserved it! He's just trying to confuse you!* He exclaimed angrily. But he had elected not to mention being jealous of Alice in his outburst.

"He *does* like Alice…he just gets jealous when we're together, he doesn't mean anything by it. The others—we both wanted to make sure they paid for what they did! It's not right that people can just go round doing what they want, and getting away with it!" He looked sullenly at Jason, almost glaring at him. Jason knew he had obviously hit a raw nerve with his approach, but it appeared to be yielding results.

"That's true Josh, people shouldn't get away with doing things that are wrong, or hurtful to other people, but we both know the way you—*and Benny*—dealt with it isn't right either, is it? It's why we are sat here right now, and it's the reason you can't go to school like you normally would, and it's the reason we are all worried about you, Josh. Do you understand that?" Jason's tone softened to try and bring Josh around. Josh was confused. He didn't *think* he wanted to hurt anyone before all this, but now…well, if they deserved it, then they should be punished surely? Did it really matter who did the punishing? The school? His parents? Him? Benny? *It doesn't matter Josh! As long as people that deserve to be punished get punished, then that's just desserts, and that's that! You are being punished right now! IT'S NOT FAIR! THE WORLD IS NOT FAIR! GET OVER IT! WE CAN MAKE SURE BETWEEN US THAT WE LOOK AFTER OURSELVES! WE DON'T NEED ANYONE ELSE! WE'VE PROVED IT!* The voice inside Josh's head grew more and more amplified as Benny ranted on. Josh looked at Jason fixedly, and echoed Benny's sentiment:

"The world is not fair."

# Chapter Seventeen

Dr Ireland had concluded the session by talking to Jen and Liam about his conversations with Josh. He told them he was concerned about his friend, Benny. And that Josh was using Benny as an excuse to enact his own, slightly unhinged method of revenge upon his peers—or at least, the ones he felt deserved it. This was no real surprise to the concerned parents. They both knew and suspected Benny wasn't helping in any way. The idea of these child psychiatry sessions was to try and eliminate Benny from the equation. If Josh's imaginary friend was the true root cause of all of this, then getting rid of him would be a massive step forward in helping Josh get back on track.

The return journey consisted of Josh withdrawn and sullen in the back seat while his mum and dad made small talk in the front, purposely avoiding anything Josh related. The few times Jen attempted to bring her son out of his shell were met with grunts for answers—until she mentioned Beth and Alice.

"I was hoping to have a day out with the girls next door next weekend, Josh—what do you think? Does that sound like a good idea?" She turned her head to glance at his reaction in the back. His eyes flashed with brief positivity, and he met her look.

"Yes, I'd like that, Mum. I always have fun with Alice. Seems like she's the only kid I get to see nowadays," he added, almost to himself. Liam's mind started working overtime on hearing the conversation between his wife and son. *This may be an ideal time to hook up with John. Could do with another chat about FMA, and see what he thinks of the stats he's got on V29,* he mused to himself. Now that Benny was becoming ever more prominent in sessions with Jason, he felt like he needed more answers from John about just exactly what goes on in the FMA labs. And what he really thought about the fire. And Sammi's death.

The Connellys were sat in the living room that evening, with Josh asleep upstairs. They had briefly discussed the day's proceedings with Dr Ireland, and had then lost themselves in their mobile phones. Jen was texting Beth to arrange the weekend with the kids, and Liam thought he had best check that it was a goer with Jen before they made arrangements. A quick confirmation with Jen gave him the go ahead, and a few minutes later it was all a done deal—John would come over on the Saturday and they would do the usual guy stuff while the wife and kids were out: Barbeque, beers, and talking nonsense mostly. With a steer from Liam on the subject of FMA, and John's recent findings…

"Where do you think you'll go with the kids?" Liam asked. Jen replied they were toying with the idea of Clayfield Woods. They hadn't been there for a while, the weather looked good, and the kids loved it there, exploring the trees, undergrowth and the stream that ran through the particular section they frequented the most. Liam thought this sounded good, and was slightly regretful he wasn't actually going himself—he could help the kids catch some minnows, frogs, and various other wildlife specimens, as he had done previously with Beth and Alex in tow last year. It had been a lovely day, and the kids were fascinated by the creatures that they caught, examining them in the jars and containers they had brought with them expressly for that purpose. But, he had another agenda that was ultimately more pressing. Liam told Jen he had arranged John's company at the house while they were out. He almost mentioned about John running some stats, and then thought better of it. Jen was way more paranoid about FMA and V29 than he was anyway, so feeding her that information would mean that she would spend all day in the woods worrying about what they were talking about at home. Liam thought it was best to play his cards close to his chest until he had the full picture.

"It may help take Josh's mind off all the recent goings on," Jen said, refilling her glass. "It feels so isolated out there, it's like you're on another planet. Hopefully, he will be able to forget about it all for a few hours and just have some good old fashioned fun with his friend." She paused, frowning, reflecting on her own words. She looked up at her husband, eyes almost pleading with him. "When will this end for him, Liam? Oh, I hope we can get him back to normal soon… I feel that if it carries on for much longer, we may not have that chance anymore. That he might be like this forever." She was visibly upset as she spilled her worries out. Liam comforted her, trying to reassure her that it would all be sorted out soon; Dr Ireland would help. But his words sounded like he was just going through the motions, saying the right things in the right places.

"Looks like I'm off to Liam's for a lads get-together on Saturday, love," John casually announced to Janet. He was looking forward to seeing his friend, and couldn't really say no, anyway—Liam knew he had info and he wanted to know what, if anything, the stats yielded. Janet replied saying that she had arrangements anyway: Phoebe was leaving work at the end of the month on maternity, and the girls had a full day planned in Brighton with a hotel overnight. John was pleased—he was off the leash. He quickly messaged Liam to confirm he'd be there with bells on. He toyed with the idea of telling Janet the real agenda for Saturday with Liam—and then decided to keep his big mouth shut, much the same as Liam had with Jen.

*What she doesn't know can't harm her...and besides, it's only a bunch of numbers. Although the numbers have a worrying similarity to some other numbers...* John quickly put this particular train of thought to the back of his mind. He would have plenty of time to chew the stats over with Liam on Saturday. He just hoped his friend's reaction would be a little more rational than his wife's thoughts about Naomi and Sammi Goodman. He himself had his doubts about the technology he dealt with in work with FMA. The few incidents he had been party to over the years did raise some uncomfortable questions for sure, but the good old John Lee logic kicked all doubts into the tall grass. He had a good, well paid job with a reputable medical company, and was hoping that it stayed that way at least for the next ten years, until he could seriously consider retirement. The last thing he wanted to do right now was jump ship to another company, a new job, new colleagues and into the relatively unknown when he had it all sewn up at FMA. He was well respected, well paid, comfortable, and settled where he was. Nothing is forever; he wanted to see out his working days in a familiar environment.

He sipped his coffee as he slowly turned these thoughts over in his mind. The only real fly in the ointment with all these thoughts and plans was the moral implication of it all. Surely if he felt there was something...well, something *not right* about FMA then he was obliged to either raise them through a formal mechanism within FMA? What about the correlation between certain sets of results he had seen? What about the 'co-incidences' that had been spotted over the years? He had told his long time technician Jez a few times that the data patterns and sometimes erratic or out of character movements of the clones within the vessels were just anomalies, and there were no particular conclusions to be drawn from these happenings. Well, if that was truly the case, then why was he questioning his own moral standing on the subject now? John decided it was time for a nightcap and to forget about all this for the minute—there would be enough FMA talk at the weekend with Liam. He didn't know whether he was looking forward to it or not.

Liam was exchanging text messages with Jason. The two men did not often do this, even though they had swapped numbers on the first meeting, what felt like an eternity ago (but in reality was less than six months), and had messaged a few times since. Jason had started this particular exchange, asking Liam some more detailed questions about FMA. It was obvious to Liam that after their last session, FMA had been internet researched by Jason. This did not come as a particular surprise to Liam—after Josh's expulsions about Benny, and Jen's apparent fixation with the twin in V29 it was only a matter of time before Jason would want to know a little more about it all. After a ten minute message swap, Liam finally suggested that he ring Jason tomorrow, as he would be able to give him some more detail on the subject.

Jason readily agreed, so Liam told him he'd phone in the morning for a chat. As he put his phone down and picked his beer up, he felt more confused than ever. All these little fragments of thoughts, ideas, and theories buzzing around his mind like disoriented moths, all underlined by an ever increasing, ever thickening blanket of dread and worry…

Liam had ducked out of the office and was sat in his car, dialling Jason. It was mid-morning, and the autumn sun shone as brightly as could be hoped for. The trees that scattered the car park and lined the perimeter were varying shades of green right the way through to brown and everything in-between. The ones that had fallen decorated the ground like a huge mosaic design with hues of amber, red, and brown all overlapping one another, adding to the depth of colour where they lay. Liam stared at these patterns absent-mindedly as he found Jason's number and put his phone to his ear. He didn't want to hold this conversation hands-free in his car—even though the car park and the grounds of the office were desolate apart from him, it still felt like he would be announcing a personal area of his life to the world.

Jason picked up on the third ring: "Hey Liam, how's things?" He sounded pleased to hear from him. It crossed Liam's mind that this was the first conversation he had had with Jason in a non-professional setting. After getting some pleasantries out of the way (Liam explained to the doctor he only had five minutes at best, as he was at work), he asked him if he would like to meet him and John on Saturday at the house. He quickly added that he was expecting FMA to come into the conversation.

Jason hesitated before replying: "I don't see why not, Liam. I haven't seen John in what feels like ages. It's a nice offer, and I think it would be good to get the insider view of what goes on there, as well as us catching up outside of Josh's sessions at the clinic. What time do you want me there...and do you want me to bring anything...?" Liam answered that John was arriving late afternoon, so anytime from then onwards would be fine, and instructed him just to bring himself.

"Look, if you'd like to stay over, it will be just us boys. Jen is staying next door with her friend Beth, and Josh is too. That way you could have a few drinks maybe...?" Jason agreed he would stay, this time a little faster than his hesitant first acceptance of the invite. With the arrangements all made, the two men (who now both felt a little more than acquaintances) said their goodbyes. As Liam got out of his car and meandered his way back to the office, he thought about what Saturday might bring—he should give John the courtesy of letting him know Jason would be there. He thought briefly about sending him a message, and then dismissed it. He could do that nearer the time. He didn't want John backing out at this stage because he felt he'd be given the third degree, and wanted time to think about how to word it to his friend. He found himself wondering already about the nature of the conversations that may happen at the weekend as he opened the glass double doors to the building.

# Chapter Eighteen

"Josh, do you know where your boots are, honey? Are you wearing your wellies, or hiking boots?" Jen hollered up the stairs at her son while she bustled around the kitchen transferring food into Tupperware containers. It was still early, eight-ish in the morning, and the girls wanted to make an early start to get the most out of the day. They had decided between them who was doing what with regards to food—Jen was on sandwich and drinks detail, while Beth had agreed to cover all snacks and sundries. Between them they would amass enough picnic food to feed a small army, as per usual. Beth had agreed to drive to Clayfield Woods; it wasn't too far in the car, about fifteen miles of straightforward A roads followed by a bit of a dirt track that led to a gravel car park, where you paid a nominal sum (last time it was three pounds for an all-day ticket). From there, within ten minutes of walking along narrow, often muddy paths, you were in what felt like the middle of nowhere. The last visit was in the autumn of last year for the ladies and their children. They would normally organise a couple of trips a year, maybe even three, but life had gotten in the way this year. The issues with Josh had been the main contributing factor to this, and Beth had stepped back a little and left Jen to suggest any get-togethers. She thought this was the right thing to do. If Jen wanted to talk, she was there, and if not, well…she was still there. The two women had not openly spoken about this unofficial approach, but subconsciously they were both aware of it. And for the main part, it had worked for Jen, at least—she knew she could call on Beth when she needed a shoulder to cry on, or even just some light relief doing something 'normal', whether it was taking the kids to the park or sharing a bottle of wine on a Friday night.

"My hiking boots…no, wait…maybe my wellies will be better if we can go in the stream?" Josh's response came from his room upstairs. He was still getting dressed after his shower, struggling to stretch his pullover over his head; his mum had advised him 'dress warm'. It was autumn after all, and even though it was sheltered in the woods, the temperature was in single figures outside. The sun was out, but its rays were significantly weaker than six weeks previous. Jen shouted his wellies will be fine and continued cutting sandwiches into triangles that fitted snugly into her boxes. She was looking forward to the day, and the evening at Beth's—an oasis of normality in her recent life of worry and turmoil. They would no doubt end up talking about Josh later after a few drinks, but Jen was determined to have a 'normal' day. Just one. Surely both her and Josh deserved that? A tiny slice of what life *used* to be like...

Liam sauntered into the kitchen, rubbing his eyes, and mumbled good morning as he kissed his wife on the cheek. It was a bit of lie in for him—usually he was awake by six thirty and up by seven, regardless of it being a weekend or not. But that was okay today; all he really had to do was say goodbye to his family, and maybe knock up a quick salad to accompany the cuts of meat he had in the fridge. He was thinking of cooking in the kitchen rather than alfresco, due to the temperature outside. All the supplies were in for the boys later on—which reminded him, he must text John. He still hadn't told him about Jason. He did this as he waited for the kettle to boil, and hoped John would be okay with it. He felt sure it wouldn't be a problem. Sure enough, by the time he had filled the cafetière, John had chirpily replied "No probs! See you later." Liam was pleased. It was all set—some good food, beer, and a couple of mates while the family are out was just the ticket for a Saturday night. He asked Jen if she wanted coffee—she said yes, while packing boxes into her large purple rucksack, still distracted by her preparing for the day ahead.

"I hope you guys have a great time today, love. I really do. Hopefully it will do Josh some good, too." He hugged his wife from behind, drawing her close to his body. She clasped his hands, and turned to face him. She smiled—it was a weak, drawn effort, but none the less, it was a smile. *There hasn't been too many, from either of us,* Liam thought.

"Oh, so do I, hon. I really need this...just something normal, just for once, so I can forget all the shit that's been going on lately. Maybe Josh can remember what things used to be like before all this, too." There was an air of desperation coupled with faint hope in her voice. They held each other close for a few seconds—just long enough to convey the emotions they shared, long enough to remind themselves that they were in this together, and they always would have each other to lean on, to rely on. As Josh came down the stairs and into the kitchen (looking like he had been dressed by elves during the night), Liam opened the dialogue with his son:

253

"Hey, Josh. Make sure you look after the girls in the woods today. You'll need to protect them from the wood people." He tipped Josh a wink as he delivered the light-hearted banter. Josh rolled his eyes.

"Dad, there aren't any wood people there! The most I'll have to protect them from is a few frogs…that's if we even see any. It may be too cold for frogs." He thought about this as he spoke. He couldn't remember the last time he had found a frog, or anything else for that matter, at the woods. It felt like another boy owned that part of his past life. Liam ruffled his son's hair—the first normal, affectionate contact in what felt like an eternity. *When was the last time I did that? God, what's happened to us?* He told Josh to let his mum sort his jumper and jeans out: "You look like a scarecrow, mate…you can't go anywhere looking like that!" he joked, determined to keep it upbeat until they left. It worked—Josh wrinkled his nose at him and wandered over to his mum, who instantly started clucking and fussing. A ray of hope pierced Liam's heart as he was briefly reminded of their previous existence. It had been all too easy to become completely absorbed in their living hell, hour after hour, day after day, ad infinitum. He made a silent resolution to somehow claw their way back to a normal family life, that simple, everyday thing that they had *all* taken so much for granted. Until it was mercilessly taken away.

Benny had left Josh alone overnight, allowing him to get a solid block of deep, uninterrupted sleep. But he had made his presence felt when he awoke, not even giving him the chance to get the sleep induced fog from his mind. *Well, today is the big day, Josh. Aren't we all going to have fun at the woods?* There was a sinister undertone to his monologue. Josh detected it instantly, and a small sliver of cold, damp fear settled in his heart. *I hope you haven't forgotten what that little bitch said about you the last time you saw 'your best friend'.* These last words were echoed in Josh's mind with the nasty bite of sarcasm that Benny had intended. *She thinks you're a nutcase! A psycho! Imagine what she's saying about you behind your back at school—I bet she's calling you all sorts of things to her shitty little friends—and to yours, too. To anyone who will listen, I bet. She's only coming today because her mum is forcing her. Do you really think she wants to be around you all day? Ha ha! You're a fool if you think she still likes you! She'll keep spreading lies about you—and me probably—until the whole world hates us both! I wonder what she's told her* mommy *about you? About us? I bet it's not good, and I bet she will tell* your *mum later, when they*

254

*are getting drunk as usual! Soon your mum will hate you too! And you're so fucking spineless; you just sit there and let it all happen.*

Josh was caught on the back foot by this tirade—he knew that Alice had been a little reluctant to give too much away last time they had spoken about any of this, but he hadn't considered that she may be talking to her parents about how messed up her friend Josh was next door, with his crazy 'imaginary friend' at the helm, getting him to beat other kids to within an inch of their lives. But this was the last thing he needed now. *Not now, Benny. I'm going to have a good day no matter what you say, so get over it.* He hoped his authoritative tone would put Benny back in his box. And it did—but not before he had the last word: *Oh yes, Josh. It will be a very good day.* And with that ominous footnote to his hate speech, he slowly receded to the depths of Josh's mind once more.

The morning was a busy, bustling one in the Connelly household, with Liam skirting around his wife and son as they made their preparations for the day's exploring ahead. He had little to do himself really—a couple of friends around later didn't mean he had to go into overdrive preparing for them, he had everything sorted anyway. He changed the bedding in the spare rooms while Josh and Jen pattered up and down the stairs and in and out of the back door, gathering all their stuff together. Liam would end up with a few hours to himself shortly, which would give him time to think about how to play the scene when John and Jason got there.

"We're all set Liam! Have a great time later on with John, I'll text you later on, come and say goodbye!" Liam hadn't mentioned about Jason coming around too. He didn't want Jen to know the agenda really; it would only add to her worry, and potentially ruin her day as she found her mind getting clogged up with thoughts about Josh and Benny. Liam finished straightening the bedding in the front bedroom and went downstairs. Jen and Josh were stood by the front door, Jen with her bulging rucksack on her shoulder. She looked a little flushed, with pinkish blooms on her cheekbones, giving her face a welcome burst of colour. As Liam looked down, she looked the epitome of an outdoor girl—jeans, chunky knit jumper, woolly hat, and hiking boots. His heart filled with love as he took her and their son in. Josh also looked well-equipped for the day, with his big waterproof jacket that nearly met the top of his boots. He looked up at his dad as he descended the stairs with large brown eyes.

"Have a great time—you got your net, kid? You may well find some fish in the stream. And maybe more…a swamp creature, perhaps! Take good care of all the girls for me—you're the big man today." he hugged his son as Josh confirmed he did indeed have the net, and pulled Jen close in too. He kissed her forehead and whispered in here ear: "I'll miss you. Have a lovely time, see you tomorrow." Jen kissed him in return and briefly held his cheek with her palm. Her eyes conveyed her love for him as they opened the front door and made their way across the drive. Liam waved goodbye on the doorstep for a short time, and finally retreated inside the house. He felt uplifted that the two of them were actually going to do something normal, something neither mother nor son had done in some time.

# Chapter Nineteen

It hadn't taken long to load Beth's car with all their stuff; Beth had put hers and Alice's gear in already. The two women chattered, almost excitedly, as they packed Jen and Josh's stuff in the back. Alice and Josh were also excited, busy discussing the prospect of catching small creatures in the woods.

"We can look under logs and rocks, as well as in the stream," Josh announced. "We may find some mice, or even a snake!" Alice nodded in agreement. They were sorting through and comparing the plethora of containers and tubs they both had to house all the creatures they would find. Beth ushered them both into the back seat of the car, locked the house, and then they were on the road. The car buzzed with chatter from both adults and children as Beth negotiated the road on auto-pilot—they were both familiar with the route. The small car park only had two other vehicles in it when they arrived. They wasted no time getting out of the car and setting off up the pathway that led into the heart of the woods. The sun peeked through the branches that overhung the path, dappling the nearly dry ground. It hadn't rained there for at least a few days, allowing the ground to firm up underfoot. The leaves and twigs crackled underfoot as the party meandered slowly upwards, and then dropped down slightly. Even though they hadn't been there for some time, both kids knew where they were going, and ran ahead of their parents. After a ten minute trek, they hit upon their favourite spot—a small clearing that had a few large tree stumps scattered around. These made convenient seats and makeshift 'tables' for food and drinks. There were remnants of a fire to the left side of the clearing, and a few beer cans and bottles still remained long after the contents had been consumed. Jen made a mental note to pick them up and bin them back in the car park. She put her rucksack down near her feet and announced to the children: "Ladies and gentlemen, we have arrived!"

Liam's phone beeped. It was John: *I'm on the way!* Jason had messaged him earlier saying he would be there by four, it was now three fifteen. This meant that the guys would be there roughly at the same time. He messaged his friend back; *Great stuff, see you soon...* There—it was done. The stage was set for what promised to be an interesting evening, and he wondered how John would react to any line of questioning about FMA that may end up at his doorstep. He would have to keep things on track. It was supposed to be a social gathering after all, not the Spanish inquisition. It might be best to get all the FMA cloning stuff and John's findings out of the way early, so they could focus on a few drinks and relaxing. Liam needed to blow off steam, after all the recent happenings. If plans had worked out differently, he would have gladly joined the girls and Josh today in the woods, but it just wasn't meant to be. He could still have fun with the guys, drinking beer, eating grilled as opposed to barbequed meat (it was decidedly too cold for eating al-fresco), and talking about everything under the sun, no doubt. As Liam pottered around in the kitchen adding more beers to the mountain that was already in the fridge and taking slabs of marinated meat out to rest, the time melted away and before he knew it the doorbell was chiming. He looked at the portly outline through the patterned glass of the front door as he approached it through the hall, identifying John rather than Jason—Jason was taller than himself, Liam put him at about six-two—and certainly wasn't carrying the weight that John was. He opened the door and ushered his friend in, who had his hands full with yet more alcohol and a few other bits and pieces, plus an overnight holdall. As the two men conversed in the kitchen, catching up on trivial matters mostly (how were the wives? And the rest of the family? Was John's father any better? How was Josh managing, etc.?), the doorbell went again. As Liam let Jason in, John greeted his friend warmly—it really had been too long, he exclaimed. They settled around the table and cracked their respective beers open (Jason declined, saying he would open a bottle of red a bit later, and settled on a coke). After fifteen minutes or so of talking, Josh came into the conversation, brought up by Jason. Liam's interest perked up, as this would inevitably be the start of what he hoped would be a revealing exchange of information. He was keen to hear what John had to say about the data analysis he had been doing, and was also keen to get Jason's take on this.

"So Josh has been okay recently, Liam? We had quite a soul searching session last time when it was just us two. He opened up a lot...and his 'friend' was discussed too." He looked at the two other men around the table as he sipped his drink.

"Yeah, he's been okay I guess. He's off today with his mum and our neighbours, they've gone to the woods for the day. I'm really pleased they're doing something normal for a change. It will do them both the world of good. And it's good for us—John and I have a few things to discuss which I'd rather do in Jen's absence." Jason's eyebrows rose slightly at this.

"Okay, well this sounds intriguing. I have to say, I'm glad that you're here, John—can we talk about FMA? I know we don't usually talk shop." he looked at his friend hopefully. "It's in the interest of young Josh." John's forehead furrowed for a second, followed by a much more accommodating expression.

"Well, yeah for sure. It's no secret I work at FMA, you both know that. I don't know how much you know about the organisation, Jason. No doubt Liam knows more than you due to his involvement, but as you know, I'm one of the head research guys there, been there for over twenty years. Watched it grow from a tiny development acorn into the mighty commercial oak it is today." John chuckled at his own statement and slurped his beer. "Obviously, a lot of information is confidential, and as an employee I'm bound by a non-disclosure agreement, but…that doesn't mean I can't talk about who I work for. All I really ask is that whatever we discuss stays within these four walls. I guess you both have a vested interest in FMA." He looked at the two men levelly. They both nodded in agreement. Liam proceeded to set the scene for Jason, filling him in on all the information that had not previously been discussed in detail, while John largely sat quiet, with the odd interjection here and there. Once done, Liam asked: "Does this give you a good background on all things FMA, and all things 'twin'?" Jason exhaled, and replied:

"Yes, thanks. It's always good to know a bit about the background of any subject you're hoping to deal with. It's sad to hear about the lady and her young daughter. But interesting that it caught Jen's imagination, Liam. What are your thoughts on the matter?" he asked. Liam hesitated before answering, and chose his words carefully:

"Well, when Jen first told me about this and that she had been to see Naomi, I thought she was being irrational and neurotic. I felt she was clutching at straws looking for a reason for Josh's behaviour. But…now I'm not so sure." He glanced at John. "There are some parallels to be drawn that maybe I hadn't appreciated before. Which has led me to ask my good friend here to look at some data in the hope of trying to make some sense of it all. Which, I'll be frank guys— I am struggling." He took a long gulp of his beer, finished it and indicated to

John for another, to which he nodded, shaking his own empty can. As he opened the fridge, John said:

"Well, I've had a look. Had some stats run on any correlation between V29 and Sammi Goodman's archived data." He paused as Liam handed him his beer. "Now, I don't want to fuel any fires here boys, but there *are* some similarities. There is elevated mental activity in the V29 dataset that looks the same as Sammi's. Both these datasets are set aside from the other twins in the lab. There's a couple of anomalies across the board, from all the current two hundred or so that are there, but nothing of note really. Just these two stick out." He inhaled deeply and opened his can. He felt distinctly compromised. *What would Dr Ellis think if he was a fly on the wall here?* An oily film of sweat started forming on his brow, which he absently swiped at with his sleeve.

"What do you think it means though, John?" Jason interjected. He was keen to find out whether it actually helped him tie anything together with Josh and Benny. John looked nervous. He didn't want to instil any falsities or assumptions into the mix.

"I don't know. I'll be honest, we don't know enough about it all. Sure, we know we have the cloning technique mastered, but as to all the possibilities for error...who knows? We haven't been doing it long enough to accumulate the data on our subjects for meaningful long term analysis. That means there's a lot of room for assumption when looking at the process as a whole. Assumptions are bad."

"Jen is convinced that after talking to that poor girl's mother, the twin at FMA has something to do with Josh's actions. John and I have discussed this, and I'm not sure *what* to think any more. It's all totally fucked up," he said to Jason. He paused. "And she also thinks that Josh's imaginary friend has something to do with this twin business. Like, this Benny character actually *is* the twin, or something. Sounds crazy, and that's exactly what I thought when she first said it, but now...well, again, I'm not so sure." John took the opportunity to jump in:

"For fuck's sake, Liam! We have no constructive proof or evidence that there is *any* truth whatsoever in that. Jeez, let's try and keep this on the level boys. This isn't a fucking horror movie." The sweat was beading on his forehead now, and he wasn't bothering to wipe it dry any more. Jason, who had been quietly absorbing all the conversation, took his turn:

"I agree John, we cannot prove any of this—but, can we *disprove* it either?" He let the question hang over the table between the men like a dread-filled mist, waiting to settle and seep into them.

"Look! There's one!" Alice pointed to a small rock about halfway up the shallow, silty bank of the stream. The clear, cold water lapped up over the rock in question, and Alice was sure she had seen the tell-tale flitting of a small body and tail dive under it. Josh was stood on the bank, just above the area Alice was pointing to, net in hand. A medium sized glass jar (complete with lid with holes punched in) sat on the top of the bank, half-filled with water from the stream. The afternoon's animal hunt had been going well—one plastic container had a small newt in it, along with some river mud and weed. The glass jar had a grand total of two small fish in it. One was definitely a minnow, and the other looked a little different; the kids weren't quite sure what it was (and neither were Beth and Jen, when shown). Josh and Alice were about twenty feet up the stream from where their respective mothers sat. They had slowly been working their way up the stream in search of new and exciting finds.

"I'll put the net in, and you see if you can scare it out—then we can catch it," Josh said, frowning with concentration as he carefully placed the net upstream of the rock in question. No sooner that the rim of the net touched the surface of the water, a small darting shape whipped out and disappeared, quick as lightning.

"Oh no, Josh! You've scared it away! You need to be more gentle with the net, or we won't catch anymore!" Alice exclaimed with disappointment. Josh looked at his friend, slightly annoyed that she was blaming him for the great fish escape.

"It's not all my fault you know, Alice! You're stood too close to it! It's no wonder he escaped!" he retorted, defending his blunder. He flushed with irritation at the thought that Alice was so quick to blame him. Benny saw his opportunity. *Stupid cow, it was her fault, not yours! She's stood right there, she must have splashed and scared it away. Some friend—happy to blame you!* Josh found himself agreeing with Benny's sentiment, but thought better of it than to feed his fire.

"Whatever. It doesn't matter, now—it's gone. We'll just have to keep looking for others," Alice stated matter-of-factly. *Who put her in change, anyway?* Josh thought angrily, but declined to say this out loud.

The mothers were engaged in a conversation about Alex and his job; he had recently applied for a new position, and both he and Beth were waiting patiently for the outcome. Every now and then, one of them would crane their necks forward to check on the kids—they could hear them faintly talking to each other, but a low hanging branch of a nearby sycamore obscured their view of them. Not completely, but enough to require some effort to see them both properly. The stream wound away to the right, and Alice and Josh were just on the cusp of the turn. There were no other people around; the mothers were happy the kids were safe, as long as they remained roughly where they were, and didn't venture too much further around the corner. They would get hungry soon, and would come scurrying back to have some sandwiches and show off their little friends from the stream, no doubt.

"There are more rocks over on the other side, why don't we cross and try there instead? I bet we'll catch loads!" Alice said, already starting to cross the stream's bed. As she took slow, deliberating steps to avoid the gurgling water flowing above the top of her boots and soaking her socks and feet, Josh heard Benny: *Seems like she's completely in control, Josh. She's telling you exactly what to do all the time, like she's your fucking boss or teacher, or something!* Again, Josh couldn't help but agree with him, as he also started spanning the bed of the stream, following roughly the path that Alice had taken moments before. She was now successfully on the other side of the bank, waiting for Josh to complete his journey—did Josh detect a slightly patronising look on her face? He couldn't be sure. But one thing he *was* sure of. She needed to stop bossing him around. And she needed to stop doing it, like, right now. As he followed her zigzag path across the stream, his right foot slipped off the rock he had stepped onto, plunging into the stream's cold, clear flow. The water instantly flooded his boot, the shock of the cold causing Josh to withdraw his foot quickly.

"Shit! My foot is soaked!" he cursed, his voice quiet, even though his mum was too far away to hear his expletives. Alice looked on and giggled. He stared at her angrily. "What's so funny?" he snapped, red blooms of colour appearing on his cheeks, partly from anger, partly from embarrassment. She continued to giggle at his misfortune, her hand moving to her mouth in the pretence of hiding her mirth.

"Should've been more careful, Josh! I did it OK, didn't I?" she goaded. In her mind, it was just a funny incident, but in Josh's, it was him being ridiculed. Benny jumped on this immediately: *She's taking the piss out of you, Josh! What, you're just going to let her get away with that? You're more spineless than I thought—perhaps you deserve it, if you're not going to stand up for yourself.*

Josh's mouth drew into a tight line of anger, and a frown clouded his expression as he stumbled the rest of the way across the stream towards Alice. She was still smiling as he approached her on the bank.

"Stop laughing at me. It's not funny—how would you like it?" he said, visibly irate at the situation. He sat down on a dry outcrop of rock and set about removing his wet boot, emptying the water unceremoniously to one side of where he sat.

"Oh Josh, don't be such a grump! It's only a bit of water, it won't kill you, will it?" she said, trying to lighten the mood. She could tell he was upset, but she thought he was being a bit of a drama queen about it all, none the less. Josh just glared at her in response as he wrung the remaining water from his sock and pulled it back onto his foot; it was cold and wet, and felt horrible. Alice picked up the net and started looking down at the stream's edge for more animals to catch. "Maybe *I'll* have more luck with this," she said casually, without looking at Josh. He continued to glare at her, his gaze boring into the back of her neck as she crouched over the water. *Maybe it's her turn to get wet, Josh...she might need a helping hand.* Benny's voice echoed around Josh's mind as the idea sank in. He quickly pulled his wet boot on and quietly walked down behind her. Alice was completely absorbed in looking at the cracks and crevices for little critters, her pink waterproof coat bunching up at her knees and meeting her pink boots. Josh was now directly behind her, and she was still blissfully unaware of him. He got as close as he dared, and glanced quickly in the direction of their mothers sat around the bend—they were just out of sight, which meant the reverse was true also—they were just out of sight too. *Do it! Just push the bitch in! See how funny she finds it! DO IT! PUSH HER IN!* Benny shouted in his head. His hands reached out, and he gave her a firm shove at the top of her back. A little whelp of surprise came from Alice as she desperately tried to keep her balance, and then she tipped forward and found herself face down in the stream's rushing water. *She's going to shout! Press her down! PRESS HER DOWN! DO IT NOW!* Josh stepped forward and stood astride Alice. As she started to struggle to get to her knees, he placed both his hands on her shoulders, and pushed her back down. He felt her struggle against his arms, and increased the pressure.

Alice's mind flooded with panic—*What the hell is happening? OH MY GOD, I CAN'T GET UP!* The shock of the cold water as it seeped into her clothes under her coat added to her hysteria. She tried to scream, but she felt the pressure on her head and shoulders keeping her head under the water. She almost drew breath, and then realised there was no air—she was underwater. *SHIT, I'M DROWNING! OH GOD NO, HELP ME!* She felt a rough, hard shove on the back of her head. It felt like someone had hold of her hair, and the side of her face smashed into the rocky bed of the stream. She tried desperately to push her head and shoulders back against the pressure, but it was no use. Her legs were thrashing in the water, and then she felt downward pressure there too. She went into shock, the nearly ice-cold water now making her face and body feel numb. She felt detached from reality, as if in an alternate universe, as she tried to make sense of what was happening: *He's trying to drown me*, she realised with panicky, sick horror.

Josh's face was a snarling rictus of hatred and determination, as he continued to apply downward pressure on his friend's head. He was kneeling on her legs to stop her from thrashing, and he felt Alice's resistance slowly ebb away. Benny was in full swing—*KILL HER! KEEP HERE THERE! THE BITCH DESERVES IT!* Anger coursed through Josh's veins, completely consuming him. He held Alice's head hard against the bottom of the stream bed. He relieved his pressure slightly, allowing her head to rise a few centimetres, and then shoved hard down again, feeling her skull bang against the rocky bed again. As he looked through her floating hair around her head, he saw a faint wisp of pink blood, quickly taken away by the current, only to be immediately replaced by more pink, slowly ebbing from the fresh cuts on her head.

*I'm dying,* Alice thought. Her lungs felt like they were on fire, and she could no longer resist the urge to draw breath. Her mouth opened and she inhaled. But instead of air, it was water. Her body reacted accordingly and tried to eject the foreign substance, but it was all in vain. She felt her energy wan away to almost nothing, and it became a gargantuan effort to move any part of her body any more. Her head felt like it was about to explode with searing pain, despite the cold water it was submerged in. As she tried to flail her legs and arms, she was dimly aware that her movements were weakened to the point of almost no movement at all. She could vaguely feel the dull pressure applied to her head and body from above, but her head was light and fuzzy—she couldn't think properly. Her last thought was: *Why is he doing this to me?* Darkness crept over her mind like thick oil, blotting everything out...then there was no more pain. There was no more *anything.*

Alice had nearly stopped moving completely, when he heard: "Hey guys! Is everything OK over there?" He felt sick as the panic of being caught red-handed flooded his head. He looked up, and saw Beth craning her head at the bank of the stream—she was about a hundred feet away. Thinking fast, he replied, trying to sound as normal as possible:

"Yes, we're fine—we're coming back now!" He hoped Beth wouldn't detect the shaky panic in his voice. He was looking at Beth, who was now bending out over the river in order to see them both better. *Oh God, please don't come up here now!* He thought. He stood up, and swapped his hands for his feet on Alice's back. She had stopped struggling completely now—*I've killed her,* he thought. Now, all of a sudden he felt confused. Why had he killed her exactly? Because she was being bossy and annoying? Because she laughed at him when he slipped? *Because she wasn't your friend at all, Josh. She never was. She lied to you all along, and tricked you. She was just a nasty, sly bitch who DESERVED IT!* Benny answered. Josh waved to Beth to indicate everything was OK, hoping she wouldn't be able to see that he was actually stood on her daughter's lifeless, drowned body. He felt sick. She hesitantly waved back (could he see a frown of doubt on her face?), and then retreated slowly from the bank. Josh felt relief wash over him. He looked down at Alice. Pink-ish traces washed away from her lifeless head and hair, downstream. He stepped away from her, his mind racing. What did he do now? His mind was reeling. Benny had all the answers, as usual. *Run back down to them and explain there's been an accident! No one saw you! Tell them she slipped and banged her head, and you didn't see it happen! By the time you realised it was too late! GO NOW!* Josh was in no fit state to make his own decisions, and this sounded like a reasonable plan. He bent down and dragged her out of the water, so that her top half was resting on the bank with her legs still in the stream. She was face down, and he debated whether to turn her over. As he looked down on her, he could see the wet strands of her blonde hair stuck to the side of her face, which looked horribly pale and somehow bloated. As he looked closer, he saw a blood-stained, purple area near her temple. Suddenly he turned to one side and violently threw up what little he had in his stomach, the acid burning his throat on the way out. He let a small moan out as he wiped his mouth with his coat sleeve. He couldn't bring himself to touch Alice. His head was spinning and his stomach was bunched into a hot, twisting ball of guilt and revulsion at what he'd done. *Too fucking late for regrets now Josh! Go back to mummy! NOW!* Josh straightened up and started walking back along the bank. He started to cry as his steps got quicker, eventually breaking into a stumbling jog. He tried to cry out, but the words came out as nothing more than a broken croak: "Help! Mum! There's been an accident! Alice is hurt!" He continued his half shuffle, half run back to the women. Initially the mothers didn't hear Josh's attempt at raising the alarm, but on his second, louder attempt, they both came into view and then started running towards him. He stopped, and waited for them to reach him. A few seconds later, his mum stopped by him as Beth raced past, shouting: "Alice! Alice, honey!" And then a loud wail of anguish as her eyes took in the scene. Jen's hand rose and covered her mouth in terror, her eyes wide with shock.

"Josh, what happened?" She asked, as she started running towards Beth. Josh remained stood where he was. He felt like an alien on another planet, like a third party watching the events unfold from another galaxy.

# Chapter Twenty

The ambulance had arrived within twenty minutes of Jen making the call. Beth was so distressed she couldn't speak properly. Once the women realised that Alice was dead after searching for a pulse, they tried the usual resuscitation techniques. They had already turned Alice onto her back from face down, Josh stood to one side near the river bank, his face almost as pale and lifeless as Alice's. The only difference was that he was alive, and she was dead. He was in shock. Benny had duly retreated to the back of his mind now their work was done, and no other thoughts were present. Josh felt so detached from the scene unfolding in front of him he may as well have not been there at all. He was numb, mentally and physically, and just stood there, motionless as his mother and her friend tried their best to bring Alice back from the dead.

"Oh God Beth, she's not breathing—there's no pulse either. Quickly, we need to try and resuscitate her." Beth didn't respond to this, her mouth gaping open and then closed again, like a fish out of water. Hitching sobs cracked from her throat. Jen took control, and started to pump Alice's chest, followed by mouth to mouth. "Come on Alice! Please…come on!" She gasped in between her efforts. She was on her knees beside the little girl, her one side and Beth the other. Both had wet, sandy mud ingrained in their jeans and boots as they crawled around Alice, trying desperately to bring the girl back to life. Jen knew it was hopeless, but continued trying nonetheless. She was functioning on auto-pilot even though she had never been faced with a situation like this previously. Her mind and body had kicked into emergency mode instinctively. Beth, on the other hand, may as well have been in a coma. She was so in shock that she was barely functioning at all. Her head span and she retched yet again as she clasped her daughter's cold, clammy hand in hers. Her eyes were wide and terrified, all blood drained from her face. There were no tears—just huge, lung-tearing sobs that sounded like they came from the deepest part of her.

Jen stopped her efforts and fished out her mobile from her jacket, punching at the screen. A minute later, she said: "Beth, the ambulance is on its way. The paramedics will help Alice when they get here." Beth looked at Jen, her eyes still terrified. Jen took her hand above her friend's dead child and squeezed, trying to reassure her through the simple gesture. Beth did not respond. She looked down at her daughter, and moved her upper body so it rested on her legs as she knelt at her side, bowed her head and silent tears rolled down her face. Jen was crying too, but trying to do it quietly so as not to distress her friend any more than she already was. The four of them stayed like this on the side of the river until the ambulance arrived.

The men were still sat around the kitchen table when Liam got the text. He looked at his phone: *Oh God Alice is dead there's been an awful accident she drowned ambulance is here will call later x* Liam looked at his phone, shocked. The unexpected bad news caused the colour to bleed out of his cheeks as he tried to process the message. What had happened? Straight away, an unsettling thought surfaced: *Did Josh have anything to do with this?* He felt guilty for thinking it, but knew in his heart of hearts that this was no accident. No more than the other incidents that had happened with the other kids over the last six months or so. *This HAS to stop!* He thought. His friends were looking at him across the table. Liam looked up. "Excuse me boys, little boys room calling." He got up and instead of using the downstairs facilities, he quietly mounted the stairs. He could hear his friends chatting over the table as he opened the wardrobe and pulled the holdall out. The gun felt heavy and ominous in his hands. He checked it was loaded, even though he knew it was. He tucked the weapon into the back of his jeans and went back downstairs, feeling giddy, confused and determined all at the same time. But, there was also a new focus that had cloaked his mind—he knew what he had to do. At the foot of the stairs he took his coat off the rack and put it on, sliding the gun into the ample pocket on the side. As he walked back into the kitchen, before he could receive questions on where he was going, he said:

"Get your coats, boys. We're going on a little trip." John looked at him, quizzically.

"Where to, Liam? We're just getting warmed up here." and tipped his beer in his direction. John placed both his hands on the table and addressed his friends.

"A visit to FMA, John. Hope you've got your ID, or we're going via your house to get it." His face was set in a stern, unwavering frown. John looked

268

visibly shocked. *What the fuck is he on about? I don't want to go to FMA now! What's he playing at?* He thought nervously. He didn't like this unexpected twist one bit.

"What? Why would we want to go there now, mate? What's this all about?" he exclaimed, gesturing with his arms. "I'm not going there now, Liam. If you need to see anyone there then you'll have to make an appointment, like any other client. No one will be there now anyway! It's all closed!" he grew gradually redder in complexion and more animated during his reply.

"Don't make this any harder than it has to be, John. I've just received some very bad news, and it's about time I stopped the source. Maybe should have done it a while ago, but now I'm sure of it. So, let's go." He took the gun from his jacket pocket. "Don't panic—this isn't for you, John. But—we *are* going. So get your coat on. Same goes for you, Jason." He looked at the doctor impassively, making it clear that resistance would be unacceptable. Jason sighed and rose.

"Okay Liam, just calm down with that fucking gun. We don't want anybody to get hurt now, do we?" He looked at Liam trying to fathom what this was about. He thought he may have an inkling.

"It's a bit late for that, Jason." He got his keys from the other pocket and put them on the table in front of him. "You're driving. Let's go." John had his head in his hands. He was getting a *very* bad feeling about this unexpected turn of events. They stood up, and filed out towards the front door, putting coats and shoes on before leaving the house. Liam didn't even bother to lock it. Two minutes later they were on the road, Liam in the back while Jason drove, and John in the front passenger seat. Liam asked him again if he had his FMA badge, and John reluctantly told him that he did.

"Good. Let's get this done, John, tell Jason where he's going. Should take no more than thirty minutes, but my advice would be let's not hang around. Get your foot down, please." Liam sat back and let the boys do the work in the front, driving and navigating. He felt cold inside, and he embraced it. It would make the task in hand easier.

The ambulance had to park in the car park where Beth's car was. There was no vehicle access beyond that point. Three of the crew hurried along the path as quickly as they could, all loaded down with carry boxes and bags of equipment from the back. One of them had a folded stretcher, while the other two had their shoulders loaded with carrying straps. The call had said a drowning accident involving an eight-year-old girl, so all their life-saving equipment was with them, although none of them felt particularly hopeful about this one—the lady calling had said no pulse and no breathing. That was nearly twenty minutes ago. They left the driver in the ambulance as they rushed towards the scene. It took them about eight minutes to get to the clearing where an hour ago, two mothers sat enjoying each other's company and chatting to each other. Form here, they could see the women and a little boy further up the river, just visible before the bend. They also saw a motionless, small body on one of the women's laps, in a pink waterproof coat. The paramedics exchanged worried glances, and ran as quickly as they could to the small gathering just up ahead. Jen looked up, and saw them coming. "Beth, the paramedics are here! Let's hope they can work their magic, hon." The sentiment fell on deaf ears. Inside, Beth was distraught with such an overpowering sense of grief, one like she had never experienced before. On the outside, this resulted in her unable to speak or move. She just knelt there like a statue, her dead daughter in her hands and resting on her lap. Her hand absent-mindedly stroked Alice's head and face, her skin still wet, cold, and lifeless. Beth's face was no longer the pretty, happy face that Jen knew and loved. All of her features seemed to sag and point downwards in grief, as if there were invisible strings attached to her features, pulled taut. Her eyes remained incredibly wide open, the horror still present in them. An occasional heart-wrenching sob escaped her mouth, which was so miserable looking it appeared to be put on her face upside down. The paramedics approached.

"What happened here?" the one at the forefront asked, as he put his equipment down on the bank, frantically opening the zips and fasteners on his bags. Beth did not respond.

"Thank God you're here at last—it was a terrible accident, she fell in and drowned, about thirty minutes ago. They were playing while we sat down there," she indicated with a nod to where the crew had just come from. "Please—be quick and save her! I tried to resuscitate her, but it didn't work. Can you help her? Please, tell me you can save her!" Jen was becoming hysterical while talking to the man, who looked at her with a sympathetic expression.

"We will do all we can," he said gravely, as he manoeuvred Alice from her mother's clutches. Beth remained impassive, motionless. Josh still remained stood a few feet away, blankly watching the series of events unfolding before his eyes. Neither his mum nor Beth had talked to him or acknowledged his presence in any way for what felt like an eternity—they were all consumed with Alice.

Ten minutes later, the crew were re-packing their equipment into its bags and boxes, while the first crew member that had spoken to Jen on their arrival explained that there was nothing they could do. The folding stretcher now had Alice's tiny body on it. Beth had wailed when they took her from her lap, and tried to keep her there with weak, flailing hands as they tried to console her in vain. It sounded like the sort of noise you might hear while crossing the bridge to Hades, the epitome of misery and suffering. One man stayed with Beth, trying to console her and get her on her feet, while the other two, Jen, and Josh moved back towards the clearing. It was over. They had done what they could, but the crew knew instinctively on arrival it was all in vain. Alice' spark had been extinguished long before they had got there. As they approached the car park, the crew suggested they follow the ambulance to the hospital. Jen told Beth to give her the key, and the three of them got into the car, one child lighter than when they had arrived a short time ago. Beth and Josh were both silent, both in shock. Only one of them was harbouring a dark secret.

Liam's BMW pulled up into an almost empty car park, just a few vehicles dotted here and there, illuminated by the Victorian style lights that glowed softly against the now all-consuming dark of the evening. Jason had no problem getting close to the entrance, when John said:

"It might be best to park around the lab side. I assume you'll want to go in via a more subtle entrance than the front doors, Liam?" The question was almost, but not quite, cynical. John was now very nervous about being there, and even more nervous at the thought of what might happen as events unfolded. He didn't press Liam on his agenda during the journey—he didn't want to aggravate the situation or Liam any more than necessary. Especially considering Liam had a loaded gun in his possession.

"Is there a separate lab entrance?" Liam asked. John nodded in the front seat, and pointed to a narrow lane that led off to the left of the main car park. Jason took his cue, and swung the car around and drove down slowly, arriving into a much smaller parking area that was not lit at all, apart from a small light above a door in the passive, white brickwork of the building. Jason brought the car to a stop close to the door, but not close enough to be lit up by the arc of yellow light thrown out from above it. He was also playing the game, like John, unsure of what they were actually doing here—but not wanting to rock the boat at this point in time.

271

"Get your badge, John. Who's inside?" Liam asked, matter-of-factly. John sighed and replied:

"Well, normally no one, but you never know—there may be a technician doing some overtime I guess." He checked his watch. "It's still only early evening, but it's on the weekend. You'd like to think everyone is at home. Security patrol the site every two or three hours, but they're based in another building." He looked anxiously at his friend. "Look Liam, what's all this about? You're worrying me, mate." He glanced at Liam's right hand, which was buried in his jacket pocket, no doubt warming the gun-metal that lay inside. Liam looked at his two friends, both weary and nervous—it showed on his face, the shadows from the light making his features distorted, accentuating his cagey expression.

"Just do what I say, and no one will get hurt. I don't want to hurt anyone, but there's something I need to do, let's leave it at that for the minute. Jason, give me the car keys. John, let's get inside please." he said, as he watched John fumble in his wallet. "The sooner I do this, the sooner we can forget about it all. John, you go first, then you. We're heading to the lab." he said, nodding at the doctor. Liam didn't believe that there wouldn't be some fallout from this little adventure. He pushed the thought to the back of his mind: *I can deal with all that shit later...just get this done.* The door beeped, and then they were in. John led the way as instructed with Liam bringing up the rear, hand still in his pocket as if it were stitched there. A short walk down the narrow, dimly lit corridor led them to a couple of doors. Neither was marked, so Liam looked at John expectantly.

"This one is the lab area, the other will take us to the main building via another corridor," John explained in a hushed tone. He hoped to God there were no staff in the lab. This was nerve wracking enough as it was, let alone introducing more people into the potentially volatile equation. The door required him to badge it once more, and then he swung the door open. It was much brighter within, and the light flooded out onto the three men. *Thank fuck—no one in here,* John thought, with a wash of relief. Liam and Jason were both thinking similar thought also. The three computer stations to the left of the lab were empty. Above the terminals, the large plate glass windows revealed the rows of chambers within. Jason looked at them with a mixture of awe, wonder and apprehension. He had never seen anything like this before, and it was quite a sight to behold. Within the vials, the twins all remained motionless, eyes closed, as if in some eternal lifeless sleep—*But they're not lifeless,* he thought.

A shiver crept up his spine: *This is fucking creepy.* Liam scanned the large area looking for others, but also trying to remember where V29 was. *V29, or Benny?* He motioned for John to take a seat at the nearest terminal.

"Fire it up, John. The system security will need disabling." John looked at him, almost pleading, and then resigned himself with a sigh as he sat down and woke the computer. The monitor burst into life, and John started tapping at the keyboard.

"Liam, I don't know what you're doing, but please—this is serious shit we're getting ourselves into, here. I could lose my job for this. You could go to prison. Let's just get back in the car and go home, for fuck's sake!" John was desperate now. His whole body felt clammy with perspiration, and the inside of his skull pounded with every pulse of his heart, which was significantly raised above resting. His stomach squirmed with worry and dread, and he felt nauseous. He realised the full consequences of what was happening now they were actually inside, and he didn't like it. He didn't like it one bit. Liam was bent over behind the chair, and watched as John logged in.

"Forget it, John. It's too late. This all has to stop—and I know exactly what I need to do. I'll apologise now for any repercussions on Jason and yourself, I will say I forced you both to do everything against your will, which is true. You'll keep your fucking job—if you can stand to do this ungodly shit after this, that is," he added, with bitterness. He knew that none of this was John's fault. John didn't *force* him to take out the policy with FMA, did he? They had done it of their own free will. But…without John's recommendation they wouldn't have done it, so in that respect he *was* partially responsible, surely? It didn't matter now. Liam had come here to do what he thought was the only thing left to do, given the absolute horror of the events that he had learnt about a short while ago from Jen, regardless of the consequences for him or anyone else. His mind was set. He looked at the rows of glass vessels again, searching and finally locating V29 a few rows back from the nearest. He checked the monitor—he saw that John had the security override screen up.

"Do it. And how do you open these fucking glass things?" The question prompted glances between Jason and John—finally, the penny had dropped. John's hands were trembling ever so slightly above the keyboard as he completed the deactivation steps.

"There's another screen and sequence to follow. Liam, please, I'm begging you. Why the fuck are you doing this? What do you hope to achieve from it? If you don't want anything to do with FMA or the program any more, then that can be sorted! This isn't the way!" He implored his friend, but in his heart of hearts he knew it was no use. He knew Liam well enough to know that once his mind was made up, then there was no undoing it.

"You know what to do. Unlock V29, and then badge me in there. Don't mess around, just fucking do it and let's get this done, I've had enough messing around now, and the longer this takes the more twitchy I'm getting." John started tapping, and after a few swift keystrokes he rose from the chair, walking towards the access door to the lines of vessels. Liam motioned for Jason to follow him (he didn't want anyone behind him), and then moved towards the door. "Stay here, and don't move. If this all goes to plan, it will all be done and dusted in seconds, and then we can get the fuck out and pretend nothing ever happened," he said, drawing the gun out. Even though the men knew what was about to happen, the sight of the gun still shocked them, John's eyes widening. He badged the door and Liam entered the vast containment area, taken aback by the vessels in their uniform lines. They were large and imposing seeing them this close up. He instructed John to stay put and keep the door ajar until he returned.

As he walked through the lines of glass vessels, a sense of foreboding came over him—it was weird and scary in there, all these clones just silently living their inert lives… Liam felt like he was in a science-fiction movie, or a *Doctor Who* episode, or something. As he approached V29, the foreboding turned to dread. The last time he had been here Josh had been unborn, and the contents of the vessels hadn't really meant that much to him, at least physically or visually—now, he was looking through toughened glass and fluid directly at a carbon copy of his eight-year-old son. He glanced back to make sure the men had not moved, and then fixed his stare once more on the clone in front of him. There were some differences—the hair and the perceived texture of the skin, plus the overall pallor. This helped Liam focus. It wasn't his son. It wasn't a poor imposter; it was a scientifically created, very sophisticated mimic. An abomination.

He looked at the vessel curiously. There was what appeared to be a safety catch mechanism at the top, where the lid met the body of the glass. He studied it briefly, trying to figure out what would happen if he disengaged it, and then its eyes opened. Liam was startled by this, and drew a sharp intake of breath as he noticed movement from its lower quarters—it was moving its legs in order to turn and face him. As the watery eyes came to rest on Liam's face, he had to suppress the urge to scream: *What the FUCK IS THIS the bastard is fucking*

*LOOKING RIGHT AT ME...just KILL IT!* His mind screamed at him. He reached for the safety catch and flicked the mechanism.

A green LED lit up and he pressed the button directly underneath it: RELEASE. He heard a small escape of gas and pressure from the top of the vessel as he continued to stare at the clone, mesmerised by its gaze. Its mouth was now slowly opening as if to scream at him, but of course the scream was silent. Liam was staring bug-eyed and in complete horror at the living being inside the glass, as if hypnotised: *SNAP OUT OF IT! GET IT DONE!* His mind screamed at him once more. He kick-started himself into action at last, breaking the locked-in stare of the twin. He pushed the rim of the lid upwards, and all of a sudden realised that the vessel was too tall to give him the position he needed. He looked around and saw a small footstool to his right, obviously for that very purpose.

As he pulled it close and stood on it, his eyes became locked briefly once more with the twin—the eyes were identical to his son's, apart from the hatred emanating from them—he could feel it, sense it. He looked away, and as he brought the handgun in line with the top of the vessel he felt his emotions culminate all at once into a crashing crescendo of momentary madness. He aimed the barrel directly at the top of the thing's skull. There was no room for error. It was close quarters, and when the gun went off, the report was so loud it appeared to fill the entire lab space for what felt like eternity, echoing off the walls and the glass, bouncing around endlessly.

Liam looked down on the vessel, and wished he hadn't. The liquid within was no longer clear, but a vivid pink, gradually getting darker and darker. The clone had sagged within its confines, and now slumped to the bottom half of the container, blood from its head mixing with the fluid. As Liam looked partly in fascination, partly in horror, he could see flecks of grey, soft-looking material slowly making its way out of the ragged hole that had been newly formed in its skull. He felt his stomach clench and fought back the urge to vomit, quickly looking away. It was done. It was dead. He snapped out of his shock reverie of what he had just done and stepped away from the vessel, stumbling slightly as he made his way back to his friends. They both looked completely horrified at what they had just witnessed, stood motionless with almost comical expressions frozen onto their faces.

# Chapter Twenty-One

While her husband was being driven to FMA by Jason, Jen was driving Beth's car to the hospital. Her head was spinning with grief and disbelief, and there was a nasty undercurrent of *what* had actually happened with Alice and Josh underneath it all. She didn't want to think the worst (what even *was* the worst?), but she couldn't help but question the events that ultimately led to Alice's demise. Those events involved her son, as he was present when it happened, but she hoped and prayed with all her heart that his only involvement was being there...no other engagement. She felt terrible for even thinking these doubtful thoughts, and they only served to make her feel even worse than she already felt, which was already becoming more than difficult to manage. None of the occupants of the car had spoken a word since they left the woods, and that remained the same as they pulled into the hospital behind the ambulance.

The hospital was busy and bustling with activity as the women and Josh followed Alice's stretchered body down a wide corridor to a room on the left. A doctor politely asked Josh and Jen to wait outside; there was a small line of chairs against the wall opposite the room. Beth went inside, still completely shell-shocked. She looked briefly at her friend—her eyes had absolutely nothing behind them, and were devoid of virtually all expression. Jen looked at her friend with renewed agony and grief, feeling completely helpless. A solitary tear ran down her cheek. After about ten minutes of sitting in the most sombre silence imaginable with her son, a doctor came out and approached them. Jen stood to talk to him.

"Mrs Connelly, my name is Dr Ashworth. I am so sorry about what's happened to your friend's daughter—what an awful accident. We have a few procedures and protocols to follow here when something of this nature happens, as I'm sure you're aware. The best thing for you to do now would be to take your son home—it's been a terrible shock for all involved. There's nothing you can do for your friend here. We intend to keep her in under observation, as her grief has affected her severely, understandably." The doctor paused, allowing this information to sink in. Jen just blinked at him, her expression blank. "There are taxis outside, but we will need Mrs Gleeson's car keys, please." Jen fumbled in her bag and handed the keys to the doctor, still silent. Her and Josh stood up, and after a croaked 'thank you' to the doctor, they walked towards the exit.

It seemed to Jen that someone else was actually in her body—she felt completely detached from everything. The journey home was almost dreamlike, and once she and Josh were inside, the detached feeling remained with her. She turned to look at her son as they sat together on the sofa. She asked him if he wanted some hot chocolate, and Josh simply nodded. As she set the cup down on the coffee table a few minutes later, she turned to him again.

"Josh, what happened with Alice? I mean, really...? Was it an accident?" Then, quietly: "Was Benny there?"

Josh stirred and a flicker of emotion crossed his troubled face—the first emotion he had displayed since the whole thing began. Benny was stirring too. He didn't like this line of questioning, and needed to make sure that Josh said the right thing. *Remember Josh—it was an accident, she slipped, the stupid bitch just slipped! You couldn't help her! You tried but it was too late! Remember?*

He looked at his mother, tears welling in his eyes. "I'm sorry Mum. I really am sorry... I never wanted her to die!" As he exclaimed this, a wail of angst escaped his lips.

At that very moment, Liam was pulling the trigger into the vessel V29 at the FMA lab. Benny knew it was coming—he could see Josh's dad level with him, and then he was staring at his chest as he lifted the lid: *NO! NOOOO! Please don't hurt me, you BASTARD! GET AWAY FROM ME!* As the bullet left the barrel and entered the skull of the twin, Josh felt nothing. Just a huge, black cloak of nothingness. No pain. No nothing. Just a huge, endless nothing—everything black and silent.

Jen stared at her son as she saw his life ebb from his eyes, her own face twisting into a rictus of terror and agonising realisation as her brain processed the fact he was dead. Before his lifeless body had a chance to reach the back of the sofa as he slumped backwards, she grabbed him in a fierce embrace, and brought him close to her own body: "NO! NO, NOT MY LOVELY BOY!" she wailed in a pain—stricken, high-pitched tone. She sat there rocking him gently back and forth as she sobbed uncontrollably, her shadow mimicking her movements on the living room wall behind her.

A short time later (an undetermined length of time for Jen—it could have been ten minutes, or ten days), she vaguely heard noises outside on the drive. She had been rocking her dead son, swaying with the motion, but now she slowly came to a halt, looking up at the window. She saw some people getting into the cars that populated the drive, engines starting. Then they pulled away, leaving just Liam's. She heard the front door open, and her husband entered into the hall. He looked dishevelled and shocked to her—like he had been through some kind of ordeal of his own. As he closed the door behind him, he looked at his wife and son. Instantly, he knew something else was wrong. Josh wasn't moving—Jen looked up at him and simply said: "It's over. He's gone. Forever, now. I hope he has peace."

Liam joined them and embraced them. The three of them sat in that locked state until the blue lights started to beam in through the window as the police cars pulled into the drive.

# Epilogue

Jen watched the slow, rolling waves as they crashed hypnotically against the shore. The wide-brimmed hat she wore stopped the blazing sun from giving her heatstroke and the worst sunburn imaginable, and the palm tree she was situated under at the top of the beach offered welcome respite from the heat also. Liam had gone to get them some drinks and would be back soon. It felt so strange to be back in the Caribbean, just the two of them—the same as they had done before Josh had been conceived.

The last twelve months had been traumatic for the couple to say the least. It felt like a dream, and Jen was happy to allow it to *keep* feeling like that—she had decided that in order to move on with their lives (which had felt impossible for what seemed like an age), she had to compartmentalise the tragic events to some kind of Pandora's box, lock it, and throw away the key. Metaphorically that's what she had then done—apart from Josh's room. That had remained exactly as it was right up until the day he left the world. The door remained closed, but she went in there every day. Sometimes she cried, sometimes she smiled to herself as she reflected on the good times they'd had with their beautiful son. She never reflected on the bad stuff. Ever.

After Josh's death, a lot of things had happened. The police charged Liam with possession of a firearm and criminal damage. They couldn't charge him with murder, or even manslaughter of the twin—after all, it wasn't a real human being, was it? At least, that's what the defence argued, and they'd won. Luckily, he'd escaped with a suspended sentence and no jail time (Jen was convinced he would go to prison, and she would be left alone in her living hell). Josh's death had been the result of "massive brain trauma—the cause of injury undetermined." Both Jen and Liam knew the true cause. They didn't discuss it, and didn't mention anything about Benny or the twin to the authorities. After all, they didn't want to be diagnosed as insane. They were both aware of how ridiculous it sounded, so the unspoken agreement between them remained secret.

Things had deteriorated between Beth and Jen. This was inevitable, given what the mothers had been through, each of their own stories full of tragedy and loss. They slowly stopped speaking to each other (the few times they had talked, it had ended in tears on both parts), and eventually Jen and Liam saw the 'for sale' sign go up on their neighbour's lawn. The two women had wished each other all the best and good luck on the moving day, and that was the last time they had seen or spoken to their neighbours—maybe the separation would help with the closure of it all, a line drawn under part of their past that both couples wished to forget as best they could.

They had decided to return to the Caribbean for a three week holiday, and to try and reset their lives. They had booked the same hotel as their previous visit, and intended to do nothing for the whole time, hoping that the holiday would work as a kind of circuit breaker for them. Maybe things would be a bit easier to cope with on their return.

That evening, as Jen and Liam walked hand in hand over the soft sand of the beach, evening sun low in the sky sending bright orange rays across the water, they saw the fire ahead. As they approached, Liam said: "I wonder if it's the same locals we saw last time, all those years ago? What was she called again… Calemba or something?"

"Cazembe was the old woman," Jen corrected him. "Kadisha was her granddaughter. And yes, it looks like it's them," she said as they got close enough to make out the locals more clearly. They were sat and stood around the fire, maybe ten people in total, talking and drinking. One young girl glanced up at the approaching couple and squealed with delight.

"Ahh! It's the English couple! It's been so long! You have returned at last! Come, join us!" This was Kadisha, who had grown into a beautiful, lithe young woman. Liam and Jen looked at each other and smiled, walking towards the group. Kadisha had turned away from them to talk to the old woman sat on a large driftwood log set back from the blaze. The old woman beckoned them over, and they wandered over and sat down next to her. She remembered them well, and talked to her granddaughter in Portuguese—Kadisha translated what she was saying.

After a short time of catching up with the two women, Kadisha leant in and whispered in Jen's ear: "Grandma has said she can sense the glow on you again."

Liam was sat the other side of his wife and couldn't hear what was being said. Jen stiffened and looked over at the old woman, smiling hesitantly. She nodded kindly in return and motioned her to sit closer. Jen got up and sat next to the old woman, and they clasped hands as Cazembe muttered kind-sounding words to both her and her granddaughter.

"Let her touch you there and she will know!" Kadisha said excitedly. "Remember? The same as last time!"

Jen nodded apprehensively, and the old woman grinned a toothless smile as she extended a leathery hand towards Jen's abdomen. Jen let her feel her stomach gently, watching her face as she did so. After a few seconds, she beamed at Jen and started talking hurriedly to Kadisha. Liam looked on with curiosity as the old lady babbled in an animated fashion.

"What's she saying to you?" Jen asked.

The young woman turned to her, a huge smile lighting up her pretty face. "She says you are with child! But it's very early. She also says—it's twins! Boys, too!"

The sun cast its final rays across the ocean before it finally blinked out and allowed the night to reign.

Printed in Great Britain
by Amazon

39817248R00156